Love After Death

To Jikye,

Thanks for supporting me
in reading my first novel.
I hope you enjoy it. May
it inspire your walk as a
Woman of God and speak to
your spirit in some way.
God Bless!!

Love
Nanette
Ramsay

Love After Death

A Novel

Nanette Ramsay

iUniverse, Inc.
New York   Bloomington

Love After Death
A Novel

This is a work of fiction. All of the characters, names, incidents, organizations, and dialogue in this novel are either the products of the author's imagination or are used fictitiously.   ·

iUniverse books may be ordered through booksellers or by contacting:

iUniverse
1663 Liberty Drive
Bloomington, IN 47403
www.iuniverse.com
1-800-Authors (1-800-288-4677)

ISBN: 978-0-595-45979-7 (sc)
ISBN: 978-0-595-70017-2 (dj)
ISBN: 978-0-595-90280-4 (ebk)

Printed in the United States of America

iUniverse rev. date: 10/21/2010

Acknowledgments

Greatest thanks to the one I serve, the one who has saved me, and the true author of this novel; with you I am all things possible - without you I am nothing... my Savior Jesus Christ.

Bendicion Bita - yo gracias tanto para hacer todo hace para mí y para todos en la familia. Significa tanto a mí. Está por su ejemplo por qué yo puedo ser una mujer resuelta y capaz de cuidar de mi marido y a niños también. Yo sólo espero que parezca tan bueno como usted cuando consigo más viejo. Te quiero mucho, su nieta Nanette.

Hi Mom, I did it! Finally... and I couldn't have done it without your help too. You've shown me in more ways than one that I can be more than just a girl from the hood. You not only believed in me, but you gave me pure and unconditional love. And even though I get on your nerves sometimes – you still manage to be the kind and caring Mom I've always known you to be. Words can't express how much I love and appreciate you. But, here it goes again – I LOVE YOU MOMMY! And thanks for always being there.

Love, peace and thanks to everyone who has supported me on this Journey; especially my god-mommies Auntie Lori and Aunt Gerry. To all of my beautiful, intelligent and strong Divas: Symoun, Ayisha, Marcia, Nadia, Chanel, Nikki, and Genevieve – I appreciate all of the extra support, advice, help and love you have given me. To Theresa and

Adrienne, thank you for taking the time to read and give insight with the book, before its final stages. I love you all.

In lieu of my past, I'd like to express my gratitude to my Father for establishing a relationship with my family and re-establishing himself into my life. Thank You...

To all of my family, cousins, brother and sisters - I love you all. A special thanks to Titi Ana, Titi Carmen, Tio David, Titi Judy, Tio Robert, and Titi Lucy for being who you are and were in my life. I love you.

I'd like to also thank the staff at iuniverse who helped to bring my manuscript to fruition. I am especially grateful to one of the most kind, patient and considerate consultants at iuniverse, Mr. George Nedeff. I appreciate you taking out the time to explain any and everything to help get me through to the end. You gave me confidence when I needed it most. Thanks and May God Bless You Always.

Deb Sugar, if you're out there thanks for giving me my first official writing job for the school newspaper at Kingsborough Community College, my alma-mater. You took a chance on me, and it reminded me of my passion. Thank you soooo much!

To my sons and daughter, Mommy loves you! Thanks for letting Mom get her work done. And asking when is the book going to be finished, every month. You've definitely kept me on my toes. You are amazingly fun and I am proud to be your Mom.

Last but certainly not least, I dedicate this book to my husband Junior, You inspire me to be not only a mere wife and mother, but also a woman of God. You've helped me accomplish my dreams and for all of these things I am grateful. I am proud to call you my husband, look forward to spending the rest of our lives together, and treasure our friendship and our marriage. I love you for Always, Nanette.

Contents

The End Is Near

N o, no, no, no, no, please don't leave me. Baby, please. Hang in there! Nurse, we need help! I love you, Dee. Nurse! *You can't give up now!* Hang in there, *Baby*!

"*Code blue! Code blue!*" That's all Myra Lopes-Harris could hear over the loudspeaker and her heart beating in her ears. She thought things like this only happen in movies, but never once did she think she'd experience this firsthand—especially at this point in their life.

"Mrs. Harris, you have to step aside now. Mrs. Harris, I'm sorry, but we need to work on your husband," says one of the doctors.

Wearing an all-black ensemble, Mrs. Harris held on tighter. One of the nurses in the flower-filled room tried to pry the petite, full-figured Mrs. Harris away from her husband's side. But to no avail. The doctors finally aggressively shoved her out of the way to revive him. Myra, now draped over the nurse like a wounded soldier, begins to have one of her episodes. The nurse then noticed a handsome young man in the corner, watching in fear. He stood six feet three inches tall, resembling the man in the hospital bed, but much younger. He stood shaking, with tears rolling down his face. The nurse signaled the young man to come and help. He hesitated at first, as if paralyzed. He finally took soft baby steps, gently grabbing his mother in a bear hug, whispering, "Come on, Mama. Let the doctors work."

The nurse looked on in shock. Although the boy looks like the man on the bed, Mrs. Harris didn't look old enough to be his mama. As the two walked out of the room, the nurse held the door open, following them to the waiting room. There she handed the boy an inhalation mask to help Myra breathe. Being caught between the two, the young man didn't know what was happening. First his father's heart flatlined, then his mom had an episode. That's what they called it at home, ever since his father was admitted to the hospital six months prior. He wasn't quite sure what it was, but his aunt, Myra's sister, referred to it as an episode. So he, his brother, and his sister followed suit.

After breathing into the apparatus for ten minutes, Myra was back to breathing normally. Devon then grabbed his head as he sat down beside her.

This was a day he and Myra would never forget. And although she was very spiritual, the question she kept screaming in her mind was *why? Why now, God! Why would you do this now?* Her knees grew faint as she wept in sorrow. Devon held her tight as they sat in the waiting area. Who knew her life would come to this? She was just about ready to start her career, and now this. Myra continued to weep as all of these thoughts entered her mind. Devon looked on in fear, wondering what would happen if his father died. He dare not bring it up since doubt was a word refrained from in their family. Besides, his mom was upset enough. There they were, Myra looking at the floor weeping, while Devon looked at the ceiling in anger. If looks could kill, God would be—well, you know. Devon was at the moment quietly angry with this so-called "God."

Myra and her husband Dee had it all figured out. Only thing was, it wasn't a part of God's plans. It all started about twenty-three years ago. Myra was a junior and Dee was a senior in Eastside High. And although they had never spoken, she became aggressive in her approach one fateful night at a championship party, after finding her then-boyfriend dancing closely with someone else. As Dee walked by at that very moment, Myra grabbed his hand in an exotic grope of dirty dancing. And even though he was lost in translation, he never questioned her. The rest was history.

Myra saw Dee all of the time while they were in school, but he wasn't her type. He was the captain of the football team, top of his class, handsome, and knew it. She, on the other hand, was the total opposite. Myra, down-to-earth, passionate, yet aggressive, was a radical, whose philosophy was cultivated in a spiritual foundation. All of this combined made the attraction to Dee close to null and void. In her mind, Dee was all looks, with no substance. However, Dee Devon Livonius Harris was not a person of many words, but he was smart and used it well. He wasn't into quitting or giving into any shortcomings. As a matter of fact, to him there was no such thing as a shortcoming, just imperfections not yet enhanced. He was charismatic then as he was now. His eyes spoke words only Myra understood. And when he stood up, you knew he was somebody, because he had the physique of a "Greek God" and the posture of a "soldier boy."

While everyone in the school called him Von, Myra called him "Dee." Some say they were a match made in heaven; others (especially the females) thought they wouldn't last; and then there were the rest, who couldn't care less. Myra had the look of a model, very well proportioned. And like Dee's eyes spoke to her, her body spoke to him. You could say they had a language all their own. No one could learn it, comprehend it, or break it. They spent most of his last year in high school in their own communication, talking about their hopes, dreams, and plans for the future. Myra went to his prom, and he went to hers. All was good. There weren't any issues, problems, or strife. At least as far as they knew, love was in the air, and that was all that mattered.

After dating for one year of high school and surviving a long-distance college relationship, Dee graduated at the top of his class and became a lawyer at one of the top law firms in Maryland. Myra received a degree in marketing and fashion design. She became a stay-at-home mom with the understanding she would develop her own career after their first son (Devon Jr.) was old enough to go to school. Instead, four years later, they had another son, Trevon. They called him Trey for short. So Myra held on a little longer. And before long, another three years had passed, and they had the princess of the family. That is exactly what they named her, Princess Malina Harris. They were happy, full of blessing, and complete. At least, that's what they thought.

Dee being the mighty breadwinner made Myra the unhappy stay-at-home "soccer mom." And even though they both knew very well that her housewife position was temporary, Dee became complacent with the idea of Myra staying home. Of course, feeling stifled with dependency and loss, Myra continued to live day to day satisfying her family's every need—even to this very day, frustrated with her incompletion. And while friends and family alike saw Myra as having it all together, they still had no idea she was mourning her own death.

Growing up, she was taught to be strong, independent, and full of faith. Somehow, it all changed when love became the huge benefactor on her priority list. Sadly, loving herself came at a cost without a payoff. The balance of family and career was inevitable, but would it come at the price of death? If it did, Myra definitely wasn't ready. A couple of more years would be perfect, in Myra's eyes. In one year, Princess would be in school full days, Devon would be off to college, and Trey would be starting junior high and going to school on his own.

Dee had never had any health issues until he ventured off and headed his own law firm. A few years later, he was diagnosed with high blood pressure. He began taking medication, but inconsistently—which lead to this moment where Myra and Devon sat waiting for the doctor's prognosis. Myra sat quietly, with fear and trembling. She didn't know what she would do if she lost Dee. He was all she'd ever known.

Devon, on the other hand, stood pacing the floors, while occasionally looking at his mom with worry written all over his face. He walked by Myra in his last pace across the floor. She looked up, and their eyes met. Myra's stare was empty, yet filled with pain. At that moment, she knew she should have told the kids about Dee's condition. And just then, in her private thoughts, she remembers the first time Dee was taken to the emergency room, like it was yesterday.

Janice, Dee's assistant and paralegal at his office, called with news that he had collapsed after giving her the assignments for the day. Myra couldn't believe what she was hearing. Janice gave her every detail of the incident with a shaky voice as if she was paralyzed with fear. There was a long pause on the phone. Myra's whole body became numb. The phone dropped out of her hand. Internally Myra was screaming, but lack of breath kept her from letting anything out. She could still hear Janice on the other end of the phone asking if she was still there. And even though Myra was there, she was far away from what was occurring. Myra could only question if death was going to be what parted them. It became apparent how much people often took the words "til death do you part" for granted.

"Mom, Mom, snap out of it. What are you thinking about?" Devon demanded, gently nudging Myra from her thoughts. Myra, suddenly blinking her eyes, looked at Devon, seeing his face masked with concern. She stared at him before responding, "I was just thinking about your dad and the first time he was rushed to the emergency room." Devon, confused, looked at his mother and said abruptly, "What! What are you talking about?"

"Devon, I can't help but think I ..." Myra couldn't even get her words out.

In a worried, sincere tone, Devon ignored Myra's last statement, mumbling, "Look, Mom, I know it's hard to see Dad like this, but do you think Dad is going to make it?"

Without hesitation, Myra smiled slightly while responding, "Oh, yes, baby, he's got the strength of God inside him."

Even though Myra smiled, Devon could see past it and knew she was just as scared as he was.

"God, how can God be on his side? He's the reason why Dad ended up here. Don't even mention God right now, Mom." Devon threw his hands up as if that was the last thing he wanted to hear. In his mind, he couldn't believe his mother had the nerve to mention God, as if "he" really cared.

Myra walked up to Devon clenching her teeth, while gripping his chin, and whispered aggressively, "Now you listen to me.… God does decide who lives or dies, but he is not responsible for putting your dad here. So don't you dare place blame in the hands of the one who gives and spares your life every day, or you will definitely be sorry. Do I make myself clear?"

Devon stepped back, looking down, and responded, "Yes, Mama, it's very clear. It's clear you want me to believe something you don't even believe. You walk around talking about God and having faith, but yet you're wearing black every day … as if you're just waiting for his death. How am I supposed to appreciate life when you act as if Dad is already dead?"

Myra couldn't believe the words coming out of his mouth but knew every ounce of it was true. Her mind was thinking one thing, but her heart felt something entirely different. She just didn't know it was that obvious.

"You just don't understand … Dad isn't supposed to be here. It's not fair! I want him back home with us."

"I know, baby, I know." Myra hugged Devon tight, weeping heavily.

Suddenly Myra noticed the doctor walking toward them, so she wiped her tears and tried to maintain her composure.

"Mrs. Harris," the doctor said in a low tone.

"Yes, Dr. Levy." Myra looked straight into the doctor's eyes.

"We were able to revive and stabilize your husband, but I regret to inform you that he is still in a coma. I'm sorry."

Myra dropped into Devon's arms, screaming and crying like a baby. Devon took one look at his mother, then yelled at the doctor, "What do you mean he's still in a coma? Do something, man! You're a doctor, do your damn job, man!"

The doctor started to explain further, but Myra managed to compose herself enough to interrupt him and ask how long the coma would last.

"It's hard to say; comas can last anywhere from a few days to weeks unto years. There's really no telling. We need to run a few more tests, and then we can know more or less what you have to look forward to."

The doctor looked down at his chart and, with a sorrowful voice, he told Myra again how sorry he was to deliver the news. Then he went over the tests they had to perform.

Myra quieted down, wiped her tears, and said, "Thank you, Doctor, for all of your help. Can we see him now?"

"Yes. And whatever you think you can say or do to bring him back, feel free to be as open as possible. At this point, you and your kids are probably the only ones that can bring him back and …"

Interrupting the doctor, Devon grabbed his jacket and said, "Mama, you go ahead …"

Confused, Myra screamed out, "What, where are you going, Devon? Don't you want to see your father?"

Devon put his head down and said, "No, Mom, I just wanna remember him the way I saw him last."

"Oh, who's acting as if Dad is already dead now, Devon?"

Devon rolled his eyes up in anger, "Then what is he, Mama, what is he?"

"You know what? Lower your voice right now, you hear me?" Myra grabbed his arms.

"Yes." Devon looked away.

"Yes, who?"

"Yes, Mom."

"Now I'm going in to see your father. You could either come with me or wait in the car, but either way, you stop with the negative foolishness right now. It has to stop somewhere. I guess I'll be the first."

Devon pulled away, walking off. On the way out, he kicked the garbage can further down the hall. Myra jumped, then shook her head while looking up, whispering, "Lord, help him." Myra walked toward the intensive care unit slowly. As she entered the dimly lit ICU, where Dee was now located, she looked around at all the other patients in similar conditions. She stood in one spot, sweating profusely. Then her hands began to shake nervously like an old person. She then started to pant and breathe heavily again. It was almost as if she was having another one of her episodes. She thought to herself, "Okay, Myra, breathe in and out.

You can do this, just breathe." Suddenly Myra heard a woman humming the old spiritual "Amazing Grace" beside her. She felt the woman grab her hand as she whispered to Myra, "Need some company?"

Myra smiled and said, "No, thanks, Ma'am. I think I can make it."

Responding as if Myra were her daughter, the woman said, "Baby, if you're still standing, I know you can make it. Just trust and keep the faith."

As Myra turned to look at the woman's face, she noticed there was no one beside her. She looked around the whole unit, scanning for an elderly woman walking around. Somehow there wasn't anyone fitting that description. Confused, Myra walked slowly toward Dee. As she approached his bed, she grabbed his hand, placed it on her cheek, and began to shed tears. Myra looked at him with so much pain, yet passion. As she began to speak, her voice cracked, then returned to her raspy, sexy tone. "Hey, baby, I know you're not awake, but if you can still hear me, I want you to get all the rest you can get right now. Okay, baby … You know, while you have a chance; because when you come out of this hospital, you have a lot of stuff to get back to."

Myra gasped for air and continued to ramble, "Let's see: you have to clean out the garage and finish building the cabinets I asked for months ago. Oh, and you have to get your home office organized." Now, Myra knew he wasn't coming home to do all of those chores, but it didn't matter as long as she spoke enough that her voice was recognizable. In her mind, she knew her voice could do something to change his condition.

Just then, Myra stared at him, whispering, "But first things first … you have to wake up, okay, baby."

Myra closed her eyes tight as she continued to speak. "The Lord has truly blessed us, Dee. And I know he would never forsake us, so come out of this okay because I need you. Better yet, we need you. Your family needs you, Dee."

And with regret in her tone, Myra rubbed his smooth but brittle cheeks and said, "Bye, baby, sweet dreams."

Myra took another look at him and around the room to find that woman who was humming, so she could thank her. But she didn't hear or see anything. The room was very still and quiet. And the only thing making noise was the machines the patients were hooked up to. Myra at this point found it strange that she didn't see the woman again. After a few minutes of waiting for her to show up, it became futile, so she just assumed the woman had left. She then gathered her purse and jacket and walked out.

In the elevator riding down, Myra sobbed incessantly. Not having Dee around became harder and harder every day. Everything she and the kids did together, over the past six months, as a family was meaningless without Dee. Whether eating dinner together or going to church, there wasn't any point. Even praying together every night became a task. And these days it diminished. Before, they would pray every morning and night together as a family. Now, the tradition of praying as a family was the furthest thing from her mind. All she could do these days was run errands and run Dee's office—or rather, run it to muck. Between taking the kids back and forth to school and to their extracurricular activities, visiting Dee, and going to Dee's office to make sure it was running smoothly, Myra hadn't been able to keep her head straight, much less pray.

As Myra walked through the parking lot searching for Dee's Jaguar XJR, which she'd been driving since his hospitalization, she mulled over her plans for the next day. In deep thought, Myra walked past one of the security posts before realizing she had already passed the car. She made an about-face and saw the Jag a few cars down. Finally at the car, she saw Devon reclined in the passenger seat, sleeping. She pressed the code to open the door, then abruptly opened it. Devon jumped up from his sleep, quickly asking, "So, how's Dad?"

"Why do you want to know? It's not like you couldn't find out for yourself," Myra snapped.

"Oh, Ma, please, can I just feel the way I do without you making me wrong?" Devon answered back.

"Boy, please, I'm not making you wrong, you wronged yourself.

You just finish telling me how you want your dad back home, but you couldn't even visit him and let him hear your voice. At least, let him know what he would be coming home to …"

Cutting her off, Devon assertively answered back, "Mama, I can never win with you. If I'm honest about what I'm feeling, you say I'm wrong; and if I stay to myself, I'm more wrong. When am I going to be able to just be myself without your idea of what I should be?"

"Boy, are you coming out of the closet?" Myra asked with her eyes wide open. She knew that wasn't what he was trying to say, but she couldn't help but be facetious.

"What? No! I just want you to let me do me and be proud of it."

"Now, you know I am very proud of you," Myra says as she started the car and pulled out.

Shaking his head in disagreement, Devon explained he rarely knows when she's proud of him. He then goes on to say, mocking her voice, "All I ever hear is, 'Why didn't you do this' and 'You can do better than that, Devon.' But for once, can you just say, 'Great job, Devon!' Or just say 'Devon, I'm proud of you!'"

"Devon, I'm always proud of you," Myra responded calmly, trying to ignore his fallacious details of Myra's attitude toward him.

Looking at his mother in disbelief, Devon uttered, "Whateva …"

"Excuse me. I'm talking now, Devon," Myra scolded.

"Sorry …"

"Every time I buy the sneakers you like, take you on vacation, or just give you money to hang out with your friends, that says I'm proud …"

"Yes, Mama, but it's not the same as hearing you say it …" Devon turned to look out of his window.

Myra sighed heavily. She hated being put in her place or, even worse, called out on her faults. But this was one time when she couldn't allow her pride to take the lead. So she gently grabbed Devon's hand, and with tears in her eyes, said, "Devon, I am very proud of you … When I get on you, it's because I know what you're capable of. You're just like your father. Baby, you have it all—looks, a brain, and charm. I just want you to use it."

"I get that, Mom. And don't get me wrong, I know when you look at me, you see Dad, but I'm not like Dad. I'm just myself. So please stop giving me grief as though I should be just like him."

Devon took a deep breath, finally feeling he got that off his chest, but Myra didn't pay him any attention, shrugging off his comment.

"Well, I don't know what you're talking about, Devon, because the only thing your father and I expect you to be is yourself, so stop with all the semantics."

Devon looked at his mother, disappointed at her attitude. Feeling like the weight of the world was on his shoulders again, he mumbled, "Okay, fine, Mama."

"Thank you." Myra continued to drive.

Devon laid his seat back, putting his iPod on. He didn't mind riding in the car, but he wasn't about to listen to the one station Myra played in the car, gospel. It was the last thing Devon wanted to hear. Ever since Dee had been in the hospital, this was her new ritual. Somehow she gave the impression the music made her stronger. And to a certain extent, it did. However, on days like today, there wouldn't be any song that could give her the strength she needed to face this battle. She was weak in the knees, and the only thing that could cure it was a miracle. The problem was, over the course of the months, she started believing it didn't exist. And prayer, again, wasn't a practice in her life these days. Anyone would think as a Christian, how could prayer not be a part of her practice? But when you live vicariously through your husband's spirituality, it's easy to be a traditional Christian and forget the relationship with Christ. Most times Myra stuck to the usual—go to church, pray in the morning, at night, and pray over food or when there's a problem. This had been the biggest issue between Dee and Myra. He felt Myra was just going through the motions. Truth is, that's exactly what Myra was doing. There was no doubt that she loved the Lord, but that's all it ever was—just love. There wasn't any discipline, obedience, and most importantly, relationship.

*   *   *   *   *

"Mommy, you're home." Princess ran toward Myra like she hadn't seen her in a week. In fact, she saw her this morning before school. Princess looked just like Myra, only with Dee's complexion and light brown eyes. And when she looks at you, her eyes radiate with life. It gives new meaning to the old saying "If looks could kill," because one look at her and you could just die; she's just that captivating. And her name was nothing short of true. Everything from her looks and attitude to her behavior screamed Princess. Dee knew she would be like royalty from the time she was born. And like he read in the bible, "A name is more precious than silver and gold." So, Princess Malina Harris fit perfectly. And Myra, more than happy, stood in agreement. Just having a girl was all she had prayed for, ironically.

Before Myra could come out of her heels, Princess jumped into her arms. Gasping for air, Myra picked her up.

"Hey, Princess. How was your day?"

Now Myra knew that one question would lead to five minutes of nonstop talking. And as luck would have it, Princess started to ramble. "Fine. Auntie Cissy played dolls with me, gave me lots of snacks, and she bought me a dress with shoes. I was thinking to wear it to see Daddy. But I'm not sure yet. Oh, and Mama, you have to make brownies for my Girl Scout meeting. Um, and I have to stay after school tomorrow for the class play …"

Myra was so tired she didn't even have the energy to say anything. To her, Princess sounded like the teacher on Charlie Brown. The only thing she could manage to vent out was, "Oh, wow, and did Auntie give you dinner, too?"

*   *   *   *   *

In walked "Cissy," Myra's sister, whose real name was Celeste Marie Lopes. Cissy was opposite in every way from Myra. As a matter of fact, the only thing they had in common was their parents. Cissy didn't go to college like Myra. Instead, she opted to take her college money, go to beauty school, and open her own spa/salon, Celestial Hair. Cissy was Myra's younger sister by age, but older in spirit. Cissy, being the loud, outspoken, and willfully independent one of the two, wasn't afraid to show her true feelings with anyone. These were just a few good qualities of Cissy that Myra admired.

Although she was never married and didn't have any intentions of marrying or having children, Cissy loved the idea of one day acquiring both a husband and children; maybe one day she would meet a man worthy of her love and time. As far as Cissy was concerned, men were good for two things: screwing and paying bills. And thus far, she was able to do both without any help. Her beauty/spa salon was in the downtown area of Baltimore, Maryland, and very lucrative. She had the best of the best beauticians, masseuses, and facial specialists. Born and raised in Maryland, it was nice to own a business in the heart of Pennsylvania Market, where mostly African-American-owned or operated businesses were located. And although Cissy had her own business to run, she always made it her business to help Myra with the kids, especially after Dee's hospitalization.

Cissy took Myra aside, teasing, "Of course, I gave her dinner, Sis—cereal."

"Ha-ha-ha … real funny, Cissy, but I'm not in any mood to joke right now," Myra snapped.

After hearing the serious tone in Myra's voice, Cissy just stopped and looked at her.

"Oh, my God, did something go wrong at the hospital, Myra?"

Without wanting to alarm Princess, Myra nonchalantly replied, "We'll talk later; right now, I want to read my little Princess a bedtime story."

Holding Princess's chin, Myra looked into Princess's eyes as she smiled. Princess had no clue how serious the situation was, but she blurted out anxiously, "When is Daddy coming home, Mommy? I wanna show him my new dress Auntie bought me."

"He ain't coming home!" Devon walked in grabbing a can of soda from the refrigerator.

"*Devon!*" Myra screamed in disbelief.

Shrugging his shoulders as if he didn't know what he was saying was so wrong, he swaggered across the kitchen floor, sarcastically saying, "What! It's true. Or are we not into telling the truth now, either? I mean the doctors did say he's in a coma and probably won't wake up, right?"

Devon knew exactly what he was doing. He was making sure Myra was feeling as bad as he felt on the car ride from the hospital. Devon drank the soda while staring at his mother in anger. Myra rolled her eyes, trying to comfort Princess as she cried.

"Stop lying, you stupid head. He is coming home!" Trey shouted, as he stood at the kitchen entrance, with his fist balled, panting heavily through his nose. You could see the smoke coming out of his ears, in a manner of speaking. And even though he was less than half the size of Devon, he had heart and wasn't the least intimidated or fearful of him.

Devon knew Trey could not hurt him, so he smirked while repeating, "He's not coming home, Trey."

"Yes, he is coming home, and if you say that again, I'm going to …"

Devon laughed out loud. "You're going to what, li'l man, you can't do nothin' to me." That's what Devon always called him when he intentionally wanted to get Trey mad. And that's just what Trey became—mad. Trey started to snarl angrily, charging at Devon after grabbing the broomstick. He started swinging like he was at the batting cage, but missed. Devon, laughing profusely at Trey, began taunting him, playing catch-me-if-you-can around the marble countertop island in the kitchen.

"*All right now!*" Myra yelled as she stepped in front of Devon, giving him a threatening look. But Devon turned away, avoiding eye contact. Myra turned to Princess and Trey, sending them to brush their teeth and get ready for bed.

Looking confused, Princess paused. "But I wanna know when Daddy is coming home. And what's a coma?"

Myra picked Princess up and lovingly told her, "You will see him soon, and I'll explain everything to you later. Right now, you need to brush your teeth and get some rest for school tomorrow."

Unsatisfied, Princess asked Myra again, "But when will I see him?"

Trying to get to Princess too, Devon snidely remarked, "That's easy, never."

Myra turned around to Devon, grinding her teeth, and mumbled, "Devon, if you don't *shut up* …" Then turning back to Princess with a comforting smile on her face, she said, "You'll see him soon. Now go get ready for bed."

Myra patted her on the butt as she walked out, and then turned to Trey and gave him a kiss. Before they reached the top of the staircase, Myra shouted, "Good-night, Princess. Good-night, Trey."

They continued to run up the stairs while simultaneously shouting back, "Good-night, Mom."

Myra waited until she heard the water running in their bathroom before turning to Devon with a look of disappointment and disgust. After noticing the lack of sorrow on his face, she walked up to him slowly and said, "Devon! Just who do you think you are, to talk that nonsense? The last thing I need you to do is make the situation harder for Trey and Princess right now. You know, things are complicated enough without you teasing and aggravating them. Instead, you should be giving them hope. That's what they need."

Standing next to the stainless steel refrigerator, Devon opened it and grabbed another can of soda, while pointing to her and saying, "Does that include lying to them?"

"Excuse me!" Myra slammed the fridge shut, just missing his head. Devon turned to walk away, but Myra pulled Devon's shoulder back to get his full attention. She wanted to see his eyes, because she couldn't believe the words were truly coming out of his mouth. After a moment of silence and a hard stare between them, Devon said with conviction, "I'm sorry, Mom, but I can't sit by watching Trey and Princess ask for Dad to come home, knowing the docs say he might or might not wake up."

Myra raised her hands as if she had given up on him. "That's not the point, Devon!"

"Then what is the point, Mama? Since you have all the answers!" he shouted back.

"Oh, now you know better—lower your voice when you're addressing me. You will watch your tone. You hear me?"

"Yes, Mama." Devon looked down at the floor.

"Now, whether or not your father makes it, is not my point. Because whatever the case will be, I need you to comfort—not torture—your brother and sister."

Devon saw his mother in despair, but ripped into her more. "Maybe so, but what you call torture, I call the truth."

Myra grabbed Devon by his T-shirt, slamming him into the mahogany-stained cabinets by the refrigerator. "*Truth! Truth!* Here's the truth, Devon, we're going to pray your father gets through this. And *you* are not to mention again what the doctors are saying, or your truth will meet my high five. Understand me?"

"Yeah," Devon whispered.

"Excuse me! I can't hear you."

"Yes, okay, Mom." Devon looked away angrily.

Myra let go of his shirt, dismissing him. "Now, good-night. I've had enough of you today."

Cissy had been looking on in shock. Myra and Cissy always got along fairly well together. Except when Myra would act like Cissy's mother instead of her sister. As Myra looked at Cissy, she saw the pity all over her face. This was something she couldn't stand for anyone to have on her—pity. Shaking her head back and forth, Myra said, "No, don't …"

"Don't what?"

"Don't pity me! Dee's going to make it! Don't share your condolences yet." Myra walked off, changing the subject. "You know, I have to get my hair done, you have any time tomorrow? Oh, which reminds me, I have to go through the mail."

Cissy couldn't see how hair could remind Myra to go through the mail, but she knew it was just Myra's nerves talking. Myra continued to ramble while cleaning the kitchen. Cissy walked over to Myra to get her attention, but Myra walked over to the stove. As Cissy walked over to the stove, Myra walked to the fridge. Finally Cissy stood right behind her at the refrigerator, confronting her face-to-face, grabbing her hand. "Myra, I know it's hard to face the truth, but you have to realize ..."

"*Realize what?*" Myra pulled her hand away.

"You need to realize, Dee's been like this for six months now. You have to come to terms with him staying that way. I mean, having faith isn't being in denial, too. I think once you understand the difference, you won't feel so helpless."

"Oh, please, Cissy, you're the one in denial. My faith is just what it is—faith. I refuse to give up."

Myra walked away to unload the dishwasher. And as she moaned a melody to tune Cissy out, a glass slipped out of her hand. And like the glass, Myra broke into pieces, crying. Cissy rubbed her back, trying to console her.

"What do you expect me to do, Cissy? He's the only man that I've ever loved. He is everything to me—my best friend, my love, and my soul mate. I don't even know how to start a life without him, it's not supposed to happen this way ..."

"I know." At this point, that was all Cissy could think to say.

"I don't know if I should prepare the kids for the worst or not," said Myra.

"I know, and there's nothing wrong with having faith. It's what Mama tried to instill in us. I just don't like to see you wait in vain. But, of course, how could it be waiting in vain if all of what God does is never in vain, but for a purpose. Listen, just scratch what I said and continue what you're doing—having faith, hoping, and praying. It's like Mama used to say, 'No sense in praying if you're going to worry. And ...'"

"'No sense worrying if you're going to pray,'" Myra joined Cissy as they looked at each other and chuckled.

"Thanks, Sis. It's just that all I keep thinking about is, we were supposed to grow old together," Myra said as she started to stare in a daze and remember the very day she and Dee moved into their first apartment. In her mind, she recounted that moment like it was yesterday.

("Myra, I love you."

"I love you more. Dee, do you think we'll grow old together?"

"Mimi, why would you ask me that? You know I want to grow old with you even if you end up looking like your mother."

"Um—excuse me! You know my mother looks good."

"Yeah, baby, after she puts on her wig and makeup and removes her mustache."

"No, you didn't, you little ..."

"What! It's the truth, no need for the abuse."

"You know that's my mom's real hair and natural beauty, Dee."

"Is that her natural mustache, too?... I'm just kidding, but baby, I'll be here for always ... till death do us part."

"Till death do us part, huh ...")

A tear rolled down Myra's cheek as the memory faded.

"Oh, Myra, don't cry. Dee is going to make it." Cissy hugged Myra.

"What am I going to do, Cissy? I'm losing my will to live," Myra wept.

"Myra, listen to me, you're going to be okay, I'm not going to let you go through this alone. Come on, girl, you're my big sis. I can't let you fall apart. Believe that God is in full control. And if you want to see Dee live, you have to get yourself together. Trust that he will bless you no matter what the circumstances. And you have to see Dee every chance you get. Let him know you're here waiting for him. You know I'm here to help with the kids. So, just let go and let God. Whatever comes out of this, you will be okay. God is not going to leave you alone."

"I know. You're right. I just can't help but feel like I'm a part of the reason why Dee's in the hospital to begin with." Myra looked at Cissy with guilt in her eyes.

"What! Are you serious? You can't be serious. You did all you could to help Dee. He knew how vital his health was. The only thing you could have done more is force him to take his medication ..." Cissy said while giving Myra a dirty look.

"Yes, but maybe I didn't remind him enough to take his medication, Cissy."

"Humph, and how could you, when every time you did, he would tell you he's not one of the kids and he's capable of remembering to take his own medication. So what, you were supposed to mash them up and feed it to him, too? Dee is in the hospital because of Dee. Not you or anyone else is the reason for his lack of responsibility. Dee was an a—"

"Cissy, please, not now."

"I'm sorry, but he just pisses me off sometimes."

Myra continued, speaking over Cissy. "Why can't I see him teach our boys to be men? I want him to live. I feel like without him here, it takes every breath away from me—he is my life. Where do I go without him? He told me forever—forever! How can he just ... just give up on life?"

With tears rolling down her face, Cissy consoled Myra. "Please relax, stop working yourself up. You're going to make yourself sick, and the kids need you right now."

At that moment, Devon entered the kitchen looking worried. He walked over to them, whispering, "Mama, you okay?"

Myra wiped her face and walked over to the dishwasher to finish what she had started. Devon walked over to see her face, but she didn't bother to look at him. Instead, she brushed him off gently and sent him to bed. Before turning around to leave, he paused and, in the most apologetic tone, said, "Uh, Mama, I'm sorry about earlier. I just don't want to see ..."

But before he could finish, Myra knew he was sorry, so she gently stroked his baby-smooth cheek and said, "Baby, it's okay, I understand."

"I love you, Mama," Devon replied after kissing her cheek.

Myra held his lips on her cheek. "I love you, too, baby."

Then she watched as her firstborn son walked out of the room with the same physique and commanding posture Dee had. She could not believe the possibility of her husband never recovering could be happening now, just as Devon was transitioning from a boy, attending his last year in high school, into a young man embarking on a life-altering journey to his dreams—college.

Since Myra was as Christian as the next person, she usually prayed when she felt it was necessary. And even though this was one of those times, it wasn't going to happen. She was more angry with God than anything else. She knew prayer would only lead her to give him a piece of her mind. And at this point, she didn't want to do anything to keep Dee's coma going on.

After unloading the dishwasher, she looked at the mountain of mail on the small work space from an open view from the kitchen to the living room and dining room. Just looking at the mail made Myra weak, and she knew if she opened them to find bills, it would just overwhelm her even more. Myra walked over to the mail, shook her head in disbelief, then made a quick exodus out. It was a job that had to be done, but it wouldn't be tonight, she thought, as she locked the door behind Cissy. Right now she had a headache, and tomorrow was a new day. Hopefully she would make it as well as Dee.

Oh, Happy Day!

℘ઽ

The sun was bright and beating on Myra's back when the alarm rang. "Good morning, people! It is time to wake, wake, wake, the heaven up! It is Tuesday morning, and it is two play hits on WLI—"

Myra slammed her hand on the alarm, took off her eye mask, and rose from the bed. She grabbed her silk robe and walked into her bathroom, washes her face, brushed her teeth and put her hair into a pony tail. She then walked out of her room and into the kitchen. Upon entering, she saw Devon and Trey eating their cereal.

"Good morning."

Devon, who was not a morning person, snapped, "What's so good about it?"

"Uh, excuse me, Devon, I thought we had an understanding," Myra responded.

Devon shrugged his shoulder in an I-don't-care motion.

"Okay, since you feel like letting the devil ride your back, how about you go back to your room and start all over again, Devon. And this time you will enter the kitchen and say good morning."

Devon looked at his mother as if she were crazy.

Myra continued, "Yeah, you heard me. You know better than to greet the devil in the morning."

21

"That's right, because God gave you another day to live, right, Mom?" interrupted Trey.

Trey quickly gave his input, while secretly making faces behind Myra's back.

"Shut up, Trey!" shouted Devon.

"No. you shut up …"

Myra intervened again, "How about you both give it a rest? And Devon, apologize to Trey for being rude."

"But …" Devon hissed.

"But nothing, Devon, the only but I want to hear right now is yours doing what I said. Now go upstairs, like I asked you to!" Myra snapped.

In a mumble, Devon replied, "Sorry."

"Sorry who?" interrupted Myra.

"Sorry, Trey."

"It's okay, I know you can't help it, you meanie," Trey responded as he stuck out his tongue.

"What!" Devon barked as he grabbed Trey by his collar, lifting him from his seat.

"Mama, help!" Trey yelled.

With her eyes closed and her head toward the ceiling, Myra ground her teeth, uttering, "Devon, let go of your brother and do what I ask you to do, now!" Devon let him go, then walked out.

"Good morning, Mommy. Look, I didn't wet the bed," Princess announced as she entered the kitchen with her wide smile and mismatched socks.

"You didn't? Good job. And what do we want for breakfast?"

Princess paused, putting her pointer finger over her mouth as if to be in deep thought, and said, "Um … how about cookies?"

"Uh, I don't think so. Try again."

"Cereal?" This time Princess made a look as if she smelled something bad.

"Good answer. Do you want any fruit with your cereal?" asked Myra.

"Yes, thank you," Princess politely answered.

Knowing he could get Devon in more trouble, Trey sarcastically remarked about his brother taking a long time to return.

"Devon is surely taking his time upstairs. Boy, I wonder what he's doing?"

Myra looked at Trey from the corner of her eye as if to say "I know what you're up to," but the only words she offered were, "Trey, mind your business."

Trey responded by shrugging his shoulders and staying quiet. Myra, infuriated with Devon's lack of respect, began to yell at the top of her lungs for him to get back downstairs. Devon yelled back in a frustrated tone that he was getting dressed.

Myra continued to shout, now at the foot of the stairs, "I believe I asked you to start your morning greeting over … not get dressed!"

As Devon began to walk down the shellacked wood stairs, he impolitely responded back, "Mama, why are you yelling? I'm not deaf."

Myra walked halfway up the stairs and jumped so close to his face their noses touched. She pointed her finger to his forehead and said very angrily, "Excuse me, I can yell if I want to, I am the parent, not you. Do I make myself clear?"

And although Devon was aware of his mother's upset, he continued to confront her with sarcasm and replied, "Yes, and I can hear you clearly."

Myra looked him in the eyes, "Oh, really, if you can hear so clearly, do you hear this?"

"What?" Devon answered.

Myra slapped the side of his head.

"Ooh, I know you heard that," Trey joked as he grabbed his book bag and ran out the door to practice his basketball while waiting to be dropped off to school.

Devon, on the other hand, was not fazed by Myra's hit at all. Instead, he responded, "Fine, good morning. Is that better?"

Myra then raised her hand again.

"Boy, you better come correct before I knock you straight into good-night."

Although Devon knew he was taller than his mother, he also knew she would make good on her word, so he looked at her calmly and said, "Good morning, Mama."

"Now, was that so hard, Devon?"

"It's hard when there's nothing good about your morning," Devon replied.

Even though Myra understood how Devon was feeling, she responded, "You have one thing that's good about this morning."

"What, Mama?"

"You're here, right. He didn't have to spare your life, but He did."

Myra tried to convince Devon that he should be happy to have good health and life, but he didn't feel it was enough. All he could think was that his father had neither good health nor life right now. Having no interest in his mother's "happy to be alive" speech, he looked down at Myra and said, "Mama, can I leave for school now? I'm going to be late."

"Yes, go before I change my mind and you meet your maker."

Myra got halfway to the kitchen, then yelled, "Oh, don't forget to pick up your brother and sister from school."

Devon mumbled, "Okay! Bye, already."

Myra shook her head, looked up, and whispered, "Lord help him."

"Mama, I'm done," Princess said.

"Okay, great, get your shoes on and get in the car. And tell Trey to get in the car, too."

Myra quickly goes to the room, throws on a pair of black tights, her white Donna Karan blouse, and black tall boots and lets her hair down. Normally a ponytail would suffice, but today she felt like looking sexy. She looks quickly in her full mirror, applies some make-up, then grabbed her purse and keys and headed for the two-car garage. Upon entering the garage, she paused briefly as she noticed Dee's S CLASS

Mercedes beside her Navigator. Typically Dee would be gone when the kids left for school, so seeing his car only reminded her of his absence. She realized then that she had to go back to the hospital to bring some recognizable items in case he awakened. All of sudden, Trey yelled out, "Mama, come on, we're going to be late."

Myra, caught off guard, looked at the kids and asked them if they were buckled in yet. Princess and Trey yelled out "yes" in an annoyed manner, as if to say "Come on already." Myra proceeded to get in the car and had just started it when Trey asked her if she has the lunch money for his class trip. Already in the motion of pulling away, she pressed down the brake abruptly and responded, "Shoot, Trey, why didn't you tell me sooner? Now I have to go to the bank."

"Sorry, I thought you'd remember. I mean, how would I know you'd forget?" Trey replied.

Myra continued to pull out, when all of sudden, Trey remembered he had birthday money he could use. What a relief, Myra thought to herself, as she realized the time. Her intention was to drop Trey and Princess off quickly, so she could go to the hospital early to spend the day with Dee. She handed Trey the keys to the house, so he could get the money from his room. As Myra looked at Trey in the rearview mirror, she assured him he'd get his money back.

Trey then responded to Myra, "Okay, but don't forget."

Looking at Trey in disbelief, Myra replied, "Boy, do I ever forget?"

Trey looked back and shouted, "Sometimes."

"Oh, really? Well, this time I won't forget, and if I do, please remind me."

"Oh, trust, Mommy, he will remind you all day long," interrupted Princess.

"That's right, because it's my money," Trey contested while walking away.

"Boy, be quiet and go get your money." Myra looked back at Princess, then whispered, "Your brother has ears of gold, he can hear anything."

"I heard that, too," yelled Trey as he approached the door.

Knowing Trey was being nosy, Myra shouted out, "Well, I hope you hear me when I start to drive off and leave you."

Trey ran quickly to his room, went in his closet, and looked in one of his sneaker boxes hidden in the back on the top shelf under his comic books. He took out a ten dollar bill and kissed it up to God. This was one of the things he had picked up from his father. Even though Dee paid his tithes, this was Dee's way of saying thank you to God for always providing. Trey ran to the garage, jumped in the car, and put on his seat belt while announcing he was back. Myra, being pressed for time, sped off into the street and clumsily knocked over their trash cans—something she always did and Dee always complained about. However, this time he wasn't home to do just that—and all of sudden, Myra pressed the brake, threw her head on the steering wheel, and began sobbing like a baby.

Trey and Princess sat back and watched in confusion. They knew their mother was crying, but didn't know why. They looked at each other and, without making it noticeable to Myra, signaled to each other, "What happened?" At the same time, they shrugged their shoulders and began pointing at each other to comfort her—but neither of them wanted to. Finally Trey said, "Mama, are you okay?"

Then Princess followed with, "It's okay, Mama, you don't have to cry. We won't tell Daddy you knocked over the trash cans."

Wiping her face, Myra couldn't help but laugh at the thought of Princess thinking she was crying because she was afraid to get in trouble with Dee for knocking down the trash cans. So Myra wouldn't get Princess upset about her father's true condition, she responded, "Thank you, baby."

Myra drove off.

Upon reaching their school, Myra looked back at Trey and Princess and said, "Well, here we are. You kids have a good day today, okay?"

They both answered, "Okay. You too."

Trey opened the back door so they could get out.

After closing the door, Princess walked to the front passenger side and said, "Mama, I love you!... and tell Daddy I said hi and I miss him."

"I love you, too, Princess, and I'll tell him," Myra replied as she leaned over to kiss her on the cheek.

Then Trey with his bionic ears realized that Princess was sending her best wishes, so he interrupted and yelled out to Myra, "Tell him I miss him, too, Mom."

"Okay! Now go in before the late bell rings," Myra said to both of them.

On the drive to the hospital, Myra heard her wedding song "Always and Forever." She started to reflect on her wedding day. How happy she was on that day! She couldn't believe it would be almost twenty years of marriage in a couple of months. And she remembered their day like it was yesterday. Dee had on his navy uniform because at that time he had just graduated from the military. She wore a beautiful Princess-style wedding gown because nothing was too good for the firstborn princess in her father's eyes. They picked "Always and Forever" because that's exactly what they intended on being—always and forever together. But these days, she was not so sure.

When Myra finally reached the top-rated hospital in Baltimore, Johns Hopkins, she parked in the outside parking lot. Since the landscape was so beautiful in the spring, the nurses made sure to take the patients for walks around the premises. She entered the main entrance. Heading straight for the elevators, she went to the ICU floor. When she got there, she looked around, confused because the room looked different. But in actuality, she just didn't recognize any of the patients. So she walked up to the nurse on duty to ask where Dee was. Before she could ask her question, the nurse pointed her in Dee's direction. Myra was trying to figure out how the nurse knew she was there to see Dee. Then she remembered she had left his wallet-size picture of her and the kids on his bedside table. She walked over to him, leaned over, and planted a gentle kiss on his forehead. She fixed his pillows and sheets. Myra started talking to him as though he was just sleeping—which to her was the case.

"Hi, honey. I went to your office yesterday, and it was busier than ever. It seems like things can't run smoothly without you being there. Baby, you have to wake up now. They need you … Your Princess said the funniest thing to me last night as I tucked her into bed. You know what she said? She said, 'Mommy, this boy in my class asked me to be his girlfriend, and I said no, 'cause he's not smart like my daddy. I told him he gotta do all of his work first and show me he's smart—then maybe I'll think about it.' Can you believe it? She already knows what she wants even though she's not old enough to have a boyfriend. Hmm, and funny enough, it's someone like you. She misses you, baby, you hear me, your little Princess misses you. Now, Devon Jr. has been a little difficult. He can't handle you being like this. I know he misses you, but he seems more angry than sad … I know you would know what to say to him, you know your boys. Trey is … well, you know he's a trooper … he has the love of God in him. He's always telling me, 'God is going to make a way, just keep the faith, Mom.' He loves the Lord, Dee … Our boy is going to be a preacher … Baby, I need you. I want you to come back to us … You have to come through this okay. If not for me, then come through for the kids … they need their dad. Okay, baby …"

Myra laid her head on Dee's chest, looking down at his fingers. All of a sudden, she saw his hand move a little. Yelling in happiness, Myra belched out, "Dee! Dee! Nurse, call the doctor—my husband just moved his hand."

The nurse paged the doctor, then walked over to check Dee's vitals. Myra started shouting "thank you" in excitement. The nurse tried to quiet her down, but to no avail Myra continued on. Only this time, she did it in a whisper, so she wouldn't disturb the other patients. When the doctor arrived, he removed the breathing apparatus for a minute. He noticed Dee breathing on his own and noted it down on his chart. The doctor turned to Myra and said, "I don't know how you did it, but whatever you're doing, keep on doing it because it's working."

Myra smiled and responded, "I didn't do anything special. I just talked to him a lot. And did some praying too...."

Myra knew she didn't do any praying. She just hoped God wouldn't count it against her.

"Well, keep doing that, because this sudden movement doesn't usually happen after what occurred yesterday, being so close to dying," the doctor replied while checking Dee's pupils.

Myra looked down at Dee and rubbed his cheek in amazement. In her eyes, this was one small step toward the healing process. As exciting as this news was, she didn't want to tell the kids just yet, but she had to tell someone, so she went for a walk to call Cissy. After the phone rang about three times, her voice mail came on, and Myra began leaving her a message. "Cissy, you need to call me back. I have good news. Where are you anyway? I'm calling the shop and there's no answer, so call me back as soon as you get this message."

Myra walked back into the hospital and went to the gift shop to buy some flowers—but as she went to pick up a bundle, she saw a little bear with a heart attached to its hand. It looked pretty simple, but when she read the tag, it had instructions showing how to make a personalized message with your own voice. She instantly took it to the cashier to purchase it. Myra thought it would be great to record the children's voices on it for Dee to hear, since it would be awhile before she'd bring them for a visit. When Myra reached the ICU, she saw Dee for the first time breathing on his own. She stood by his bed, astonished at his ability to come this far so fast. Myra then sat on the bed and held his hands. She held them in case there was any movement again. As Myra talked to Dee, the nurse walked over to change Dee's fluid bag. The nurse turned to Myra and said, "I know you must be ecstatic now that your husband is breathing on his own."

"Oh yes, absolutely. This is definitely a good sign that he's going to make it," Myra replied while continuing to stare at Dee.

"Can I ask you a question if you don't mind?" asked the nurse.

"Sure," replied Myra.

"You had a young man with you the other day that looked at least sixteen or seventeen years old, and I wasn't sure how he was related to you because you look too young to have a teenage son …"

Myra interrupted the nurse and said, "No, that's my son—at least one of them."

"Get out of here. You mean you have another son?" the nurse replied.

"Actually, I have another son and a daughter," Myra shared.

The nurse looked back at Myra quickly, gave her the up-and-down, and said, "Well, whatever you're doing to stay looking so young, keep it up, girlfriend. There are many women fighting to look so good after having one child, including me."

Myra looked at the nurse and said, "Fortunately it's an inherited trait, because I'm definitely not responsible for half my looks …"

"That's because God made you just the way I like it, beautiful."

Myra suddenly jumped up from the bed and belted out, "Oh, my God, baby, you're awake …"

But when she turned around to look at him, she realized the compliment didn't come from Dee. Myra rolled her eyes and started fixing Dee's sheets, ignoring who it was coming from. Mr. Travis Dewitt. This was her ex-boyfriend in high school. And he was also the cousin of her best friend, Michelle Dewitt. He said, "I'm sorry, I didn't mean to startle you."

"Trust me—you didn't. What are you doing here anyway, Travis?" Myra led him away from Dee's bed.

"I'm here to question a patient that was shot in an undercover case I was working."

Travis was the complete opposite of Dee. He was more rugged in his looks, but in a pretty-boy kind of way. He stood at 6 feet 3 inches tall and about 185 pounds. And it was all muscle. His smile was captivating and contagious. And surprisingly enough, being a detective didn't age him one bit. Myra tries to play it off as though she wasn't really interested, but everything about her disposition screamed, "How you doin'?"

"I thought you lived in Atlanta now."

"I did, but I was promoted, and the transfer came with it. Plus the pay was even better." He placed his hand on her back, but Myra moved away, crossing her arms. She looked at him and said, "Well, congratulations …"

"Yeah, um, thanks."

They stood for a minute in silence, then Myra excused herself to go back to Dee. Travis nodded his head and watched her walk back to Dee's bedside.

Myra stared at Dee, rubbing his hand. Then she put her hand over his chest. She wanted to make sure she wasn't seeing things. With a sigh of relief, she exhaled deeply. It was surprising how quickly he was bouncing back, but then again, anything was possible with Dee. He was a fighter, and he didn't believe in giving up. That was what Myra loved most about him. He never threw in the towel. Instead, he just used it over and over again, hung it to dry, then used it some more. She wanted to say a prayer, but didn't know where to begin. Dee always led their morning prayer, the prayer over the food, and the nightly prayer with the kids. Myra tried to think of what she could possibly say to God that wouldn't be hypocritical. And, of course, nothing came to mind.

So she looked for the nurse that helped her the day before. When Myra asked the nurse on duty about her, she had no clue who Myra was describing. There wasn't anyone like she described on staff. Myra walked away disappointed, holding her head down. The nurse then asked Myra what she needed. Myra turned to her, signaling for her to come closer, then she whispered asking if she could help her in a prayer. The nurse grabbed Myra's hand and began walking over to Dee. The nurse was tiny and short, but had a strong grip. And standing next to Myra, she practically looked like a midget. Myra wasn't that tall herself, but with stilettos, she was an easy three inches taller.

At Dee's side, the nurse started praying while tightly holding Dee in one hand and Myra in the other. Myra's eyes were shut, but with a few peeks here and there. She always had a problem with being in total submission in prayer, especially when it came to closing her eyes. It was as if she had a trust issue. And as Dee's health was slowly getting worse, her trust was doing the same. Oftentimes Myra felt like she was living a lie. She didn't know how she could preach faith and trust to her children when she herself lacked it. But no matter what she would preach to Devon, he would do just the opposite. This, in turn, made her feel accountable and guilty.

As the nurse ended the prayer, Myra took a peek and saw and felt Dee's hand squeeze hers. A tear rolled down her cheek, dropping on his hand. They said "Amen," and then Myra turned to the nurse, giving her a hug and saying thanks for the powerful prayer. The nurse assured her it was no big deal. Instead, the nurse expressed her happiness to share with her in spirit. Myra didn't think of it so deeply; she was just happy the lady was there to help say the prayer. The nurse went back to her post as Myra said her good-byes to Dee.

On the way down, Myra thought about stopping by the gift shop again to see what else she could pick up for Dee. But as she approached the shop, she heard her name. And even though she was sure she heard it, turning around would only confirm that it wasn't worth answering to. Out of nowhere, Travis was on her tail and sought to speak, begging for her attention. Even though Myra didn't want anything to do with Travis, she was enjoying the chase.

"Myra, slow down, I just want to …"

"You just want what, Travis? Can't you see I have a lot to deal with right now? I don't have time to socialize, or better yet, take a stroll down memory lane with you!" Myra rolled her eyes away, but not as nastily as before.

"Well, then, it's a good thing I didn't stop you to do either." Travis didn't crack one smile, proving he wasn't trying to have a social call with her. "Listen, I never got to send my well wishes to you, and you know …"

"His name is Dee, and thank you. Are you done?"

Exhaling deeply, Travis said, "Yeah, I guess. Just keep your head up. See you.…"

"Bye."

Myra walked away happy, but annoyed at the same time. Although Travis did aggravate her nerves, he couldn't wash away the fact that Dee was getting better. Everything was starting to look good again, and not Travis or anyone else could damper her feelings. Just then, Myra's phone rang. It was Devon's school. Normally they only call for two reasons. And lately, one of them had been his behavior. Great! She thought to herself, *Dee is getting better while Devon is getting worse.*

"Hello?"

"Hello, Mrs. Harris. This is Coach Barnes."

Myra was strangely at ease. Although a call from Devon's coach didn't mitigate her concern for the call, it somehow made her think that whatever the issue was, it wasn't so serious, or else it would've been the principal on the other end.

"Yes, Coach Barnes, how are you?"

"Excited to let you know that I received a call from the head coach at Clarke Atlanta University, and he will be coming down to watch Devon play in the last game of the season."

"Oh, wow, I guess that's a good thing?" Myra questioned the coach. She didn't really know much about the sport, nor did she care to know. Football was really a Dee and Devon thing. And just as well it should be, being that Dee played it in high school and one year in college.

"No, this isn't just a good thing, but a great opportunity, Mrs. Harris. And not just for Devon to show his skills, but if he impresses him enough, he could get a full scholarship there."

"This is great …"

"Yes, and not only are they interested in his athletic skills, but they are astounded by his academic average so far. I didn't tell Devon yet. I want you to be the first to know in case you get a call from the university …"

"That's okay, I understand. Thanks for the great news and the heads-up. And you know what? I'd like to tell him the news, if you don't mind."

"By all means, I'm sure Devon will be excited no matter what. Enjoy the rest of your day, Mrs. Harris."

"You do the same. Bye."

Myra put her phone in her purse, smiling. The thought of her firstborn attaining such a goal made her proud. To her, it meant everything she and Dee sacrificed and did to this point was a confirmation they were doing something right. And now all the family needed was for Dee to wake up and join in this great news. As a matter of fact, she couldn't wait to share it with him, but Devon needed to know first, since this was his life's passion and decision to make. Suddenly Myra totally forgot about the gift shop and walked out to the car. Once she reached outside, the sun was so bright she realized it was almost midday.

The ICU was so dimly lit, it gave the impression of being nighttime. This was one of Myra's pet peeves. In fact, at home she made a point of opening any and all blinds and curtains. In some way, she believed letting the sun in made a difference in the aura of the atmosphere. Of course, this was something she would have to get over on her hospital visits. The only way she could control its ambiance was if by chance Dee recovered enough to get a private room. But first things first—Myra was just happy to know that Dee was making some improvement.

Outside, Myra admired the hospital grounds. It was well kept. She thought whoever did the landscaping truly had a green thumb. The grass was manicured in all its greenery, the flowers were a multitude of assorted colors from the brightest pinks and oranges to the palest yellow and lavender, and with the spring air breeze, you could smell each scent. It was a beautiful day for a walk. Unfortunately Myra couldn't take advantage of it. She had to buy the groceries, catch up on the laundry, and cook. Cissy was very good with the babysitting, but she didn't have a domestic bone in her body; which didn't leave room for Myra to fully depend on her. But in all fairness, Cissy made sure the kids walked a straight line in every way while under her care.

On her daily run of errands, Myra stopped by the local supermarket to pick up the ingredients for the paella she was preparing for dinner.

While going through one aisle, she heard a familiar voice coming from the other, so she proceeded to follow it. And just as she thought, it was a familiar voice. Myra wasn't quite sure why she was seeing him again, but it became apparent that it was becoming more and more of a coincidence.

"Travis, what are you doing here?" Myra looked around to make sure she didn't see anyone else who would misconstrue this chance meeting.

"Well, it's a supermarket, and I do have to eat ..."

Myra didn't care for his sarcasm, so she looked him up and down, "Oh, really, Sherlock, I didn't know that."

"What else would I be doing here?" Travis smirked while pretending to intensely look for something on the shelf.

"I don't know, but if I didn't know better, I would think you were following me ..."

"*What!*"

"Sssh, lower your voice, Travis." Myra looked around again.

"Give me a break. Are you serious? I am a detective. I catch the bad guys; I'm not one. You may be beautiful and all, but don't be so full of yourself. I live here now, and me being here has nothing to do with you, so you can relax. I'm not stalking you ..."

Travis found what he was looking for, then tells Myra good-bye and leaves the aisle. Myra regrettably watched him walk away. She wasn't trying to insult him, but the way they broke up left her wondering why he would come back to a town where he didn't have such great memories.

After his father died, Travis dropped out of school. He went into the military, then into the police academy. It was a hard time for him and his family, but somehow he made it through. Myra stopped thinking of Travis and continued to shop.

*   *   *   *   *

At home, Devon was giving Trey and Princess a snack before starting to work on his college applications. It was only yesterday that he was running all over the house like a little tyrant until he'd fall and hurt himself. Now he was all grown up and getting ready for college. Although Devon knew football was his thing, he would have never thought he'd have the opportunity to follow his dream of becoming a football player. The years went by so fast. If Myra could turn back time, she would without a doubt do it. Myra wasn't by any means prepared for her older son to leave for college soon. Although she wanted him to go to a college locally, she knew going away to school would be best. The experience of being away from the parents always pushes someone into maturity, which she had experienced herself twenty-two years ago. Devon might not know how to take responsibility now, but he'd learn it fast in college.

Myra pulled up to the house and saw the trash cans still at the curb knocked down. She became angry with Devon for not bringing them in, but then she remembered she had good news for him. So she figured she could let him get away with it this time around, though normally he would be called outside and scolded about his responsibilities and the lack thereof. Instead, she picked them up and rolled them back to the garage. However, she did call him out to help with the groceries and dry cleaning. The dry cleaning consisted of Dee's work shirts and suits, and Myra didn't know why she had bothered to pick them up. Bringing them home somehow helped her hold onto his coming home from the hospital.

"Hey, Mom, you're home early." Devon came running out with his undershirt showing his sculpted arms and shorts hanging down below his boxers. Myra took one look at him up and down, then stared at him briefly. Devon looked back at her, knowing automatically to pull up his pants and put on a shirt once they were in the house. If there was one thing Myra didn't allow, it was Devon to follow the ignorance of certain so-called "hip-hop" styles. She let him have his own style, but not at the expense of looking like a typical street-boy with an attitude to top it off.

As soon as Myra put the groceries down, Princess came running to kiss her. Myra picked her up, kissing and hugging her tight. Myra glanced at Devon as he came into the kitchen and smiled, "You look so handsome when you're dressed properly." Then she grabbed his cheek, squeezing it tight.

Devon smiled. He didn't know why Myra was so happy, but he was glad to see it. "Mama, I thought you were going to be with Daddy all day?"

"I was, but then he ... Well, I'll tell you the good news over dinner."

Myra wanted to share the news about Dee, but realized she didn't want to get their hopes high. So she diverted the conversation.

"So, how was school today?"

The kids were so enthused with the snacks in the groceries that they totally ignored Myra's question.

"Oh, don't all answer at once ... Hello!"

"Mama, the trip was cool. We went to the wax museum and saw wax statues of historical and famous people."

"Wow, that is cool, Trey. And Devon, how was your day?"

"It was okay."

"Just okay? Why?"

"Well, I had a major science test, which was hard, then my English teacher decided to assign a very hard project due at the end of the week. The only good thing that happened today was the coach let me leave practice early. And even that was sort of crazy because the coach doesn't ever do that."

"That was a good thing, because now we can have dinner together as a family again."

"Yeah, the only thing, Dad ain't here too ..."

"Excuse me."

"Oh, I mean, he isn't here to have dinner with us. How is he anyway?"

"He's okay."

Myra smiled at Devon while looking in his eyes. Devon had no idea why Myra was smiling, but whatever it was, he just wanted to relish in the moment. Deep inside, he had a feeling it had something to do with his father. But he didn't want to ask, just in case that wasn't it. The last thing he wanted to do right now was get into another argument with his mother. As far as Trey and Princess, they weren't even paying attention to the conversation.

Myra started pulling out her pots and pans to cook. At the same time, Trey and Devon sat at the island and continued to do their work. Princess, however, ran around the island trying to get Myra's attention. As she ran, she started singing loudly. Finally Myra slammed down one of the spoons and told princess to have a seat. Princess stopped, jumped in fear, and held her head down while walking to sit down. Suddenly Myra walked over, picked her up, and repeatedly apologized for scaring her. Princess cried softly, but it cut Myra more. She couldn't believe she was so aggressive toward her. Myra promised herself the day she had Princess, she would never show her daughter any form of aggressive or abrasive attitude. But here she was, slamming and screaming at her little daughter as if she shouldn't be running free, as any child often does. After a minute, Princess wiped her tears and told Myra it was okay. Myra went back to cooking, only she changed the menu. Instead of paella, she heated up the premade rotisserie chicken she bought at the supermarket. Then she continued to stir the rice. And all she has left to do now was make the vegetables.

As dinner was cooking, Myra started going through the mail. In it she found a letter of discrepancy with an account she wasn't even aware Dee had opened up. She read it with her eyes wide open in disbelief. Then she partly crumpled the letter in her upset. This was one of the reasons why she wasn't prepared for any tragedy. There was too much she didn't know about. This was her fear. Even though she was partly to blame, her expectations were leading her to point the fault at Dee. In her mind, she played out all of the ways Dee never made it his business to keep her up-to-date with the finances.

In the background, Devon yelled, "Mom, Mom! The rice is boiling."

"Huh," Myra somewhat replied.

Devon tapped her shoulder, "Mom, the rice. It's boiling."

"Oh, oh, yeah." Myra turned the flame down, stirred it a little, and ordered Devon and Trey to set the table.

As Trey went for the plates, Devon aggressively redirected him to get the forks and spoons. Trey continued to go for the plates. Devon then pushed him out of the way, making Trey trip and hit his nose on one of the counter stools. He screamed, grabbing his bloody nose. Myra quickly grabbed a paper towel, wet it, and then ordered Trey to throw his head back. Standing by in disbelief, Devon shook his head as if Trey made his pushing him harder than it had really been. Myra looked at Devon in rage. Trying desperately not to lose her temper, Myra dismissed Devon from the kitchen. She knew he didn't do it intentionally, but it didn't matter, because everyone knew how sensitive Trey's nose was. All she could think of was why did he push him, knowing he could get hurt? But, of course, this was how Devon was with Trey when he felt like being in charge.

After ten minutes passed and the fuse died down, Myra called Devon back down. He came down looking embarrassed, took a seat, and intentionally waited for Myra to instruct them to hold hands to pray. Lately she hadn't been home for dinner, and when she was, prayer was not at the top of her priority list, now that Dee was in the hospital. Myra sat down, picked up her fork, and began to grab a forkful. Devon hissed loudly, frowning, and ordered Trey and Princess to pray.

"But Mama didn't pray," Princess protested.

Devon, looking upset at Myra, said, "So! What did Daddy teach us?"

"To pray before our food, then thank him after we're full," Trey replied.

"So that is what we're going to do. Now grab each other's hand and pray!"

Even though Myra knew she was the one in charge, this time she felt like she was the child being corrected. Devon looked at Myra, waiting for her response. Most of the time Myra didn't like to admit her wrongs or apologize to the kids, but today she felt an apology was in order. She looked up at each of the kids and apologized for not leading them in prayer. In the same breath, she thanks Devon for taking a stand for consistency in one of their daily prayers. Devon didn't give in to her so-called sincerity. He just stared unresponsively. Myra tread softly so as to not devalue his attempt to get the family back on track, but she felt this was the best time to mention the call she had from his coach. As she told the good news, Devon jumps up in excitement, not letting her finish completely. He acted as if he knew what she was going to say next. Myra smiles with joy. Devon danced and jumped around. Finally, he landed a big wet one on Myra's cheek. She continued to share the details. Devon boasted some more, chanting, "Oh yeah, Oh yeah—Got game, don't hate—Slap me five—Too late," taking his hand away from Trey when he gave him a five. Trey pushed Devon. Devon patted his head like a puppy and said he was sorry.

This was the best news Devon had received since his father's hospitalization. He'd been waiting for this moment since he was a freshman. Here he was, a senior varsity being considered for college football and, more importantly, a scholarship to one of the best schools in Atlanta. Dee had been instilling this in him from the time he was three and could throw a ball with strength and precision. Clarke being Dee's alma mater and football being his favorite pastime, it was bound to be the road Devon also traveled. It didn't matter to Myra at all what sport Devon took on, as long as he made it a point to put his education first. Once it became the other way around, she made it clear football would be over.

Myra and Dee agreed that having an education was the best backup. Devon didn't think of it that way. He thought there was no need for a backup. He believed a talent was a blessing and education was a treat. You could take it or leave it. The only thing was, this opportunity came with good grades. Without it, he would lose out, but with it, he would win all the way around. Myra sat him down to have a heart-to-heart talk while Trey and Princess cleared the table.

Devon listened attentively to Myra's lecture. This was something he hadn't heard before from her and more importantly his father. He understood why they felt the need to talk about blessings and rare opportunities and being humble. She called him out on his cocky attitude. Devon admitted he gets a little arrogant. But he chucked it up to an uncontrolled desire to make his father proud. He dug further in a rare feeling to share and told Myra he wished Dee was around to hear the news. Myra was taken back by his honesty. She offered to share the news when she got to the hospital. Devon nodded his head in agreement, then asked her to give him some time, so he could sit with everything. Myra got up and kissed him on the forehead.

As Myra entered the kitchen, she witnessed Trey picking Princess up to help her put the cups away. Trey hemmed and hawed trying not to drop her. Myra rushed to his aid, grabbing Princess, and then closed the cabinet door. Suddenly Myra slipped and fell. After the loud thump of Myra's butt hitting the floor, Devon ran downstairs. Myra hadn't noticed the floor was soaked from Trey and Princess attempting to mop it. Devon looked at her sitting on the floor, then began to laugh hysterically. Myra joined him, along with Trey and Princess. Five minutes passed, then Cissy walked in, looking at them on the floor laughing. She didn't know what had happened, but knew whatever it was, of course, wasn't serious. She walked over to Myra, grabbed one of her hands, and with Devon holding the other, pulled her up.

Myra excused herself to change. Cissy cleaned up the mess, sending Trey and Princess to brush their teeth. Devon finished putting the dishes away while telling his aunt the great news. Cissy stopped mopping, screaming with joy, and hugged him tightly. Devon chuckled and blushed from the love she exuded. Myra entered the kitchen, grabbed her keys, and poked fun at their aunt-and-nephew moment. Devon retaliated by making fun of her fall. Myra then grabbed her purse off the counter, leaving them on that note.

Life Goes On

&

"Hello …"

"Hey, beautiful, what's up?"

"Devon?"

"Of course! Who else would it be?"

"I don't know … my new boyfriend …"

"Ha-ha-ha, real funny … You're a comedian now, huh?" Devon lay back on his bed.

"Well, since I haven't heard from you in a few days, I didn't recognize your voice."

"Shalise, you know what I've been going through. It's not like I'm hanging out. My pops is in the hospital."

"I know, but you don't have to be a stranger …"

"I just don't see the point in calling you when all I'm gonna do is be on the phone with you dwelling on my father, you know."

"But I'm your friend, too, if you need to talk, you know …"

"So, you marking me now?" Devon looks at the phone.

"No, baby, I'm just playing, you know how I do."

"You're playing, huh? Well, I'll see how much you're ready to play tomorrow …"

"Oh, whatever! So I guess I'll be seeing you at our spot?"

"Yep." Devon smiled as he looked at her picture.

42

"Same time?"

With a calculating laugh, Devon answered yes. Shalise stayed silent, listening to him snicker. After a few seconds, Shalise took a deep breath, "Are you finished? What's so funn—"

"Devon, get off the phone. I have a call to make!" Cissy slammed the phone down.

"Oooh, well, I guess you better go." Shalise started laughing.

"It's not funny!"

"Ha-ha-ha, whatever! Tomorrow, baby."

"Later, love."

*   *   *   *   *

Myra entered the ICU, recognizing no change in Dee. She became discouraged. She sat down beside him, wondering if this would be the day he woke up. The same nurse who prayed with her earlier, checked his vitals for the last time before ending her shift. Myra thanked her for all of her devoted work. Then she began praising her for nursing him back to life. The nurse stood in shock over the mistaken credit Myra was giving her. The nurse told her gently it was all God's doing and continued writing her notes on the chart.

Although Myra was a Christian, she seemed to have a hard time walking with that recognition. She did very well in the traditional ways of being a Christian, even though lately she hadn't been going to church, praying, or acting in faith. Somehow Myra believed that through the deep relationship of her husband to the Lord, she would also somehow have the same relationship. She respected the Lord's position, but didn't understand it. And she wasn't about to start figuring him out now. She looked at the nurse and said, "You know, I just meant because of God blessing you with your skills, my husband is slowly healing."

At this point, the nurse's disposition went from gentle to outright abrasive. "Now, I told you anything done to your husband came from God and only God. The sooner you receive it—the sooner he, you know, the Lord, can fully bless you and your family, so don't praise me for anything because he does it all. Are we understood?"

The nurse looked at Myra with her piercing eyes as Myra looked down in shame. Then she answered in a soft tone, "Yes, Ma'am."

The nurse gently pulled Myra's chin up. "The spirit of the Lord is within you, just open up your ears and heart and let him in. I do thank you sweetie for trying to give me all the credit, but you have to pay credit where credit is due. Now, I'll be back with the doctor."

Myra then sat on the bed beside Dee.

"I guess she told me," she whispered. Then she went on about the rest of the day. She started with the events that occurred at home with Trey's nose and her falling on the floor. Myra laughed incessantly as she remembered the moment. She tried to maintain her composure as she began telling him about the phone call from Devon's coach. Myra spoke in specifics all the time. This time wasn't any different. She looked up, closing her eyes to hold back her tears and recall the conversation. The more she spoke, the more her eyes filled up with tears. With her eyes still closed, she smiled and said, "So, with God's blessing, our son will be going to Clarke Atlanta University …"

"So, why… are you crying?"

Myra opened her eyes, making sure she was hearing correctly. Lo and behold, she heard right.

"Oh, my God! Dee, you're awake!" Myra hugged him tight. Dee let out a moan. Letting him go quickly, she apologized. "Baby, you gave me the scare of my life. I didn't know if you were going to make it. I mean, I wanted to believe you would, but all I kept seeing was you laying here."

In a whisper, Dee strained to speak. "What happened to, "he inhales again, "the faith?"

"Honey, please don't force yourself to say anything. When the doctor gets here, he will remove the tubes from your nose so it's easier for you to talk." Myra gently pushed his hand down.

Dee tried again to remove the tubes from his nose. Although he was groggy, Dee knew Myra was evading his question.

Myra stopped him dead in his tracks. "What are you doing, baby? I told you the doctor will do that ... I just paged him."

Dee then responded passively, "What happened?"

Myra took a deep breath and began explaining everything that had happened. Of course, precisely the way it did. "Well, you were at work, and I don't know if you were having a bad day or just under a lot of stress, but you were giving Janice a list of things to do, then you just collapsed. Janice then called the ambulance to take you to the hospital ..."

"Yeah, I remember that ... I was going to a meeting," Dee whispered in pain.

Myra told him to save his energy for the doctor. And in perfect timing, the doctor entered, speaking in his usual loud voice.

"Hello, people. Hey! Welcome back, Chief."

"Hey, Dr. D'Angelo," Dee whispered.

"Well, you remember my name, but say no more until I remove the tube," the doctor ordered.

"You're about the only one that can order him around like that," Myra intervened.

The doctor chuckled while Dee shook his head no in disagreement. Myra couldn't believe Dee's denial, even though he knew it was true. He also knew if he had just listened to Myra about taking his medication, this would have never happened, but that was neither here nor there at this point.

The doctor broke their stares, explaining his condition. "Now here's the thing, Mr. Harris, you had a stroke, which led you to go into a coma. You've been in the coma for about six months, and at one point you weren't breathing and you were attached to a breathing apparatus. Now this morning, you made movement with your fingers. And you began breathing on your own. So here we are, you're awake and hopefully on your way to recovery. Now we can remove this tube from your nose."

"Thank God. It's … uncomfortable," Dee murmured.

"If discomfort is all you feel, that's good, because you came pretty close to death," responded the doctor.

Myra quickly interrupted, "But God is good all the time, and all the time God is good. He knew we needed you more, baby. So, Doctor, where do we go from here? How soon will he recover?"

"It depends. First, we have to observe him and do some neurological tests—a CAT scan and MRI. We need to make sure he hasn't suffered any brain damage. We will also be doing an echocardiogram, which is a sonogram of the heart," replied the doctor.

"Well, we know he hasn't lost his memory. He remembers your name …"

The doctor interrupted Myra, "Yes, but we still have to make sure the brain is fully functioning."

"Well, it has to be if he's talking. I mean, thank God, he even woke up," Myra said, speaking as if Dee was not present.

Again the doctor tried to explain, "Yes, Mrs. Harris, but due to his inconsistency with taking his blood pressure medication, it led him to having the stroke and possibly other health-related issues that we may not be aware of. We can't consider him fully recovered just yet."

"Okay, so how soon will he have these tests taken?" asked Myra.

"Well, most of the tests will be done tomorrow morning," responded the doctor in a blasé tone.

Anxious to know what could be done for Dee, Myra immediately asked how soon they would get the results of the tests. If any physical therapy was going to be necessary, she needed to know as soon as possible. The doctor nonchalantly said the results would be in soon, "but it will take time."

Myra went from being anxious to being dissatisfied with the doctor's laid-back attitude. Aggressively she asked, "So, how soon is soon?"

The doctor grabbed Dee's chart to note down his vitals and, without making eye contact, responding, "Oh, probably within a day or two."

Myra stood up from the bed and approached the doctor in a face-to-face manner, commanding his full attention. She said, "Oh, no, that will not do ... We need those results the same day."

"Mrs. Harris, as much as I would like to have the results the same day, the tests have to be read by another group of doctors, who unfortunately have their own schedules," the doctor replied.

"Well, if this other group of doctors is too busy, then maybe we need to find a new set of doctors, including you, to get what we want. I mean it's not like we don't have insurance that's paying for it. All we're asking for is prompt test results."

Interrupting, Dee strained, "Relax, baby ... he's just doing his job ..."

"No, I can't relax, because I don't understand how doctors are too busy to give prompt medical diagnoses. This only shows lack of compassion and care for the patient," Myra responded, crossing her arms while tapping her feet.

Dee then tried to sit up—to no avail. He dropped back down. He grabbed his head as if he was in pain. Myra ran to his side in fear, asking him if he's okay. Dee stared at Myra, annoyed. "Myra, you're acting like I can't speak for myself. I'm here in the room." Dee stops to take another breath before continuing to speak. "If I feel the doctor isn't showing quality care, I'm more than capable of making it known with my own mouth," he inhales again, "not to mention you're behaving uncivilized."

"Well, excuse me, I guess I'll let you handle things now. Since I'm behaving uncivilized ... I'm going for a walk before I lose it." Myra grabbed her purse to leave.

"Oh, as if you haven't lost it already... You always find a way to take things to the extreme," Dee responded.

Myra paused for a second and gave Dee a snide look, retorting, "Like I said, you can handle it now. I'll be back!" Myra rolled her eyes. The doctor began to apologize to her for not having the answer she wanted to hear, but as he looked up, he realized she's already gone. The doctor resumed with his evaluation.

"So, what if anything do you remember about the day you collapsed?"

"I remember asking my secretary, Janice, to do a few things for me. Then I turned around to collect my things. And as I stopped to ask her to do something else." Dee paused, grabbing his head in pain. "After that I don't remember what happened."

"Well, it's a good thing you remember that much; at least we know now that the stroke hasn't affected your memory. And definitely hasn't affected your speech. We just need to find out if it's affected you physically."

"So, Doc, how did it get this far?"

"Mr. Harris, you can't be serious. I mean, it can be a number of things, but your inconsistency with taking the blood pressure medication is how it came this far ..."

Dee shook his head in disbelief and confusion.

"Mr. Harris, not to insult you, but it's pretty ignorant for you to believe it's okay to miss taking your medication. Prescribed medications are just that, directing a necessary course of treatment with patients such as yourself in dire need of it."

"Yes, I understand. I guess I just didn't think it was that serious," answered Dee.

"So, you're not ignorant, just in denial?" asked the doctor.

Dee chuckled at the doctor's sarcasm and said, "All right, I get your point, but honestly speaking, how am I going to be?"

"Honestly, it depends on what we see on the tests. And while we are doing that, I want you to get as much rest as possible ... Oh, and please apologize to your wife for me. I just hate to see a woman upset with me even if she's not my wife," the doctor pleaded.

"Okay, what time will I be going for my first test?"

"Your first test will be around ten in the morning," answered Dr. D'Angelo.

"Okay, thanks for everything, Doc, I know you're doing everything possible to help me ..."

As the doctor shook Dee's hand, he replied, "You're welcome, and I'll be back before I leave my shift to check on you. By then you should be in a private room. And I'll have the nurse let your wife know where it is …"

"Okay." Dee lies back down holding his head.

*   *   *   *   *

In the interim, Myra walked out to the hospital grounds to call Cissy and the kids at home. As the phone rang, she made mental notes of what the kids should have done already. She hoped Cissy would be the one to pick up the phone. Then, breaking her thoughts, the phone picked up, and she heard Devon say, "Yo, whatsup?" with music blaring in the background.

"Uh, excuse me, Devon, how did I tell you to answer my phone? And why are you chewing like a cow on the phone?"

Immediately Devon apologized, "Sorry. Ma, I thought it was my girl calling me."

"And that's how you address your girl? You know better than that, I don't care who you think is calling. When you answer my phone, you say hell—"

Devon interrupted Myra's speech, saying, "I know, hello or good evening, I know, Ma."

Annoyed with his I–know-everything attitude, Myra quickly said, "Um hmm, well, if you know so much, try doing what I ask you to do next time. Okay?"

"Okay, Mom, I heard you the first time," Devon sarcastically remarked.

"Uh-uh, do not get fresh with me. You are not too old to be put in your place," shouted Myra.

"All right, Ma …"

"Okay, well, I have some good news."

"Okay, what?" Devon replied.

"Your dad woke up, he's talking and everything," Myra said excitedly.

Shouting over the phone, Devon screamed, "For real? Mama, that's great! When can we see him?"

Holding the phone inches away from her ears, Myra suggested, "How about tomorrow morning?"

Devon replied, "You serious, Ma—you mean we don't have to go to school?" Devon knew his mother was dead set against absences from school, so this came as a shock.

"I don't see why not. I think visiting your father takes priority right now. I don't want to take anything for granted anymore. Life is too short, and we have to take advantage of our time here together."

Devon replied, "Cool. Hey, guys! Guess what?"

Trey and Princess yelled in the background, "What!"

"Dad is better, we can go see him tomorrow."

Trey and Princess began shouting, "*Yea!* Oh, yeah … oh, yeah … oh, yeah … oh, yeah."

Myra listened proudly, happy to hear the kids excited again. "Okay, so I'll see you guys in the morning. And make sure all of you brush your teeth and pray before you lay your head to rest."

"Okay, Mama … And say hello to Dad for us."

"I will … Good-night."

As Myra hung up the phone, she took a deep breath and began walking back to Dee. She remembered how annoyed she was at Dee, but having no time to stay aggravated, she had to change her attitude quickly. She didn't want to continue with any arguments. As she got to the room the nurse told her, she took a quick breath in, releasing all of her frustration. Pushing the door open, Myra smiled, hiding all form of upset. "Hi, baby, I'm back. Oh this is nice, all you need are some flowers to add more life to the room. "

Now if there was one thing Dee was good at, it was leaving things in the past. He was good at having a disagreement, making his point, and moving on.

Myra, on the other hand, was more dramatic, but in this instance, she could not be bothered. Enough time had already passed with Dee being in a coma for six months. She often wondered how he could move on without staying upset. Either way, it worked. It always seems to soften her up. And this time wasn't any different.

"Hey, beautiful. How are the kids?" Somehow Dee knew she called home while she was out.

Myra blushed, looking down. "They're okay, they send their hellos. They're excited to hear you're okay."

Dee gently grabbed Myra's chin, looked into her hazel eyes, and said, "So, now that you're back, you want to give me some luscious?"

With her eyes filled with tears, Myra quickly responded, "I've missed you so much. I'm sorry I allowed myself to get upset earlier."

"That's in the past, now come and show your husband some love."

Myra planted a nice wet one on him.

"Um, now that's a kiss I can never forget." Dee looked at Myra as if she was the only woman in the world for him.

"I'm so happy God gave us a second chance, because honestly I was losing hope," said Myra.

"What's that I'm hearing, lack of faith?" asked Dee.

In her raspy voice, Myra replied, "Nooo, more like I was unsure." Myra knew she was lacking in faith, but didn't want to admit to it. In fact, she didn't have to. Dee knew all too well.

"I don't know, baby, it sounds like you were thinking worldly with 'ye of little or no faith?' And I know you're stronger than you believe, so please stop thinking negative, okay?" pleaded Dee.

Now this, this was strange even for Dee to be so calm and encouraging, Myra thought in her head. Usually he was judgmental and his patience would run low. However, this time, Dee didn't allow his dislike for spiritual doubt to overshadow their discussion. Comfort ensuing, Myra was led to take advantage of Dee's calmness and speak honestly about her feelings.

"Well, maybe I had a little loss of faith. I had to question why this was happening to us. I just couldn't believe that God would bring us this far. Then take it away. I wanted to believe the Lord was going to bring us through, but every time I tried to get closer to God, I became overwhelmed with the thought of being left alone. I mean, I wouldn't know how to go on. I have no work experience. I don't know all the bills we have. And how to pay them. I just don't know how I could face it alone ..."

At this point, Dee interrupted, "That's just it—you were not alone. The Lord is with you, always. Having little faith is not acceptable when you have the foundation we have. I think you need to repent and ask for forgiveness. Especially after going off on the doctor like you did."

"I know ... I was just a little upset," Myra whined.

"Well, being upset is not going to accomplish anything, Mimi."

Myra looked up at Dee, surprised, with tears in her eyes. Mimi was the pet name he gave her when they began dating.

Dee continued, "It's amazing what comes back to you when you're on your deathbed. I had the weirdest dream, you know ..." Dee leaned over, grabbing his head.

"Are you okay?" Myra looked at Dee with worry.

"Yeah, it's just my head hurts. It feels like a debilitating migraine. I'm okay though ... it'll pass. Now, as I was saying, I had a dream we were both in high school again, and you were in your cheerleading uniform ..."

Interrupting Dee, Myra remarked in her fabulous, self-absorbed way, "You mean the one I can still get into?"

Closing his eyes with a slight smirk, he replied, "Yes, Myra. Now, as I was saying, you were looking out to me from the sidelines ... and all I remember thinking was *that girl is going to be my wife someday*, but as soon as that thought entered my mind, you disappeared and I was gone. I couldn't even feel anything ... just a great sense of loss ... and I couldn't understand what it was or meant."

"Wow ... it's like we were thinking alike, because that's exactly what I was feeling when you were in the coma. I felt like I not only lost my husband, but my best friend. And although I'm a wife and mother, I felt like I was losing myself to life. We never communicated what would take place in this kind of situation. You are my whole entire life, and when you were in a coma, I felt if you died, I would die right along with you, Dee."

Feeling uncontrollably upset, Dee commenced giving Myra a piece of his mind. "Why would you say that? Who would take care of our kids? I mean, you have a lot of life in you without me. God gave you life!… I didn't know I married a woman so dependent … What kind of Christian woman allows circumstance to consume her so much that she can't see beyond death? The last thing I want to hear is you giving up because I'm not around …"

Myra looked at Dee like he had lost his mind. He was scolding her as if she was one of the children. She then shouted back, "That's easy for you to say. I didn't do anything after I graduated college … you did. When you married me, I had dreams, and we put them off, remember … to help embark on your dream of having your own law firm … and to answer your question, you married the kind of Christian woman whose love for her husband goes beyond what he's afforded her …My love for you runs deep."

Dee gave a sarcastic chuckle and replied, "So much for love … you can't even see how vague and ignorant that statement is."

"What! How can you say that?"

"Myra, how can your love run deep for me when all you mention is how you can't make it on your own if I die—or go as far as to mention how you put your dreams off for me?…"

Myra put her hands on her stomach and said, "So, having your children meant nothing in this whole equation?"

"Damn it, Myra!" Dee slammed his fist on the food tray so hard it made Myra jump in fear; then to calm himself down, he took a deep breath and continued, "You don't get it … If you truly loved me, then you would know how to embrace any circumstance with faith and know that whether in life or death, all that we accomplished together was for something much greater than you and me …" Dee began to tear and continued, "I want to know that your love for me comes from a much

greater source and not from circumstances ... because it is in that you will accept everything given to you or taken away. I mean then, and only then, Myra, will you be able to see beyond what is occurring to you and be able to live life."

Myra wiped Dee's tears and said, "I'm sorry, it didn't occur to me that you had your own concerns about the possibility of you dying ..."

"Correction, that's not my only concern. I'm concerned more that you're not living in excellence and faith ... you have the power, Myra, just do it."

"Do what?"

Happy that she asked, Dee responded, "Start by getting closer to the Lord again, building that relationship. Use him to work on you and what you want."

"I can't now. You need me here with you, Dee."

"You're telling me you can't build a relationship with the Lord? Come on, Myra, you can do it. God doesn't give you more than you can handle."

"Of course, I can and want to build a relationship with the Lord, but as far as going after my goals or desires right now ... with you just recovering, it's highly unlikely."

"You can do all things through Christ. You're strong, smart, serious about your passion, so combine the three S's with the Lord, and you can do anything you set your mind to. Look, Myra, I want you to be happy, and right now you're not happy."

Myra lay beside Dee and put her arm around him like she used to when they were at home in bed after a grueling day of running around and working. Myra played with his fingers and said, "I'm happy ... I'm just not ready to lose you."

"No one ever is, but you can't let death stop you, because it's all a part of life. I mean, in order to have life, there must be death," Dee responded.

Myra looked at the mahogany wooden clock on the wall and realized how late it was. She wanted to go, so Dee could get some rest, but at the same time, she wanted to stay in his arms—where she hadn't been in a long time. Contemplating what to do, she finally rose from the bed and said, "Speaking of life, since God has given you a second chance at it, I want you to get some rest, and I'll be back in the morning."

Dee gently grabbed her hand and asked her to stay. Myra explained that he needed his full rest. But Dee wasn't having that, so he told her to spend the night with him. Myra still wasn't convinced about staying. So Dee stroked her cheek, which he often did when he wanted some affection or attention, then he whispered in his godforsaken sexy, deep voice, "Would I ask if I wasn't? I need you here with me tonight. I want to feel you, touch you, and smell your not-so-good morning breath."

Myra shoved him because, as usual, Dee was trying to be suave and funny at the same time. Then she responded, "Oh, please, your breath doesn't smell like vanilla—just slide over and make room."

"I love you, Mimi."

"I love you, too, baby."

Visiting Day

I t was testing day as the morning sun filled the floral-decorated hospital room. Although Myra had been up since before dawn, the brightness awakened Dee. He woke to find Myra looking out of the window, at the view of the pond outside. As he stretched his arms out, he interrupted Myra's thoughts and said, "Good morning, Mimi. How did you sleep?"

Holding onto the diamond and ruby-studded necklace Dee gave her for their tenth wedding anniversary, she softly said, "Good morning," but followed with what she thought was an intriguing question, "Dee, you ever wonder where the sun is rising from if its place is in the sky?"

Laughing to himself, and looking at Myra crazily Dee said, "No, because it's not the sun that's actually moving, Myra, the earth is … You know that."

Myra catches herself, replying, "Of course, I knew that; I was testing you to see how much you know. Anyways, how did you sleep?"

"I slept great with you in my arms. Again, how about you?"

Myra walked back to Dee to lie down beside him. As she snuggled back under his arm, she kissed his bulky, carved chest and replied, "You know, sleeping by your side is always a pleasure. I've missed you at night. You know, having that feeling of protection and warmth made me appreciate you even more as I was looking at you sleep. Dee, I don't want to take us for granted anymore, so maybe after you get better, we could plan a getaway trip for just you and me."

Dee rubbed her back, but made no agreement to Myra's suggestion. And as silence filled the room, Myra looked up at Dee and asked him what he thought. Dee turned away and said, "We will have to see ..."

Myra knew Dee was about to say the "No one is promised tomorrow" statement, so she cut him off, got up quickly from the bed so she wouldn't show her disappointment, and said, "I have to go take care of some things; I'll be back later."

Dee looked at her suspiciously and replied, "Oh, yeah, what?"

"Just errands; don't worry, I'll be back by the time you're done with the tests. Now God bless you and I will see you later, kisses?"

Myra grabbed her purse and practically ran out of the room. As she grabbed the door to walk out, she put her face in her hand to let out a tear without making it obvious to Dee. Dee then yelled out, "Come back, okay, and I love you!"

In her shaky and raspy voice, Myra responded, "I will, love you, too."

Myra passed Dr. D'Angelo as she was walking out. He held the door for her, saying, "Good morning." Myra returned the greeting and tried to catch the elevator, conveniently diagonal to Dee's room.

Curiosity killing the cat, Dr. D'Angelo turned to Dee and asked, "Is everything okay?"

"Sure, she just went to run some errands, I guess."

While checking Dee's pulse, Dr. D'Angelo began to explain the line of tests for the day. He picked up Dee's chart to make notes, explaining that the first test would be an MRI of his head, the second would be a CAT Scan, and the last would be an echocardiogram, which was a sonogram of the heart.

He went on to say that if they did not see what caused the coma, then they might have to perform a nuclear test. But for now, he told Dee to be ready for the transporter to take him in the next ten minutes. The doctor then asked Dee if he got plenty of sleep the night before.

With a slight smirk on his face, Dee responded, "I got all the rest I could get with my wife by my side."

Dr. D'Angelo continued looking down at Dee's chart, focusing on the task at hand. He made no comment back to Dee's last statement and said, "Now, as a result of the stroke, you may need some therapy to build your muscles up, depending if you have any numbness. Do you have any loss of feeling or numbness?"

Dee tried to move his right arm, but had trouble. He looked at the doctor and said, "My right arm is hard to move and slightly numb, but my left arm I can move and feel."

"Okay, and do you feel this on your leg?" Dr. D'Angelo asked, applying pressure to his lower leg.

"Yes, I do," Dee replied.

"Can you move your leg at all, Mr. Harris?"

"Yes, but not as strongly as before." Dee tried to lift his leg, but was only able to lift it up an inch from the bed before plopping it back down.

The doctor took out his pen to note his condition and said, "After being in a coma for six months, I'm surprised you can move at all. I'll be back after your tests are done to check on you—and good luck."

"I don't need luck, Doc. I need a blessing, but thank you for everything. I do appreciate all your well wishes."

"You're very welcome. It's what I love to do. See you later, Mr. Harris," Dr. D'Angelo responded.

*   *   *   *   *

In the meantime, Myra reached home to find it in disarray. Typically everything was in its place, but over the past few weeks, she had had very little time to think about cleaning or even organizing. She grabbed a sponge to wipe the spilled milk on the counter and shouted, "Hellooo! I'm home!"

Trey was the first one down the stairs. He grabbed his cap and anxiously shouted, "Hi, Mom! Let's go."

"Wait a minute, Trey, you can't go in your team uniform."

Trey whined back, "Why not? It's clean."

"Yes, baby, but it's not ironed."

"Uh! Mama, I really wanted Daddy to see my jersey from my basketball team."

"Okay, but please, at least put on jeans instead of the shorts. It's chilly this morning."

"All right, I'll be right back."

Devon then walked down the stairs and approached Myra to give her a kiss on the cheek. As he bent down to kiss her, Myra ranted, "Devon! Where were you?"

Devon smiled slightly, showing his dimples, and passively replied, "Hey, Ma, I was helping Princess put on her new dress."

Myra immediately checked her frustration and thanked him for helping to get his brother and sister ready. While grabbing his cheek, she said, "Thank you, baby. So, are you ready?"

"Yeah," Devon replied.

If there was one thing Myra didn't like, it was lazy speech, so she snapped her neck and gave Devon a once-over look that clearly said, "Um, excuse me."

Devon changed his response to, "I mean, yes, Ma."

"Much better. Now can you please bring in the groceries I picked up?"

"No problem."

Devon's helpfulness raised an eyebrow from Myra, but she didn't say anything. She just knew something was always in the works whenever Devon was being very helpful.

Before going to the car, Devon said, "Oh, Mom, what time are we coming back from seeing Dad?"

And here we go, Myra thought to herself. She knew Devon had something up his sleeve. She grabbed the pile of mail and hesitantly asked why.

Devon said, "Because I wanted to go with Kilo and dem to the movies."

"Listen, boy, when you are speaking to me, please use English and real names."

"Oh, Ma, please, you know it's just a nickname," Devon said with a deep voice.

Myra could remember a time when Devon sounded like his younger brother, and now he was talking like a man.

Myra continued, "I know it's a street name. And just why do they call him Kilo?"

"He says he's tryin' to get 'killa' millions," Devon explained while rubbing his fingers together.

"Oh, really, and how is he supposed to make millions when he can't speak English? And are you sure that's why they call him that? Because it better not be some gang or drug thing, you hear me?"

"Yes. Ma, God! His name is Kevin."

Myra snapped her neck again, this time giving Devon the evil eye for uttering God's name in vain. And Devon, rushing to his own defense, apologized, giving his mother the baby-face smile. This was something he did to get what he wanted. Myra turned back around and continued looking through the mail until she came to an urgent letter from a bank, not their bank, but another one. She started speaking slowly and softly, "Well, you guys should be back home by 3:00 or 4:00 PM ..."

Devon notices the change in Myra's attitude and said, "What's the matter, Mom?"

"Huh? Oh, nothing," Myra replied, but she knew something was up because this was the second time she saw a letter come from this bank. The last time it came, she just gave it to Dee in hopes that he would explain what it was, since his name was on this account. At that moment, she contemplated opening it, but didn't want to do it in front of the kids, so she put it in her mail drawer to look at later. Devon was waiting in the wings for Myra's response to going out with his friends. When she looked up, Devon was right in front of her. She gave him one eye and said, "But I'm not coming back home, so ..."

"So I have to watch my brother and sister until you get back, right?"

"You don't have to do anything, Devon, just like I don't have to buy those sneakers, clothes, or everything else you have."

"Man, I just want to hang out with my friends," Devon blurted out.

Myra looked Devon up and down, pointed her finger, and said, "First and foremost, there is no man in front of you. And, second, all you do is hang out. Now I understand you want to go with your friends, but do not overlook that we are family and we do things for each other. I'll ask your aunt this time to stay with your brother and sister, but don't ask me to do this again, especially at the last minute, Devon."

"Thanks, Mom, you're the best."

Devon smacked a kiss on her cheek and ran out to get the groceries.

"But I'm not making any promises Aunt Cissy will babysit," Myra screamed out.

"That's okay, I'm sure Auntie will do it!" Devon yelled back.

"Now where are you going, Devon?"

"I'm going to get Trey and Princess in the car."

"Okay, because we have to leave in the next five minutes," Myra warned Devon.

Myra couldn't shake the feeling that something was up with this letter because Dee would not talk about it. It's not like she never asked him, but when she did, he'd tell her, "What! You don't trust me?" Her first thought was to scream, "Hell, no, Negro, why do you think I'm asking?"

But putting a lock on her mouth, she would say, "Dee, it's not that I don't trust you, I just don't want any surprises."

And being as stubborn as always, Dee would come back with, "Well, surprise, I'm not telling you, it's business and that's all you need to know." Myra smiled to herself because now that Dee was in the hospital, he couldn't stop her from doing her detective work. Myra grabbed her keys, got in the car, and pulled out. Again she knocked over the trash cans, so she stopped short. Only this time, she laughed out loud. And the kids joined her as she drove off. As they reached the hospital, the kids were amazed at the ambiance, because they had been told that hospitals are usually smelly and somewhat dirty, at least the ones in the inner city. In this hospital, the floors were clean, it didn't have a smell of sick people, and every floor had a floral design with a flower arrangement in the lobby area. They kept walking and looking around until they came to a room. They realized by the look on Myra's face that it was their father's room. Suddenly they went running toward his bed, yelling, "Hey, Dad! We miss you!"

And Myra, being protective as usual, said, "All right, kids, be careful."

Putting his arm around all three, Dee told her, "It's okay, Mimi, I haven't seen these guys in so long that I just want to hold all of them."

Trey looked up at Dee and began speaking first. "Daddy, I'm on the basketball team."

"Oh, really."

"Uh-huh, that's why I'm wearing this jersey. It's the uniform."

"Wow! I'm so proud of you, Trey."

Then Dee turned to look at Devon, now standing six feet three inches tall, and said, "And what is my row dog up to?"

Shocked by his father's recovery, he smiled and said, "What it do, Dad?"

Myra gave Dee a nudge, signaling him not to encourage the boy with the slang

"Oh, Mimi, relax, I'm just having fun with my big son-aka-ironman-aka-next man in line."

Devon joined in and chanted, "What what! Big dogs in the hizouse."

Myra rolled her eyes up and mumbled, "Lord, help them for they know not what they do—you guys are making too much noise … there are sick people here."

Ignoring Myra's request, Dee continued to speak to Devon. "Anyway, Devon, what's up? How's school? Tell me everything."

"Well, I made first cut on the junior varsity. And we just received news yesterday that Clarke Atlanta University will be coming to check me out in the last game."

"What! Now that's what I'm talking about, just like his father—all skills."

"I am passing most of my classes, except for English ..."

"Oh, I wonder why," Myra sarcastically added.

"All right, Ma, chill," said Devon.

"Excuse me." Myra looked at Devon and raised her hand, but before she could slap him in the back of his neck, Devon quickly apologized and said, "I mean, please relax while I talk to Dad."

"See what I mean, Dee, when you talk slang, it encourages him to do the same."

"I know, Mimi. Devon, your mother has a point; please do not talk to her that way."

"Okay, Dad. Oh, and I gotta nice shorty."

In shock, Myra blurted out, "Devon!"

"I mean I have a nice girlfriend ... It takes some getting used to, Ma."

"Is she pretty, a Christian?" Dee asked.

"Oh, yeah, most definitely, Dad. She is both fine and divine."

"Good, that's what I like to hear." Dee then noticed the look on Princess's face and said, "Now, what's wrong with my little Princess? Come here, baby girl."

"Hi, Daddy ..."

"Why you look so sad?" Dee attempted to pick her up, but one of his hands gave way. Devon quickly stepped in and helped her up.

"Because ..."

"Because what, baby girl?"

"Well, because I don't have any news to tell you ..."

"You must have something you want to share with me ..."

"No, I don't." Princess poked her mouth out more.

"Well, how was your day at school yesterday?"

"Okay …"

"It was just okay?"

Princess put her finger on his lips. "Hmm, well, I went on a trip to the library."

"Oh, yeah? What did you read?"

"I didn't read. An author came to read to us."

"Yeah, well, who was that?"

"Maya Ang … I don't remember her last name, it's too hard to remember."

Princess intentionally stalled, knowing she remembered the name.

"Was it Maya Angelou, baby?"

"Yeah, how did you know, Daddy?" Princess smiled brightly.

"Well, she is my favorite author in the world."

"Really, Daddy?"

"Yep, you know what else? I have almost all of her books."

With her eyes wide open, Princess reached for the book on the table. "But do you have this one?"

"Wow, baby girl, I don't have this …"

"It's for you, Daddy." Princess badgered him to look at the book. "Open it up, Daddy."

"I'll read it later, Princess." Dee laid his head back. Myra rushed to his side.

"Are you okay, Dee?

Dee nodded his head yes, but signaled Myra to prevent drawing attention to his pain. Meanwhile, Devon noticed and tried to get Princess off the bed. Of course, without a budge, she ignored Devon. Instead, she continued to press upon Dee to open the book to the front page at least.

"No, Daddy! Open it up now."

"Okay, okay …"

Dee opened the book to the front cover and saw a little note of encouragement and a signed autograph from Maya Angelou herself. He looked in disbelief and said, "Oh, my God, I can't believe it."

"What, Dee?" Myra waited anxiously to hear what Dee was staring in awe of.

"Mimi, she had it autographed for me."

"What, really?"

"Here, look for yourself." Dee passed the book to Myra and grabbed Princess closer to kiss her forehead—this was his usual sign of affection with his baby girl. Suddenly he realized this was the first time Princess actually played him … "Hey you—you tricked me."

Princess giggled, "Yep, and you fell for it, ha-ha-ha … Do you like it, Daddy?"

"Like it?… I love it. Thanks, baby girl."

"Yeah, and even though everybody got the same thing in their book, I was the only one to ask for a different one."

"Wow, Princess, now that makes it more special. I love you, baby girl."

"Love you, too, Daddy."

Dee and Princess locked into a long embrace. As they hugged, a tear rolled down Dee's face. Devon and Trey began to feel melancholy. Suddenly, with a knock on the door, Cissy peeped in, "Knock-knock …" Cissy waited for a response.

"Come in, Reject," Dee snapped sarcastically.

Cissy snapped back, "Who are you calling a reject, you has-been? Have you learned anything from being laid-up? You know I put you here." Cissy placed the flowers she brought in on his table.

"That's because I took one look at you and collapsed," replied Dee.

"Yo, Mama …"

"Now why you have to go to the Mama jokes?" Cissy knew Dee could only say Mama jokes when Myra wasn't around because she would get overly sensitive. The last time they had a "Yo, Mama" match, Myra stopped speaking to Dee for a week. Here they stood looking at each other. Then out of the blue, they started laughing.

"Anyway, Dee, how you feeling?"

"I'm okay, little sis."

"Hi, Aunt Cissy," the kids simultaneously said before Myra started to call them on their manners. If there was one thing Myra was a stickler for, it was manners. She didn't tolerate the kids being rude or behaving as though they had no upbringing. Saying hello when someone entered the room, excusing yourself when people were talking, and taking off your hat upon entering a place were just a few things she expected the kids to remember. Cissy always said it was "old-school," but to Myra old-school was the best school. And it was what made Myra and Cissy the great women they were today. Although Cissy was younger, she was just as strict, only she kept up-to-date with the new ways and trends.

Cissy said hello back to the kids. Then she turned to Myra to give her a hug and kiss, then asked, "How you doing, Sis?"

"I'm fine, but I'm shocked to see you here. What brings you to the hospital?"

"I came to see my brother-in-law now that he can't move around; I figured I'd mess with him."

"I may not be able to move around, but I can still move my mouth. By the way, are you still looking for a man to take you in?"

"For your information, I am not looking for, nor do I need or want a man ..."

"Oh, no, don't tell me you leaning the other way now, Cissy."

"Shut up, Dee!" Cissy scowled at Dee.

"Ooh, you said a bad word," Princess cut in to remind Cissy.

"Yes, Princess, Auntie was just playing. She won't do it again," Myra explained as she gave Cissy the evil eye.

"Sorry, kids," Cissy apologized, but Trey and Devon didn't pay them any attention. At this point, they were immune to their kind of humor. They knew their father and Cissy had a love/hate relationship.

"Uh, Aunt Cissy, let me holla atcha for a minute." Devon put his arm around Cissy and began to plead his case about her babysitting.

"What do you want, Devon?" Cissy rolled her eyes at him.

"Man, Auntie, why you gotta say it like that?"

"Because she stup—"

"Dee!" Myra loudly interrupted, nudging Dee at his leg.

"Oh, my bad. She's ignorant."

"Uh, excuse me, who's the one lying up in the hospital because he didn't use half his sense to take better care of himself?"

And if looks could kill, Dee would die because Cissy gave him the hardest stare.

Myra then intervened, putting her hands up between Dee and Cissy. "Hush now! Aren't you guys tired of fighting after all these years?"

"Oh, please, she knows that I'm just playing with her. It's all in fun, right, Cissy?" Dee fakes a smile, to sort of lighten the situation for Myra.

Waving her hand at him, Cissy mumbled, "Whatever."

"Anyway, Auntie, can you stay with Trey and Princess tonight? I wanna chill with my boys."

Cissy. now aggravated, wasn't going to make it easy for Devon.

"I don't know. I have plans tonight, Devon."

"Please, Auntie, just for tonight. I had these plans for a long time."

Cissy crossed her arms, looking at Devon in disbelief. "Now how could you have had these plans for a long time with your father in the hospital?"

"I wasn't even expecting for him to—you know."

"No, I don't know, tell me, Devon."

"You know—get sick. I knew this movie was coming out before all of this happened. And me and my boys want to go see it today, since it's Friday and not a 'school night.'"

"So, now that your father is better, you want to go hanging with your friends?"

"Man, it's just the movies. Watch the kids for the boy, it's not like you have a date." Dee tried to help, but Devon, behind Cissy, signaled his father to quit.

Cissy, looking at Dee, pointed her finger while giving him the "black woman's neck roll" and said, "You know what, Dee, you lucky my sister married your ignorant behind because my father was dead against her marrying such an incredibly dumb jock."

"Awww, poor Cissy, the truth hurts, doesn't it? Don't worry, the men's shelter is still open. And from what I hear, they accept senior citizens, but be careful now because they don't accept retards."

Walking toward him, Cissy stuck out her two hands, heading for his neck, and said, "No, but they're about to accept a handicap if you don't shut—"

"Okay, stop it, guys," Myra interrupted.

Devon again ignored their twisted tit-for-tat bumping of the heads, and said, "So, Auntie, you'll babysit?"

The three of them stopped and looked at Devon as if he had two heads for interrupting with such an unimportant question. Devon quickly stepped back. To break the silence, Cissy told Devon yes, but warned him to give her notice ahead of time the next time he wanted to go out and needed her to babysit. Devon ran up to her, kissed her on the cheek, and hugged her while thanking her over and over again.

"All right, kids, let's go get some lunch, then come back." Myra ordered them to gather their things.

"Wow, that sounds great, what are we getting, Mimi?" Dee asked.

"Uh, I don't think you should get anything. You have a special diet you have to follow, Dee."

"Are you really going to let me suffer with this hospital food?"

"I don't know if eating outside food is a good idea, sweetie. Not now anyway."

All the "sweeties" in the world could not cool down Dee's upset.

"So, why don't you go ask the doctor instead of making assumptions? Isn't he the person to make the final decision?"

"Yeah, I guess so," Myra answered him, with doubt weighing on her heart.

"What do you mean you guess so? You must know, since you said I have a special diet, right?"

"Dee, why are you being so rude? Kids, wait for me outside with Aunt Cissy."

The kids had never really witnessed their parents in a disagreement before, so they watched in shock, just staring at both of them. Myra then shouted, "Go. Now!"

Being very narcissistic, Dee tried pushing Myra's button further. "Why are you sending the kids out of the room, Mimi? Afraid to give the wrong impression? I mean, everyone knows you can be a 'Ms. Know-it-all' when you want."

"Oh, I'm not the one giving any impressions, but you're most certainly giving the impression of being a big jackass..."

"Wooo, okay, kids, cover your ears and walk quickly out the door," Cissy interrupted.

"Oh, you're just innocent, aren't you, Myra?"

The two continued as if they were alone in the room.

"You know what, you just came out of a coma and already you're acting rude and obnoxious. I'm not going to even respond to your disgraceful attitude because you always tend to blow things out of proportion and make me feel like the bad guy." Myra shook her head in disbelief as she gathered her jacket and purse.

"Listen, nobody makes you feel like anything. You do a great job of it yourself."

"Oh, really? Well, since I'm the obvious problem here, I'll leave you alone.

"Do whatever makes you happy. Walk away as usual."

"Have a good day, Dee."

"Don't be cordial now, just leave," Dee said as he waved his hand at Myra to leave.

"Oh, you don't have to ask me twice. I was already leaving, A—"

"Myra! He's not worth it, let's go," said Cissy, grabbing Myra's hand. She quickly pulls her out the doorway before she could call him another name.

"You're right, let's go before I really go off. Have the nerve to talk to me like this after all I do for him. He must be out of his mind. You know what?" Myra aggressively grabbed Princess and headed for the elevator.

Dee knew he had struck the wrong cord in Myra when she started to curse at him.

Cissy tried to calm Myra down.

Myra fanned herself, saying, "Oh, I'm cool … Hurry up, kids!"

"Okay!" Princess and Trey mumbled.

Cissy just shrugged her shoulders, knowing Myra was anything but cool because the kids were practically running to keep with her. At this point, Myra was through with Dee and his attitude. It was too soon for him to start acting his old ridiculous self. After waiting several months for him to come back to life, she started to think, "Do I want him back?" And as soon as the question came to mind, she stopped walking and asked Cissy to take the kids to the car. Cissy looked into Myra's eyes with concern. "Cissy, please, I just have to use the bathroom," Myra said. But Cissy knew better.

In a sympathetic tone, Cissy said, "Sure, Girl … take all the time you need."

Myra dashed into the private ladies' room. She locked the door behind her, then slid down to the floor, weeping. She couldn't believe after all of the begging she did to God to bring him back, that he was behaving so cruelly. After a few minutes of weeping, she picked up her cell phone to call the one person who understood her the most, her best friend Michelle. She was the only person who would listen to her let off some steam, not be so critical, and still be able to give an impartial opinion.

"Hello, Dr. Duvois' office. Dr. Duvois speaking."

"He-llo, you're answering your own phone now?"

"Myra? What's wrong, sister girl? Is Dee okay?"

"Oh, Dee's doing fine now. I'm the one having a breakdown."

"Wow, what's going on?"

"Well, he's out of the coma …"

"Oh, my God! To God be the glory. Thank you, Jesus."

Silence overpowered the conversation. Myra looked at herself in her compact mirror. She grabbed a piece of tissue, wiping the running mascara staining her face. Michelle listened on the other end as Myra cleared her throat. Intently listening, Michelle knew this was her signal to say something. Being friends for so long, they knew how and when to speak.

"Myra, why do you sound so sad when you should be so happy?"

Myra didn't know what to say. She felt like pouring out her feelings, but at the same time, she didn't want to appear ungrateful. Michelle began spewing out questions as if Myra was one of her patients. However, Myra didn't respond. Instead, she rambled about Dee's miraculous awakening. Michelle clearly heard the shakiness in Myra's voice as she spoke. Mildly interrupting, Michelle asked, "What did Dee say to you, honey?"

"It's not what he said, it's how he said it. I mean, after all I've done for him and all I've gone through, I can't believe he would be so abrasive. I was only suggesting he eat healthy food …"

"I know he can be condescending, but you have to understand he's going through his own guilt, girl. You know he didn't take good care of himself before he went into the hospital …"

"And apparently nothing has changed …"

"Well, I guess not …"

"I don't know. Maybe I should just give up getting him to do right …"

"No, sweetie, don't give into the devil."

Michelle tried hard to speak words of wisdom. She, along with Cissy, didn't care for Dee's character too much. At least, the way he acted with Myra. Although he did well for himself, it was evident he believed Myra was only a small entity to his success. And though publicly he was good with paying her full credit, he patronized her in any way he could—whether it was about how she dealt with the kids, the house, or even herself.

"Myra, most times it's not the person, but the spirit behind the person. And not the Holy Spirit either. You hear what I'm saying?"

"Yeah, I hear you …"

"Girl, wipe your tears and keep being you. The loving, thoughtful, and courageous you."

Myra then stood up from the floor to get herself together. She looked in the mirror, wiped her tears, and put on a fresh coat of lip gloss. Then she calmly said to herself, "God is good all the time, and all the time God is good."

*   *   *   *   *

As Myra approached the car, she saw Cissy talking to a guy and taking his card.

"Great. I ask you to watch the kids, and you're out here giving numbers."

"Uh, correction, I'm getting numbers. I don't give anything but my time, which I don't have right now. I have a client waiting for me. I'll see you at the house later!"

"Okay, bye!"

Myra got in the car and told the kids to put on their seat belts, but Princess couldn't help but want to know what happened between her mama and daddy.

"Mama, why are you and Daddy fighting?"

"We're not fighting … Daddy is just not happy right now, Princess."

"Why?"

"Because he wants to be with us. He misses hanging out with his family, but you don't worry about it. He's going to be okay. Now, what do you kids want to eat?"

"McDonalds!" shouted Princess.

"No … Burger King," Trey blurted out.

"Listen, I just want to go home and get ready, I'll eat later," Devon slipped in.

Myra in aggravation replied, "Devon, we will be home soon! Now let's try this again. What are you guys going to eat?"

"All right, let's get McDonald's since Princess wants to," Trey offered.

"Thank you, Trey!... Hey, you're supposed to say 'You're welcome,'" Princess said.

"Oh, gosh! You're welcome. Now leave me alone, Princess!" Trey retorted.

Myra couldn't stand it when the boys spoke roughly to Princess.

"Stop talking to your sister that way … it's rude. Say sorry."

With his lips poked out, in his most upset voice, Trey uttered, "Sorry!"

"How about saying it nicer, boy?" Myra criticized.

Trey didn't like having to say "Sorry," but he despised being scolded, so he tells Princess he's sorry in a calm tone.

"It's getting late. I have to meet them at 7:00, Ma," Devon cut in.

"Devon, if you mention anything again about going out tonight, you will not be going anywhere."

Devon murmured to himself, "Whatever."

"What did you say?"

"Nothing, Ma."

"We are almost home anyway, Devon; just be patient."

Confused

❦

"Well, hello, Mr. Harris, how are we feeling?"

"Yea ... yea, hi, Dr. D'Angelo ... You can call me by my first name."

"Why are we so sour?"

"Listen, I'm tired of this hospital and the food ..."

"I know the food has no taste, but you have no other choice if you want to get better."

"Whatever. I just want to hurry things up. I have accounts and clients to get back to and a staff waiting for my return. You know what that's all about, Doc."

"I know, but right now you need to concentrate on your recovery, more importantly, your family. So far you're returning to normal, your heart rate is good, and pressure is normal. And aside from your attitude, you're doing very well for someone who just got out of a coma ..."

"But, Doc ... I keep getting headaches—what's that all about?"

"I can't answer that right now, but tomorrow I'll have the results of your tests, and we'll find out then. For now, get some rest."

"I will. Thanks, Doc."

Dee laid his head back, closing his eyes in meditation. Praying being a large part of Dee's "walk," he resumed with a prayer.

"Lord, I know you are the most sovereign, most high Lord, and any circumstances that comes my way is pre-ordained by you. I pray that you continue to bless my wife and children, my practice and my health. Have your way with me, Lord. I leave it in your hands. In Jesus' name, I pray. Amen."

Dee continued to meditate until he began to fall asleep. His hope was that Myra would return to the hospital before he'd fall asleep. He thought 'It's a slim chance", but he had hope. That was the one thing he always had, is hope. Even more than hope, he had faith. Plus, knowing Myra has always had a soft spot for him made it more likely than not she would come back. He couldn't see how she would've changed much while he was in the coma. He started to breathe in and out slowly. That alone helped his headaches subside.

*   *   *   *   *

At the house, Myra was busy getting the laundry done, helping with projects, and cooking dinner. This Of course, made it easier for Cissy, since she was not a cook. She was great at cleaning and organizing. But cooking was more up Myra's alley. Yeah, Myra could get down in the kitchen. As children, Myra was the helpful one, always chopping, grating and seasoning by her mother's side. Cissy was just the opposite. The closest she came to helping in the kitchen was when she tried to make scrambled eggs one morning. But instead they came out more like crunchy eggs from all the shells left in the yolk. Thereafter, she vowed her place wasn't in the kitchen. And everyone else agreed.

After putting one load in, helping Trey with his math project, and checking the chicken in the oven. Myra went to Devon's room. As usual, it was atypically clean, neat and organized for a boy his age. Myra walked in to find Devon standing there with a towel around his narrow waist.

Looking in the mirror, He noticed Myra standing at the foot of his bed. Sarcastically he tells her sit, get comfortable since she didn't knock. She ignored him, staring in disbelief. Her firstborn was turning into a young man, going out on his own. Myra then started giving Devon the rules for going out.

"All right now, Devon, make sure you come home at a decent hour like eleven and no later, do not hang out in the street, and go directly to the movies, to eat, and back home."

"Okay, Mama."

"Mama" was his form of endearment toward Myra when she made him happy.

Then Myra started to leave, but remembered one more thing.

"Oh, and Devon, make sure you have your ID on you."

"Okay, Mama."

"And another thing, how are you getting there, Devon?"

"Kilo—I mean, Kevin—is driving."

"Really ..."

Myra stared. Devon stared back. He noticed her second-guessing the whole outing now, so he began giving her the lost-puppy look.

Myra, looking back in suspicion, let go of her doubt. "All right, well, there better not be any drinking tonight."

"Mom, I don't drink ..."

"That's right, but if your friend does, you better n—"

"Not go in the car, I know, Ma. Now, can I get dressed, please?"

"Yes, and ..." Myra started walking out, then turned around again. However, before she could get a word out, Devon planted both hands on her shoulders, turning her back around, and led her back out the door. "Mom, don't worry, I'll be careful. You know the Lord will take care of me."

"Devon, do not use the Lord to your convenience with me. I was just going to say have fun tonight."

Devon then leaned in, giving Myra a kiss on the cheek. "See you later, Ma, and tell Dad I'll see him tomorrow. After school."

"Okay!"

Myra walked downstairs and noticed Cissy's car in the driveway. She grabbed her purse and jacket and headed for the door. "Cissy, I'm heading back to the hospital now!" she shouted.

Cissy shouted back from her car, "Okay, see you later!"

Myra jumped in the car and took off. She realized she had only a few more hours to visit Dee before he fell asleep. And she didn't want to spend it discussing what happened earlier. Her wish was that he'd already be asleep. To her, that was when he looked most angelic. And that's exactly how she wanted to enjoy him, in peace.

On the car ride, Myra tuned into the traffic station on the radio. Traffic was one of many things that agitated Myra most about driving. Whether the reports were accurate or not, she lived "religiously" by the station, so to speak. Ten minutes in, she noticed a backup on the freeway and thought *So much for the traffic station*. Myra turned the radio off, put on her Yolanda Adams CD, and exited. She decided to take the surface streets instead. Myra hummed along to the first track.

After two songs and fifteen minutes of driving, she pulled into the hospital parking lot. Before going in, Myra takes a quick walk around the grounds. She figured a walk would help clear her mind and give her peace.

As she stopped to look at the cathedral-style building, she took in small gulps of air. She then closed her eyes, imagining herself in the wooded mountains outside her cabin. All she could think of was how much she loved going there on weekends and holidays with Dee and the kids. There were even times they didn't want to go back home. Today would make six months since they'd gone to the cabin. And although Dee was just getting better, Myra and the kids had been planning to go for the summer, to spend time with Devon before he left for college in the fall. Keeping that thought in mind, Myra opened her eyes, looking straight at the dome on the building. She took in her last breath of fresh air and began to walk into the hospital.

In the lobby, she watched as different people walked around with gifts, flowers, and balloons in their hands to visit their sick family members. Usually this would encourage her to do the same, but today was not a usual day. Myra walked to the elevator diagonal to where she was standing and waited for its arrival. After two minutes of humming while waiting, it came. Myra boarded it with hesitation. She asked the lady next to the buttons to press the button for the floor Dee was on.

*   *   *   *   *

Myra walked quickly to the room, hoping he was asleep. She finally got to the door, opened it, and thankfully found him asleep. She took a sigh of relief and mumbled, "Oh, good, he's asleep."

"No, I'm just meditating, Mimi."

"You heard me—I mean, you heard that?"

"Yes, I did, and I can't believe you're relieved to see me asleep."

"I'm not relieved. I'm just at peace. You need your rest …" With all intentions to not show how disappointed she was in his behavior earlier, Myra looked down to the floor with a repressed expression. However, Dee already knew Myra's feelings about arguing in front of the kids. And he could see this hadn't changed with Myra. Dee gently brought Myra's chin up.

"Listen, baby, I apologize for being so hostile…."

"Yes, you were definitely on a warpath—" Myra tried to interrupt, but Dee stopped her.

"Wait, let me finish. I know you've been through a lot, and I want to be your refuge, not your burden or enemy, so I promise to make this situation better for both us and the kids."

Myra, not so impressed, asked, "Are you done, Dee?"

Dee replied, "Yes," with his puppy-dog eyes and handsome smile.

"Dee, I know it's hard for you, not being able to move around the way you want, but it's a sacrifice for all of us. In order for you to get back to some sort of normalcy, you have to set some priorities on your health. So, please, promise me that whatever you want to do from now on, you'll address it to the doctor first. And to me, that will make your stay at the hospital better and shorter."

"I can definitely do that. Now you promise me something."

"What, Dee?" Myra blushed.

"Promise me you'll continue being the beautiful blessing you are. And ignore me when I act like a donkey's you-know-what."

"Well, of course, that's why I'm here, baby."

"I honestly thought you were going to stay home tonight. Especially after seeing how upset you were at me earlier."

"Now, since when is your wife that stubborn?"

"I don't know what I was thinking; I'm just glad you're here. Now, can you please lie down next to me?"

"Sure. Move over, Big Daddy."

*   *   *   *   *

Hours passed, and the television in Myra's living room started blaring. Cissy jumped up from her sleep only to realize she had laid her head on the remote. She turned down the volume, looked at her watch, and made out 1:55 in the morning. Frantically aware of the time, Cissy started talking to herself.

"I know this boy is not still out there. Okay, let me not jump to conclusions, and check his room."

Cissy went to Devon's room and saw his bed empty. "Humph, just what I thought." Cissy then went to the kitchen and started pacing the floor, mumbling words, and looking out the window in anticipation. Finally she saw headlights from a car entering the driveway, and she rushed to the door to confront him as he walked in.

Two minutes passed, and Cissy began to huff and puff as if she was going to blow the house down. Suddenly Devon opened the door, and Cissy rushed him. "Boy, where were you? It's two o' clock in the morning, Devon."

"Ssh, Aunt Cissy. You're gonna wake up Trey and Princess."

"Boy, don't you shush me … I will smack the life out of you. Now I said, where were you?"

"I went to my friend's house, and we were just chillin … What?"

"*Excuse me!* What do you mean, what? Just who do you think you're talking to?" Cissy whacked him in the back of his head with the rolled-up newspaper she found on the console behind the door.

"Ouch, Aunt Cissy. What was that for?"

"For being rude with your mouth. Open your mouth like that to me again, and the next hit will be with the bat your mother keeps in the closet. Now, let's try this again: Where were you?"

Devon looked up with a don't-care expression and said, "I was at my boys' house."

"Boy, you think I'm playing with you, right? Wait right here! Talking to me like you're grown, you must be out of your doggone mind." Cissy went to Myra's bedroom to get the bat out of the closet. Looking in disbelief, Devon stood in his place with his fist balled in. Cissy came back with the bat in the air ready for aim. She knew she wasn't about to hit him, but he didn't have a clue what she was about to do. And this was exactly how she liked it to be.

"Aunt Cissy, nooo! I'm sorry."

"No, don't say sorry now, Devon. You're grown, you're tough, and this won't hurt at all ..."

"Okay, okay, just put the bat down, please ..."

At this point Devon was holding his hands out in front of him, with his eyes wide open in fear. He continued to beg her to put the bat down. After a few seconds of gathering herself for the big swing, she finally put it down and said, "Now, are you going to answer my question in a civil manner, or am I going to have to beat it out of you? Then your mother will find out, and you know that kind of crazy is a sure thing."

"Okay, I was at my friend Kevin's house. We went there after the movies because no one had any money to go anywhere else and you know how my mom doesn't want me in the street."

"Who is 'we,' Devon?"

"Huh?"

"Don't huh me ... who is 'we'?"

"Kevin, his shorty, two of my other friends and their shortys, and ..."

"And let me guess, you and your 'shorty,'" Cissy interrupted with sarcasm.

"Huh?"

"Boy, if you huh me one more time, I'm going to beat the 'huh' out of you." Cissy picked up the bat again.

"No, my girl wasn't there … I mean, not the whole time … she had to be home by eleven o'clock."

"Okay, so if she had to be home at eleven, why are you just getting home at two o'clock?"

"Because I took her home, then went back to Kevin's house."

"So, let me get this straight, you went to Kevin's house, hung out, took your girlfriend home, then went back to Kevin's house?"

"Yes."

"You went back to Kevin's house to do what, Devon?"

"So we can chill and talk."

"No, uh-uh, that doesn't even sound right … Boy, do you see stupid written across my forehead?"

"Aunt Cissy, I'm telling the truth …"

"Oh, yeah? Well, since you're telling the truth, what time did the movie start, Devon?"

"It started at nine."

"What time did it finish, Devon?"

"It finished at ten-thirty."

"And you had time to go to Kevin's house, drop your girlfriend off, and go back to Kevin's house again, but now here you come waltzing in at two in the morning. Now, what's wrong with that picture, Devon?"

"Nothing … because it's the truth."

"Urr … wrong answer; it's not true. It's made-up, make-believe, you know, a lie you made up—liar!"

At this point, Cissy jumped right in Devon's face, putting the fear of God in him. Devon looked in disbelief. He couldn't understand why his auntie didn't believe him. She had never treated him suspect before.

"But, Auntie, I'm not lying."

"Were Kevin's parents home?"

"No. They went out …"

"So, your girlfriend's parents were home to meet you at least?"

"Yes, but …"

"But let me guess, you didn't meet them either … just like you and Kevin spent the rest of the night 'talkin and chillin' … Yeah, you must think I'm stupid … and since you think I'm stupid, do not ask me to cover with babysitting anymore."

"But, Aunt Cissy, why?"

"I will not be your opportunity to mess up! That's why!"

"But I'm not messing up … please, don't stop babysitting …"

"Nope … I can't do it. You ought to be thankful your mom didn't get home yet …" Cissy walked away, leaving him standing there with a dumbfounded look on his face. Devon knew if he didn't come straight with the truth, then he would lose all freedom to hang out. And at this point, Aunt Cissy was his ticket to that freedom.

"Okay, okay … Aunt Cissy, my girlfriend and I hung out longer than that … but we didn't do anything."

"Yeah, right …"

"It's true, Aunt Cissy."

"Boy, do you know that whatever you do in life impacts the people around you? Especially at this stage of your life … you have a brother who wants to be like you, a sister who looks up to you—who, by the way, will one day be 'talkin and chillin' with her friend/boyfriend just like you. And let's not forget your parents, who bust their behinds to give you everything. And if you get caught out there, they'll wonder where they went wrong. One slipup and a possible baby can transform your life forever. You won't be able to hang out; you will have to get a job to pay for the girl and a baby. And college may be out of the question in the beginning because taking care of your baby will be your first priority. Not to mention you would disappoint your father, break your mother's heart, and leave a big question mark for your future. So, do you see how one slipup can cause a breakdown for not only you, but for everyone else around you, too?"

"Yeah, I see what you're saying, Aunt Cissy."

"Do you? Because you have to understand that life is what you make it, and it's just not about fun and hanging out with your friends. It's what you create. Whatever seed you sow will determine what you reap. So if you sow a seed of foolishness, then you will reap being a fool or vagrant; if you sow a seed of 'talking and chillin' with your friends over doing your schoolwork, then you will reap being a dummy; and if you sow a seed of being a player-player, then you will reap ..."

"Let me guess, I will reap becoming a baby Daddy."

"No, you will reap getting a butt-kicking because you know better than to become a baby Daddy!"

Devon chuckled while shaking his head. "Aunt Cissy, you're crazy, but I got you ..."

"Now take some pride and respect in yourself; be a leader and not a follower."

"I hear you, but Aunt Cissy, what's a vagrant?"

"It's a homeless person. You know, what you were about to become a couple of minutes ago. See, if you did more studying than hanging out, I wouldn't have to tell you what it is."

"Please, I'm straight, Aunt Cissy."

"I know that's right, but we're not talking about your preference right now, we're talking about your grades."

"Good one, Aunt Cissy, but I'm talking about how your smart and handsome nephew made the honor roll."

"Oh, so your school just gives it to anyone these days ..."

Devon then stopped dancing and smiling, but gave Cissy a serious stare.

"Just joking, I'm very proud of you. Now go to bed before your mother gets home."

"Good-night, Auntie."

"Good-night, Devon."

Devon ran upstairs to do his ritual of washing his hands and face and brushing his teeth. He then walked into his room. He took his shirt off and hung it in the order of color in his closet. He took off his jeans, folding them precisely at the inseam, and put them on the shelf with the other dark jeans in his closet. He put his basketball shorts on, leaving on his white mariner undershirt. If he could sleep in his boxers he would, but his father wouldn't have it. Dee's philosophy was "The only man that can sleep in his boxers is the man paying the bills." Devon respected his father's wishes no matter whether he was home or not. After making sure everything was away, he got on his knees at the foot of his bed and prayed. These were the few things Dee had impressed upon him, which his militant father had taught him. Dee made sure Devon understood disorder, clutter, or sloppiness was all a frame of mind and nothing more. He always said, "If your mind is filled with things, nonsense, and ungodliness, then it shows publicly in your walk, in your presence, and in your lifestyle."

And because Devon looked up to his father so much, he paid close heed to Dee's advice. Devon got into bed and fell asleep with those thoughts in his mind and a smile on his face. Minutes later, Myra walked in to see Cissy in the kitchen drinking tea. She put her keys on the hook by the door. She put her bag on the counter, then grabbed a mug to join her sister in tea.

"Hey, Sis, how was babysitting?"

"Girl, you know I can handle these kids."

"Did Devon come home on time?"

"He came in a little late …"

"What! And you didn't call me?"

Myra jumps up without hesitation to confront him, but Cissy stopped her. She let her know she took care of it. And Devon assured her it wouldn't happen again. Myra looked in disbelief. Cissy gave her a serious look as if to say "You know I don't take crap." Myra then sat back down with relief on her face and said, "Girl, you know I don't care what time it is. I would beat him out of his sleep."

Cissy snickered, replying, "I know that's right. Anyways, how was the rest of your visit? Being that Dee was acting like a real jerk earlier."

Myra put her hand up. "Cissy, don't start."

"What! You know it's true."

Myra couldn't stand it when Cissy talked bad about Dee, especially being he'd always had nothing but love for her. Almost as if she was his little sister. Dee just found her annoying at times, but he loved her in any case, hence making sense of the little sister/big brother rivalry. And although Cissy always said belittling things about Dee, Myra knew the majority of the time, Cissy had love for him, too. Myra just wished they'd stop arguing all of the time.

Cissy continued, "So, what did the selfish ingrate have to say for himself?"

"Well, we talked and …"

"And what?" Cissy gave the "let me hear this one" look.

"We have an understanding, Cissy."

"As always, Myra, you have the understanding while he makes demands on you."

"No. I think we really have an understanding this time. I understand that he can take care of himself and ask the doctor his own questions about what he can or cannot do, and he understands that I care about his health and want him to take a more active role in it."

"Oh, really, and what about taking care of *your* health?"

"Cissy, what are you talking about? My health is perfectly fine."

"Is it, Myra? You are constantly stressed, not eating properly, and on top of that, you act depressed most of the time."

"Oh, please, that was when he was in a coma. I'm fine now, and you have nothing to worry about." Myra grabbed their mugs and put them in the sink to avoid eye contact.

"Oh, I'm not worried … because I'm not the one who's crazy; but you, on the other hand …"

"Excuse me," Myra responded in alarm. For some reason, she thought maybe Cissy knew about her inner debate to seek professional help. She wouldn't have to go far, since her best friend Michelle is a psychiatrist.

"I'm just playing, but you are my sister, and when you're not feeling good, I can sense it," Cissy explained.

"Cissy, I've been doing just fine with the help of the Lord. And you and Devon have been a great help, too. I know I've been blessed."

Cissy got up, kissed Myra on her cheek, and said her good-byes. Myra didn't want Cissy to leave because she wanted the company. Even though Cissy had explained time and time again that sleeping in her own bed was more comfortable, Myra figured she'd try again and ask her to sleep over.

Cissy shook her head no, saying, "I don't want to stay … I want to go home and sleep in my own bed. I'll be careful, Mrs. MamaD #2."

MamaD is what Myra's kids called their grandmother. And this is what Cissy called Myra whenever she started acting like their mom. Cissy also knew it aggravated Myra. And, as always, Myra waved her hand in an "I don't care" motion, and said, "Bye then, hef—"

"See ya," Cissy interrupted, closing the door quickly to cut Myra off from calling her out.

Myra checked in on the kids. Then she went down to her room and changed into one of Dee's work shirts. She walked out to lie down on her new bed, the couch. Ever since Dee was in the hospital, sleeping in their bed only reminded her of his absence. However, wearing his cologne-scented shirt made her feel closer to him. As she lay on the couch, she programmed her phone to remind her of the schedule for the next day. The first thing to do was take the kids to school. Then she could go to the gym, shower, and get ready to meet Michelle for lunch. Michelle was the best person to speak to because it would be like talking to a friend, who happens to be a psychiatrist. Seeing a psychiatrist was a big no-no in her family. As a child, Myra remembered her father stubbornly telling her mom, "Terry, black and Spanish people don't see psychiatrists for their problems—they drink them away." Then her mom would elbow him for making such an ignorant statement.

And even though Myra knew better, she often still wondered if it was true, because most of her dad's family were alcoholics. Myra looked at the clock on the mantle over the fireplace and saw three o'clock. She rolled over to go to sleep. Five minutes passed, and Myra sat back up and put on the television in hopes that it would help her fall asleep. After not finding anything to watch, Myra finally fell asleep to an infomercial.

*   *   *   *   *

The next morning Myra woke up to Devon gently shaking and calling her. Myra jumped up in a panic, fearing that she woke up too late. Devon calmed her down by making her aware of Trey and Princess being ready. Then, he told her, all she had to do was get herself together. He gave her a peck on the forehead and walked himself, Trey, and Princess to school. And although going to the gym was on her agenda this morning, she scratched it off her list of things to do and got up to take a shower. She took a fifteen-minute steam shower. She dried herself, lotioned her body, then sat at her vanity to put on her make-up.

Finally, she opened her walk-in closet, searching for something nice to wear. It was one thing to dress sexy for Dee. But today she was having lunch with her best friend. She had to look "fantabulous." It was one of those "Looking Good" images that occurred often in their friendship. In everyone else's eyes, it looked as though they were competing with each other. But to them, they were just making sure they stayed looking "fantabulous" no matter what age they became. Myra put on her black Donna Karen palazzo pants, white Brooks Brothers shirt with her pink diamond cuff links, and her pink stiletto heels. She pulled out her rollers and brushed her wavy long hair. And for the final touches, she put on the diamond earrings and friendship necklace Michelle bought her two Christmases ago. It was must-wear whenever she was going to hang out with Michelle.

Suddenly Myra noticed the time passing, so she grabbed her jacket and walked out to grab her purse and keys. On the way out, she noticed her coffee jug out. She looked inside to find a fresh cup of coffee still hot with the aroma of hazelnut in it. Myra smiled at the thought of how considerate Devon could be at times. She could honestly say she was blessed with all of her kids, especially him. Myra grabbed the jug, took a sip, and left with it to drink on the drive.

In the car, Myra put the radio on the morning praise and worship station. It was her boost at the start of the day. She pulled out, making her way to the bank, the cleaners, and Dee's office. She had to do a daily check at his office for any messages. Although Dee had a partner, she felt obligated to make sure everything was running smoothly without his presence. And although she didn't have any knowledge of law, she knew how the office should run. Anything to do with the office as far as correspondence, messages, and organizing files didn't take a law degree to handle. Myra's only concern was taking over the firm. It didn't pique her interest at all. More importantly, it wasn't her passion. To her, there was no point in getting involved with something that you have no real interest in. If she had her way, by the time Dee got out, she would be able to start her own business. Though she didn't know how, her hope was that Dee would support her in every way. Whether financially, physically, or just with spiritual help, it would give her the encouragement she needed to live out her passion. This would make her completely happy.

*   *   *   *   *

Cissy pulled into the salon parking lot; she gathered her purse, jacket, and box of products she bought the day before for the salon. While attempting to close the door, she lost her balance. The box slipped.

"Wooo, I got that, baby."

"Lance! What are you doing here? I told you I'm done with you."

"What do you mean, you're done? You know you don't mean that …"

Cissy put up her finger while snapping her neck. She looked at him crazy and said, "Look, Lance, I know very well what I mean, so don't tell me—okay? One thing is for sure, I want you to crawl back to the chicken coop you came from and go back to the chicken head claiming you now. And that I mean from the heart."

Lance never saw Cissy this upset. She had always told him not to cross her the wrong way, but he never thought for once she meant it. He didn't know what to do without Cissy. She was his muscle. His strength was in being with her. However, it didn't make a difference the night he cheated. They had been dating for almost two years up until six months ago. Three and a half months prior, they had a big fight. Lance stormed out, vowing he would never come back. That, of course, lasted two months. By the third month, he was back to calling and begging to see Cissy again. And she took him back.

"Cissy, please! I miss you, I'm not eating or …"

"Good. Starve to death if you want."

"Cissy, come on, look at me …" Lance grabbed her forearm as she turned to open the salon.

Clenching her teeth, Cissy tried to snatch her arm back. "Get your filthy, disgusting hands off of me." Cissy stared at him coldly. Suddenly, without hesitation, he let go of her arm.

"Can you please hear me out?" he begged.

"No, Lance, because giving you any time to speak is a waste of my time. All you're going to do is give me a lame excuse as to why you can't keep your penis in your pants …"

"Cissy, just, please, I know I made a big mistake. I'm so sorry. I really regret it …"

"*Shut up, shut up, shut the hell up!* You are a sorry excuse for a man …"

"I love you, Celeste Marie Lopes!"

Cissy started crying. She followed with shaking her head in disbelief. The last thing he said to her before walking out the first time was "I don't love you enough to settle." Of course, she took in what he said and to this day couldn't believe he could formulate those words. In her mind, all she could think was maybe he really loved her. If he couldn't bother to say it for two years, why would he say it now if he really didn't mean it? All of sudden, two of the beauticians, Jasmine and Val, walked in laughing. They stopped as soon as they saw Lance on his knees with his hands around her waist. Val stood there chewing her gum with an attitude. Jasmine just shook her head as she walked to her booth.

At this point, Cissy didn't know what to do. Those three words touched her to the very core. However, seeing the girls gave her some strength to dismiss him. Lance looked up, stood to his feet with his face wet from crying, and tried to get Cissy to look at him. Cissy turned her back on him. Lance wiped his face, breathing heavily. He then walked out with his head hanging down in shame. As soon as the door closed behind him, Jasmine and Val rushed to Cissy's side to console her. She knew her opportunity to make amends with Lance had just passed, and it hurt so much. Lance was not a man of many words. However, this time she knew he was laying out his feelings. And her denial caused him to quit.

*   *   *   *   *

Myra sped into the parking lot behind Michelle's office. On the way in, she almost ran into another car. She looked at the driver as if it was his fault, then kept going. She parked her car and got out, furiously looking around to find the other driver. But all she recognized was his jacket. She grabbed a bottle of apple cider champagne, which happened to be Michelle's favorite. When she finally got in the building, she ran to the second floor and opened the door to Michelle's office. Out of breath, Myra blurted, "Hello, is Dr. Duvois in?"

"Uh, yes. You can have a seat while I buzz her—"

Michelle came out before the receptionist could intercom her.

"Myra!" Michelle put out her arm for a hug.

"Michelle!" Myra hugged her, then kissed her on the cheek.

"Hey, lady, it's been awhile...."

"You look fabulous, as always," Myra said. In return, Michelle stepped back while holding Myra's hands and checked out her ensemble. Myra let go and did a quick catwalk and turn. They started laughing, then went into the office.

"Let me just gather some files, then we can go eat," Michelle said.

"I see you're still taking work home with you. Girl, I don't know how you do it ..."

"Easy, I make Jeff do everything at home!"

They looked at each other and burst out laughing. Just the thought alone of him doing all the work was so true. Michelle was very good at having her way, especially with her husband. They continued laughing.

"No, but seriously, Myra, it's just about having balance. There's a time for everything, if you plan it out right ..."

"That's a given, but you are doing it all. Work, mom, wife, and you make time to be on the PTA at the kids' school. And on top of that, you have your own medical practice. I don't know. I just don't know if I could do it ..."

"What are talking about—you're doing it! Aren't you organizing and cleaning the house?

"Yes ..."

"Well, that's work. Aren't you taking the kids to all of their activities and being class mom every year in one of the kids' classes? Well, that's being a mom. And haven't you been at your Dee's side every day for the past couple of months? Quite honestly, I don't know how *you* are doing it. I have help; you, on the other hand, are taking care of things by yourself."

"Oh, please, I'm just doing what any wife would do for her husband in a coma. I just thank God he's back ..."

"Maybe now you can get back to doing what you want to do in your life."

"I wish, but I can't do anything until Dee is fully recovered ..."

"Well, I know that, and after he recovers, you are going to put yourself first, no matter what!"

Myra stopped looking at Michelle and walked over to the window. As she looked out, she tried to imagine herself with a career. But the only thing that came to her mind was Dee in the hospital bed.

"Okay, girl, what is going on in that head of yours?" Michelle asked.

"I'm not so sure if I want to take the time to start doing anything. I don't know …"

"Please don't start second-guessing yourself. You could do it, Myra.…"

Michelle joined Myra at the window. She placed her hand on her shoulder. Just then, a tear rolled down Myra's face. Michelle turned and grabbed a tissue off her desk, then handed it to Myra. Myra apologized, but Michelle waved her hand, letting her know there wasn't any need for apologies. She understood Myra's confusion. One thing she knew was that Dee wasn't supportive enough to let Myra focus on herself. He talked a good game, but when it really came down to it, he always managed to get all the attention on himself. However, this time, Michelle was going to see to it that Myra stuck to her plans. A couple of minutes passed, and Michelle broke the silence, telling Myra she had one more phone call to make and then she would meet her downstairs. Myra cleaned her face, freshened her makeup, then grabbed her purse and walked out.

On the way down, Myra recognized the same guy from the parking lot earlier. At least his jacket, but again, she didn't see his face. As he came closer to Myra, she ducked into another corridor. She peeped out and squinted her eyes to get a better look. He pushed the elevator button. And as he looked down at his watch, she thought to herself, *He really looks familiar. Oh, my God, that's …* All of sudden, the stranger blurted out, "I see you looking at me, so why don't you come out and get a closer look?"

Myra stepped out, recognizing his voice, and sarcastically said, "Oh, please, like you're something to look at."

"Myra! Oh, my God, I can't believe it."

"I knew that was you, Travis.… What are you doing here? Are you visiting Michelle?"

"No, I saw her yesterday. Actually remember the case I was investigating?"

Myra pretended to remember, "Uh-huh …"

"You have no clue what I'm talking about, right?"

"Sorry, I have a lot of things on my mind."

"I understand you're dealing with a lot. I was actually picking up some files and lab reports. Are you coming from my cousin's office?"

"Yeah, we're about to go to lunch."

"That sounds good—too bad I can't join you two."

Myra acted as if she was really sorry that he couldn't join them. Travis smiled. Myra turned her head and licked her lips. His smile just had an effect on her.

"It's been awhile. And the last time I saw you, I didn't get a hug, much less a nice greeting."

Myra leaned in for a hug. He hugged her tight. Myra took in his cologne, then pulled away.

"So, let me get a good look at you." Travis looked her up and down. Then he said, "You still look good."

Myra blushed. Travis was definitely a charmer and a womanizer at the same time. Myra noticed him trying to flirt, but ignored it and agreed, "I know … I still got it."

"What are you doing later? I have some time after work. Maybe we can get some coffee and catch up." Travis smiled again, hoping Myra would say yes.

"Oh, I don't think so, Travis. I have a lot of things to take care of today, but maybe another time."

With disappointment in his tone, he noticed her obvious two-carat wedding band and said, "I'm sure your husband wouldn't be happy, either, huh?"

"Oh, please, this has nothing to do with my husband. I just have a lot of things to do."

"Then I'm sure you have at least a few minutes for coffee."

Travis was still the same, always trying to use his charm for persuasion. He never forced her, but he did this thing with his lips while tilting his head to the side, which, of course, worked most of the time. Only this time it wouldn't work.

"Travis, now you of all people should know that anything that comes out of my mouth is the real deal. If I have things to do, then it is what it is."

"I know, I'm sorry. I'm just so happy to see you that I want to catch up."

"I understand, but I can't …"

"Well, before you go, here's my card; give me a call sometime," Travis replied while looking into her eyes.

"Okay, but I can't promise you anything, Travis. I have a lot on my hands right now."

"By no means am I holding you to anything. Just call me when you have the time. I know your situation."

Myra looked at his card, noticing he did exactly what he set out to do. He was now chief detective. Now all she needed to know was why he was back in town. Myra knew she had no time to play catch-up now, but she put the card in her wallet, saying, "All right, Travis, I'll catch up to you later; take care." Myra got on her toes and gave him a peck on the cheek.

"Okay, take care …"

As Myra walked off toward the stairs, Travis stood gazing in awe at how beautiful and maintained she was after all these years. But to add insult to injury, Myra gave him the "sock-it-to-him" walk. This was a name her sister and friends gave it, when they wanted a man to realize what they had missed out on.

Travis took a deep breath and mumbled to himself, "Um, um, um, how did I let her slip away?" At least, he thought he said it to himself— because Myra paused, smiled, and continued giving him the walk until she reached the stairway. In the stairway, Myra sat down for a few minutes to compose herself. For some reason, she was feeling flushed from seeing Travis again. She couldn't believe that after all these years, Travis still had an effect on her. After a brief episode and butterflies in her stomach, Myra walked down the stairs slowly to prevent falling in her stilettos.

When Myra finally reached the car, she noticed a note on the windshield with a package on the passenger seat. She was in such a rush to see Michelle that she didn't realize she had left her doors open. She opened the card and read, "Myra, I remember your infatuation with purses, so here's a small pouch from Dooney & Bourke. I hope you like it. I have a friend in the industry, and it's from the summer line coming up. Think of it as a small token of appreciation for not holding the past against me. I always believed you had class, and I hope you will give me a call sometime so we can catch up."

Myra opened the box, which looked too big to have just a pouch inside. And just as she thought, she saw a purse inside. Myra smiled— the purse was hot, but she knew it would be out of place to keep it considering their past. She also knew that this was his way of getting her to call. Whether she kept it or not, her sense of etiquette would lead her to call and say "thank you" or "no, thank you." But for now, she couldn't give it much thought because she had other fish to fry, figuratively speaking. Right now she was going to lunch with her best friend, getting her hair done, and going back to the hospital to visit Dee.

Finally Michelle came down. She signaled Myra to follow her. Myra pulled up behind her. They drove for about ten minutes, when Michelle pulled up to a Mexican restaurant. This was definitely Michelle's favorite food. And Myra didn't mind it at all, being that she was practically raised on Mexican food. She pulled in behind Michelle. She saw her come out as if they had valet.

And lo and behold, a man came out to park their cars.

"This is nice," Myra commented.

"Yeah, I love this place."

"Girl, tell me why I saw your brother coming out of one of the offices in your building …"

"Oh, yeah, he was probably on a case, because he definitely wasn't there to see me."

"Oh, I know. Oddly enough, he left a card and gift in my car. And I don't know …"

"Well, you know why …"

"Girl, please. He has been the furthest thing from my mind …"

"That may be true, but you know he's always had a thing for you."

"Whether or not that's the case, I know I have to give it back!"

"Why?"

"Michelle, think about it. What would Paul say if you kept a gift from another man?" Myra gave Michelle an eerie look. Michelle looked back at Myra, shaking her head in agreement, completely seeing her point.

The waiter came to get their order. Michelle ordered her usual chicken burrito, while Myra looked over the menu, undecided on what to eat. Finally she looked up at the waiter and asked him in Spanish for black beans and a chicken taco salad. The waiter smiled and left them to continue chatting. Michelle, taken aback, asked Myra if she'd been practicing her Spanish. Myra didn't want to toot her own horn, but she let Michelle know she'd been brushing up for a while. Michelle couldn't say anything, but she slapped Myra a high five. Anything that had to do with growth, prosperity, and determination, Michelle loved to hear. She couldn't be bothered in any way with idle people. Michelle and Myra continued conversing and eating the nachos on the table. Myra began spilling out her guts about Dee, his health, and life when he returned home. At first, Michelle listened intently, and then followed with a slew of questions about Myra's plans. Although Myra knew her concern as a friend, she grew agitated with Michelle's questioning. She couldn't understand why Michelle didn't see her point of putting her career off until Dee recuperated. After an exchange of opposing words and an "agreement to disagree," the two moved on to a different subject.

*   *   *   *   *

The spring weather made it easy for the seniors in Devon's school to leave for "Senior Cut-Out Day." This was the day the seniors cut out of school and went to a party, which was typically held in the captain of the football team's house. Since this was Devon, it was re-routed to the cocaptain's house, since everyone knew of his situation. Besides, Devon wasn't participating in it. Instead, he left to visit his father. And although this was a thing everyone who is anyone did, Devon's girlfriend didn't give in to the hype of cutting out. Her plans to be a success in life kept her in school. Devon, of course, couldn't be happier knowing she didn't follow the crowd and had her own mind. Somehow, it reminded him of his mom.

On the way to the hospital, Devon had time to read over some notes. He took a seat on the bus and pulled out his notebook. Five minutes later, he found himself thinking about college. He always wanted to go away, but since his father's illness, he wasn't so sure anymore. The last thing he wanted to do was go away and have something happen again. Then his mother would be doing everything by herself. He didn't know what he was going to do; going to CAU—aka Clarke Atlanta University—was an opportunity of a lifetime. But he didn't want to go to the expense of his mom suffering alone.

The bus pulled up to the hospital. Devon got off. He entered the hospital, looking around lost. The security guard asked him if he needed help. Devon explained that he was there to visit his father. The guard asked him for the name, looked it up in the computer, and gave Devon the room number. Devon turned around and ran for the elevator. On the way, he got nervous. He didn't know what to say to his father about his college decision. All he knew was that his father was going to want an answer. CAU, being Dee's alma mater, Devon was expected to go there. Devon entered the room, but the bed was empty. His heart beat quickly. Suddenly Dee came out of the bathroom, asking, "Hey, Devon, what are you doing out so early from school?"

"Today is Senior Cut-Out Day, plus I get out at lunch anyway …" Devon told Dee everything. This was just the kind of relationship they had. Dee always made Devon feel like he could tell him anything.

"Wow, it's Senior Cut-Out Day already, huh?" Dee chuckled.

Devon asked him what was so funny. Dee then went into his Senior Cut-Out Day. He told him about trying to convince Myra to cut out with him, but she refused. So he went anyway. However, he got caught up dancing with another girl. Somehow it got back to Myra, and she didn't speak to him for a month. Devon opened his eyes wide, smirking. Dee continued, "Yeah, as you know, your mom is not one to play with ..."

"Yeah, I know. So how did you get her to speak again?"

"Well, I did what every other man does when he's wrong ..."

"What's that?"

"Beg."

They looked at each other and burst out in laughter. One thing Devon enjoyed about his father was his honesty. He never held back. And he never pretended to have total control. Dee let him know when he was messing up, without the anger and hysteria. He left the dramatics to Myra.

They continued to talk and laugh for a few minutes. When Devon started speaking to Dee about his indecision to go away to college, Dee listened intently. Devon expressed his concern for his dad's health. Dee let him finish. Then he reassured him that he was okay. And that no matter what, staying home wasn't an option. He let him know that if he stayed home, it would actually do more damage than help. He reiterated the importance of his education and going for his passion. Devon heard him out, then finally agreed. Devon was still concerned, but at more ease after hearing his father's thoughts. Devon then changed the subject to talk about other things going on in his life.

*   *   *   *   *

Myra walked up to the salon, where Cissy, Jasmine, and Val were standing taking a break.

"Hey, Myra, you're looking good, girl. How's Dee doing?" asked Jasmine.

"Aww, thanks, girl, Dee is coming along great, thanks for asking. And you ladies should talk—you're looking sharp yourselves …"

Cissy grabbed Myra by the wrist and said, "Come on, Myra, let's get started. Val, don't forget your two o'clock client is here."

"Um, Cissy, can you let go of me? I can walk fine on my own." Myra pulled her hand back.

"It's not your walking I'm concerned about. It's your mouth. You know once you start to talk, you can't stop."

"Oh, please, Cissy. You should talk!" Myra rolled her eyes.

Cissy leaned in, whispering, "Myra, I'm just saying this is not the place to speak your personal business. Plus you know you can't carry a conversation to save your life without saying too much or something wrong."

"Now that's where you're wrong, Cissy, because anything coming from my mouth is the truth, and there's nothing wrong with the truth."

"I beg to differ. Sometimes the truth hurts, Myra."

"I can't help it if I'm blunt."

"Anyways, where are you coming from looking all dressy?" Cissy smiled.

"What are you trying to say? This is how I usually dress," Myra remarked.

"I know, I just haven't seen you like this for a while."

"Well, you know I've been overwhelmed lately. Besides, you make it sound like I was walking around in house clothes."

"No, I'm not saying that. Anyways, you look good. Keep it up."

"Thanks. And guess who I ran into this morning—you'll never guess," Myra quickly changed the subject. She couldn't hold back a run-in with Travis anymore.

"I don't know, the mailman," Cissy joked.

"Cissy, I'm serious. Take a guess."

"Rob?" Cissy asked in an uninterested tone.

"Who's Rob, Cissy?" Myra replied aggravatingly.

"My ex-boyfriend."

"Now why would that be news coming from me? I didn't like the guy, much less know him," Myra snapped.

It was clear that Cissy wasn't in the mood to play the guessing game, so she responded, "I don't know, Myra, who?"

"Travis …"

"What!" Cissy screamed.

"Sshh …" Myra put her finger over her mouth. She didn't want to draw any attention.

Cissy was just finishing middle school when the two were dating; Cissy and Travis were really close. He spoiled her like "milk" back then. And Cissy loved every bit of it, until he broke Myra's heart. Then she became his number one enemy aside from their mom. From that moment on, she wouldn't speak or defend him to Myra.

Cissy asked Myra where she saw him. When Myra told her it was coming out of Michelle's office building, Cissy jumped right in, "Wow, what a cowinkadink!"

"What are you trying to say, Cissy?"

"Uh hello, he is Michelle's brother …"

"Oh, well, as I was saying, when I pulled into the parking lot, I almost hit his car, but I didn't recognize him—I just noticed his jacket. Then when I was coming out of Michelle's office, I saw him again in the hallway …"

"Is he still fine as can be?" Cissy cut in.

"Let me finish … so I see him walking toward the elevator, and before he turns to press the button, I ducked into the corridor."

"What did you do that for?" Cissy asked as she washed Myra's hair.

"I didn't want him to see me. At the time, I just thought he was the guy I almost hit. I didn't know it was Travis."

"So you hid?" Cissy chuckled.

"Cissy, please let me finish."

"Okay, go ahead." Cissy rolled her eyes up as if Myra was taking too long to get to the punch line in a joke. Only this she didn't find amusing at all.

"So, as I was peeking at him, he catches me and says 'I see you looking at me, so why don't you come out and get a closer look.'"

"Oh, yeah, that sounds like something Travis would say."

"You know it. Now you know I had to come back with something, so I said, 'Oh, please, like you're something to look at.'"

"Wow, you really told him, Myra," Cissy sarcastically remarked.

"Oh, shut up, Cissy. That's all I could think of...."

"Why is it you can be blunt with everyone else but Travis? You know damn well he is something to look at and more, but you come back with that corny line."

"What are you talking about? I'm like that with Dee, too."

"You are, but to a certain extent; and only because you don't want to argue with Dee. But with Travis, it's different."

"How, Cissy?" Myra asked in a knowing but not willing to hear kind of way.

"For one, in high school, Travis could convince you of anything and everything to do. He made you weak in some ways. Personally, I think you respect him more."

Myra quickly interrupted and said, "Well, that was when I was young and naïve. I'm grown now. Besides, I think handled him well today."

"Okay, Myra, whatever you say ... keep going." Cissy rolled her eyes up again, hoping she was finished.

Myra sensed Cissy's impatience and sped up. "He asked me to coffee, and I declined. Then he put it off on me being married because he saw my ring. I reminded him that I was never the type of woman to say one thing but mean another. And anything coming from my mouth was the real deal. So he tried again to coerce me to go out with him, and I turned him down. He gave me his card, and I walked away."

"That's it, Myra?"

"Yeah. What did you think?"

"Well, did you at least give him the 'sock-it-to-him' walk?"

"Girl, you know I did, and he mumbled something like 'I messed up, or why did I let her go?' I have to say I held my own the whole time until I got in the stairway. Then I became flushed and jittery. Cissy, he is still fine. And when we hugged, I felt ..."

"Hug! You didn't mention any hug. Why would you leave out the hug part and tell me about some unnecessary hide-and-seek crap?"

Myra looked at Cissy like she was crazy. She couldn't understand why Cissy was getting excited over a hug. Myra then sat up after getting her hair washed and walked with Cissy to her chair. There she calmly said, "Oh, did I leave out the hug? I'm sorry. Well, after my comeback, he asked for a hug, and I don't know if it just felt good because I haven't had sex in a long time or if it was just the way he wrapped his arms around me. Either way, I held my composure. God knows I wanted to stay in his arms. I mean, I definitely had to repent."

"What for? It's not like you had sex with him, Myra," Cissy interrupted.

"No, but I felt lustful ..."

Cissy jumped right in to rationalize Myra's thoughts. "Oh, please, it's not like you undressed him with your eyes or imagined yourself with him, right?"

"You're right, but I did have a 'what if' moment, Cissy."

"So, that doesn't mean anything. People have 'what if' moments all the time. It's just a question asked when someone wonders what their life could've been ..."

Myra wasn't satisfied and continued to be hard on herself. "I just think God knows my thoughts. No, as a matter of fact, I *know* he knows my thoughts."

"Of course, he does, but it's not your thoughts he's concerned about—it's your heart. In your heart, did you want to do something with Travis?"

"No, I just wondered if my life would've been different ..."

"Hell, yeah! Your husband wouldn't be in the hospital."

Myra couldn't help but laugh. Cissy always knew how to make a serious situation seem like nothing. Myra elbowed Cissy, saying, "You're crazy, Sis. Anyway, look at what he left on my windshield." Myra handed Cissy the note and the box, waiting to see her reaction.

"Ooh, he wrote a note. And gave you a bag. A Dooney & Bourke one at that—you go, girl. See if you can get one for me."

"You think I'm keeping it?"

"Why not, Myra, it's just a friendly gift, which happens to be really expensive. I'll tell you what, if you don't want it, then pass it this way."

"I don't know. I'll think about it ... Michelle said the same thing until I asked her would Jeff accept her bringing in gifts from other men ..."

"I know she changed her answer quick."

"She sure did ..."

"What is Travis here for?"

"He was recently promoted to chief detective. And was transferred here ..."

"Really, out of all places to be transferred to ... he lands here."

"You know, isn't it crazy?" Myra gave Cissy the eye. Cissy repaid her with the same action.

"Well, I think you should go for coffee," Cissy said, giving Myra a nudge.

She took Myra's cape off, letting her know she was done. Myra took a look in the mirror, smiled, and gave a thumbs-up on the curly hairdo. Cissy was happy to see the good review. Myra completely ignored Cissy's comment, gathering herself together. Cissy, knowing Myra was avoiding the subject, asked her if she was going to go for the coffee. Myra used the question as the perfect exodus away from the discussion.

"See you later, Cissy, I have a lot of things to take care of." Myra bolted out quickly. Once outside, she jumped in her truck and took off for the bank.

*   *   *   *   *

A couple of hours later, Myra surprisingly ran into Devon at the hospital. As she entered Dee's room, she caught him sharing a joke with Devon.

"Well, hello, Devon, what are you doing here?"

"Ma, I told you I was visiting Dad today ..."

"Hey, Mimi, how was your day?" Dee politely asked Myra.

"Oh, it was fine, baby, and yours?" Myra asked as she leaned over to give him a kiss.

"It was boring until Devon came. We were just exchanging stories and similar experiences with each other."

"Oh, really? What experiences could you two be talking about?"

"You know, just guy talk, nothing that you would relate to," Devon quickly replied.

"Oh, excuse me ... so I guess Mama can't know what you guys talk about. Even though I'm guessing it's about sports because that's the only thing I can't relate to."

"Ma, it's not like that. I mean, you don't see us asking what you and Aunt Cissy or your girlfriends talk about ..." Devon threw out this thought—with regret, of course, after seeing Myra's facial expression.

"Excuse me, Devon, who are you talking to? Don't get fresh with me."

"He's just joking, Myra, stop bothering the boy," butted in Dee.

Myra couldn't believe Dee was telling her to stop bothering Devon. As if Devon had said nothing wrong. *Here he goes giving Devon the impression that he can pretty much say anything he wants, with no regard as to how he says it*, she thought to herself. She then asked herself if this was a conversation she wanted to have now in front of Devon or when he was gone. Like her mother always said, "Baby, you need to know when to choose your battles. Choose what's worth tolerating around your husband and children. If you fight for everything and anything while in front of the children, you'll end up giving them leverage. They will use your different points of view to get what they want. Remember, they will grow and go on their own. Then you and Dee will be looking at each like strangers because you're divided and not joined. God is your foundation and not a limitation—use him when you need to address your family." So Myra chose to let it go. At that moment, Devon decided to go home.

"All right, Dad, I'm out. I have to get Trey and Princess."

"All right. Be careful going home and call as soon as you get there."

"I will, Dad," Devon responded while giving his father a pound and hug.

"Devon, go straight home; do not make any detours," Myra ordered before Devon walked out.

Devon remarked in an annoyed tone of voice, "Okay, bye …"

"Uh, aren't you forgetting something, Devon?" Myra asked.

Devon turned back and gave Myra a peck on her cheek. Myra leaned in while reminding him to have all of his work done by the time she got home. As Devon walked toward the door, he mumbled, "Don't I always?"

Myra gave him a look and said, "Excuse me, is there something you want to share, Devon?"

"No, I'm just humming to myself." Devon quickly walked out of the room. As the door closed, Dee looked at Myra and asked, "Why are you so hard on him?"

Myra, keeping her cool, answered, "Because Devon does silly things, so I need to stay after him."

"No, what you need to do is give him a break, Myra," responded Dee in an abrupt manner.

Myra immediately thought to herself, *And you need to stop acting like a donkey's behind. Over here trying to make me look like the bad guy …*

Myra, still deep in thought, vaguely heard Dee say, "Myra, if you continue to ride his back, he's going to stray away, and then we'll have a bigger problem on our hands."

Myra, being the presumptuous woman that she was, acted untouched and distant at the same time. She knew in her heart of hearts that she was doing the right thing by staying on top of Devon. Although Dee didn't agree with her, he knew it too. He just hated to admit that she was doing a great job no matter what. But Myra kept her cool while Dee continued to lecture her on how to raise their son, until he made a lousy comment about her being too controlling. At this point, Myra became livid. She stood up from the bed and shouted, "Oh, so you think I'm controlling. Are you aware that he is my son, who I pushed out after twenty-three long hours of labor pain? And are you aware that I am the one who made sure he stayed on track while you were in a coma? Huh? And when he started to act out as a result of you being here, I set him straight on what is expected of him, so until he leaves our home and is on his own, yes, I am in control. Because I take care of him, and he is my son, too ..."

Dee shook his head back and forth in disbelief, then asked Myra if she was finished. Myra looked Dee up and down as if he was crazy for interrupting her and continued sternly, "Please excuse me for not trying to be friends with our kids, but being a mother is what I do. I have enough friends, so I don't need their friendship, only their respect. And quite honestly, that can only come from our direction and partnership. Now you can either show the kids you support me, or you can continue to play good cop/bad cop. But either way, you need to realize they will have friends who come and go, but a mother and father are forever. And that's what's most important, Dee."

Being his reasonable self, Dee paid no mind to Myra's attitude and passively replied, "True, but when are we going to allow our kids to be themselves no matter what that is? They have to make their own choices."

"Humph, when they stop making foolish choices and have a place of their own ..." Myra retorted, rolling her eyes.

"Look, I'm just saying if you continue getting on Devon's case for every single thing he does and says, he will leave sooner than you think."

Pleadingly, Dee asked Myra to understand his way of thinking, but to no avail. Myra made her position clear, and nothing would change her mind. Dee threw in the towel, knowing there was no way of getting through to Myra once she got upset, so he told her to change the subject before things went too far. Myra couldn't believe he was being so nonchalant about Devon's lackadaisical behavior, but *like father like son*, she thought to herself while sarcastically mumbling, "Talk about controlling ..."

"You see, you're taking what I'm saying personal now."

"No, I'm not, Dee. It just sounds like you want to control what discussions we have as always, when you're not getting through to me."

"No. I just want to enjoy my wife's visit without an argument."

"Well, if that's all you want, why did you even question me?"

"I did not question you, Myra. I just simply asked you to give our son a break from your mouth."

"Oh, excuse me, I misunderstood. I will be going home now. So you can get a break from my mouth." Myra turned to walk away, but Dee grabbed her hand at the same time and asked, "Is that all you can do when you hear the truth?"

"No. This is what I do when I am being told to shut my mouth."

"That is not what I said ... I said ..."

"No, I know what you said. And for your information, it was my mouth that kept Devon in line when you were in a coma. It was my mouth that kept him from failing in school. And it was my mouth that kept him believing in himself when you couldn't do it, so as far as giving our son a break from my mouth, it will happen when hell freezes over, because quite frankly, even when I'm dead, he won't get a break from my mouth."

Dee covered his face, hiding his quiet laugh. He couldn't believe how upset Myra had become. As he put his head up to look at Myra, he couldn't help but burst out in laughter at her wrenched-up face. He thought she was the cutest when angry. Myra grew more frustrated, but his smile broke her down. As Dee reached for Myra's hand again, he jokingly replied, "I hope I get a break from your ..."

Myra pulled back her hand and warned him to not go there with the corny jokes. Dee didn't think it was something to become so intense about, so he gently pulled Myra to sit beside him to reason with her. He softly rubbed her cheek, knowing this always calmed her down. Then he leaned over, kissing her on the lips. After they kissed, Myra looked into his eyes.

"Mimi, I get your point. I just want you to understand that Devon is becoming a young man. And he's at a crucial point in his life. Turning into a man is taking responsibility over his actions while discerning what and what not to do. And learning the distinctions in life can only be taught by example and by giving him free will to choose. We could either chastise him until we're blue in the face about what he can or cannot do, or we could allow him the freedom to determine right from wrong on his own. It is my hope that before he goes to anyone or anything for solace, he goes to God or one of us. Whether I'm alive or not."

"Oh, please, don't talk like that, Dee …"

"It's a part of reality, Myra. I want him to have a close relationship with you and even a closer one with God, no matter what happens."

In hearing this, Myra thought Dee must have already received the results of his tests. He assured her, though, that he had no clue what the diagnosis was. However, he made clear that they should be fully prepared either way. Myra became very emotional at the very mention of his possible death. Dee tried to calm her down by saying it was a blessing they were finding out about his health condition now, rather than not knowing at all. Myra didn't see it this way. She couldn't see what plans God had for their lives. Myra then lied down beside Dee in the bed. As they lay there, Dee rubbed his fingers through Myra's hair as she listened to his heartbeat. They held each other tight. "The Lord has blessed us, Myra. And I'm fortunate to have you. I appreciate you staying with me tonight. There's always a light at the end of the tunnel. I see it now."

Myra, confused, asks, "What do you mean?"

"I mean Cissy is home with the kids, making it possible for us to be together. Even if it is in the hospital."

"You always see the brighter side of things, Dee."

"I love you, Myra," Dee whispered.

"Love you more."

*   *   *   *   *

"Good morning, sunshine."

"Good morning," Myra replied with a yawn.

"How did you sleep?"

Myra covered her face from the sun and sarcastically joked, "Well, you know it's always better to sleep at home instead of here in your arms."

Dee pulled his head back. "Oh, really?"

Myra loved teasing Dee, especially when he was annoyingly happy in the morning. She liked seeing his reaction whenever she pretended to be unaffected by him. No matter how serious she pretended to be, Dee knew she was trying to be funny. Dee stretched and gave Myra a kiss on the lips, then said, "Hopefully soon I will be going home with you."

"I hope so because I need you home to tame those kids of ours. Speaking of which, I have to call home and see if they're up and …"

"Didn't you already speak to your sister about the kids?"

"Yes, Dee, but I know our children, and they would do everything in their power to pull the wool over Cissy's eyes to get what they want."

"Mimi, you don't need to worry about the kids. I think Cissy can handle it …"

Interrupting them both, the doctor walked in with the results of Dee's tests. As he walked in, Myra greeted him to avoid another disagreement. The doctor, taken back by Myra's kindness, returned the greeting. Dee interrupted, asking the doctor for the results with a slight hesitation in his voice. Myra grabbed Dee's hand. But he pulled back.

He didn't want to get emotional. As the doctor delivered the results, Myra's eyes welled up with tears. Her gut feeling was saying the doctor didn't have good news, but she pretended to be optimistic. "Okay, Doctor, let's hear it," said Dee.

Well, you were in a coma. This was caused by a small rupture or breakage of an enlarged artery in your brain, called an aneurysm. The good news is that it didn't completely rupture and cause more bleeding in the brain.

Dee took a deep breath and put his hand on his head, and then he looked at the doctor and said, "Okay, so how do we get rid of it, Doc?

"Well, there are two ways we can carefully treat this issue. We can attempt to effectively manage your blood pressure lowering the chance of another coma. Or we can correct the aneurysm with a procedure where we would insert a supportive material that would prevent the aneurysm from breaking again... The risk with this procedure however, is the possibility of a stroke occurring during surgery. All things considered, we are suggesting you have the surgery done. Do you understand everything I have explained to you?

Dee shook his head in disbelief, but replied, "Yes, I understand."

Happy to hear Dee was in full understanding, the doctor quickly moved on, while making notes on Dee's vitals at that moment.

"Good, we can schedule the surgery first thing tomorrow morning...."

At this point, the information was so overwhelming that Myra became agitated at the speed with which the doctor was explaining everything. She held her hand up signaling him to stop and said, "Wait a minute, can you just slow down? This is a lot of information to digest."

The doctor looked up briefly enough to notice the tension building in the room.

"I understand this is a difficult decision to make. We just want to do everything we can to help your husband, Mrs. Harris."

"I'm sorry Mrs, Harris if all of this seems a bit rushed, but this is not something you want to sit on…. " The doctor looked Myra straight in the eye.

I do empathize with you and your husband. However, I would like to schedule the surgery as soon as possible."

"And I understand the rush, but I also understand that this is a decision my husband and I need to discuss. And as much as it is your concern to quickly resolve this illness. Compassion should also be attempted at least." Myra said as she rolled her eyes.

The doctor opens his eyes wide, and then replied, "I most definitely care for all patients. It's only out of habit that I am conditioned to give the patients results, state the facts, and execute the solution at once…"

Myra then changed her disposition, lightening up and advising the doctor that habits sown reap character from those habits. Then in so many words suggested the doctor's character was speaking volumes at that moment.

The doctor again apologized calmly. Meanwhile, Dee sat zoned out and paid no attention to Myra or the doctor. He started to think about what plans to set in place with the Law firm, the bank accounts, and his boys. As he continued thinking, the doctor and Myra continued to discuss Dee's condition without his involvement. All of a sudden, Myra looked at Dee to see if he was still paying attention—but instead she noticed his tears. She rushed to his side, grabbing his bold head, bringing it to her chest, and comforting him.

"Oh, baby, it's going to be all right, we will get through this."

Dee began crying out loud, holding her tight. Myra didn't know how to respond because she never saw him cry like this. She was at a loss of words. Dr. D'Angelo put Dee's chart on the hospital tray then looked to excuse himself.

"Mrs. Harris… Mrs. Harris," the doctor mumbled.

"Huh, I'm sorry. Just give us a few minutes, please?"

"Okay, I'll come back in a few minutes to answer anymore questions you may have."

As the doctor turned to walk out of the room, Dee lifted his head, wiped his face, and said, "I'm okay, Just let the doctor finish, so we can make a decision already."

"Are you sure, Dee?" Myra asked with hesitation.

"Yes I'm sure. I just want to get the information I need so I can decide what to do."

Myra didn't want to get Dee more upset about not including her in the decision making, so she just stayed quiet and allowed the doctor to continue. And although this was the usual way things functioned between them when making life-altering decisions, Myra no longer felt the need to oblige Dee and his ego. Instead she was going to stand up for her point of view this time, no matter what.

"Okay so with the surgery, you run the risk of possibly going into stroke…"

After hearing this, Myra thought that would be the best time to intervene and voice her opinion and decision at the same time. The doctor then realized the impact of that occurring left the wrong impression of how helpful the surgery could be.

"Mrs. Harris, I could see why you would be a little apprehensive. However I can assure you that while you may think the first treatment would be the safest, it is not the most effective at this point. The lack of taking the pressure medication consistently has already caused damage. I don't want to run the risk of your husband not utilizing the treatment as prescribed then incurring an even worse or irreversible damage. Plus, I must say I have perfected this surgery …"

Myra rolled her eyes in annoyance over the doctor's last statement, then boldly responded, "Uh, excuse me, Dr; D'Angelo, I don't mean any disrespect, but if we were looking for perfection there would be no purpose for using the surgery, much less you. We could just depend on the almighty perfect God that we serve. And clearly you are not Him."

Feeling now annoyed with Myra's attitude, the doctor recants sarcastically, "Hmm, I'm aware that I'm not God, nor have I ever claimed to be. However, I know that it is because of God why I can say I've been able to perform each and every surgery with perfection."

Just then Dee interrupts to tell the doctor of his decision to do the surgery. And even though he knew the risk, he was only interested in doing what will keep him alive longer. Myra, on the other hand wanted numbers.

"So tell us doctor, how many patients do better with the surgery as supposed to medication, diet, exercise and etc?" Myra asked sternly with her hands on her hips.

"There are patients that do very well with those kinds of treatments, but it is all relative to the commitment of each individual patient to the lifestyle change. In more severe cases such as your husband, surgery is the best solution, in my opinion. Now you are free to get a second opinion, but time is of the essence and the longer you wait to do surgery – the worse the aneurysm will get."

Myra knew in heart that the surgery would be best, but was not willing to take the risk. She stood staring in a daze as the doctor and Dee spoke some more. Finally, Dee tapped her and asked her if she had any more questions. After being caught off guard and confused, Myra asked the doctor how soon the surgery could be done. The doctor then smirked and reminded her the sooner they agree to the surgery, the sooner Dee will be scheduled for it. Once she saw the doctor's expression, she realized how silly her question was. She thanked the doctor for the quick test results then politely asked him to give them a moment to make a decision. The doctor graciously smiled and left them to talk and read some of the information he printed for their own knowledge and better understanding. Once the doctor was out of the room, Dee gently led Myra to lie down beside him. Myra put her ear to his chest to listen to Dee's heartbeat. It was one of the things that soothed Myra.

*   *   *   *   *

At the house, Trey and Princess were driving Cissy crazy with their arguing over everything. With all the yelling, they managed to give her a headache. Thank God it was Sunday, she thought. And she could leave them in Devon's care soon so she could go take care of some things at her shop. Suddenly she heard a glass break. She ran into the family room, where she witnessed Trey and Princess having a tug-of-war over a game. Somehow they had managed to knock over one of the lamps on the end table.

"Give it back!" shouted Princess.

"No, you had it all day yesterday, Princess," Trey shouted back.

"But it's mine, and you have your own to play with, Trey."

"I let you hold my Game Boy, and now it's your turn to share," Trey argued.

"Hey, hey, what are you two arguing about now?" Cissy intervened.

"Aunt Cissy, Trey has my Game Boy and won't give it back."

"Trey, don't you have your own Game Boy?" Cissy asked.

"Yes. But I couldn't find it. She played with it yesterday and didn't put it back. Plus she wasn't even using hers, so I took it to play with it."

"Yeah, but you didn't even ask me, Trey," Princess interjected.

"Now you know better than that, Trey. You are older," Cissy said with a probing look.

Trey didn't like when he was given the look, so he immediately apologized and then asked Princess for the Game Boy. Princess, on the other hand, wasn't bothered by Cissy's look and told him no.

"You see, Aunt Cissy, even when I ask her, she says no … I always let her play with my games," Trey whined.

Cissy got on her knees to make eye contact with Princess. "Okay, Princess, you know that we share in this family. If you don't share with your brother, then I'm sorry, but we'll have to take your toys away. And everyone else won't share with you. Do you want that?"

Princess whispered no and gave the Game Boy to Trey—however with a time limit of five minutes. Cissy gave Princess an unpleasant look, letting her know that her response wasn't acceptable. So Princess gave in and told Trey to give it back when he finished.

Cissy thought to herself, "Okay, so now that that's settled, what is Devon up to?"

Cissy shouted, "Devon! What are you doing?"

"Right now?" Devon yelled.

"No, *tomorrow*! Of course, right now, Devon!"

"I'm on the phone, Aunt Cissy."

Cissy went to his room with an attitude and said, "Well, aren't you supposed to be doing homework or studying for your exam on Monday? I mean, that's why I'm here watching Trey and Princess. Not so you can talk on the phone all day to your raggedy friends."

"I already did my homework, and I did all my studying during the week," Devon answered while smirking.

Cissy gave Devon a suspicious look as if to say she didn't believe him. Devon didn't pay her any mind and said, "Aunt Cissy, I'm passing most of my classes."

"Um, excuse me, but most is not good enough; we need you to pass *all* of your classes." Cissy signaled him to cut the conversation he was having on the phone short.

"Aunt Cissy, nobody really passes all of their classes unless they're nerds."

"You see, that's the problem with you kids today—you're more concerned about your reputation instead of your education. You want the bling bling without knowing a damn thing!"

Devon then covered the receiving end of the phone. "Aunt Cissy, I'mma get off soon."

"No, get off the phone now, or I hang it up for you."

"Hello, Shalise, I have to call you back. My aunt is buggin ..."

"Oh, I'm buggin? If you don't hang up the phone, I'm going to show you just how much I'm buggin, Devon!"

Devon hung up, then plopped down on his bed.

"Aunt Cissy, I know you want the best for me. Believe me, I'm trying..."

"Well that's your first problem. We don't try in this family—we 'do'."

"And what's the point of doing anything when at the end you can still end up like my father; starting over, unable to take care of yourself or your family, and close to death?"

"Hmm! I see, so you figure because your father turned out the way he did, you shouldn't do anything at all, Devon?"

"Yeah, basically …"

"Okay, well tell me something. There are many Christians in this world, our family being one of them, who believe Christ is Lord and Savior, and that's the only way to get into heaven, but what if it's all in vain?" Cissy posed.

"What do you mean?" Devon replied in confusion.

"What if choosing Christ isn't the only way to get into heaven?"

"Well, if that's the case, then I guess we're believers for no reason …"

"Okay, so we should just have no beliefs, do what we please, when we please despite the possibility of hurting our family, ourselves and most importantly the one who gave us life."

"No…"

"So what are you saying?"

"I'm saying, why should I spend my time becoming anything when my father might not be here to see it.....""

"Exactly!" Cissy exclaims.

Devon looks on, confused and upset. He had no clue where Cissy was going with her point.

"The key word in all of what you said is 'Might'. Your father might be here—we never know. However one thing I know is if I die believing in something that might happen, there's no loss if it doesn't, but if condemnation be the result of my not believing then I rather live for a lost cause then die in the fiery pits of Hell! Get my drift?"

Devon then goes from a puzzled look to smiling slightly as if his Aunt made a valid point.

"So you see, being a Christian in the end can only help you, not harm you. You have nothing to lose, but everything to gain. Just like with your education. If you were to ask your father about his life based on his illness today, I know he'll never say that it was a waste to get his education; because it's his education that takes care of his family. He really lost nothing. Even if he doesn't overcome his illness, you guys will reap all the benefits of his getting an education. And that, Devon, is what life is really all about—what you make it. And remember: 'Draw near to God and He will draw near to you.' James 4:8."

"I feel you, Aunt Cissy. I never really looked at it that way. I was so into what people would say about me that I didn't even stop to think what God was thinking of me."

"Well, today is a good start, so pull out your books or notes and study them—you never know what tomorrow will bring."

"Okay, Aunt Cissy, I got you."

"I love you, Devon."

"I love you, too, Aunt Cissy."

Cissy then hooked Trey and Princess up with some snacks, and soon after started to leave for the shop. Before going, she left Devon a set of rules for himself and the two younger ones. As far as dinner was concerned, Cissy told Devon to order out again, since she wasn't sure when Myra would be getting home. At this point, Devon was tired of ordering out. His preference was home-cooked meals. This was what they were used to eating because Myra constantly stayed on them to eat healthy. So they weren't the kind of kids you could bribe with outside food often. As a matter of fact, you couldn't bribe them with anything but sweets. And Cissy only did that rarely to avoid from hearing Myra's mouth.

Cissy got in her car and raced to the shop to get everything done quickly so she could get back and spend the night with the kids. At the shop, Cissy was able to make all of her phone calls and reorganize the supply closet. She was happy to know that the shop was running smoothly without her presence. After everything was done, she had a brief meeting with the hairdressers to let them know that she appreciated their help in running the shop. She assured them that as soon as everything returned to normal, they'd receive a bonus. Then she left orders for one of the ladies to lock up no later than ten o'clock. Cissy closed out the meeting with a prayer and then dismissed them.

Cissy then raced to her condo to pick up some more clothes and necessities. As she was packing her bags, Lance called. He asked to stop by for a visit, but Cissy wasn't having it. He continued to plead, and Cissy continued to shoot him down. Finally she hung up the phone and started weeping. She couldn't believe he had just called. She thought she wouldn't hear from him again after what occurred at the salon a few days ago. Lance was supposed to be the one, but he cheated on her. And on top of that, he became a daddy. And even though he was not with the mother of his child, she couldn't accept herself as being the afterthought and not the prospective. With all of the men she dated, not one of them came close to getting a commitment from her. She knew she was a good woman. She had her own business, car, and apartment. She definitely looked good. So why was she still single? She just couldn't understand why she wasn't someone's wife yet. Suddenly she heard her mother's voice in her head, giving one of her lectures on not just finding a man, but keeping one: *"Baby, sometimes you have to let a man be a man. You can't keep running the show and expect him to just watch. Men like to know that you not only want them, but need them. If you keep acting like you can do it all, that's exactly what you'll be doing for the rest of your life. I promise you that."*

Cissy fell to her knees, wiping her tears. She realized how ridiculous she was being and where she went wrong with Lance. So she called him back, explaining the situation at hand with Myra and Dee. They spoke for a few minutes before she let him know she forgave him. She even went as far as to say they could talk some more after things returned to normal so they could have closure. Lance was so happy, thinking he was in again, but before hanging up Cissy made it clear that she was not interested in taking him back, but just having closure. Cissy then hung up the phone and took a minute to compose herself.

*   *   *   *   *

The following morning, Cissy jumped out of bed, realizing she woke up late. After brushing her teeth and washing her face, Cissy started shouting, "Okay, you kids get in the car. You have to get to school. Devon! Trey! Princess!"

"Yes!" they shouted all together.

"Where are all of you?"

"We're in the kitchen getting our lunch, Aunt Cissy."

Cissy walked into the kitchen with a baffled look saying, "What do you mean? Don't you guys get lunch in school?"

"Yes, but we are not allowed to eat it because Mom says their food is old and unhealthy," replied Devon.

"You have got to be kidding me, so what are you supposed to get for lunch, and why am I just finding out now that you guys take lunch to school?" Cissy responded while holding her head.

Devon continued to explain the order of things. "Mom usually prepares the lunch a day ahead for us, but she didn't this time. I mean I'm good because I can go out to lunch, but Trey and Princess usually get a sandwich or chicken nuggets and rice."

"What is so healthy about sandwich meat or processed chicken nuggets?... You know, your mother is too much," Cissy retorted.

"You don't have to tell me. I already knew that, Aunt Cissy," Devon replied.

"All right. By the time I'm done here, you guys should be in the car," ordered Cissy.

"You know what, Aunt Cissy? I could walk to school, so you don't have to worry about me."

"Okay, but please don't make any detours, Devon ... because I don't want to hear your mother's mouth."

"All right, see you later. Oh, before I forget, who's picking Trey and Princess up from school, Aunt Cissy?"

"I'm not sure yet, but you can definitely get them if you don't have anything to do after school."

"All right ... so you both better wait in the front of the school," Devon said as he pointed to Trey and Princess.

"Okay, let's go, you guys—we don't have much time."

"Okay! Let's go," Trey blurted out.

At the car, Trey pushed Princess hard, making her fall and hit her chin on the floor of the car. Princess started crying profusely. Suddenly Cissy jumped out of the driver seat, rushed into Trey's face, and screamed, "What did you do, Trey? Answer me!"

In a soft tone, Trey said, "I pushed her over. She was in the way, and I'm tired of her doing things on purpose. She gets me so sick."

"Listen, I told you already she is a girl and smaller than you, so you do not put your hands on her. You understand?"

"But she keeps acting like she is the only one that ..."

Cissy was so fed up with Trey talking back, she began threatening him. "Listen to me, I know you heard what I said, so don't touch her again. If you do, I'll make sure to do to you what you do to her. You hear me, Trey? I mean it."

"Okay, okay ..." Trey answered back as he breathed heavily.

"Boy, you better relax. And Princess, get in your seat and put on your seat belt, now."

"Okay, Aunt Cissy," Princess replied.

As Cissy got back into the car, she continued to lecture them on their behavior. "You guys are driving me up the wall with all of this arguing. Brothers and sisters are not supposed to be fighting so much. I tell you one thing: if you don't stop, I'll put a stop to it for you, by whipping your tails. You hear me?"

The kids hardly responded with a yes, so Cissy stopped the car, looked back, and gave them the "look." Trey and Princess knew the "look" was a warning, so they said "yes" louder and faster. They knew when she meant business. So for the duration of the drive, they kept quiet, making sure not to get on her nerves. As she pulled up to the school, Trey and Princess said "bye" and jumped out of the car quickly. Cissy laughed to herself, knowing she had scared them with her attitude. However, it didn't faze her one bit because it worked, and that's what was most important. She then pulled off to go back to the house, shower and get dressed.

Decisions, Decisions

This was Myra's second day staying at the hospital. She lay in Dee's arms awake, but not saying so much as a Good Morning to him. Up to that point, they hadn't given the doctor their decision. However Dee was pretty sure he was going to go with the surgery. Even though he knew Myra had something else in mind. He wondered if he should bring it up, knowing the discussion would head in the same unfaithful way all over again. Finally he broke the silence, asking, "Mimi, what's up?"

"Nothing, I was just wondering what we should do."

Dee sighed in relief that her mind wasn't on any sob story of doubt. "Well, you can put your mind at ease because I'm definitely going to do the surgery."

Myra jumps up in hysterics, "What! How can you go with a surgery where the risk is a stroke? Quite honestly, I'm not ready for that, especially knowing there's a possibility you may die as a result of having a stroke."

"Then Dam it Myra, it's meant to be." Dee reacted abruptly.

"How can you say that? You act as if changing your lifestyle wouldn't work just as well..."

"So basically you rather I live with the aneurysm and risk it possibly rupturing next time.... Uh-uh, no way."

"But Dee, changing your lifestyle is what you'll have to do ultimately, anyways. Once the surgery is over and you survive, you'll still have to take better care of your health along with prescribed medication. I mean surgery resolves the aneurysm, but it doesn't take away your high blood pressure… And besides, who knows if with God's help and a lifestyle change you'll get totally healed…"

"Oh please Myra, you don't even believe that… either way I go there's a risk. But at least with surgery I won't have to suffer through these head-wrenching migraines. The surgery is better in the long run. If I survive it, great. If not, then like I said, it isn't meant to be."

"Exactly … if you survive it, Dee. That's a big if. We can't afford to take that chance."

"Mimi, when did it become 'we'? I'm the one who's sick and going into surgery. By the way, where is your faith?"

Myra got out of his bed and passively responded, "I have faith. I just have my concerns too."

Speaking roughly, Dee gave Myra a piece of his mind. "Oh, really? Well, I would like to see the faith more than your concerns, Myra. Because what you show and say are two different things."

"What!"

"Yeah, you restrict Devon like you don't believe the Lord will take care of him. You are constantly telling me how much the family needs me, but if you truly believe the Lord is on our side, then the only person our family needs is God. That is what I want my kids to depend on, Him and not me … and I wish you would do the same."

"Oh, excuse me for wanting you alive rather than dead. You act as if you never had a doubt in your mind."

"No, I may have had doubts, but never did I act defeated." Dee grew upset.

"Yeah, well, I can't help it if I need you in my life, Dee. And you may not feel the same, but my life has always been about you … since high school."

"And that has always been my problem with you. You fail to find your own way. I mean, don't get me wrong, I appreciate all that you are in my life, but what I really need is for you to make your own way aside from me and not in spite of me. If I die, I would be more at peace knowing you can take care of yourself and our family. I don't want you to be stagnant ..."

"Oh, excuse me. I didn't know you had a problem with me ... And just so you know, I could take care of our family whether you're here or not."

"What about you, Mimi? When are you going to focus on yourself and what you want out of life?" Dee questioned.

"You know what? I will get to me in due time. Right now it's about you, the surgery, and the kids," answered Myra.

"No. It's not about me or the kids. It's about creating a balance."

"I get your point, Dee. Now it's time you get mine—you need to pull through this and stop talking like you are preparing for your death."

"I'm not preparing for my death, but I am preparing for the chance that it may be my time to go. I definitely don't want to fight for life and suffer. I'd rather die in peace, Myra."

"Well, I don't want you to die at all, Dee."

"Myra, you do realize that death is a part of life. You can complete your life despite it."

"I realize that, but I also know that you complete my life." Myra put her hands on top of his.

"No, I don't, Myra. You were complete before I married you. That is why God put you in my life. Myra, I want the best for you. I want you to focus on your own destiny. It's time ..."

Avoiding Dee's plea, Myra interjected, "Okay, so what is our decision."

"The surgery ..."

Myra, though not happy, realized she had to support him no matter what she felt. She began thinking to herself.

Interrupting her thoughts, Dee held onto Myra's hand. "Mimi, I understand you don't want to take a chance on losing me, but I want to do a method that has a better outcome ... I love you, and I don't want you to go through any more grief and heartache because I'm in the hospital."

"I understand, Dee. Whatever you feel more comfortable with, I support you."

"Thank you."

Myra went to the nurses' station to have the doctor paged. On the way back, she called Cissy. The phone rang three times before Cissy finally picked up.

"Hey, Sis, you finally found time to call," Cissy said sarcastically.

"What do you mean? I always call at some point to make sure things are going okay. Are they?"

"Myra, with your busy a-- kids ..."

"Wait, before you continue, please don't get ignorant with me."

"Excuse me! As if you don't have your moments after dealing with your crazy-acting kids."

"Oh, I always have my moments, but I'm mature enough to not allow it to change my whole aura, much less my vocabulary, Celeste."

"You know what, Myra? Since you think I'm not mature, then you don't need me to watch your busy a-- kids."

"Why do you always have to go there?" Myra shouted.

"No, why do you always have to act like you're better than me? Just because you're older does not mean you have to talk down to me, Myra."

"Well, maybe if you were to stop using three or four letter words to express yourself, then maybe I wouldn't talk down to you."

"You know what, Myra?..."

"No, you know what, Cissy? I can't talk right now. Sadly enough, I'm busy accepting the fact that Dee now needs surgery. A surgery that could take his life, but you don't worry about the kids. They're my responsibility, not yours—because you don't have any! Have a nice day. Bye."

Myra closed her eyes in shame. She knew the minute she mentioned Cissy not having any children, that it was wrong. But it was too late to take it back. Mad at herself, Myra slammed the door open and sat on the chair beside Dee's bed, shaking her legs. Dee gave her a strange look and said, "What took you so long?"

"Listen, I'm not in the mood right now. Whatever personal stuff you care to discuss, go ahead."

"Oh, boy, who pissed you off now, Mimi?"

"Nobody. I don't want to talk about it, Dee."

"Okay, I just didn't want anything negative to disturb our flow of conversation," Dee said with reluctance. He began talking about his plans for the family and the law firm.

"Fine, so I call Cissy to see how the morning went and …"

Dee knew Myra wanted to talk about it, so he put off his concerns.

"I thought I told you it wasn't necessary to call her. She knows what to do with the kids, Mimi."

Myra gave Dee a snide look, then said, "Are you going to let me finish, or you just want to hear yourself speak?"

"Oh, excuse me, zipping my lips," Dee responded, while motioning his fingers to zip his lips.

But Myra paid him no attention. She continued to express her frustrations. "You're excused. As I was saying, I asked about the morning, and she made some comment about me finally calling her, and before I knew it, she starts getting all indignant, cursing. She knows I don't like her to act that way. Then she had the nerve to say I act like I'm better than her just because I'm older … how dare she!"

"Um …" Dee responds cautiously.

"What is that supposed to mean, Dee?" Myra interrupted before he could say anything.

"It does not mean anything, I'm just listening," Dee said calmly. He knew better than to cross Myra when she was upset.

"Yeah, right, I know when you say 'Um,' you are in agreement with the other person." Myra then rolled her eyes in anger.

"You don't know anything because I'm just taking it all in for now. I will tell you what I think after you're finished."

"Dee, I don't want to know what you think because I already know what you're going to say."

"Oh, yeah? I didn't know you were psychic," Dee retorted.

"Anyways, she needs to stop acting so ignorant and childish."

"What did she say, Myra? It must have been something really bad for you to be this upset."

Spelling it out, Myra said with an attitude, "A-s-s...."

"Are you serious? You guys are arguing over a donkey?" Dee started laughing hysterically.

"It's not funny, Dee. It's not the word I'm mad at, but the context in which she used it."

"What was the context?"

She said verbatim, "Girl, with your busy a-s-s kids...."

"Um, the kids are pretty busy, Myra."

"That's not the point, Dee. She didn't have to curse."

"I don't think that's half as bad as some of the things I have heard Cissy say."

Myra became more agitated and told Dee to stop making excuses for Cissy. Dee, on the other hand, told Myra she was overreacting because it wasn't something to argue over. Myra didn't agree. And one quirky thing Myra was adamant about was the use of unnecessary foul language. Dee continued to aggravate Myra with his composed attitude, as he said to Myra, "You have to learn to tune out other peoples' ways, especially your sister. You need to decipher what's more important— your relationship or the flaws. And remember we all have our moments when we lose it and use foul language."

This was Dee's way of telling Myra in so many words she should not be the pot calling the kettle black.

"I see what you're saying, but I think I'm more upset with myself."

"Why?"

"Because I made a comment about her not having any kids ..."

"Wow, that was a low blow." Dee shook his head, letting Myra know what she said was wrong.

"Anyways, let's just change the subject. I'll call her later to apologize."

"Are you sure you're okay now, Mimi?"

"Yes, Dee, say what's on your mind."

"Well, what's on my mind is kissing you. And please stop letting people steal your joy … they should never have that much power in your life." Dee leaned in and kissed Myra on the lips. They stopped kissing, then Dee began talking about what he wanted to set out to do. Dee paused, then started, "Well, in case of my untimely death, I want you to take over the law firm …"

Myra jumped back in shock and said, "Um, what about Charles? I don't think I can do that. No, as a matter of fact, I know I can't … I mean, give me a break, Dee. I have no experience. And besides, I was hoping at some point I would be opening up my own business."

"I understand that, Myra. I just want you to watch over things until the law firm reaches its seventh year of operation." Dee tried to convince Myra.

"Baby, I know that's the plan, but you have to understand that if you were to die, I don't know if I could throw myself into the law firm. I mean, you're forgetting one thing!"

"What, Myra?"

"Uh, I don't know law … Come on, Dee, you were the one that told me that I should start with myself. And after thinking about what you said, I realize that's exactly what I want to do." Myra walked to the window.

"Mimi, I'm not asking you to put your life on hold, but for the sake of financial stability, I think it's best that you at least give it one more year. Then, by all means, you could begin your business. As a matter of fact, that would work out even better because you'll have the money for it."

Myra paused, thought, then said, "Well, I will give it some thought and get back to you."

Dee became annoyingly dissatisfied with her answer and demanded, "What, are you scared, Mimi?"

"Dee! What is wrong with you? First you tell me to make myself a priority, then you spring this idea of my taking over your law firm … And now, when I'm taking a stand for myself, you think I'm scared. I wish you would make up your mind. As always, you act in the moment for your convenience and no one else's."

"I'm just asking if fear is the reason why you don't want to take over the firm."

"Dee, I told you the reason … I also said I would get back to you on my decision. Now, do you have anything else you'd like to discuss?"

"Yes, as a matter of fact, I do—our finances and properties. I would like to transfer the house into Devon's name, since he is the oldest."

"Uh, excuse me, that house will remain in our name unless I'm on my deathbed." Myra gave Dee a threatening look.

"Myra, why are you fighting me on everything?"

"No, don't make this my issue. You're the one making ridiculous, careless decisions. And I will not have our house be put on the line because it suits you, Dee."

"How could our house be on the line? It's just a name. I don't want to hold you back. If you want to start the business, you won't have the house on your credit to hold you back from getting a loan."

"Now, why would that hurt my credit? If anything, having the house will show financial responsibility and stability. And why would I need a loan anyway, Dee, if we have more than enough money in the business account?"

"Well. I don't expect you to use any of the profit from the law firm if you don't decide to take a position as vice president."

"Wow … wow …" Myra placed her hand on her forehead in shock. She looked up to the ceiling, wondering if Dee's aneurysm was now affecting his brain. She dared not say it, though. Instead, she gave a little chuckle. "So I support you through school, have your three kids, and all you can do is manipulate me into doing what you want."

Dee sat up sternly, looking at Myra without batting an eye, unrelenting. Myra watched how inexorable Dee was on his position, so she just threw her hands up.

"Okay, well at least I know where you stand now, Dee."

"Yeah, I guess you do." Dee looked the other way. Although he did feel bad about giving Myra an ultimatum, he didn't budge.

"Okay. Well, you know what? It's not going to work this time. I'm not giving in this time." Myra started gathering her things.

"Listen, Myra, I'm not trying to manipulate you into doing anything. I just think it wouldn't be fair for you to use money you didn't work hard to make."

"Excuse me! I may not have spent the hours in the office researching cases and counseling clients, but if I hadn't stayed at home with our three kids, supplying their needs, taking care of the house, bills, and everything else you were too busy to do yourself … you wouldn't have been able to spend those long nights at the firm to make that hard-earned money. And you know what? You're right—you're not trying to manipulate me … You are manipulating me."

"Myra, I don't think we should talk right now. It's obvious that you're still frustrated with your sister and not thinking clearly in this conversation."

"No, I'm thinking real clear, but we agree on one thing—we should talk about this another day because right now I have a headache and don't want to lose it in here."

"Okay, so are you hungry?" Dee asked, hoping it would break the tension.

"No, I'm not, but I'm going to leave now. I have to get some groceries for the house and run some errands as usual. You know, the things not considered working."

Dee ignored her comment. Instead, he softened his tone. "Do you have to do that right now, Mimi? The doctor will be here soon."

"Yes, Dee, I have to do that right now, since I don't work long hours. I just have this silly notion to make our kids a home-cooked meal. And I get this crazy thought like balance the checkbooks, pay some bills, and go to a school board meeting to organize the senior prom for our son Devon."

"Okay, Myra, you made your point. You're busy …"

"Busy, who? Me? No, I'm not busy—I'm just home eating bonbons all day!"

Dee tried to act concerned. "Well, I guess I'll see you later. Try to get some rest."

"Yeah, later ..." Myra swung the door open abruptly.

"Bye, baby ... love you ..." Dee yelled out.

Myra stormed out. She was enraged at the nerve of him to say that she didn't work hard to make his income. She never thought she'd see the day when Dee would say something so chauvinistic. As she walked to the elevator, she thought to herself, "Leaving his presence is the best thing for me to do before I say something I regret. I'm not going to even shed a tear over that man. So why are my eyes so watery? Don't cry, Myra, don't cry." But all of a sudden, Myra began sobbing. She wondered why she kept falling for his bullcrap when she knew that was his nature. He'd never be different because it was what it had always been—about him. She understood he was trying to make a way for the family, but why talk one way out of one side of his mouth, then another way from the other side?

At this point, she didn't know what to do with her life. Myra couldn't understand why her life was so unclear. When she pictured her life before marriage, she definitely didn't see this coming. But, of course, who could have predicted this, other than the Lord above? Myra got in the car and sat for five minutes to clear her mind. This was her way of drawing a line from one upset and not putting it off on someone else, especially the kids.

As she drove along the expressway, she noticed the diner where she and Travis used to hang out after school. Instantly her mind ran on him. She wondered what he'd been up to over the past twenty years. She thought to call him, but felt the need to think of what to say. She didn't want to sound foolish on the phone. After rehearsing a few times, she finally dialed the number on the card he had given her. The phone rang a few times until a woman picked up. Suddenly Myra froze and didn't respond. When the lady hung up, Myra looked to see if she had dialed the right number. The last thing she needed was his wife to be upset from her calling him. Myra sighed in relief when she realized it was his office phone. So she dialed the number again. She hoped this time that Travis would pick up. As the phone rang, Myra mumbled, "Come on, Travis, pick up the phone."

"Hello, Detective Dewitt …"

Myra's heart was racing and she froze again. Travis said hello again, waiting for a response.

"Hello," Myra answered in her raspy voice.

Travis knew it was she, but still he asked, "Myra, is that you? How did you like my gift?"

"The gift is really nice. You definitely know what I like. I just can't …"

"Hold on, Myra, I have another call."

While Myra waited for his return, she contemplated keeping or giving back the gift. She loved the purse, but didn't want to give Travis the wrong impression by keeping it. Even after trying to rationalize why it was okay to keep it, it didn't feel right to her.

"Hey, Myra, sorry, that was my daughter."

"Oh, wow, how old is she?"

"She's seventeen going on thirty. She acts so grown."

They shared a laugh.

"Well, they all do—my son is the same way. And he's the same age."

"Yeah, so what were you saying?"

"Oh, no, I was just saying I can't keep the gift."

"What? Why?"

"Because I don't think it's appropriate. I'm married, and I don't want to give you the wrong impression …"

"You're not, and it's just a gift. So your husband doesn't let you receive gifts?"

"I mean, how would you like it if your wife accepted a gift from another man?"

"I wouldn't mind the gift. It's the sleeping around that I can't tolerate."

Myra got silent. She knew Travis was being forthcoming with his personal information, but she didn't want to push the subject. So Myra switched the topic.

"So, you have your own office?" Myra asked in confusion.

"No, my partner and I just use this line for personal calls, but the majority of the time, I'm on the go. That's why I also gave you my cell number."

"Okay …"

"So, back to the gift."

Myra sighed.

"Yeah, you thought I would forget? Listen, just tell your husband Michelle bought it for you. I mean, we go way back, you know I don't have a motive … I'm sorry, can you hold a moment, Myra? I have to take this other call. My partner insists that it's important."

"By all means, go ahead."

"Okay, I'll be right back."

Myra hummed to the jazz music playing on the radio. She thought to ask Travis for coffee, but then she didn't want to seem like she was interested. Although it would be nice to experience something other than hospital visits, Myra decided against it. Just then Travis returned to the line.

"Listen, Myra, it turns out this call is really important, so can I call you back?"

"Sure, but you don't have my number, Travis."

"Don't worry, I'll find you," Travis responded in a flirtatious voice.

"I bet you will."

Before Myra could say good-bye, Travis went to the other line. *Now what do I do?* Myra thought to herself. She already did the groceries and went to the bank yesterday. There was really nothing else for her to do at this point. Around this time, she would still be at the hospital with Dee. Only he didn't deserve another visit after what he said to her. She could always go home, since the kids were in school and coming home after four. She decided to go home, get comfortable, and get some shut-eye.

*   *   *   *   *

In the meantime, at Devon's school, Devon was being summoned to a meeting with the principal. Over the loudspeaker, he heard, "Will Devon Harris come to the principal's office?"

"Ooh, Devon, you're in trouble," snickered some of the students in his class.

"Mind your business," replied Devon.

The teacher motioned the class to be quiet. "All right, class, calm down. Devon, you can go now; take your books with you just in case the bell rings for the next class. Oh, and don't forget tomorrow is the midterm."

"Okay, Mrs. Dougherty," Devon respectfully responded.

Devon grabbed his books, jacket, and book bag and headed for the principal's office. On the way there, he ran into his girlfriend, so he stopped to talk. He gently grabbed her hand as she tried to pass him by.

"Where you going, baby?" he asked while licking his lips.

"I'm going to the library. The better question is, where are you going?"

"Come here, let me get a hug." Devon gave her a bear hug, ignoring her question.

"Don't try to avoid my question."

"I'm not … Damn, you look good right now. Can I get a kiss?" Devon gave the same cute smile Dee did when he wanted something from Myra.

"Not until you tell me where you're going, Devon."

"Ooh, say my name again," Devon joked.

"Devon, I'm not playing. Answer the question."

"Okay. I got called to the principal's office. Now can I get a kiss?"

"What did you do now?"

"Give me a kiss first." Devon softly pulled her chin closer. They started tongue kissing. After a few seconds, Devon realized he was unable to control himself, so he pulled back.

"What's wrong?" his girlfriend asked.

"Um, nothing …"

"So, why did you stop kissing me?"

"Nah, it's nothing. I'm good. You should go to the library before you're late, Shalise."

"Okay, but give me a kiss good-bye first."

Devon leaned over, leaving space between them, and gave her a peck on her lips.

"Devon, you can do better than that."

"Nah, I'm good. I'm straight. I'll talk to you later; go to the library."

Devon tried to maintain his composure as Shalise walked off. Her body was definitely calling him. Devon turned around and continued to the principal's office. Upon reaching the main office, Devon bumped into the captain of the cheerleading squad, his ex-girlfriend Joy. They stopped, gazed at each other, and smiled.

"Hey, Devon, you look cute in those jeans," she said, looking him up and down.

"Oh, please, you know you're not looking at my jeans. So, what do you want, girl, with your fine self?"

Twisting her loosely curled hair, Joy reached over to grab his butt and said, "I want what I had last summer."

"Come on now, stop playing, Joy."

"Who's playing?," she asked with a seductive look on her face. Joy was nice to look at but very superficial, unlike Shalise.

"Joy, you know the only reason why you're interested in me is because you can't stand to see me with anyone besides you."

"True, but what I can't stand more is looking into those sexy hazel eyes while you suck on my ..."

"Devon Harris, you were supposed to be in my office ten minutes ago. Get in here now!" the principal interrupted as he held the door open. Devon thought *Thank God*, because he knew he was about to do something stupid.

Joy held onto Devon's hand for a second, staring at him. She gave him a look she knew made him melt, then whispered with enticement, "Meet me after school."

"Joy, let go of the boy's hand and go to class," the principal yelled out from his desk.

"Okay, Mr. Hall. "

In the moment, Devon imagined himself with Joy again, not in a relationship, but definitely sexually. Joy then gave him a kiss on the cheek and walked away. Devon closed his eyes and took a deep breath to prevent looking flush in the face upon entering the principal's office. After Devon retrieved his composure, he quickly addressed the principal.

"Principal Hall, you wanted to see me?"

"Yes, it has come to my attention that you've missed half of the semester of your biology class. And your grades thus far reflect a possible C in that class. Do you care to explain yourself?"

"Sir, the only explanation I have is my father has been in the hospital, on his deathbed, and biology is not exactly on the top of my priority list."

"I understand, as your mother did make me aware at the beginning of the school year. However, your mother has also made it clear to me that under no circumstances are you to be excused from maintaining your high grade point average. Now I'm going to give you an opportunity to vindicate yourself and get back on track, but you must do it by the end of the next marking period or you will be cut from the team. And to show you I mean business, I've already spoken to the coach. We agreed to suspend you from the next two games, so that you're able to focus on your studies."

"Mr. Hall, you can't do that—there are scouts from colleges coming to see me play. If I don't play, they won't get to see my skills and offer me a spot on their team!" Devon replied excitedly.

"I'm sorry, but I'm afraid you have buried yourself deep this time."

Devon looked at the principal as if he was the enemy, pleading his case, but to no avail. The principal made it clear why this was his final and only offer.

"Listen, Devon, if you don't increase your grades overall, those colleges or college scouts won't even look at you because they want the whole package. And quite honestly, you're lucky I'm even giving you a chance to bring up your grades, because once you're in college, you won't be getting this kind of guidance. So at this point, your grades and overall lack of participation in some of your classes don't leave me any other choice …"

"You always have a choice. Mr. Hall, please let me play," Devon begged.

"I'm sorry, but unless you pass your next two exams in biology, you will get cut from the team altogether. However, on the upside of things, when you do pass, you will be able to play in the final game—which happens to be the most important game of the year…. So, can I get your word that you'll hold up your end of the deal?"

"Yes, Mr. Hall," Devon replied with a disappointed look on his face.

"All right, so we are done here. You can go to your next class."

"Mr. Hall, does my mother have to know about this?"

"Unfortunately, I'm afraid a notice has already been sent out a couple of days ago. I just wanted to bring it to your attention."

"Man, she's going to kill me …"

"Look, right now all you should be thinking about is studying and staying away from anything or anyone that hinders you from doing that, okay?"

This being said, Mr. Hall gave the eye, hinting at what he had witnessed between Devon and Joy. Devon smirked, catching Mr. Hall's drift completely.

"All right, see you later, Mr. Hall."

"Devon, I know you can do this. You are intelligent, talented, and capable of doing anything you put your mind to. And I hate to see you waste it." The principal put his hand out to shake Devon's hand.

"Thank you, Mr. Hall," replied Devon as they shook hands.

Devon left the principal's office with mixed emotions. He was frustrated, confused, and sad all at the same time; he couldn't understand how his life could go from being on top to slowly falling to the bottom. He was on the honor roll and all-star varsity and making his family proud. Now he just felt like a failure, a letdown. While walking to his last class, he saw Joy again. She waved, blew him a kiss, and motioned him to meet her after the next class. Devon tried to ignore her and continued to walk to class. All of a sudden, Shalise popped up from behind and planted a kiss on his cheek. Devon jumped, in fear that Shalise had seen what just happened.

"What was that for?"

"I just wanted to kiss you. Can I kiss my man if I want to?"

"Yeah, I was just caught a little off guard. I'll see you later." Devon held his head down.

"Okay, cutie …" Shalise softly pinched his cheek.

Devon blushed, then entered his next class. He was trying to figure out what he was going to do about his biology class. And aside from that, he didn't know what he was going to do about the Joy situation. He definitely didn't want to give Joy the wrong impression. And although he was over their breakup, he was still very much physically attracted to her. However, Shalise was the one that had all the qualities he loved. But it was Joy's athletic body and experience that really had him hooked. He went back and forth on what to do for the duration of the class.

Finally, after a good thirty minutes of boring math equations, the bell rang. Devon left the classroom still in heavy contemplation. He headed for the exit doors, where both Shalise and Joy stood waiting for him. The two were very much aware of the other's position, but unaware of Devon's. They watched as Devon stopped at the top of the stairway and, making eye contact with the two of them, he turned around. Suddenly a rush of students came through the doors, making it impossible for both girls to see where he had gone.

Outside of the school, Devon walked to pick up Trey and Princess. He saw Shalise waiting for him at their spot in the park. They looked at each other, smiled, and grabbed hands. The connection they shared definitely spoke volumes through their eyes.

"So, Joy wants you back," Shalise said, keeping her head turned the opposite direction.

"Yes, but I want you." Devon brought her face toward him for a soft kiss.

"I know … I'm just worried about you. You seemed out of it earlier."

"Nah, I just got a lot of stuff on my mind right now."

"Is it about your dad? You know you can talk to me, Devon."

"I know. It's not about my father …"

"So, what's it about?"

"It's about me failing biology. If I don't pass the next two exams, I'll be kicked off the team."

"Okay, but that's not something we can't fix," Shalise responded with a smile.

"Oh, yeah, how's that, Shai?" This is what he called her when they were having a serious conversation

"I can help you, and I have a cousin who does tutoring on the weekends."

Devon stopped walking and pulled Shalise to him. "Girl, you're always looking out for me. I appreciate it, so how about I return the favor now? Come over to my house, and I'll help you study."

"Nope. I don't think so … I know that's not all you want to do. Thanks anyway; I'll pass."

"You see? I didn't even say all of that. I just want to help you get your study on."

"Devon, since when you study?" Shalise chuckled at the mere thought.

"Well, I have you know that I do study, so come over." Devon got serious.

"I can't today."

"Why? You have to babysit again?" Devon began to have an attitude.

"No, Devon. I have dance class, remember?"

"Oh, yeah, true dat, true dat … I forgot, you have to get your dance together for the competition." Devon wrapped his arms around her waist.

"Wow, you remember my competition?" Shalise responded, thinking it was sweet.

"Of course I remember, you only told me like a hundred times already."

Shalise elbowed him. "Oh, stop, it was only ten times."

Devon stared at Shalise for a minute, realizing for the first time he had strong feelings for her. He never felt this way before, not even with Joy. Shalise was patient, but aggressive. She was kind, but not at all naïve. She was mature and inexperienced at the same time. She even knew what she wanted out of life. Never once did she ever mention him being a part of it. Suddenly he let her go, with his eyes filled with water. Shalise looked at him, trying to figure out why he let her go.

"Devon, what's wrong?"

"Oh, God! Why is this happening?" Devon blurted out.

Shalise was unsure why he was so upset, but she hugged him tight, consoling him.

"Devon, it's going to be okay. I know you're going through a lot, but I got your back."

Devon shook his head, mumbling, "No, no, no … I can't do this right now."

Devon pushed her arms down and began walking off.

"Devon! What are you talking about?" Shalise called out to him. Then she walked after him. When she caught up, she pulled his arm back to get his attention.

"Devon, talk to me, I don't understand …" Devon snatched his arm away.

"Shalise, go home. I'm not good enough …"

"I know you're not, but you're good for me, Devon."

"No, I'm not. I can't promise you a commit—"

Shalise cut him off. "Who said you have to promise me anything? We're just seventeen, Devon."

"That's my point, Shalise. At the rate we're going, I know we're going to end up in some sort of committed relationship. And I can't handle that right now."

"Devon, did I ask for a commitment?"

"It's not you, Shalise; it's me. I can't be with you when I know in college I may not be able to stay faithful."

"Devon, I'm not sure where you're going with this, but if I'm too much for you, then maybe we should just be friends."

Shalise walked away. She rubbed her face, wiping the tears from her eyes. Devon kicked the garbage can in, frustrated at himself. He couldn't believe he just messed up the only good thing going on in his life right now. He turned around, looking at Shalise again, and tried to fight the urge to go after her. Unsuccessful, he ran toward her, shouting her name. Shalise kept walking without responding. Devon caught up and grabbed her, hugging her tight and smelling her hair. Shalise stood stiff, then pushed him off.

"Shalise, wait up!" Devon cried out.

"Devon, go home! Isn't that what you said to me? I mean ..."

Devon gently put his finger to her lip. "Sshh, let me speak."

Shalise stopped, then looked away, shaking her leg in anticipation. She didn't want to hear anything he had to say at this point.

Devon brought her face to his attention. "You're everything good for me, and it's scary to know that I may not be the same for you. I really do want you in my life. I mean I can't promise you forever right now, but I can without a doubt work to make it forever."

Shalise stepped back. "Look, Devon, are you sure? Because I'm not into the games, the back and forth, or whatever you want to call it. I have my whole life ahead of me to choose when, where, and with whom I want to settle down, so relax, I'm not asking for anything more. I'm happy just taking it day by day."

"I know. I don't know what I was thinking because I definitely love you, girl," Devon replied with a smile on his face.

"Uh, excuse me, did you just say you love me? Because you have a heck of way of showing love, Devon."

"I'm sorry, I act dumb sometimes."

"You said it!" Shalise pushed him in the chest. "Now, can I get a hug?"

"What do you think?" Devon blushed as he went in for a hug. They kissed, then Devon sent Shalise off to her dance class.

"I'll call you later."

"Okay, bye. Oh, and Devon, I love you too!" Shalise hollered out as she walked away.

Devon just smiled as he watched her walk down the street. Before she turned the corner, they took another glance at each other and waved good-bye. Then Devon started making his way to get Trey and Princess from school. While their school wasn't too far, it was a nice walk. He didn't mind much; Devon thought of it as his opportunity to mull over things. His first thought, his father. Then he thought about school and college, and pictured himself at Clarke Atlanta University. By the time he got to his next thought, he reached Trey and Princess's school.

"Finally, what took so long?" Trey yelled to Devon.

Devon grabbed his head into a gentle yoke, "Stop complaining, li'l man, and let's go home."

Devon let him go, picked up Princess, and placed her on his neck as they started walking home. On the walk, Devon and Trey joked around, talking about everything under the sun. Even though they fought a lot, they had their moments of unity, unlike Trey and Princess who were not close at all.

At the same time, Princess loved her Devon. So much so it was as if he was a father to her. He couldn't go anywhere without her knowing. And when he went out, she'd cry like someone was taking something from her. Trey didn't have the same effect on her; Princess's love for him was different. Trey was her go-to sibling—the one she could go to and get anything just to keep her from crying. Trey would actually give her anything, from a toy to the last cookie. If he had a snack, he'd give it up, too. Everything Princess wanted, she could have so long as he didn't have to hear her cry. So there they were, the three stooges, the three amigos, walking home together happy for the first time in a long time.

Sister to Sister

Cissy was feeling unbelievably guilty about writing Myra off yesterday morning, which was a first for her, being that she never felt guilty about anything ever. Cissy's mantra always was, "Any negative done is gone, and any negative said is dead." Living a guilt-free life always gave Cissy peace of mind. Only this time, she felt compelled to make amends with Myra. So Cissy called her. The phone rang several times. She supposed Myra saw her number, but didn't want to pick up. Finally Myra's sleepy voice said hello.

"Hey, Sis, how's Dee?" Cissy went straight into a conversation about Dee, thinking it would lighten Myra's attitude. That is, if she had one. It was Cissy's way of breaking the tension.

"He's fine, Celeste." Cissy, after hearing her actual name Celeste instead of her nickname, confirmed her assumptions. In fact, she found it humorous that Myra always let her frustration show in that way. When she was upset with Dee, his name became Devon; the same for Trey, who became Trevon. As for Devon, he became Devon Jr. and with Princess she used her entire name, Princess Malina Harris.

Cissy tried to joke, "Ooh, why so formal, Myra Lopes Harris?"

"Celeste, what do you want?"

"Oh, well, excuse me, I'm just calling to apologize for the disagreement we had yesterday. You know I didn't mean to curse. I know you don't like it. So I'll try to refrain from using three and four letter words around you."

"Okay." Myra unenthusiastically waited to hear more before saying anything.

"And you can count on me to take care of the kids whenever you need me."

"Thanks," replied Myra with a shaky, cracking voice. By the sound of Myra's voice, Cissy assumed something was wrong, but didn't jump to conclusions.

"Are you okay, Myra?"

"Yep."

"Myra, I'm your sister. I know when something is wrong."

Oddly enough, the same way that Cissy had her ways of dealing with matters, so did Myra. She was not the type to show when she was hurt, in pain, or having a problem. However, ever since Dee had a stroke, she couldn't seem to control her emotions.

"Are you busy now?" Cissy asked.

"No. Just lying here trying to get some sleep."

"Okay, so are you hungry? We can meet for lunch …"

"I might as well since I'm not getting any sleep."

"Okay, so get dressed and meet me at the shop," Cissy insisted cheerfully.

"Okay, I'll see you then. And Cissy—"

"Yes?"

Myra took a deep breath. "I apologize for being so judgmental."

"Don't be ridiculous, you have every right to call me on my nonsense. It doesn't mean I'll always listen, but I did get it. But you should know I don't need two mommies."

"I know that's right. And I'm not in any way, shape, or form trying to be anyone but your older sister, who wants the best for you."

Just then one of the hairdressers at the shop opened the office door with a warning, "Uh, Celeste, one of your clients is at the front desk complaining about her hair appointment."

"Myra, I have to go."

"Okay, go handle your business. I'll be there soon."

"Okay, bye."

Myra got up from the couch and went to the bathroom to get herself together. While she was fixing her hair in the mirror, she realized she looked tired, so she washed her face and put on some fresh makeup. Then she changed out of her yoga suit and put on her navy blue skinny jeans with her white shirt. After buttoning and fixing her shirt, Myra put on her red pumps, which happened to match a red 'Baby Phat' belt she had bought a couple of months ago.

She stepped inside her walk-in closet, grabbed the belt, and wrapped it around her narrow waist. And while Myra didn't intentionally try to get thin, she enjoyed her new look. She took a last look at herself in her full-length mirror on one side of the closet. She then stepped out of the closet, snatching the keys off her dresser. As she was walked toward the door, the phone rang. Myra contemplated picking it up. Thinking it might be someone important, she went to pick up the phone, then changed her mind and walked to the door. She reached the door, then changed her mind again, and walked back to the phone.

"Hello," she said as she picked up the receiver.

"Hello, can I speak to Mr. Harris?" the person asked passively.

"Mr. Harris is not here, but this is his wife. Can I help you?"

"No, ma'am, this is a private matter in regards to his money-market account. Can you have him call us?"

"It can't be all that private, I'm his wife," Myra said assertively.

"Ma'am, are you a signer on this account?"

"No," Myra replied.

The representative heard the attitude. He began feeling obligated to be extra polite.

"I'm sorry, Mrs. Harris, I can't share any information on this account since you aren't listed on it, but can you be so kind as to take my number? We would …"

Myra continued to listen to the representative explain himself, while in the same breath asked her for their address. At this point, Myra got fed up, looked at the phone crazy, rolling her eyes, and said, "Well if you have my number, you definitely have my address. So there's no need to give it again. So if you don't mind, I have a sick husband to visit. Bye."

Myra slammed the phone down and walked out of the house. On the drive to the salon, Myra started thinking about this separate account Dee had now. He never mentioned it to her before. She then started reflecting on the mail she received on this new account. She then came to the realization there was a lot more she didn't know about their finances. Burning with upset, Myra whispered, "This bastard has the nerve to have a separate account and all of this money in it."

Just then, Myra almost hit the car in front of her at the light. After smashing the breaks, she came to, immediately thinking, "If Dee thinks he's going to get away with doing something so deceitful, he won't have to worry about an aneurysm killing him, because I will. I hope he has an explanation for this."

Myra then pulled into the salon's parking lot. She was so angry she didn't bother to hold the door for the clients leaving. She just rushed in and demanded the first person she saw, "Hey, where's Cissy?"

"Uh-uh, you can't say hello, how you doin, or sumthin? Anyways, she's in her office with a client. But you go ahead back there since you can't speak, Miss Thang." Myra looked up to the ceiling, knowing how unbecoming Robert can get on some days. Myra ignored his attitude and said, "Thank you, Robert."

"Uh-uh, excuse me ... you know that is not my name, Miss Thang," Robert responded as he waved his hand in circles, snapping his fingers while rolling his eyes.

Myra continued to walk, ignoring his making a spectacle of himself. This, of course, only made him get louder. "Okay, girlfriend. 'Cause I don't know how many times I got to tell you people, I might look like a man on the outside, but I am all woman. You better recognize!"

The other hairdresser says, "Robin, you are some kind of crazy."

Robert replies, "And you know it, Miss Thang."

Myra tapped on Cissy's cracked-open door. "Knock-knock … it's me, Myra."

"Come in, Sis. I was just finishing up here."

"Are you sure? I could wait out front until you're finished, Cissy."

"No, girl, don't be silly … You know Mrs. Jean." Cissy waved Myra to sit on her lounge chair. Myra said hello to Mrs. Jean before taking a seat. Then Cissy continued to explain her case. "Now, as I was saying, Mrs. Jean, you may have made an appointment at ten, but when you come an hour after your scheduled appointment, we have no choice but to take our other clients who were here on time. I'm sorry if that upsets you. We do give our customers a half-hour grace period and sometimes longer if they call ahead of time. And if you'd like, I can reschedule you for later on today. I'll even throw in a manicure, just to assure we value your loyalty."

The woman smiled as she replied, "Well, thank you, sweetie. I do appreciate your help. I'll come back at three o'clock."

"Okay, great. And again, I'm sorry we couldn't get to you first. I look forward to seeing you later, Mrs. Jean."

"Okay, and I'll be here at three o'clock on the dot, Celeste."

"Great. See you later, Mrs. Jean."

"Bye, baby." Mrs. Jean gave Cissy a hug.

Myra waited until Mrs. Jean was out of the office to whisper, "Wow, I'm impressed. You handled her well."

"Girl, you know I got skills. I don't play when it comes to my customers. You know how I am to please. This is just what I'm about." Cissy held her hand up to give Myra a five.

Myra reciprocated, saying, "I heard that, 'Miss Thang,' as Robert likes to say. Now are you ready?"

"Yes, let me just grab my purse, lock my office, and we can go."

Cissy grabbed her Coach bag and proceeded to lock the door. Meanwhile, Myra was already walking toward the front as she asked, "What are you in the mood to eat anyway?"

"I don't know. I was thinking soul food. What are you in the mood for?" Cissy responded.

"Soul food sounds fine … Let me check my voice mail before we get in the car and start talking. My phone has been ringing off the hook all morning, and Lord knows it's probably Dee."

Myra started listening to her messages. The first one she heard was Dee, just as she had thought, sounding depressed. Myra planned to call him later because she wasn't in the mood to be worn out by his attitude. Just as Myra was about to listen to the next message, Cissy gave her a little shove, causing her finger to push the delete button. Cissy asked, "Okay, you ready, girl?"

Myra paid no attention, ended the voice mail, and replied, "Yeah, come on … my car or yours?"

"Oh you should follow me in your car, because if the time gets away from us like the last time then I'll have to bring you back to the shop and that's too much shuffling around."

"Yeah, I hear you. Just make sure you have your earpiece in so we can talk on the drive over. And, where are we going anyways?" Myra asked.

"How about King B's?"

"Okay, so I'm right behind you."

So both Myra and Cissy headed for their cars. As soon as Cissy began to pull off, she called Myra on her cell. Myra picked up on the first ring and Cissy wasted no time in asking, "So, tell me, Myra, what's been on your mind?"

Myra sighs, "Well, we found out yesterday that Dee has an aneurysm …"

"Oh, my God, I'm so sorry to hear that. How is Dee taking the news?"

Cissy held her mouth open in shock as Myra continued to speak. "At first he took it very hard. Then he broke down crying, girl, and I didn't know what to do. I've never seen him like that."

"I could imagine."

"And now he's acting like he's running out of time or something."

"That doesn't make any sense," Cissy answered in confusion.

"That's just it, *he* decided what procedure was going to be done. He didn't consider talking it over with me. And to top it all off, he chose the procedure where there's a risk of him losing a lot of blood, going into shock, and either being comatose again or dying."

"Wow, this is a biggie … So, did you explain what you feel about his decision?"

"Of course, but nonetheless he's going with what he wants, regardless of how I feel." Myra's eyes filled up with sorrow.

As they approached another red light, Cissy repositions her rear view mirror to look at Myra's face. She was making sure Myra was okay and not about to have one of her episodes. After seeing Myra was doing okay, Cissy voices her take on it. "Okay, I see his point and I see yours. And everything's going to be just the way its suppose to be … Now I see why you were emotional earlier."

"No, not even … I was emotional because he wanted to discuss some plans for the family in case he dies. His first request was to appoint me to take over the law firm along with his partner. I was honored that he chose me, but told him I did not fit the position because of my lack of knowledge with the key word being 'law,'" Myra exclaims with an attitude.

"That's understandable … So, what's the problem?" Cissy asked.

"I don't know. He just went off on a tangent, telling me I shouldn't start my business until his firm was in its seventh year of operation. I know that's what I had in mind at first. But it was while he was healthy and not in the hospital."

Myra looked disappointed in Cissy's rear view. Almost as if she just had enough or gave up on any real chance of having her dreams come true. Cissy then became aggravated at Dee for using his illness to guilt Myra into putting her life on hold again. Cissy pulled into the restaurant's parking lot and abruptly said, "Myra, since you started a life with Dee, you managed to turn your dreams upside down and around so that he can accomplish his goals. Now it's time you focus on your dream and follow it to fruition."

"I agree, but …"

Cissy turned off the car, got out, and slammed the door. She looked at Myra as she got out of her car and said, "Myra, there's no but—I mean, the only but I want to hear or see is yours, living your passion and purpose."

As they entered and sat down, one of the waiters immediately walked to Cissy's side and asked them if they were ready to order. Myra recognized his face as he stared at Cissy with the cutest smile, but Cissy didn't bother to look up as she ordered her food. When Cissy finally looked up to ask Myra what she wanted, she saw Myra giving signals with her eyes to look at the waiter, but Cissy ignored it. Myra then said, "Yes, I'll have the barbeque chicken, greens, and macaroni and cheese. And could I also have your number for my sister?"

Cissy smacked Myra's hand and mumbled, "Um, excuse me, I did not ask for his number."

"I know you didn't, I did." Myra looked again at the waiter as if she'd seen him before.

"Myra, I can ask him myself if I want his number."

The waiter then interrupted them and said, "So, I guess you don't want my number?"

Cissy started giving Myra a hard stare, but then softened up after hearing the familiar voice. Her heart beat fast as she looked up at the waiter. And just as she thought, it was him again, looking as handsome as the last time she saw him. Looking clean-cut, buff, and sexy as always, he asked for her order. She sat in shock for a minute, then asked him what he was doing waiting on tables. He explained he was helping out his uncle with a shift because one of his staff called in sick. Cissy thought it was nice of him to take the time away from his own business, even though it was his uncle who helped him start his construction company.

Myra interrupted their stare. "I'm sorry, I don't mean to interrupt, but as I'm looking at you, I know you from somewhere, but I don't remember your name. In fact, now that my sister is acting all flustered, I know I know you. What's your name again?"

Cissy turned to Myra and said, "This is Lance, Myra. You remember, I mean I only dated him for like what—three years."

Myra looked him up and down. "Oh, okay. Well I don't agree, Cissy. He's not at all that ugly. He's okay."

Cissy kicked Myra under the table, bursting out in laughter. Lance, on the other hand, was so confident he replied, "It's okay, looks aren't everything."

"Oh, yeah? Who told you that, your mama?" Myra asked.

"Well, according to my mama, God doesn't make any ugly babies. And I have to say, I agree."

"Oh, most definitely, the only thing is you're not a baby anymore," Myra added sarcastically.

"Ooh, she told you. Good one, Myra." Cissy slapped Myra a five.

Lance made the motion of scooping his face up from the floor, putting it back on, and then said, "On that note, I'll be getting your food now, ladies."

As he walked away, they looked at his butt, then back at each other. They didn't bother getting into the conversation of Lance, because Cissy wanted to talk about more pressing issues, like what Myra was going to do with her life. Cissy jumped right in and asked Myra to continue what she was saying about Dee. Myra then continued to explain that Dee wanted to put the house in Devon's name.

Cissy interrupted her, "Devon Jr.! Are you serious? And what did you tell him?"

"I told him no."

"That's right, girl … how dare him even ask you to do such a stupid thing? I think that's the most ridiculous thing I've ever heard!"

"But, Cissy, you haven't heard the best part yet. Do you know he had the audacity to say that if I'm not going to help with the firm, then I shouldn't expect to use the profit from the firm to open up my business?"

"No, he didn't! How's he going to stop you if he's dead? The dummy …"

"Ooh, good one, Cissy … Now when he first asked for the help, he did say it would help me get the money to start my business, but contingent upon my taking the position and waiting two more years. Then the money is mine."

"Oh, so he doesn't know the money is yours anyway? And furthermore he's not the only one with money. You do have Aunt Carol, Mom, and me. I mean, we do come from a line of businesswomen. Does he seriously think you should wait two more years from now to start your own business while he's dead? Shoot, he must be crazy."

Cissy slapped Myra five again while laughing. Then Myra quickly remarked to Cissy, "I like that …"

"What?"

"You didn't curse, Cissy."

"Humph, he should be thankful I wasn't there because I would've definitely given him some choice words."

"I know that's right," Myra agreed.

While they were eating, Cissy couldn't help but think of Dee's selfish proposal. As she continued to think, she became infuriated. While she chewed her food, she stopped to say, "Who the hell does he think he is? Nobody told him to leave the other firm to start his own. And you supported him through all of that mess. Girl, you need to look out for you and only you, especially if he dies."

"He is not going to die, Cissy," Myra passively reminded her.

"And if he does? I mean, he's been manipulating you throughout the whole marriage. Are you going to allow him to do the same from his grave, Myra?"

"Cissy, I don't even want to think like that: however, if it happens, you better believe I will be starting my own business, whatever it's going to be… and I hope God will provide me the strength and a way to do it."

"Please, with the money from the law firm, you could start your own department store. Shoot, who knows, you could be the next Lord & Taylor, only we'll call it Lord & Myra", Cissy joked.

"Cissy, you're so crazy."

"Ooh, ooh, no, I have a better one. Instead of people shopping at Bloomies, they'll shop at Mimi's. That's some Mimi for his A—"

"Uh, don't even go there, Cissy. You were doing so well."

Cissy took a deep breath and blew out. In that moment, she realized how hard it was to refrain from swearing.

"But on a serious note, Myra, when the time comes and you need any help, you know I'll be there to help in any way can."

"I know, thanks Sis."

Just then Myra's cell phone started going off again. Myra huffed and groaned while looking at the number.

"Oh boy, he's calling me again; let me get this…. I'll be right back, Cissy."

Cissy shook her head okay and watched from afar if Dee was making Myra upset again. After seeing Myra walk back and forth, she closed her eyes while counting to ten to calm her self down. In the middle of her counting, Lance startled her by placing the plates of food on the table. Then he proceeded to ask her how she was doing. Cissy gave him a slight cold shoulder, but answered his question. Lance then took her response as an invitation to take a seat. Because that was the type of man he was. He didn't allow his ego to dictate his heart. Furthermore, He knew Cissy's cold disposition was only her way of guarding her heart.

Meanwhile, outside of the restaurant, Myra called Dee back after loosing the connection during their discussion. After the phone rang about four times, Dee finally answered. "Mimi, where are you, anyway? I've been trying to reach you!"

"I told you I had some things to take care of. And I made plans to meet with my sister." Myra grew more annoyed at this point, but said nothing as he continued to complain about not being able to reach her for a measly hour. She couldn't believe him. First, he was giving her orders, now he wanted to try to keep tabs on her. "Give me a damn break!"

As soon as the words came out of her mouth, she knew it was bad. However, it was his continued talking that pushed her to break. Suddenly Dee stopped short and shouted, "Did you just curse at me, Myra?"

She couldn't run for cover now, so she said, "No, I just asked for a damn break. You keep fighting with me. And if you're not doing this, you're barking orders at me. And now you act as if I can't have some free time for myself."

"Oh, so hanging with your sister is free time now. And what do you need free time to do, Myra? Shop frivolously and gossip?"

"First of all, I don't gossip, Dee. And secondly, I don't have to explain what I buy because, like you, I have a job, taking care of the kids. You being the biggest one …"

Dee cut Myra off, "Oh, really, so why aren't you doing your job and taking care of me?"

"Anyways, Dee, did you call for a reason or to make ridiculous comments?"

"I would like for my wife to come back to the hospital tonight if that's not too much to ask."

"Of course, I will see you tonight, Dee. I see you every night, don't I?"

"I don't know. You seemed pretty upset earlier, and I wasn't sure if you wrote me off."

"No, I didn't write you off. I'm at King B's right now. Do you want anything?"

"Uh, yes, I could go for some catfish, greens, and sweet potato," Dee swiftly replied.

"And I'm sure you got the okay by your doctor, right, Dee?"

"Yes, Myra, I did. He says eat the foods I like but in moderation."

"Okay, so I'll see you later."

"Okay, see you."

Myra hung up and walked back inside the restaurant. Walking back to the table, Myra saw another missed call. When she checked it, it was Travis. She just smiled, sat down, and continued her lunch with Cissy.

"Okay, so where were we?" Myra asked.

"What did your husband want?"

"He just wanted to make sure that I was visiting him tonight."

"Duh, where else would you be, Myra?" Cissy shrugged her shoulders.

"That's exactly what I told him … Girl, we're on the same page."

"Well, I don't want to tell you what to do, but Myra, you have wanted to open a boutique since we were in high school. And I would be disappointed if you didn't go for it."

"Cissy, trust me, I'm not giving up on any of it. I'll find a way to somehow accomplish them both."

"Now why do you want to drive yourself crazy with two big projects, Myra?"

"Maybe it won't be so crazy," Myra tried to convince Cissy.

"Stop kidding yourself, Myra," Cissy replied.

"I'm not. Before we leave, remind me to get an extra order for Dee. This food is great."

"Please, he better hope I remind you—because he definitely doesn't deserve it right now. You are right about one thing—this food is great."

They keep eating, stuffing their faces.

"Myra, you know what I've noticed in all of this?"

"What, Cissy?"

"You haven't considered how you could make it without your husband … You keep talking as if Dee is your whole world. But I beg to differ."

"Now, how is it you and Dee can't agree on the color of the sky, but can manage to agree that I wrap the majority of my life around him?"

"Exactly. I have yet to hear what your plans are."

"How can I make plans when I have so much on my plate? The kids being one of them. Don't forget that, Cissy."

"I haven't, but apparently you have, Myra."

"What do you mean by that?" Myra looked confused.

"Relax, Myra. I'm just saying that you have a little girl growing up. And she is watching your every move. Don't get me wrong, there's nothing wrong with being a housewife, but in everything you do, you must show the commitment to yourself first. So if it's being a housewife, then it'll show in your housework. Pretty soon you'll be all she relates to, whether you like or not. Do you want her to witness you being powerless or powerful?"

"That's why I can't take the position at Dee's law firm, Cissy."

"You say it, but just a few minutes ago, you were trying to figure out how to do both."

In the midst of Cissy talking, Myra became very upset. However it wasn't with Cissy, but with herself for not pursuing here dreams. She was also upset that she decided to stay home, when in fact after receiving her degree she wanted to jump right into opening her business. At this point, she felt she cheated herself of time. Funny enough when she pictured her life, she saw life in the city with her shop doing very well, Dee's career in Law taking off, and their children going to the best schools nearby. Somehow, it turned out to be just the opposite. She couldn't be in the least surprised when all she ever did was appease Dee in every way. Dee didn't want to move to the city, so Myra agreed to live in the suburbs. Dee didn't want Devon Jr. to go to daycare, so she agreed to stay home until he could speak. But then it became until all three children could speak. Because by the time on started Pre-K, she'd became pregnant again. And finally when it was time for Princess to start school, Dee decided to leave the Law firm to start his own—only to leave Myra home in support of his new venture. And now here she was thinking about how much time she wasted, and she was angry with her own self.

"You know, I'm actually upset with myself for creating this 'woe is me pity party.' I think it's time to get cracking."

"Look, Myra, I know you have to stick with Dee through good times or bad, sickness and health, but I don't recall the marriage vows ever saying anything about you obligating yourself to only his profession."

"Yeah, I hear you …" Myra smiled briefly.

"Myra, I know you always had a lot going on in your life, but did you forget where we come from?"

"Uh, no …"

"We come from a strong line of women who make their own way regardless of any circumstances. "Isn't that what Nana and Mama taught us? It looks to me, you did the opposite." Cissy stopped to take a sip of her drink, then continued what she was saying.

"So far, you've been compromising yourself for Dee to accomplish his achievements. And the way I see it, now it's your turn. Starting here and now … You know what I'm saying?"

"Yeah, I hear you; because it really does seem like the season for change."

Myra paused, remembering how firm her mom and grandma were when they were growing up. Out of the blue, Myra came out with, "Cissy, do you remember when Mama and Nana would make us read Proverbs 31:10 almost every Sunday after church?"

Cissy quickly chuckled, shaking her head yes, and said, "Yep, I even remember having to memorize it for our rites of passage. Remember that?"

Myra, smiling, recalled that event, "Yeah, as a matter of fact, they threatened we wouldn't have a party if we didn't have it memorized by then. At that time, we didn't see the point, but if it weren't for their constant chastisement to apply God's word to our transformation from girls to women, we wouldn't have made it through college and beauty school."

"Yep, so true. And even though Mama is proud of the choices we made in our lives, I know it would make her more proud to see you accomplish your dreams, outside of you being a great mom."

Myra smirked, recognizing Cissy wasn't going to let it go. "I know, I know …"

Just then Cissy looked at her watch. "Oh, boy, look at the time. I have to get back to the shop. I have a two o'clock scheduled."

"What time is it?"

"One thirty. Here's the money for the tab, and don't forget Dee's food. And think about what I said, Myra," Cissy exclaimed. She then gathered her belongings, while casually reminding her not to give in to Dee's request.

"Okay, okay. And don't forget you're watching the kids tonight so I can go to Devon's school for the PTA meeting, and the hospital."

"I won't," Cissy replied as she planted a big kiss on Myra's cheek, then walked out.

Ten minutes later, Myra's leftovers came out, wrapped up along with Dee's order. Then she walked out. In the car, Myra called Travis back. She was wondering what he wanted.

"Hello," Travis answered with his deep voice.

"Hey, Travis, I have a missed call from you. I'm returning your call."

"Oh, hey, Myra. How are you doing?"

"Okay, and you?" Myra answered nervously.

"I'm good, a little busy, but good."

Myra thought, "You definitely sound good." Then she realized what she was thinking and nonchalantly said, "Being busy is always good."

"It can also be bad in my case."

Myra heard the agitation in his voice, then asked, "Why is that?"

"Well, my wife, um, excuse me, ex-wife doesn't agree with it much."

"So I gather you guys are divorced?"

"Fortunately, we are."

"Oh, I'm sorry to hear that," Myra said in a sorrowful tone.

"Oh, it's nothing to feel sorry about; it was definitely for the better," Travis replied, having no hard feelings.

"Maybe, but I'm just a sucker for love."

"No, Myra, you just have a big heart, something I never really appreciated when we were together."

"Oh, please, Travis, we were too young—"

Travis cut her off, "Yes, but it doesn't excuse my doggish ways then."

"Oh, is this a personal apology I'm hearing, Travis?"

Travis chuckled, "Yeah, I guess having my daughter really opened my eyes. I mean, 'cause in those days I just knew I was the player of all players, and now that my daughter is going through the boyfriend stage, I'm seeing how foolish boys are."

"That's right, Travis, but eventually they become men and learn the error of their ways."

"Yep."

"And as far as your daughter is concerned, these are the most crucial years. So everything you say has to be well thought out before you say it."

"I hear ya, thanks. Myra, I hate to cut the conversation short, but I'm about to have a meeting, so can I call you later?"

"Sure, I have to go pick up my kids anyway. Have a good day, bye."

"You too, Myra."

Myra was still uncertain why Travis called, but didn't care to find out now that she was sitting in bumper to bumper traffic on the highway. She was hoping to beat Devon in getting Trey and Princess from school, but at the rate traffic was moving she pretty much gave up on that idea. Still she began talking to herself and the cars in front of her. "Come on, people, I have to get home!."

All of a sudden, her phone started ringing. She looked at the number, seeing it was Devon. She picked it up anxiously.

"Hello, Devon, Please say you're at Trey and Princess's."

"Yes, Mom, we're at the park right now."

"Great, so after they're done playing, meet me at home. I'm going to pick up dinner."

"But, Mom, don't you have that school meeting?"

"Yes, but that's later this evening … I'll see you at home, Devon."

Devon ended the call after saying good-bye. He turned to the two, shouting, "Trey and Princess, come on, we have to go."

"Aww, man, do we have to go right now?" Trey moaned.

"Yes, Trey. Mom just called and told us to start heading home."

"But I don't want to go now," Princess whined.

"Well, we have to go, didn't you hear what Devon just said," Trey barked.

"Let's go, you guys; we don't want to keep Mom waiting," Devon yelled out. He rushed them so he could get home to check the mail for the letter the principal sent home.

Trey, on the other hand, still couldn't understand what the rush was. "I don't know why we have to go when it's still early."

"Trey, stop complaining and walk," Devon responded as he walked briskly out of the park.

"And why do we have to walk?" Trey asked.

"Do I have a car?" Devon sarcastically asked Trey.

"No, but you need one …"

"Well, next time you ask for something for yourself, Trey, ask for a car for me."

"Uh-uh, no way … it's not like you're going to take me everywhere I want to go."

"Devon?" Princess interjected.

"Yes, Princess."

"Are we going to see Daddy today?"

"I don't think so, but you could ask Mommy when we get home. Okay?"

"I hope so because I miss him a whole lot," Princess whined.

"Me too," Devon agreed.

"Me three," Trey followed suit.

Transparent

§&

U pon reaching home, Myra went through the mail and noticed a letter from Devon's school. She opened it up, reading it with her eyes wide open in disbelief. She started pacing the floor back and forth trying to figure out what she was going to do to Devon when he got home. Finally she came to the conclusion to put the letter back in the pile and see if maybe Devon would just confess. At this point, she didn't see why he would when he hadn't thus far. Especially since the letter was sent a few days ago, and he didn't bother to mention the problem he was having in school at all previously.. Myra picked up the phone to inform Dee.

"Hello," Dee answered somberly.

"Hey, Dee … did you speak to the doctor yet?"

"Oh, I'm fine, Myra."

Myra rolled her eyes.

"Yes, I did speak to the doctor. And I signed the papers for the surgery already, too, just in case you're wondering," Dee responded with arrogance.

"Well, I wasn't asking, but thanks for allowing me to be a part of the decision-making process, Dee. It's so nice to hear you being considerate of my feelings," Myra retaliated.

"Your feelings have nothing to do with my decision to fight for my life …"

"Ahh, that's the Dee I recognize ... your contemptuous attitude rings a bell. So tell me, Dee, is it your 'holier than thou ego trip' or pride that has you making decisions with no regard for your family? Inquiring minds want to know."

Dee ignored Myra's sarcasm. "Myra, I'm doing this for my family. If I can come through this, then I could provide for my family without having any more hospital situations."

"Oh, I see. You know somehow I missed the part when 'If' is a guarantee."

"Well, there aren't any guarantees. But there is faith, which apparently you still don't have."

Myra rolled her eyes up in annoyance of his repetitive reminders of her lack of faith, "Anyways, Dee ... your son Devon has a letter here from school stating he's failing biology and he's not allowed to play football for the remainder of the marking period until he brings up his grade."

"You see, Myra, that's exactly why I have to do this surgery, so I can be there for him. He's going through a lot of pressure."

"What pressure, Dee? You being in the hospital is only one part of his failing biology!"

"That may be true, but I don't recall him ever failing any subject before—"

"Well, he's coming in now, so I'll speak to you later," Myra cut in to say.

"Do not address him, Myra. I want to talk to him myself."

"Uh, excuse me?"

"Myra, I know you ..."

"Dee, I'll call you later." Myra rushed him off.

"Wait a minute, are you still coming by later?"

"Yes, I am ... Bye."

Myra hung up the phone quickly to greet the kids. As they entered, Myra noticed Devon looking around. He didn't say hello or even give Myra a kiss. So Myra asked him if everything was okay, but Devon didn't respond. He just pecked her on the cheek and plopped himself down on the couch. Princess ran to Myra in excitement. Then out of nowhere, Trey called Devon out about rushing them home from the park. Devon quickly shushed him, but to no avail. Princess grabbed Myra's attention, telling it all.

"Mama, Devon made us leave the park early. He said you told him we had to leave."

Myra looked at Devon with an attitude and said, "Now why would I stop my babies from having fun at the park? Devon, why did you rush them home?"

"Well, I thought you wanted us to come home to help," Devon said, then looked away. Suspicious, Myra looked back at Devon from the corner of her eye and said, "Well, then, you must've misunderstood, because the only help I need is in buying the groceries you run through every day. And since you don't work, I don't need your help. Understand?"

"Okay."

Myra called him out saying, "Okay what?"

"Okay, Ma, I understand," Devon replied as if he was too tired to argue.

"All right, you three go wash up for dinner," Myra ordered as Trey complained.

"Already? But I want to watch some TV first."

"Yes, now, Trey. Or would you like to go to bed now? I mean, you do have a choice. Now, as I said, all three of you go wash up."

"Ma, I think I'm old enough to know when I have to wash my hands," said Devon.

Myra stepped back, looking Devon up and down, then said, "Boy, you better—"

"I'm going, I'm going." Devon jumped up quickly after seeing Myra's reaction.

"All right, I'm going to the garage to get the paper plates. By the time I get back, all three of you should be done."

Devon thought it was the perfect time to look for the principal's letter, which is the same reason why Myra went for the plates herself. She could have just as easily asked Trey or Devon to get them, as she usually did. When she came back, they were all sitting at the table, ready to eat.

"Mom, dinner smells good," said Princess.

"Yeah, Mom, why don't you cook like this anymore?" Trey asked as he looked at the food she brought home from their favorite restaurant.

"Well, you know that's because I've been busy running back and forth to the hospital. But now that your father is better, I promise you'll have more home-cooked meals again."

Automatically Devon interjected, "Please, Ma, because if you leave it to Aunt Cissy, we'll be eatin' TV dinners every day."

"Devon, please, you shouldn't complain because you hardly ever eat my food anyway."

Trey laughed, spitting up his food. Devon gave him a mean look to shut him up. After Trey stopped laughing, Devon continued, "Ma, I'm not complaining. I'm just sayin' I'd rather eat cooked food than something that's cooked in four minutes in the microwave then tastes like rubber. You know, I have to keep my body buff and in shape for football."

Myra smiled a huge grin because Devon had no idea what he just walked into. As she swallowed her food, Myra looked Devon right in the eyes and asked, "Oh, and how is football anyway? Better yet, how's school?"

Devon avoided eye contact and said, "School and football are fine, Mama."

Myra knew how much that was a fallacy. Especially since he didn't look at her when he answered. This was one of the ways she could tell when Devon was lying. Whenever he was lying, he spoke in perfect English and ended it with "Mama." Nonetheless, she continued to question him as if nothing had happened. "Great, and when is the next report card coming?"

"I'm not exactly sure, but it should be soon, Mama," Devon replied.

Myra then thought to herself, "Yeah, I bet. Does he really think I was born yesterday? As if I don't have a clue he's not telling the truth?"

"Mommy, when are we going to see Daddy again?" asked Princess.

"Soon, Princess … soon … I'll let you know."

"I miss him," added Princess.

"We all do … not just you, Princess," Trey cut in to say.

"Trey, I don't have to say we all miss Dad, especially if I'm the only one who asked for him, so leave me alone!"

Myra held her hand up, signaling them to stop. "You guys, stop fighting. I have enough on my mind. The last thing I need is to hear you guys bickering."

"They're like this all of the time," Devon interjected.

Myra looked at Devon, then sarcastically remarked, "And let me guess—you don't stop them when you hear it, right?"

"When I'm around, I do, but besides, I'm not the one who had them, so …"

"Excuse me! Who do you think you are talking to, Devon?"

"I'm sorry, Ma, but you keep putting all of the responsibility on me when it's not …"

"Oh, yeah, well, remember that the next time you need sneakers or anything else for that matter. We'll see whose responsibility it is then, because quite frankly you can get your own job and pay for your own stuff. Your father and I do not have to do it because we only have to take care of what you need, technically speaking."

"Actually, technically speaking, you have a legal responsibility to take care of me until I'm twenty-one," Devon joked.

"Uh, wrong … until you're eighteen in this house. And even then we don't have to provide anything extra, so if you're done being sarcastic now, you can remove the TV, stereo, and computer out of your room and put them in the garage."

"What! Please, Mama, I was just playing. You know how I do …"

"Oh, like a joke. Ha-ha funny?"

Devon shook his head with a smile, hoping Myra would change her mind.

"Oh, okay. Hahaha," Myra sarcastically laughs then stopped with a serious look on her face and said, "Well, I don't get it, but you know what's really funny?" Myra asked as she really laughed.

"Ha-ha-ha ... what?" Devon replied while laughing.

"That I'm about to wipe that smile off your face because I wasn't joking ... Now get to getting on what I told you to do before I put my foot up your 'you-know-what.'"

"Mama, please, I didn't mean it."

"Oh, you didn't, huh, just like I didn't mean to see that letter from your school either."

"What letter?" Devon tried to act like he didn't know what Myra was talking about, but she wasn't letting him off that easy.

So she continued with her scolding, "Yeah, this coming from the one who rushed home to try to get it before I saw it. I wasn't born yesterday, Devon. You forget I was your age once upon a time and a lot smarter at the game too, if I do say so myself. You can't game me, because game recognize game, baby. I'm sure your father will be so proud," Myra said as she jumped in his face.

Devon, in shame, put his head down, but then tried to explain, "Mama, I have another chance to make it ..."

Myra was so furious at this point, she didn't give him the chance to finish speaking. "Devon, just go upstairs, or so help me God, you'll lose your second chance with me!"

Devon slid away from the table aggressively and ran up the stairs. Myra turned to Trey and Princess and told them to finish their dinner.

A sudden quiet came over the house. Trey and Princess made sure they ate every single grain on their plate to keep the peace. This was not the time to do anything that sounded even remotely like arguing. As Devon was bringing down all of his luxuries to the garage, Myra watched. This was her way of teaching him how blessed he was to have everything. And to top it off, she even took away his curfew and hanging out privileges. When he was done, Devon went to his bedroom and locked the door, determined to stay in there forever. Myra realized he didn't finish all of his dinner, so she called him. When he didn't answer, she went to his room to tell him. As she tried to open the door, she saw it was locked. She proceeded to bang on it as if she was the police. Devon opened the door, angrily looking at Myra.

"Boy, do you have a problem with your eyes?"

"No, Ma, why are you banging on the door?"

"Uh-uh, you don't ask the questions, I do. This is my house and I can bang on everything if I want to. You, on the other hand, are not allowed to lock any doors in this house, you understand me?"

"I didn't know this was just your house; maybe I should ask Dad if he feels the same way."

Myra looked at him like he'd lost his mind, unfolded her arms, and started walking toward him. "I don't care what your father feels. Whatever I say is what goes."

"Oh, really, that's how it is? You don't have the last word—Dad does," Devon retorted.

"Oh, really, hold that thought. I'll be right back."

Myra went to the kitchen, grabbed some tools, and proceeded to walk back to Devon's room. Cissy then walked in, giving Myra a strange look as she walked by.

"Hey, Cissy, give me a hand, please," Myra said angrily.

So Cissy began applauding, asking, "How's that?"

Myra turned around swiftly, saying, "Cissy, I'm not in the mood. Now are you going to help or not?"

"Okay, okay—sorry. What am I helping you with anyway?"

"You'll see…."

Cissy followed Myra up to Devon's room. As soon as they got there, Myra instructed Cissy to start unscrewing the hinges of the door.

Devon jumped up, racing toward the door, yelling, "What are you doing?"

"Hey, back it up, back it up. You don't want me to use this hammer on you," Myra said, looking as serious as a heart attack.

Devon stepped back, trying to plead his case to Cissy, as if she could help. But Cissy threw her hands up, letting him know she has nothing to do with this.

"Hey, I told you—your mama was crazy, but you just keep pushing her buttons, so you're on your own now, buddy."

"But, Auntie, it's not fair. She gets to take my door away for not doing well in school—what does she get for not doing well at home?"

Devon's statement was out, and he couldn't take it back. Myra and Cissy stood in disbelief, staring at Devon with an "I know you didn't go there" look. Then, out of nowhere, Myra started charging at him with the hammer swinging. Cissy jumped between them just in time to catch Myra's hand going down toward Devon. Even though he stood at six feet three inches tall, a foot taller than Myra, he was scared straight. He knew his mother didn't play, but this time, it didn't matter because he was angry.

"Myra! Put the hammer down," Cissy belted out.

"I'll hurt him, Cissy. You better let him know."

"I know, but hitting him with a hammer will kill him. Here, use this instead ..." Cissy threw the hammer aside and handed Myra a wooden bat instead. Devon looked at the two of them crazy, then grabbed his pillow to protect himself.

"Wait a minute, wait a minute. I'm sorry," Devon shouted as he tried to block his entire upper body.

"Sorry didn't say it, you did," Myra replied as she went to swing, intentionally missing.

"I know, but I didn't mean it, Mama. I just said it because I was angry."

"Now that's stupid," interrupted Cissy.

Trey and Princess were snickering in the doorway as they peeked in. Cissy looked back at them, putting her finger over her lips, warning them to be quiet. They both opened their eyes wide, then ran back to the living room.

"This is what happens when you say something you don't mean, Devon," Myra said loudly.

"Okay, I'll think before I speak next time. Mama, please ..."

"You better be grateful I have a meeting to go to. But don't think you're off the hook."

"No, actually he's off the hinges... get it, off the hing..."

Myra looks at Cissy shaking her head no.

"Oh, now is not the time either? Okay so, can I at least get a high-five?"

Myra put down the bat, wiping the sweat from her forehead, then slapped Cissy a five before walking out with the door in her hand. Devon plopped down on his bed and sighed in relief. He couldn't believe they double-teamed him. He could still hear them laughing. Just then Trey stood at the doorway and joked, "Devon, do you need some privacy?" Devon threw his pillow at Trey, letting him know he better stop playing.

Ten minutes later, the phone rang. As Cissy went to get the phone, Devon yelled from his room, "I got it, Auntie."

Cissy shouted back, "You don't have anything. You better hang up the phone, boy, and study."

"Too late, it's for Ma."

"Devon, hang up the phone now!"

"I did already."

"Watch the bass in your voice," Cissy shouted. "Hello," Cissy answered the call in an upset. The person then hung up. Cissy also hung up. Then she screamed, "Devon, I know that was one of your friends and you better tell them to stop calling here and hanging up."

Devon didn't bother to respond. Cissy then walked into Princess's room and saw her sitting up. So she sat down beside her on the bed and asked, "What's the matter, Princess?"

"I'm scared.... It's too dark in here, and I don't want to sleep alone."

"Did you see a scary movie or something?"

"No ... I want my mommy," Princess replied.

"Well, Mommy is with Daddy right now, but she'll be home soon, sweetie."

"Aunt Cissy, when is Daddy coming home?"

"Soon, baby girl, soon …"

"I wish he could come home tomorrow."

"How about you pray for God to bring him home as soon as possible?"

"Can you say it with me, Aunt Cissy?"

"Sure, why don't you start?"

"God, please bring my Daddy home very soon … and help him feel better, so he's not sick anymore. Oh, and one more thing, God, please make Mommy happy, so she won't be crying at night any more …"

Then Cissy added, "And we pray, Lord, that you bless Dee with strength and endurance. Put your hedge of protection over him and my sister, and we say this prayer in …" Cissy paused to hear Princess conclude the prayer.

"Jesus' name. Amen," Princess said.

"Amen … Now, do you want your auntie to lay down with you until you fall asleep?"

"Yes."

"Okay, scoot over—let's get some rest."

"Aunt Cissy?" Princess mumbled.

"Yes."

"You're the best auntie in the world. I love you."

"And you're the best niece in the world."

"But I'm your only niece. Aunt Cissy …"

Cissy chuckled, "Girl, you're too smart. I love you, too. Now go to sleep."

Cissy didn't hear a response, so she assumed Princess already fell asleep. When she looked down to check, Princess was knocked out. So she slid out of the bed quietly, then crept out of the room and back downstairs.

*   *   *   *   *

Myra was on a committee at Devon's school. She was on the committee long before Dee had became sick. And although she had a lot to deal with, she still wanted to be a part of the planning for the senior prom. Myra began mumbling to herself, "God, please let this meeting go by quickly, so I can go to the hospital, visit Dee, and go back home. Please make this short and sweet."

"Amen," a voice added from behind.

Myra, without bothering to look back, said, "Excuse me."

He then whispered, "Were you not praying?"

"Yes, but it isn't any business of yours."

"I'm sorry, but in standing right behind you, I heard your soft voice and couldn't help but hear what you were saying."

Myra still didn't bother to turn around. "So you just make a habit of eavesdropping when you feel like it?"

"Yes, when it's someone I'm interested in ..."

Myra became annoyed and turned around to put him in his place. As she turned around, she said, "Listen, I'm marr—*Travis*!"

Myra couldn't help but show her excitement in seeing him again. After the long day she had had, he was a breath of fresh air.

"Shhh," one of the other parents interjected.

Myra apologized and asked him what he was doing at the meeting. Travis let her know that his niece and daughter just recently transferred to the school. Travis explained he was only at the meeting because his daughter's mother was working late and couldn't make it. As Myra was about to ask him another question, the vice president of the PTA (Mrs. Greene aka Nosy) interrupted their conversation, "Oh, hi, Mrs. Harris, how's your husband?"

"He's okay, Ms. Greene. Thanks for asking."

"So, why are you here, when you should be at the hospital?"

"I made this commitment prior to his condition, and I like to follow through on my word."

"Uh-huh, and who's this handsome guy?" She put her hand out, waiting for an introduction.

"Ms. Greene, I'm Jaylin's father, Travis Dewitt. I was just here last week with her mother for the parent-teacher conference."

"Oh, of course ... How is your daughter?"

"She's fine."

"You guys must be a tight-knit family, because we hardly get the husbands into these kinds of meetings."

"Well, no, we just have an understanding," Travis replied discreetly.

Unaware of his situation, Ms. Greene interjected, "Marriage is give and take."

Travis knew what she was getting at, so he put her curiosity to rest. "Oh, we're not married."

"Oh, really? Well, let me know if you have any problems or need any information; I will be happy to help in any way I can."

Myra thought to herself, *I'm sure you will. Every man that comes in here, you jump at them ... Thank God, Dee's already taken, or you would've gone after him, too.*

"Mrs. Harris, I'll see you later." Ms. Greene tried to dismiss Myra. But Myra didn't budge. Instead, she stayed there just in case she had to save Travis.

"Okay, bye."

"And Mr. ... I'm sorry, I didn't get your last name," Ms. Greene responded while sticking her hand out again.

"Dewitt, but you can call me Travis."

"Oh, okay, Travis; a strong name—for a strong man. Well, have a good night, and remember if there's anything you need, don't hesitate to call."

"You have a good night as well, Ms. Greene."

"Wow, that couldn't be more forward," Myra said to Travis.

Ignoring Ms. Greene's come-on, Travis replied, "Yeah, but I'm sorry to hear about your husband."

"Thanks, I just hope he pulls through. He'll be going for surgery in a couple of days."

"Oh, I'm sure he'll pull through, Myra."

"What makes you so sure?"

"He has you to come back home to ... just keep your faith," Travis smiled.

"Thanks for the compliment, but my faith has been minimal lately. What about you?"

"I'm not an atheist, but let's just say I'm not walking with Jesus, either," Travis replied.

Myra attempted to give him some words of encouragement, but Travis interrupted her to say, "Like I said, I'm not a heathen now."

"I didn't say you were ... Don't be so defensive ... you always did take things personal."

"What are you talking about, Ms. Know-it-all?" Travis joked back.

"Excuse me," Myra looked him up and down.

"Anyway, whatever happened to that stupid football jock you left me for?"

"He's on his deathbed. You know, my husband."

"Ooh, I'm so sorry, Myra."

"It's okay. You couldn't have known ..."

Travis then said to Myra, "I hope he knows what he has, and if not, I could let him know for you."

"No, I think he knows."

"So, how about we go for coffee after this?"

"Travis, I don't think that would be appropriate under the circumstances."

"Um ... I didn't ask you for a date, just two friends going for a cup of coffee."

"Tonight, I have to go to the hospital," Myra responded with a flirtatious smirk on her face.

"So, how does tomorrow sound? For lunch?" Travis continued to ask.

"I'll think about it."

"Okay, just give me a call when you know the best time," Travis smiled, while looking for a seat.

"A little cocky, are we?"

"You and I go way back, Myra. You don't have to play coy with me. Now just give me a time and place, so I can find a seat."

"I'm not giving you anything, and you can go find your seat, thank you."

"Okay, but I know you'll give me a time—"

Myra, trying to shoot him down, cut him off, "Travis, stop being so narcissistic."

However, Travis wasn't bothered by her comment. Instead, he teased her, "Ooh, I love it when you use big words …"

"Travis, have a good night," Myra replied as she started to walk away. Travis gently reached for her hand and said he was just joking and she shouldn't take him so seriously. Just then, Myra couldn't help but to compare him to Dee. Whenever she became upset with Dee, he would let her stay angry. And if she'd walk away from an argument, he rarely chased her, unless he felt he was wrong—which wasn't very often. Myra didn't have anything else to say but, "Travis, I have a husband who I need to visit; which means I do not have time to play cat and mouse with you all night."

"I understand, but how often do two old friends get to see each other? Come on, I'm just asking for a cup of coffee." Travis gave Myra a sad face. He knew this would work.

Myra instantly became annoyed with his persistence and said, "News flash, Travis, this is not high school. And I am no longer a sixteen-year-old with a crush."

Travis stepped back, "Excuse me, did you say crush? I didn't know what we had was just a crush."

"Oh, stop smiling like that … it doesn't work anymore, Travis." Myra turned her face to avoid making eye contact with him.

"Oh, really?" he asked while bringing his face down to look in her eyes.

Myra continued to stand firm to her no. But Travis believed her eyes were saying yes, so he asked one more time to see if she'd change her answer. Myra paused, then said, "Okay, but only this time, Travis. And don't think it's because of your smile either. I just really need a cup of coffee after the long day I had."

"Great, I know the perfect diner, which happens to have the best coffee." Travis hands her the diner's business card.

Myra took his word for it and put the diner's card in her jacket. She watched him as he walked away with a smooth swagger as always. Out of nowhere, breaking Myra's stare, Ms. Greene showed Myra to a seat across the room from Travis. Myra took her seat, knowing her intentions. However, she didn't let it bother her. Myra knew very well that Ms. Greene wanted to take a seat right next to Travis. The meeting continued over the next two hours as they determined everyone's responsibilities. After the meeting, Ms. Greene instantly began talking to Travis. Travis politely listened, even though he was ready to go for the coffee with Myra.

Myra locked eyes with Travis a few minutes later. They smiled at each other, then he signaled for her to save him. Myra shook her head no and laughed at him. Travis then signed to Myra that he'd see her at the diner. Myra picked up her jacket and purse, then made her way out the door. On the drive over, Myra took the long way to mull over some things. She thought having coffee with Travis would maybe bring her some clarity.

*   *   *   *   *

Myra finally reached the diner. And she suddenly heard, "Hey, Myra, over here."

Myra walked to the booth.

"I thought you were lost for a minute," Travis said as he watched her sit down.

"No, I just took a longer way, so I could—"

"Let me guess, think," Travis finished her sentence.

Myra gave Travis a suspicious look before saying, "Yeah, you know I don't get to think often enough because of my hectic schedule. I mean, between hospital visits, paying bills, school meetings, and the kids' activities, I don't have a chance to take a breather from the everyday hustle."

"Okay, Myra, stop right there. As much as I like that you have wonderful kids and a wonderful marriage, I want to hear about you and how you're doing."

"But hearing about me is my family and marriage …"

"I disagree, it's only part of you. I want to hear what you, *Myra*, have been up to."

"Travis, my family is all I've been up to. I don't have anything else to talk about."

"Okay, so how about you start by telling me how you're doing with Dee being in the hospital."

"I'm just hoping Dee makes it through the surgery. I went through a lot the last couple of months between Dee collapsing at work, going into a coma, and now coming back. It's been really crazy. Sometimes I don't know whether I'm coming or going. I go home to an empty bed and can't sleep. I wake up in the morning and I can't eat. I don't know …"

Myra paused to wipe her tears. Travis was at a loss for words. He placed his hand over hers while handing her a tissue. He wasn't trying to make her feel sad. So he changed the subject.

"I remember distinctly you wanted to design clothes and open up your own clothing boutique—what ever happened to that?"

Myra took a deep breath to compose herself and said, "Well, it went out of the window when I had my first son. Dee received a great position at a lucrative law firm …"

"Well, why did you let it go out of the window?"

"It just made perfect sense for me to stay home … since I was the one carrying and having the baby, you know what I mean."

"And your husband, was he okay with that? What's his take on all of this?"

"He definitely supports my dreams, but at the time, he was working hard on making partner. And after working blood, sweat, and tears, he realized that the firm wasn't going to make him partner and decided to open up his own law firm …"

"And, let me guess, you ended up helping him with his new venture. Instead of focusing on yourself."

"Well, yes and no. I'm hoping his law firm can finance the boutique."

"Myra, ever since I met you, all you ever talked about is the boutique you want to open. I mean, you have waited your whole entire life to reach your dream, literally. It doesn't sound like you to push it off for so long. This is definitely not the Myra I used to know."

"I know.…"

"I mean, you even talked about me heading the men's line of suits or everyday wear, and we would call our company 'My-T Looks.'"

Myra looked at Travis, smiling and giggling. She took a sip of her coffee and said, "Yeah, those were the days."

Travis replied, "Myra, you know you could do it. I mean, you're already ahead of the game. You have a degree."

"And how did you know that?" Myra was taken back.

"Um, I have my sources …"

"What sources, Travis?"

"Let's just say, anything I want to know I can find out."

"Is that part of the detective advantages?"

"Something like that."

"You know, as a woman, my life has a lot more going on. Taking care of my kids is always my first priority. You men have it easy. You don't have to take care of children full-time."

Travis wasn't convinced by Myra's statement, so he cut her off saying, "Blah blah blah, you women kill me."

Myra leaned back, "Excuse me."

"You're excused. Just so you know, I raised both my daughter and son while going to work and school because their mother was in medical school and had a heavier load."

"Wow, big handclap, you're one out of a thousand men who actually step up."

"Wait a minute, I'm not done. Don't assume …"

"Travis, I'm not assuming anything. I just happen to witness more men doing their own thing than helping their wives. I don't know why it is, but I know one thing, no matter what the outcome of the surgery is, I am planning to start my own business, whether Dee's on board or not."

"It's due time you do that, Myra. So, do you have a business plan in place already? A location in mind of where the boutique would be located? Do you know what style of market you're planning to sell to? And what is the profit margin for that market?"

"Whoa, slow down, Travis. I didn't get to that yet."

"Well, what have you been doing all of this time? I mean, even though it wasn't the right time to start your business, you should've at least had the proposal in place, research done, so you can be ready for action. As the saying goes, 'If you fail to plan, you plan to fail.'"

"True … I see your point. I'm going to start right after the surgery. But right now, I have to get to the hospital."

Myra looked at her watch, finished her coffee, and picked up her purse. Travis, looking confused, asked, "You're going right now?"

"Travis, I told you I had to visit my husband, but thanks for the coffee. It was really good." Myra got up, walked to his side, and stretched her arms for a hug.

"Okay, well I just assumed since it was late …"

"Well, you know what happens when you assume, Travis. It was nice seeing you again."

"Thanks for the company, call me."

Myra walked out of the diner and quickly got in the car. She didn't realize the time had gone by so fast. She knew no matter how many shortcuts she tried to take, there would be roadwork traffic. All of a sudden, Myra felt guilty and began beating herself up for not going straight to the hospital and choosing to have coffee with Travis first. She was trying to think of what to say to Dee if he asked her why she came so late. Nothing came to mind, and quite honestly, she didn't want to make it that much of a big deal. As long as she made it there, that was good enough. It wasn't like she'd done this before. She just needed some time away from the hospital. Besides, there wasn't any point in being with Dee if all they were going to do was argue over the decisions he made or wanted to make. Now if she could just figure out who she's trying to convince, herself or Dee.

As Myra pulled into the parking lot, it dawned on her that she was ready to make some changes in her life, starting with doing what was necessary to start her business. Whatever she decided, she'd talk to Dee after the surgery about making the adjustments in schedules. Myra turned off the car, looked in the rearview mirror to make sure her hair and makeup were still good, then grabbed Dee's food. Myra got in the hospital and started running toward the waiting elevator. After catching it, her heart started to beat fast, partly from being out of shape, but mainly because she was anxious to see Dee.

"Hey, baby, sorry I came so late, but that meeting was so long." Myra walked in avoiding eye contact with Dee. But Dee retorted with an attitude. Myra took his attitude in stride, calmly changing the subject and explaining her plans to go to Devon's school to speak to the principal. Dee, however, didn't agree with those plans. He looked at Myra crazy saying, "Myra, didn't I say I wanted to handle this situation with Devon?"

Of course, Myra could only hold her composure for a minute before retorting bluntly, "Um, excuse me, but how are you supposed to handle anything from the hospital? And, by the way, you are not my father. You're my husband, so need I remind you on how to address me?"

But being the brute Dee was, he answered back with just as much of an outspoken attitude as Myra and said, "I know I'm not your father, but I am Devon's father. And as his father, I said I will handle it. Now I don't think my mouth is mute, just like I don't think your ears are deaf."

Myra turned her head quickly, squinted her eyes like he was the enemy, then rolled them up as if to say "Lord, give me patience." She took a deep breath, then said, "You know what? I'm not going to argue about this. Devon is not just your son, but ours. and I would like to think you trust me to handle our son's situation."

And even though Myra threw in the towel, Dee had to make sure he screwed the screw tighter, so he said, "Uh, you would like to think, but your brain once again is fighting the feeling. You see, because you're not capable of handling situations—you more likely to control situations."

Myra jumped back, then Dee jumped back, mocking her behavior. Myra couldn't believe her ears. She became livid at his condescending attitude and began to fight fire with fire, saying loudly, "No, control would be when you limit or restrict someone from doing something, and that would be what you're doing. I would be the one trying to keep abreast of our son's schoolwork by, you know, uh, 'helping'!"

"Okay, since you feel like defining words, Myra. What do you call a wife who wants to do what she wants to do and not submit to her husband's request?"

Myra was still aggravated. Raising her voice now to screaming, she said, "You mean demands, because you don't make requests. So don't try to put this on me. You're just being a dictator, as usual."

"Oh, really, now I'm a dictator. So what are you?"

Dee wanted to continue with his frank attitude, but he realized Myra was becoming more and more upset. So he grabbed Myra's hand after making his statement, to gently rub it as they talked. This always worked in the past, so he waited to see if he still "had it" to calm her down. Myra, on the other hand, knew what he was up to. She enjoyed when he cared enough to soothe her anguish, whether or not he put her there, So she looked down while he continued rubbing her hand and said in her normal tone, "Okay, right now it makes no sense to argue about this. You have a lot to deal with, so please, just let me handle this situation, Dee."

"Myra, I want you to understand that just because I'm in the hospital and having surgery does not mean I can't handle the kids," Dee pleaded as he put his hand on her cheek softly.

Myra loved it when Dee was gentle; hence, she lay her cheek into his hand more. She closed her eyes to enjoy the moment, then said, "I know you can handle the kids, and you have nothing to prove to me or anyone else, so please relax. And rest your mind and body."

Dee appreciated Myra's concern. But he didn't know how to say it any way other than to be argumentative, so he replied, "Myra, stop telling me to relax, when I am, all right."

Myra opened her eyes, lifted her head, and then said, "Okay, clearly you feel like arguing with me tonight, so I will be back in the morning."

"Wait, Mimi, don't leave, I'm just frustrated that I can't be there for the kids. I want you to stay, I've missed you all day today …"

"Baby, I missed you, too. And you're going to get a lot of opportunities to be there for the kids, after the surgery, but for now just concentrate on getting mentally ready… Now, scoot over so I can join you."

"My pleasure. So how was the rest of your day?"

"It was okay. Somewhat hectic, but the lunch I had with Cissy made up for it."

"Good, I'm glad you had a chance to actually do something other than being in the hospital all day with me."

"The only thing that I had to deal with was Devon's attitude. He had the audacity to say to me that he did not make Trey and Princess, so why should he be responsible for them when I'm not around? I mean, he was actually allowing them to argue and fight with each other, Dee."

"Oh, really, well, I hope you set him straight, Mimi."

"Oh, you know I did, and after telling him to clear out his room, I had to call him out on the notice we received from the principal."

"I bet he had that stupid look he always gets when he's busted."

"He sure did. Do you know the dingbat had the nerve to try to hide the letter, thinking I didn't see it? I guess he was busy trying to be a sneak; he didn't realize I had already opened and read it."

"Wow, that was retarded."

"He's been acting up since you were hospitalized, Dee."

"Hey, you know what? Why not bring the kids tomorrow so I could have a talk with all three of them."

"That would be great, because they wanted to visit you again anyways, especially Princess."

All of a sudden, Dee screamed out in pain. Myra jumped up, frantically asking if he was okay. Dee slowly answered back that he'd been having a sharp pain in his head off and on all day. Myra immediately jumped into her "mother nurturer" role, as Cissy would call it, and asked Dee if he had eaten. Grabbing his head, he weakly tried to get out that he did eat, but not enough because he hated the hospital food. Myra knew this already, but she couldn't help but fight the prankster in her and say she forgot his food. Although Dee was in pain, he was able to speak without strain, asking if she was kidding. Myra didn't feel right teasing him, so she told him she'd be right back. She went to the cafeteria to prepare a dish. As Myra left, Dee excitedly anticipated Myra bringing the food.

While Myra was out, Dee put his head back to relieve his headache. He started praying for relief from the pain, at least for tonight. He just wanted a couple of hours of pain-free time with his wife. Unbelievably, as soon as Myra touched the door to come back in, Dee's headache went away. Myra walked over to him and kissed him on the forehead, then gave him his food. Dee grabbed the fork and began gulping down the food, confirming he hadn't eaten all day. In between spoonfuls, Dee managed to get out, "Thanks, baby, what would I do without you?"

"Uh, find another wife," Myra tried to play it off.

"No way, God has already given me a virtuous woman."

"Oh, yeah, I guess that would be me?" Myra jokingly remarked.

"Of course, it's you, Mimi."

Dee continued to eat fast, then Myra said, "Slow down, you're going to give yourself indigestion, Dee."

"I can't help it—this food is so good. Thanks, baby, for getting it for me." Dee leaned over to kiss her, but his mouth was greasy from the food, making Myra back away from his kiss. She wanted the kiss but hated getting her person dirty, so she said, "No problem. Just give me the kiss after you're finished eating."

Dee shrugged her blatant reaction off and continued his conversation. He went into the discussion he had earlier with the doctor and their decision to have the surgery early the following week. Myra was surprised at the time the doctor scheduled the surgery, so she asked, "Why so far away?"

"Well, because he wants to conduct the surgery with another specialty surgeon. And that surgeon can only fly in by early Monday or Tuesday morning." Dee wasn't fazed by the time span.

However, Myra felt the days were too far away. And even though it was about four days away, she wanted the surgery to be done sooner. Dee didn't give it a second thought. Instead, he moved forward with their discussion by requesting that they reach some sort of consensus as to his proposal of what he wanted done in case of his death. Dee then asked Myra if she'd given any thought to his propositions. Myra shook her head yes, but told him she hadn't reached a decision, when in fact, she had, but she did not have the courage to tell him just then. So she told Dee she'd let him know the next day after his visit with the kids. And surprisingly enough, he agreed. After Dee finished up his dinner, he wiped his mouth and hands while motioning Myra to come closer for a kiss.

As Myra got closer, Dee said, "I can't wait to go home so I can just hold you, rub you, and ..."

Myra put her hand over Dee's mouth and replied, "Less talking and more kissing, baby."

Dee said nothing more and continued kissing and caressing Myra, until she started to pull away from him.

Dee was so excited at this point he began to plead, saying, "No, no, no, please, Myra, don't stop. Why are you pulling away?"

Myra found it hard to stop, too, but she knew she didn't want them to start something they very well couldn't finish while he was laid up on a hospital bed. Dee tried to reassure her that none of the nurses would be coming in for the rest of the night. And in spite of how convincing Dee was, Myra wasn't persuaded. So Dee finally gave up and said, "Okay, so when you come tomorrow, why don't bring something nice to sleep in?"

"Dee! Are you sure we can do that?"

"Myra, I can do anything. Remember, I am a dying man. And a dying man deserves his last wish."

"Oh, God forbid, Dee … Are you sure you're up to it?" Myra knew this was his way of influencing her to do what he wanted. She even found it quite funny. And in the middle of her laughing hysterically, he said with a serious face, "Mimi, look at me and tell me if I'm up to it."

Myra took one look down and said, "Oh no, we have a very serious problem on our hands."

Dee huffed in an upset, and Myra immediately told him she was just playing. They locked eyes. Dee started kissing her, but this time he couldn't stop. It felt so good to him that he started grabbing her sensually. As he kissed Myra's neck, she whispered, "Ooh, baby, that feels so good. You know that's my weak spot."

Dee replied, "I know; that's why I love kissing you there."

"Okay, let's stop right here before we go too far, Dee."

"You're probably right, but the only problem is I can't stop right now, Myra."

"All right, as long as you know that the sooner you stop kissing my neck is the sooner I could go home, come back tomorrow, and you could have the real deal."

Dee said okay, but he didn't stop. So Myra took a deep breath and tried again, saying, "So, stop, Dee."

"I will …" he whispered while continuing to kiss her neck.

"Uh, now, Dee …" Myra somehow whispered, in between her sighs of pleasure. Myra then pushed Dee away, hoping he would stop.

Finally Dee gave up and said, "Okay, one last kiss because it is getting late."

"Okay, so I will see you tomorrow; get some rest tonight. You're going to need the energy for those kids of ours," Myra reminded Dee.

Dee put on his shy-boy voice—a voice he only used when he was in the mood—and asked Myra for a hug. Myra agreed but insisted that it just be a hug. They began to hug, and Dee told her to be careful going home. Then he squeezed tighter and reminded her to call when she got home. All the while Myra was saying she would, but Dee had yet to let her go. Finally Myra managed to gather enough air to mumble, "Um, Dee?"

Dee answered, "Yes."

"You're on my neck again, Dee."

Pretending to not notice, Dee said, "Oh, yeah, that is your neck, right?"

Myra looked at him in disbelief, then said, "Oh, yeah, right, like you didn't realize you were on my weak spot again, Dee."

"Oh, I noticed, I just ..." Dee leaned over and grabbed Myra into a hug again, cutting himself short.

Myra hugged him back. However, she fought her urges, saying, "Baby, please let me go."

"All right, all right, I'm done, but you smell so good. And you look so beautiful."

"Thank you, but I really have to go, Dee. So, good night."

"Good night, Mimi."

Myra grabbed her purse, looked back at Dee, and said, "And just so you know, I miss you too, baby."

Dee watched as Myra walked out. He couldn't shake the feeling he wouldn't be getting any more hugs. Every night for the past couple of days, he'd had this reoccurring dream of him dying on the operating table. Then he saw Myra screaming while Devon was holding her and saying, "It's okay, Mama, I got you, we'll be all right." At the end of the dream, he woke up with his heart racing and face sweating. He couldn't believe that this could be it for his life. With tears rolling down his face, he felt guilty for not taking better care of himself. At that moment, he made a promise to God that he would appreciate his life and health if he brought him through the surgery alive.

*   *   *   *   *

As soon as Myra got in the door, she heard the phone ringing. She dropped everything on the floor to run for the phone so it wouldn't wake up anyone. Myra knew that was Dee on the phone, making sure she reached home okay. She picked up the phone. "Hey, Dee, I'm home …"

"Hey, Myra, how's it going?"

"Travis! How did you get my home number?"

"After we met, some of the parents and I had a phone conference to organize the assignments for the school dances. Ms. Greene nominated me for the music and band performance. So I then let her know that you would be my partner since you were the only one I knew out of everybody."

Myra was now perturbed by his having her number, so she replied, "How convenient, but you still haven't told me how you got my number."

"Well, Ms. Greene, however reluctant, was kind enough to give me your number. Why, is there a problem, Myra?"

"No, I'm just surprised she would give my number without my knowledge. I'm going to have to speak to her about that. On the other hand, you could've just worked with Ms. Greene herself. I mean, she is single. This is the perfect way to get to know her better. Lord knows she wants to know you better …"

"Oh, please, she has a lot on her agenda. And besides, I have no trouble in the 'getting to know people' arena. Nor do I need help finding anyone, Myra."

"Excuse me, but I wasn't trying to help. I was more like trying to get rid of you, Travis," Myra replied sarcastically, but in a joking way.

"Ha-ha-ha, Myra, but that's not funny. Plus, she's not my type."

"Oh, please, Travis, like you have a type."

Travis was left dumbfounded, so he said, "What's that supposed to mean?"

"Um … from what I recall in high school, you chased after anything that had two legs, arms, and tatas to match."

"Myra, that was over twenty years ago. I have stepped up since then. Not to mention I was a young boy with a lot of game—what young boy wasn't playing the field?"

"Anyway, Travis, what do you want?" Myra blurted out.

She was looking forward to arguing with him. Travis, on the other hand, was not the arguing type. He was the exact opposite of Dee. He never used words to hurt people or fight fire with fire.

"I'm sorry if I'm upsetting you. Let's just change the subject. Anyways, can we meet again tomorrow for lunch to discuss some ideas for the music and band?"

"Unfortunately, I won't be able to meet tomorrow because I'm bringing my children to see their father."

"Okay, so how about Sunday?"

"No, not Sunday, either.… Listen, Travis, I'm pretty much already overwhelmed with my own situation. My husband is probably going to have the surgery on Monday, so I am not a good person to be a partner with right now."

"I understand if you need a few days. You can give me a call if you're ever ready."

"I will probably be caught up for a while. I will help in any way I can, but my husband is my first priority. Besides, I think this is something we can do over the phone."

"You have a point there, so listen, don't worry about meeting me. I'll call you when I have a list of DJ's and bands."

"Thanks, Travis, for your understanding."

"No problem, I'm here for you regardless. I am and always will be your friend. And I want you to remember that, Myra."

"Ditto … have a good night," Myra said peacefully.

"Good night," Travis replied softly.

Myra left the phone call smiling. She was thinking of Dee's way of trying to calm her down, which almost always led her to be more infuriated, as supposed to calming her down. Travis was different in that respect. He never would and still doesn't let their disagreements go too far. She always liked and appreciated that about him. After changing into her silky nightgown, she went upstairs to let Cissy know she was home. As she walked to the guest room, now Cissy's room, she passed Princess's room and saw Cissy sleeping beside her. Myra tiptoed to Cissy, gently shaking her while softly saying, "Hey, Cissy, I'm home."

Cissy awoke confused, but aware of the last thing she was doing, putting Princess to sleep, so she whispered back, "Sshh … I just got Princess to fall asleep again …"

"Why, what happened?"

"She woke up from her sleep yelling my name. She said she was scared, and she wanted you …"

"And how did you calm her down?"

"I just explained to her you were with Dee and would be home soon. Then she asked when her father was coming home."

"And?" Myra asked, anxiously waiting for response.

"And what, Myra?"

"And what did you say, Cissy?" Myra asked with concern.

"I told her soon and that she should pray to God for him. Then she asked me to pray with her, so I did …"

Myra sighed in relief and said, "Thanks, Sis, what would I do without you?"

"Well, thank God you don't have to do anything without me," Cissy said while motioning Myra to start heading out. As they walked downstairs, Myra asked if she missed any important phone calls. Cissy smirked, then answered, "Michelle called to say you bailed out on lunch and she was concerned." Myra didn't immediately respond. Instead, she grabbed her head in disbelief for forgetting lunch. Cissy watched Myra's reaction, suspiciously concluding it wasn't a typical lunch. After listening to Myra babble about some other nonsense, Cissy finally cut her off, demanding her full attention. "Why would Michelle be so concerned? Were you meeting her for lunch or session?"

Myra snapped at Cissy, basically telling her to mind her own business. To Cissy, this was a confirmation that Michelle and Myra were not just meeting as friends, but this time as doctor/patient. Cissy knew something was up, but she didn't want to push too hard, so she asked, "I know you guys were meeting, Myra, but what for?"

"It's nothing important, just leave it alone ..."

"Uh, Myra, I would like to know if you're sick or something you would tell me."

"Cissy, I'm not sick. I may need someone to talk to from time to time, but I'm not sick."

"So you'd rather talk to a friend, who happens to be a psychiatrist, than your own sister?"

"You could say that. I started talking to her about three months ago ..."

"What do you need a psychiatrist for when you have me?"

"Cissy, please, you're making it out to be more than what it is. Sometimes I don't want to burden you with my problems. Especially when you're overwhelmed with your own drama ..."

"Listen, Sis, there is nothing too heavy in my life that I can't make room for my big sister, okay? And even if I do have a lot going on, there's nothing that your baby sister and a glass of wine can't fix."

"Please, Cissy, don't be ignorant like Daddy ..."

At this point, Myra was annoyed at Cissy's sense of humor. She didn't understand why Cissy found talking to a psychiatrist so amusing, so she took a seat at the counter and began to explain her point. "I've been going through so much. Between Dee taking ill, Devon being rebellious, and now Dee wants me to take on his law firm. I think my life is a warpath between the devil and God. I hate my life. My husband, the kids keep adding to my frustration. I flip at everything. I can't seem to stay happy or be joyful. I'm depressed, lonely, and don't know what to do with my life outside of the kids and Dee. I am so consumed with emotion and fear that I'm beginning to lose my faith. I speak faith when it comes to Dee, but my heart holds a different kind of truth, and that alone drives me crazy. Here I am a Christian, but I act just the opposite. The only good that's coming out of this is that I'm professing what's in my heart."

"Well, you know, it's like the pastor says, 'Out of the abundance of the heart, the mouth speaks; listen to yourself.'"

Myra and Cissy said the last part together. Cissy then continued, "Myra, you're not doing a lot of things you normally do, like going to church, the women's prayer meetings, and you stopped praying with the kids because Dee's in the hospital. Girl, you know if you break up the spiritual foundation, you're bound to lose the faith …"

Myra looked down at her fingers and said, "You're right, Cissy."

"I mean, to this day the church has no clue how bad Dee's health is—you've secluded yourself from the church family …"

"But—" Myra said, trying to cut Cissy off. But instead, Cissy cut Myra off, saying, "No, let me finish. I know I am not the best person to speak on spirituality, but if this is the path you and Dee chose, don't you think you need to be consistent, now even more so in these circumstances? You know the power of prayer. You need to call the pastor and ask him to send a word of prayer out to the congregation."

Cissy grabbed the Bible off the phone shelf and placed it in front of Myra. She didn't say another word, but Myra knew exactly what Cissy was conveying just then. Cissy knew just what to say to Myra without making her feel wrong or foolish.

"Myra, I'm not saying that you're failing, but in order to sustain the full glory of God, you must honor him and know that he's always there, whether disaster, celebration, sickness, or health. It's like Pastor says, 'You see, congregation, the storm is temporary, but the Spirit and the word of God is forever. When you carry the two through the storm, your heart will automatically fill with power, wisdom, and faith even without knowing what's to come.'"

Both Myra and Cissy looked at each other and laughed at Cissy's imitation of the pastor. Then Myra stopped to say, "Yeah, when did you become so holy?"

"Uh-uh, no, you don't. I am not in any way, shape, or form 'holy.' I'm just in a relationship with 'Him'. And even though I have a foul mouth sometimes, I definitely talk to the man above. Shoot, we talk all the time, especially when I come out of character."

"I hear that," Myra replied.

"And just so you know, this advice didn't come from your friend the psychiatrist, but from your sister who loves you dearly no matter what we go through. So take advantage of the moment, because next time I might have to charge you."

"And you call me crazy, Cissy? You're the one who has a few screws loose."

"I'm not the one using her friend the 'psychiatrist' to talk to ..."

Myra immediately nudged Cissy in her side as she replied, "Girl, don't make me hurt you."

"I'm just playing, but in all seriousness, I have another bone to pick with you."

"What's up?"

"I've been observing you, and it seems like the only time you have a relationship with God is when you are with Dee. You know, in the Bible it says every man is responsible for themselves ..."

Myra interjected quickly, "Now that's where you are wrong, Cissy. My relationship with God is not dependent on Dee. I have my own way of relationship with him."

Cissy put up her hands in a stop motion, "All right, but if that's the case, your faith wouldn't be questionable."

"True. I receive that."

Myra didn't have a response for Cissy. She knew it was true what Cissy was saying. To change the subject, Myra ended the conversation with her plans to call the pastor in the morning. She saw Cissy yawn and began to do the same. She looked at Cissy saying, "So, now are you going home or spending the night because it's late, girl?"

"I wasn't planning on going home, but if you're kicking me out …"

"Oh, please, Cissy, I'm going to bed. Thanks again for all of your help."

"Oh, stop thanking me, that's what family is for. Just remember all of this when I have my kids."

"Uh-huh, but first you need to find a man."

"No, what I need is a prayer to find a man worthy of my eggs."

"Amen to that," Myra agreed.

"I'm not worried. It will happen when it happens," Cissy intuitively responded.

"I know … Good night, Sis."

"Good night, Myra."

Myra turned the light down in the kitchen and checked the front door before going to her room and getting into her bed; for the first time, in a long time. As she grabbed the picture of Dee and herself, embracing it to her heart, she looked up at the ceiling and began to pray. "Lord, keep me in your heart … Give me the courage to face this surgery and the outcome. I don't know what you've planned, but help me to receive it and follow it with full obedience, discipline, and faith. I know, God, that I haven't been a faithful Christian, but you know my heart and all that I want to accomplish in my life, so please …" The phone rang. Myra jumped, took a deep breath, then answered the phone. She couldn't believe someone was calling the house at one o'clock in the morning.

"Hello! Who is this calling my phone at this time?" Myra answered in aggravation.

"Hey, Mimi, I'm glad you're okay. You didn't call me, and I was worried."

"Oh, sorry, baby. As soon as I got in, Cissy and I started talking. I didn't mean to forget to call you."

"It's okay. I just wanted to make sure you were okay … I'm relieved to know that you are."

"I'm okay, baby, how are you doing?"

"Well, I had a headache until I heard your voice. I miss you already."

"Aww, Dee, I miss you too. I can't wait to see you tomorrow."

"Me, too, how are the kids doing?" Dee asked with sorrow.

Myra could hear from his voice that he was concerned and missing them. She wanted to make him feel at peace, so she assured him they were fine and they missed him too. Dee was happy to know the kids still cared, because he always told Myra they loved her more than him. Of course, Myra felt differently, especially since she spent most of the time with them. Being at home made her the bad cop, while Dee working long hours made him the good cop—because whenever he was home, it was fun, free, and playtime. Unlike the times they spent with Myra, which was during the week when they had activities, clubs, and studying to do. Dee stayed silent on the phone for a few seconds. This made Myra uncomfortable. She didn't know whether he had fallen asleep or come down with another headache, so she called his name. He didn't respond, so she said his name again. Only this time, she said it nervously. Then out of the blue, he said, "I love it when you call my name."

Myra huffed and replied, "Dee, you play too much, that's not funny."

"What, don't tell me you were scared, Mimi?"

"Dee, you know you're not fully cured yet. I don't know what to expect from this illness; you have headaches all the time now ..."

"I'm sorry, I won't do it again. You should get some rest."

"Yes, and you should, too, because you know I'm gonna put it on you, right?" Myra said as she laughed.

Dee laughed along with her, then said good night. Myra sent her kisses and said good night. After she hung up, Myra saw her cell phone vibrating. She smiled to herself because she thought it was Dee calling her again or sending one of his freaky text messages. As she squinted her eyes, she noticed it was Travis. She fumbled, wondering if she should pick it up or not. Finally she picked it up with a sleepy voice, yawning, "Hello."

"Hey, Myra, sorry to call so late, it's me, Travis. I was just calling to make sure you're okay because you were upset earlier."

Myra took a deep breath and said, "You know, Travis, I appreciate you calling to check on me, but please don't call so late next time. I don't get enough sleep as it is already. And I wasn't that upset."

"Why aren't you getting enough sleep?" he asked in concern.

"Well, half the night, I'm crying, and the other half I'm tossing and turning from feeling restless."

"Myra, I know you're going through a lot, but try to keep the faith."

Myra in her crankiest voice snapped back, "Why does everybody keep saying that? Just step into my shoes for a moment and see how much you can keep the faith."

"Hey, out of all people, I understand. I'm not a spiritual know-it-all by any means, but I remember in high school when my mother lost my father to cancer. She went through so many feelings and emotions. Most of it being in tears, but she always kept the faith no matter what happened …"

"Yes, Travis, but your mother was a devout Christian …"

In Travis's softest, calmest tone, he replied, "Myra, you should know it's not where you are as a Christian, it's who you are—if you believe that he can bring you through any storm in your life, then it will come to pass."

"I hear you …"

"But what, Myra?"

"See, that's how much you know. I wasn't about to say but, I was going to say I'll try …"

"You don't need to try, Myra. You just need to let go. Let go and let God. Let go of the hurt, let go of the fear, and most importantly, let go of the doubt."

"It's easier said than done, Travis …" Myra answered in weakness.

"Myra, I'm only telling you this because after my father's death, I felt responsible for causing it among other things. There wasn't any time for me to be young and free how I wanted; I had to help my mother get on her feet again. She had no skills, her experience was minimal, and she didn't know where to start as far as getting a job. Now I know the last thing you or husband want is your oldest boy to miss out on his young years, carrying the burden of the family. I didn't enjoy taking that responsibility and missing out on being young. When we were dating, I thought I was a man, but I realized later that I wasn't a man. My father was a man, and his death wasn't my issue. My issue came with the burden of my mother."

"Oh, wow, Travis, I never knew you carried so much weight on your shoulders. You never shared your feelings."

"I didn't have any feelings, I had to man up. You know, I never even grieved his death."

"Really, why?"

"There was enough grieving coming from my mother and sister. And their mourning made me more angry than sad. I spent two years in therapy to realize that my lack of emotions came from not mourning my father's death."

"I guess you're okay now, right?" Myra asked in hesitation because his answer weighed heavily on her decision to cut her therapy sessions short.

"I'm fine. But you, on the other hand, have to get your rest. So just give what I said some thought, and everything will come together in his way. Get some sleep, Myra."

"You do the same, Travis."

Myra hung up the phone, remembering how helpful Travis was to her in high school. Whenever she had an issue or problem, he knew what to say or do. He was truly a friend, and she was glad they came in contact again. She had the feeling she was going to need his friendship. Travis and Myra were like best friends, only there was an attraction. Myra lay back to get the sleep she needed for her visit with Dee the next day. As she closed her eyes, she thought about her wedding day. She smiled and began to doze off.

Quality Time

ℒ

"Today is the day the Lord has made, let us rejoice and be glad in it," Myra said while walking into Dee's room with the kids.

"Good morning, sunshine!" Dee said loudly with a handsome smile.

"How's my handsome hubby?" Myra leaned in to give him a hug.

"I'm fine now that you're here. Kisses?" Dee whispered as sexy as he could.

"Sure … I'd kiss you anytime, baby."

"Ugh! Gross," Trey blurted out.

"Trey, what is so gross about Mommy and Daddy kissing?" asked Devon.

"Everything," Trey replied.

"You're only twelve; of course, you wouldn't understand …"

"Well, I understand that you and Daddy like to kiss girls."

"Shut up, Trey!" yelled Devon.

"No, you shut up, Devon!" Trey shouted back.

"Could you both be quiet? And, Trey, just so you know, I am far from being a girl. I am a woman. Now whoever Devon kisses is a girl," Myra peacefully interjected.

"I heard that, Mom," interrupted Princess.

The boys both mean mugged each other, then looked at their father to see his reaction. Of course, Dee was nonchalant, but he maintained a serious look to make them aware to stop the nonsense. Trey, being the youngest and less bothered, waved his hand at Devon, then continued to talk to Dee.

"Hey, Dad, my team won another basketball game last Saturday."

"Wow that's great, Trey. I'm so proud of you. Princess?" Dee asked as he attempted to pick her up. Myra saw him struggle, so she helped in lifting Princess up to the bed. Princess, unaware of her father's body pains, plopped herself onto him heavily, causing him to gasp for air.

"I'm okay, but you don't look so good," Princess said as she referred to his being attached to IV needles and looking unshaven. Everyone began to laugh at her remark, but she looked in confusion as if to ask "What's so funny?" Then Dee looked over at Devon and asked how his head man in charge was. Myra didn't agree with his labeling and quickly commented, "Dee, please don't give him any ideas—he's already trying to behave like the man of the house."

"Mimi, he is the man of the house when I'm not around," Dee said as he stared at Devon.

Myra put her hands on her hips, then replied, "No, he will be the man when he gets a job, pays some bills, and buys all of the things we provide."

"Ma, when are you going to start realizing that I'm practically a man?" Devon asked jokingly.

Myra, maintaining her seriousness, shot back, "When you stop practicing and actually become a man, because a real man handles his business."

Devon couldn't believe his mom just called him out in front of his dad. The last thing Devon wanted to give his father was the impression he was not taking care of his business—with school, that is. Devon got upset, then took a seat as he replied in annoyance, "Oh, come on, I fail one class, and it's a big deal. Give me a break."

Myra rolled her neck back saying, "Excuse me … You see, Dee, he already thinks he's 'a man.' Look at the way he talks to me."

Dee didn't want the visit to turn into an argument or therapy session so he calmly addressed Myra's problem saying, "Devon, when I say you're the man of the house, I don't want you to think you can start disrespecting your mother. It doesn't mean you can be rude to your family and be irresponsible in school. I say you're the man of the house for you to protect your mother, brother, and sister. To be a strong and dignified position in the home that leaves your mother proud and not ashamed. You know better than to fail any class, much less one science class, with all of the resources you have. So, please, son, do your best always, no matter what."

Devon looked at Dee with tears in his eyes and said, "I know. And I have a chance to raise my grades. That's what I'm trying to do."

"Don't try, just do. Trying is the rationalization of not accomplishing goals in life. Like when someone says 'well, I tried to pass, but it was too hard.' When you do something without trying, it leaves no room for excuses, and the outcome shows. For example, when you play in a football game, you don't try to play, you just play. And your doing leads to touchdowns and tackling until you win. But when you try, that's when you start fumbling the ball, losing yards, and then you lose the game. And it's as simple as the Nike commercial, 'Just do it.' You give me your word."

"Yes, Dad, I give you my word," Devon replied as he smiled at his father.

"Now come here and give your father a pound. Thanks, Devon, I'm counting on you."

"No problem, Dad ..."

This was the kind of relationship Dee and Devon had; Dee did more talking than yelling unlike Myra. As it was quiet in the room for a few seconds, Dee thought he would break the silence and ask them why they were there. Princess automatically blurted out they were there for a visit, when Dee interrupted to say they were doing more than visiting. He went further, to explain that he wanted them to know about his illness and what the doctor had to do to heal him. After he let them know he had a brain aneurysm; they looked at him in confusion, wondering what he was talking about—until Princess finally asked, "Daddy, what's an aneurysm?"

"Well it's a little difficult to explain, but the simplest way for me to explain is basically there's an artery in my brain that ripped apart..."

"Huh?" she mumbled, sounding even more confused.

"Okay, so picture this artery being a rubber band. And if you pull on it real hard, what does it eventually do?'

"Rip apart!" shouted Trey.

"That's right trey,

"So who was pulling on your artery, Daddy?" Princess innocently asked and waited for his response.

Dee chuckled a little, and then replied, "Well it wasn't exactly pulled, but because it is a blood vessel that carries blood throughout the body; it's important that we take of our body so the artery won't be strained by not eating right or exercising. The good thing is the artery didn't totally break off; because if it did I could've died."

"Die! I don't want you to die, Daddy. Please don't die," Princess yelled as she began to cry.

"Well, that's why I'm having surgery, so I won't die, Princess."

Myra rushed in to comfort Princess by caressing her back, as she lied down beside Dee. She knew once the kids heard the news, it would be hard for them to accept. Dee continued to comfort Princess as he explained the procedure the doctor would be using. Once he was done explaining, Devon jumped right in and asked, "What kind of material is the doctor going to use?"

"I don't know, Devon."

"So, you're going to put something in your head and you have no clue what it is? ...Great," Devon snapped.

"No, Devon, I am doing what's best. I would like to go back to normal. And this surgery can get me there."

"Well how are they going to do it, anyway?" Devon looked on in anger.

"They have to make a small incision in my head to get to the artery, locate it then insert the material they're going to use."

Devon couldn't help but jump out of his seat and yell, "Oh, hell, no!"

"Boy!" Dee reacted in anger.

"I'm sorry, Dad," Devon pleaded. He knew whenever his father raised his voice, it meant business. Devon tried to further explain his outburst, "It just sounds like you signed up for death. I might have failed science, but I know enough to know that cutting the head open is not going to keep you alive. What are you trying to do, kill yourself, Dad?"

"Get over here! Now! Now you listen to me, I did not have to share any of this with you, but I wanted my family to know about my sickness and what we decided to do about it, so you wouldn't be left out in the cold. And the last thing I need is for you to mention death again in front of Trey and Princess."

"All right, Dad, get off my shirt, I'm sorry," Devon replied, looking his father square in the eyes.

"And I'm sorry I lost it on you, but you left me no choice. Your faith has to be stronger, that is what we taught you, Devon."

After snatching himself away, Devon continued to speak aggressively. "Listen, my faith went out the window a long time ago. And as far as you choosing to share this issue with me, you should have just left me out. At least then I wouldn't have to listen to this and keep my mind on myself. Man. I'm outta here."

"Devon!" Myra yelled as Devon headed for the door.

"No, Mimi, let him go. He's just scared right now."

All of a sudden, Princess started to cry again. Trey grabbed and attempted to pick her up. At the same time, he said, "Princess, don't cry, Daddy's going to be okay."

Then Princess looked up at him and replied, crying, "I know, I just don't want Devon to be upset."

"Okay, you two, don't worry about me or Devon. Today we're going to have fun, and that's all," Dee suggested. Myra jumped right in to agree, then recommended they go to the cafeteria to get ice cream and other snacks, then come back to the room to hang out. Princess slowly stopped crying when she heard ice cream. Dee caught Myra's attention to thank her for helping to alleviate the emotions coming out. Even though Dee was known for his aggressive, sarcastic, and slightly neurotic attitude, he had a heart of gold. He was very sensitive. Not just with his feelings, but with the feelings of others. And as Myra stared back at him, she noticed the tears in his eyes. Now where other people have to try and figure out why he was tearing up, Myra knew exactly what he was feeling. She knew he was upset for Devon, Trey, and Princess—especially Devon. Devon was the closest to becoming a man, and this was a crucial time in his life. And instead of Devon having to be concerned with the key elements of becoming a man, here he was facing the possibility of losing his father. Dee never wanted his kids to experience death, and now the odds were becoming a reality. So he put his head down to hide his face from Trey and Princess, but Myra noticed and told the kids to wait by the elevator.

As soon as the kids left, Myra grabbed Dee's head to let him cry it out. And when he was done, Myra grabbed her purse and went to the elevator, where she met Trey and Princess. As soon as Myra found good reception, she called Devon on his cell phone. She wanted to make sure he knew how important it was for him to spend some time with Dee before the surgery. She listened as the phone rang, then went to his noise-making message. Myra hung up, then tried it again. This time, Devon answered, "What's up?"

"Hello, Devon."

"Yes, Mom …"

"Where are you?"

"Right now I'm in the lobby contemplating if I should go home or stay."

"Well, you need to get your butt back up here to spend some time with your father. The surgery will be on Monday …"

"What do you mean on Monday? Why is he having it so soon?"

"Maybe we want him to get better sooner than later, Devon. What do you think?"

"Man, I can't believe you're letting him do this …"

"Excuse me … Your father is his own man. He's looking out for the best interests of the family, so in the long run we won't have to go through any more hospital visits and he can be home with us. Now you need to get upstairs and spend some quality time with him."

"All right, Mama."

"See you at the room, Devon," Myra ordered as she quickly hung up the phone.

She went to the cafeteria to get the ice cream for the kids and Dee. As she was getting the ice cream, Travis called, but she couldn't bring herself to pick up the phone so she ignored the call. She finished getting the ice cream and headed back to the room with Trey and Princess.

"Okay, here we go, Princess picked out this ice cream for you, Dee."

"Thank you, Princess."

"You're welcome, Daddy."

Once everyone started eating their ice cream, Dee began to ask them how school was.

"Okay, Trey, you first, how's school?"

"Fine, I have a lot of fun in art and music class. The teacher gives us a lot of fun things to do."

"Oh, yeah, like what?" Dee asked.

"In music class, we get to play the drums and piano and bring in our favorite music to share with the class. And in art class, we made a collage of everybody in the class, and it's in the lobby of the school …"

Then out of nowhere, Princess interrupted to say, "Guess what, Daddy? I know how to say the colors in Spanish, want to hear?"

"Yes, but you have to wait until Trey is finished. You just interrupted him, Princess."

And although Trey knew she was trying to steal the attention, he didn't mind, so he said, "It's okay, Dad, I'm finished."

"Okay, Dad, you have to say a color, and I'll say it in Spanish ... go ahead," Princess ordered as if she was Myra. Dee always said "Like mother, like daughter." Princess was going to be bossy like Myra.

"Red."

"Rojo."

"Blue."

"Azul."

"Yellow."

"Amar ... Amar ..."

"Amarillo, Princess," Myra interrupted.

"Amar what?"

"Repeat after me, Ama."

"Ama."

"Rillo, and roll the 'r,' okay?" Myra coached Princess to say.

"Rillo."

"Now say it together, Princess," said Dee.

"A-ma-rillo."

"Good job, baby," Dee applauded.

"Thanks, Dad."

"Hey, can I join you guys?" Suddenly Devon entered the room.

"Devon, you're back!" shouted Princess as she ran and jumped onto Devon.

"Of course, Princess ... wow, you're getting heavy."

"What bought you back here?" asked Dee.

Devon turned to head toward his father and said, "Dad, I'm sorry for being so rude. I just don't know what I'm gonna do if you're not here ... I mean I didn't even know the surgery is Monday."

"I understand, Son, and everything is going to be all right," replied Dee.

"So, what are we doing, anyway?"

Dee filled Devon in, then asked him how things were for him, both in and out of school. Devon took a seat on the chair by the bed and said, "School is fine. I mean, aside from the failing grade in science, I'm passing the rest of my classes, and I have a tutor now … that Mama so graciously set up for me."

"And that was a good idea, especially if you want to play in the last couple of games of the season."

"I know, Dad. It's just that it takes up a lot of my time …"

"Takes up your time with what, or should I say with who, Devon?" Myra interjected.

"I'm not able to hang out or spend time with my girl," Devon answered reluctantly.

"Now you see why it's important for you to do well in your classes. You see, had you worked hard first, then played, and not the other way around, you wouldn't be this limited with your time," Myra said to Devon as she rolled her eyes.

Devon paid no attention to Myra's attitude and complained, "But, Dad, it's not like I want to be a biologist or doctor. I mean, half the stuff we learn in school is useless."

Dee nodded his head in agreement, but explained to Devon that although he was great at football, it didn't mean he shouldn't learn other things as a backup. And before Dee could finish, Devon cut in to say, "In case of what, Dad? You told me if I already know my purpose, that there was no need to have a backup …"

Dee cut Devon off and said, "No, what I said specifically is if you know your calling, then that is what you set out to accomplish. But in any career you have, there has to be a backup …"

Confused by his father's response, Devon asked, "Then what was your backup, Dad?"

"Well, law was my backup. You forget I was a football player, too. I made it to college football until I had a serious injury, which severed my football career. Thank God, I did well in college and already had intentions of getting my law degree, because if I didn't then, I would have never made it. Your mom helped me through all of this, too. That's why I'm so grateful to have her in my life. And whoever you get involved with, if she really cares about you, she'll understand when you can't hang out with her all of the time. I mean, I reached my goal, and now it's your mother's turn. And hopefully you could do things differently, where both you and your other half could equally accomplish your dreams, passions, and goals …"

Myra was so touched by Dee's talk she couldn't help but cut in to say, "Wow, Dee, I never heard you say that before."

"Mimi, I always knew it. I just wanted to start the law firm first, so it can help finance your business. I should've just given you the opportunity to follow your dreams, and now it's too late …"

"No, it's not, Dee. Listen, you're going to make it, and I will start my business when the time is right.…"

"Mom, I didn't know you wanted to open your own business … doing what?" asked Devon.

"I want to open up a clothing boutique and design clothes for women first, then grow into men and children," Myra replied with a twinkle in her eye.

"And you do know how to dress, Mama," Trey said as he hugged his Myra's waist.

"And you don't dress old like some of the other parents in the neighborhood," said Devon.

Myra smiled with gratitude and pride as she thanked them for their compliments. Then she picked up Princess and asked her what she thought. Princess kissed Myra on the cheek and said, "Um, I think you are beautiful, and everybody will love coming to your bouti … bout …"

"Boutique, baby," Myra laughingly tried to teach her to say.

"Yeah, that's it, and maybe we can play dress up, too, Mommy?"

"Sure, and you can even help Mommy make the clothes."

Princess opened her eyes wide, saying, "Wow, Mommy, you mean you know how to make clothes, too?"

"Well, who do you think made all of your beautiful dresses?" Myra asked.

"I thought you bought them at the store …"

Myra teared up at the amazing notion of Princess not knowing where her dresses came from. She couldn't believe that she let go of her dream so much that the kids had no clue. Finally Myra gently grabbed Princess's chin and said, "Well, your grandma taught me how to sew, and soon enough it will be time for me to teach you, baby."

Suddenly the door opened again and in walked Cissy, saying softly, "Knock-knock."

Everybody looked at the door as Myra invited her to come in. Dee then joined in with sarcasm, saying, "Yeah, come on in and do something useful with yourself, like take these kids."

"Hello to you, too, Dee." Cissy paid no attention to his obnoxious attitude.

Princess, in protest, screamed, "But we don't want to go home now."

"You're not going home now, Princess. But you will be leaving in the next half an hour, okay, baby?"

"Okay, Mommy."

"Where are you coming from anyway, Cissy?" asked Myra.

"Oh, I had a couple of clients at the shop. I finished them off, then I took the rest of the afternoon off for my niece and nephews."

"Yeah, right, Aunt Cissy, you know you came to get us, so Mom and Dad can bump and grind."

"Devon Livonius Harris Jr., why you always have to open your mouth? Especially when not spoken to. You need to take a step back and stop being so damn grown before I knock you back into your infant years." Myra ranted as she got in his face.

Dee interrupted, "Hold up, Myra. You don't even have to go there, because I got this one. Boy, come here. You may be sixteen going on seventeen, but you are not too old for me to knock you out, understand me? You have a responsibility to be respectful to your elders. That includes your mother, aunt, grandmothers, and anyone else, for that matter."

"You have to give respect in order to get it, man,…." Devon remarked freely.

Up until this point, Devon could freely express himself around Dee, but this time it wasn't expression in Dee's eyes. He believed

Devon had crossed a significant boundary between adult and non-adult conversation, so he motioned for Devon to come closer, while saying, "Boy, who are you talking to?"

"Dee, don't …" Myra tried to intervene, but it was too late.

"Myra! I'm handling my son right now," Dee said in frustration.

"Dad, you're hurting him," said Princess as she tried to cut between them and pry Devon from Dee. But to no avail. Dee only grabbed tighter to Devon's shirt as he said forcefully, "Now listen to me, you will respect your elders because if you don't, I will beat you like a man. I may not rant and rave like your mother or aunt, but you better believe me, you don't want to test me. I don't use words. I use my hands. I want to know where you are getting this attitude from, because part of getting respect is learning when to shut up … Do you understand? Now, shut up!"

"All right, Dad, I'm sorry. I got you. I was just playin' in the first place," Devon replied with a lax attitude.

"Well, I'm *not* 'playin' … you hear me?" Dee shouted as he continued having a strong hold on Devon's shirt.

"Yeah," Devon answered in his nonchalant attitude.

"What did you say?" Dee drew Devon closer.

"Yes, yes, Dad."

"I want you to be on point, Son. I'm depending on you to show Trey and Princess how to carry themselves at all times, okay?"

"Yes, I heard you," Devon said with an annoyed attitude.

"Okay, kids, are you ready to go? I want to take you to eat and get some movies to watch at home," Cissy interjected to break the tension.

"Aunt Cissy, can we get McDonald's?" asked Princess.

"Princess, I actually want to take you to a restaurant and not Mickey D's."

"Okay," Princess easily agreed.

"Say good-bye, you guys, so we can go eat. I'm starving," Cissy pleaded.

"Bye, Mom; bye, Dad," both Trey and Princess shouted.

"Good-bye, Princess; good-bye, Trey," Dee and Myra shouted back.

"Good-bye, Dad … and I'm sorry for being disrespectful." Devon leaned in to give Dee a pound and hug.

Dee put his right hand on Devon's left shoulder while holding the other hand in his and said, "Devon, I accept your apology, but please, don't do it again."

"I won't, Dad, I promise."

"All right now, because I'll be checking up on you tomorrow, okay?"

"Yes."

As Devon walked toward the door to leave, Dee stopped him, saying, "And, Son, I'm still proud of you …"

Devon smiled as he replied, "Thanks, Dad … Good-bye, Mama."

"Good-bye, baby."

"Ma, stop with the whole baby thing, please," Devon begged.

Myra shrugged her shoulders saying, "What? You'll always be my baby."

"Bye, Sis; bye, Dee. I'll keep you in my prayers," Cissy said.

Dee looked at Cissy with love and said, "Thanks, Celeste."

"Oh, please, Dee, since when do you call me by my name?"

"I don't know, but it's all love. Anyway, I want to thank you for helping so much with the kids. I really appreciate it." Dee held his arms out, motioning for a hug.

Cissy hugged him, saying, "No problem, you're my family, that's what family does for each other."

Cissy came up from the hug, then Myra gently pulled her into a hug and thanked her again. After Cissy left the room, Dee pulled Myra closer, whispering, "Alone at last."

They started to kiss, but Myra, feeling uncomfortable, came up for air. Then she walked to the door to lock it. When she walked back to the bed, she took out her red silk nightgown and motioned she'd be right back. Dee, with a big smile on his face, rubbed his hands together and signaled for Myra to hurry up. "I'll be right back," Myra assured him. While Myra was in the bathroom, Dee beeped the nurses' station to bring in the candles and Myra's favorite mixture of Exotic/Casablanca lilies. Then he set them up around the room. While Myra was turning the knob to come out, the nurse helping him quickly left the room so she wouldn't see her. Myra finally walked out, and, with her eyes wide open, she said with a smile, "Aww, baby, they're beautiful. You're so sweet … Where did you get them?"

"I had one of the nurses 'hook me up,' as they say, but forget about that, baby, you look beautiful."

"Thank you.… You like?"

"I more than like it, I love it. Can I take it off now?"

"Dee, you're crazy …"

"No, I'm not crazy, I just miss my wife," Dee replied in excitement as he started to kiss her neck.

Myra enjoyed it, but couldn't get in the mood until she knew for sure the door was locked, so she gently pushed him away to check it. He showed her it was locked, then told her to come closer and give him some luscious, as he liked to call it. Then out of nowhere, Dee grabbed his head, belting out, "Ouch! Damn it, not now …"

Myra jumped in fear, then put her hand over his as she asked what was wrong and if he was okay. At first, Dee couldn't respond. So he leaned his back against the wall and whispered, "My head, it's pounding. I can't believe this is happening now …"

"It's okay, baby, let's just call the nurse."

Myra walked over to the phone. But before she could pick it up, he abruptly said, "No, Myra, I don't need a nurse. I need these headaches to stop."

Myra didn't bother to argue with him; she just put his arm around her neck, slowly walked him back to the bed, and told him to lie down and try to relax. Dee followed Myra's orders, but couldn't help but want to bring her down with him. And as he lay back, Myra somehow fell on top of his chest. Then Dee looked her in the eyes and said, "Sorry, baby."

"Dee, you don't have to apologize. You did nothing wrong. As a matter of fact, you did everything right. And I loved it."

Dee was in shock by her response and said, "But we didn't get to do anything."

Myra stroked his smooth, clean-shaven cheek and said, "That's right, and that was the best part, because today I realized you really know me and what I like. And that in so many ways turned me on even more, Dee."

Myra then lay down with Dee; and though Dee was in pain, he couldn't stop thinking he had disappointed Myra. Myra lay her head on his chest. She loved to hear his heartbeat. Although they weren't aware of each other's hurt at that moment, they silently cried together until they both fell asleep. Through the night, the candles burned and the flowers reflected in the light. And one hour into his sleep, Dee awoke to the scent of Myra's hair close to his nose. He realized his headache had gone away, but then his other body part was pulsating, so he began to caress Myra in her sleep. Myra squirmed, then opened her eyes. She looked up at Dee, and they kissed. They then spent the rest of the night making love, holding each other and talking until the sun came out.

"Good morning, sunshine," Dee whispered.

"Good morning, baby. How are you feeling?"

"Great, and you?" Dee asked in all happiness.

"Well, I feel a little tired, but I'm okay. Hmm, but last night was a night I would never forget. It was like we were home again. I haven't felt that good and safe in a long time."

"I know, Myra, and I promise you it will all come to an end soon. But for now, what's up for today anyway?"

"First, I'm going home to spend the day with the kids, get them ready for the week, and finish organizing the house. But I will be back bright and early in the morning."

"Mimi, I want to thank you for always being there regardless of the circumstances. You pulled through in so many ways that I've lost count, and for that I am grateful to God that He has blessed me with you in my life."

"Thanks, Dee, I feel the same way."

Dee looked at Myra's smile with enjoyment, then said, "Oh, please, I haven't done half as much for you in the years we've been together."

Myra rushed to Dee's defense, saying, "That's not true, Dee, you have provided a home and not just any home, but the kind of home that has a lot of love, support, and even peace. You have never let us go without, and you were the strength and security we needed, so much so we can't imagine our lives without you."

In amazement, Dee said, "Wow, even though I haven't been the most considerate, you continue to not only encourage me but compliment me. I never thought of myself like that, and I appreciate it."

"Well, maybe because I never shared that with you before, but I want you to know how I feel before tomorrow. I want you to always remember that I love you for who you are and not what you do."

"I love you, too, Mimi."

Myra and Dee embraced each other. Myra got up to wash up and change. Dee followed suit, and they took a nice shower together. It felt like old times when they would shower together all of the time. In the shower, Dee washed Myra's hair, and Myra returned the favor. After fifteen minutes of washing each other completely, they made love again, only to wash up and get out before the doctor came to speak to them. As soon as they finished getting dressed, there was a knock on the door. Myra walked back into the bathroom to finish getting ready while Dee answered and opened the door for the doctor. The doctor looked at Dee with a smirk and said, "Hello, good morning, am I interrupting anything?"

"No, Dr. D'Angelo, please come in; you know you're always welcome," said Dee.

"Looks like someone stayed over last night. I hope you let him sleep well," the doctor said.

Myra blushed, putting her head down. Dee, on the other hand, commented, "No, I didn't sleep, but who needs sleep when you have a beautiful wife like mine? Anyways, I know you didn't come to have bed talk, so do we know what time the surgery is tomorrow?"

The doctor started to take Dee's vitals, then replied, "Yes, as a matter of fact, I was coming to tell you the details of everything."

"Great, do tell, we're really anxious at this point," Dee said in excitement.

"Well, Mr. Harris, we will begin the surgery at exactly seven o'clock in the morning. The surgery will take about four or five hours, after which you will be transferred to ICU, and then Mrs. Harris will be able to come and see you. During the surgery, we will keep your wife posted on the progress of the surgery, and if all goes well, it will be the last time you need surgery. Are there any questions?"

"No. I just need something for these headaches I'm having. Otherwise, I think we understand everything, right, Myra?"

"Yes, I'm pretty much at peace with everything except for the headaches," Myra replied.

The doctor finished writing on Dee's chart while saying, "Uh-huh, all right, so I'll send the nurse in to give you something for the headaches; and once you have the surgery, the headaches will go away. Okay, great, so I'll be going now. Enjoy the rest of this beautiful day. And get plenty of rest."

"Thanks, Dr. D'Angelo. You do the same," Dee replied.

"No, thank you, for being a gracious patient. Well, see you later, Mr. Harris," the doctor said as he shook Dee's hand.

"Bye, Doc."

"Well, I'm going to get going, too. I will call you later, baby, so you can speak to the kids." Myra pecked him on the cheek and grabbed her purse and overnight bag.

"I'll see you in the morning?" Dee asked.

Myra ran her hand over Dee's cheek and said, "Yes, baby, I will be here an hour before the surgery. Dee, why are your eyes so glassy?"

"I don't know, but don't worry about it. Go on home, you have enough on your hands."

"Okay, so I'll call you later; get some rest. You'll need it for tomorrow. Love you."

"I will, baby. I love you, too, Mimi."

Myra walked out, then headed for the elevator. On the ride home, Myra began talking to God. "So, this is it, Lord, my husband is about to have surgery, and now he's in your hands. This is the part I don't enjoy, because I just want to have a sense of knowing. Knowing he'll be okay and what will happen—but, of course, you're in control. Just help me to be a source of strength for my kids ... Oh, boy, who is this calling me now?"

"Hello," Myra answered in annoyance.

"Hey, Myra."

"Uh, Travis, this is definitely becoming a habit."

"Don't worry, I just called to tell you that my prayers are with you and your husband."

"Okay ... thank you," Myra hesitatingly answered, wondering how he knew when the surgery was.

Then he quickly replied, "You said his surgery was tomorrow, right?"

"Yes, I did."

"Okay, because the way you sound, I thought for a minute I had my dates wrong."

"No, I'm just surprised that you called to send your well wishes for Dee."

"Why?"

"Travis, do you have a girlfriend to keep you company?"

"No one serious, but I'm seeing someone. Although I have to say, girlfriend or no, Myra, it has nothing to do with calling up a friend to wish them the best."

"No, I just find it strange that I would be on your mind so often when—"

"Let me interrupt you there. I have known you since we were in junior high. I cared about you then, and I care about you now, regardless of our commitments to other people. I told you I'll always be a friend to you. And any person that comes into my life has to accept it or move on."

"Okay, okay, I get your point, Travis. Thanks for calling. I really appreciate it."

"No problem, and please let me know how well it turns out."

"Now, how do you know it's going to turn out well?" Myra asked.

"Well, maybe because there's a higher being, which you believe in and have faith is going to make everything work out right?"

Myra, not enthused at having the spiritual talk with Travis, agreed, then switched the subject to talk about his plans for the day. Travis ran down his plans to take his daughter to a movie and lunch, then asked her if she wanted to join them. Myra let him know she has her own plans to go home and spend the day with her kids, but Travis quickly told Myra to bring them, too. Myra took the phone away from her ear and looked at it strangely. She couldn't understand why Travis would even think she would go to the movies with him, much less bring the kids along. After hearing Travis saying hello again for the second time, Myra said, "You know what, Travis? Have a good day. Thanks for calling. Bye."

Travis didn't know what he said wrong, but he didn't push it and just told her good-bye. Myra shook her head in disbelief. She couldn't imagine why he would even ask her to go out with him and his daughter. As she was driving, she thought about how different her life would have turned out if she had stayed with Travis. She couldn't fathom not having her children. Then she realized how grateful she was for marrying Dee. She pulled up the driveway, hoping to see the kids playing outside, but they weren't. As soon as she walked in the house, she yelled, "Hey, kids, I'm home."

She didn't get any response, so she yelled, "Hello, Devon, Cissy, Trey, where are you guys?"

"We're out here, Myra," Cissy yelled back.

"Oh, wow, what are you guys doing out here?"

"We're picking flowers from the garden, Mommy," Princess said.

"Oh, you are?... I hope your auntie is going to help me plant more flowers."

"Don't worry, I will. So, how was last night?" Cissy didn't waste any time trying to find out how her visit with Dee was.

Myra, however, was not in any rush to give details, especially in front of Princess, so she ignored the question by asking where the boys were. Cissy had sort of a clue that Myra didn't want to speak just then with heavy ears in the way. So she told her Devon was in his room and Trey was in the basement working on his science project. Myra, enjoying the beautiful sun, looked at the garage and said, "Okay, I guess I'll bring out the grill since it's nice out today."

"Yea! Can we have hot dogs, Mommy?"

"Yes, Princess." Myra pet Princess on the back.

"Okay, I'm out of here."

"Where are you going, Cissy?"

"I'm going home. I have to get ready for the hair show I told you about."

"Oh, yeah, I forgot about that; I hope I didn't make you late."

"It already started, but I didn't want to go early anyway."

"Have a good time," Myra screamed out while Cissy walked out of the yard and toward her car.

Cissy heard Myra and shouted back, "I will; we'll talk later."

"Bye, Aunt Cissy!"

"Bye, Princess!"

Myra turned to Princess and smiled while wiping the dirt off her face. Then she got up, put her hair in a ponytail, and said, "Okay, so let me get the grill and food, so we can start."

"Oh, hi, Mom," Trey said as he approached them.

"Hi, Trey, did you finish your project?"

"I did; all I have to do now is write out my cards explaining everything."

"Good. Can you get the hot dogs out of the fridge while I get the grill? Thank you."

"Princess, can you go get Devon, please?"

"Okay, Mommy. Devon! Mommy wants you!" Princess screamed.

Myra looked down at Princess and said, "I could've done that myself. I asked you to go get him, not yell."

"Here are the hot dogs, Mama." Trey handed the hot dogs to Myra as he pecked her on the cheek.

"Thanks, Trey."

"Hi, Mama, when did you get home?" Devon asked with his chest sticking out from his wife-beater T-shirt.

"About five minutes ago. What are you doing anyway?" Myra looked at him strange. She was trying to figure out when he got so buffed. Devon bent down to give her a kiss and said, "I'm studying for this biology test Tuesday."

"Wow, it's nice to see both of my boys hard at work. I figured we'd do some grilling."

"All right, you need help?" Devon offered with his deep voice.

Again Myra gave him a strange look because she couldn't remember when his voice changed from pip-squeak to Barry White. Myra turned her head toward him and said, "Yes. Please start the fire, and I'll do the rest, Devon."

"Mama, why you so afraid to start the fire?" asked Trey.

"I just don't like fires."

"Mama, I didn't know that," interrupted Princess.

"Well, now all of you know. Can you start the grill now, Devon?"

"That's what I'm doing, Ma," Devon said.

"Okay, great. Trey, you go get some drinks; and Princess, you get the plates and forks. And get the plastic ones."

"Okay, Mommy."

"Hey, Ma, the grill is started … you need anything else?"

"No, but if you're done studying, I was hoping we could all hang out here and talk."

"I have a little more studying to do, but it can wait." Devon plopped himself down on the lounge chairs.

"I'm glad I don't have to study. I'm only in the first grade; we don't have to study in my class."

"Your time will come soon, Princess," Myra told her.

"So, what time is Daddy's surgery tomorrow?" asked Devon.

"Seven o'clock tomorrow morning," Myra replied.

Devon looked at Myra in shock, as if to say, "Why so early?" Myra turned to him and explained that is the usual time for people to have surgery. Trey immediately asked to go with her to the hospital, but Myra shot him down, saying, "No, Trey, it's better if you go to school; I don't want you to miss out on any work. Plus, you will get to see him after school when he's out from surgery—which reminds me, Devon, can you pick up Trey and Princess tomorrow from school?"

"I was already planning on it," Devon answered.

"Thanks, baby."

"When can we call Daddy?"

"Later, Princess, your father is resting right now."

Devon walked over to the grill, opened it up, and announced the hot dogs were ready. Myra ran inside to make the sauce for the hot dogs, but Devon stopped her, saying, "Mama, we don't need the sauce, we could use the mustard and ketchup."

"You're sure? It only takes two minutes."

"Mommy we only want ketchup," said Trey.

"Are you sure, you guys?"

All three unanimously said yes. As soon as Myra started to take her seat, the phone rang. She sighed, grunted, then said, "Who's calling now? Devon, can you answer the phone, please? I don't feel like getting up again."

"Okay."

Devon ran inside to get the phone. He screamed from inside that the person hung up. Myra couldn't be bothered to think about who was calling and hanging up. She just rushed the kids to eat then finish their work. Then she told them when they were done, to come back downstairs to call their father and pray. The three left and went to their rooms as Myra went to lie down on the couch. Five minutes after lying down, she fell asleep. Upstairs the kids were in their rooms doing their work as Myra had asked. As Devon started getting into his studying, in walked Trey, who asked, "Devon, do you have any index cards?"

"Look, just because I don't have a door doesn't mean you can walk right in, Trey."

"So, what do you want me to do? It's not like I could knock," Trey mocked.

"No, but you have a mouth, so ask if you can come in. Look in my top drawer, on the right."

"Thanks … Ooh, what's this?"

"Just a condom; now get the cards and leave, Trey!"

"Does Mommy know you have that?"

"Trey, get out, before I throw you out!"

"Okay, okay." As Trey turned to walk out, Princess walked in.

"Princess, what do you want? Can't you guys see I'm studying? I need some peace and quiet."

"But I don't want to be alone in my room. Can I read in here?"

Devon couldn't refuse Princess, so he said, "Okay, but read to yourself."

"Okay."

"I'm out of here," Trey said as he grabbed the cards.

"Good, go," said Devon.

A couple of hours had passed, and Myra was still in a deep sleep. She was so much in a deep sleep she didn't hear her cell phone ring. Suddenly, Trey came running downstairs. He ran over to the couch and shook Myra anxiously, "Hey, Mom, wake up."

"What, Trey?"

"It's five o'clock, can we call Dad now?"

Myra jumped up, grabbing the phone, and blurted, "What! I wasn't supposed to sleep this long. Get your brother and sister while I dial the number."

"Devon, Princess!"

"Trey, I could've done that myself."

"Hello," Dee answered on the other end.

"Hey, Dee, how are you doing?"

"I'm okay, and you?"

"Well, I just woke up from a nap. A good nap at that."

"Good for you. You definitely deserve it."

"Hold on, Dee, Princess wants to say hi."

"Hi, Daddy."

"Hey, Princess, I miss you."

"I miss you, too, Daddy. I can't wait until you get home."

"It will happen soon, baby. Are you behaving?"

"Yes, Daddy."

"Good, because I want you to behave like the Princess you are. Can you put Trey on the phone?"

"Okay. Trey!"

"Princess, you don't have to yell. I'm right here … Hey, Dad."

"Hey, little man. Why do you sound so down?"

"I'm just tired. I've been working on my science project all day. Now I'm ready to just relax and go to bed."

"It's okay, it will be time for bed any time now. Just hang in there. When is the science fair?"

"On Thursday; I wish you could come," Trey sadly commented.

"I wish I could, too. Hopefully your mom could videotape it, so I can see my son win first prize."

"Okay, Dad, see you tomorrow."

"Hey, Trey?"

"Yes?"

"I'm proud of you. And I love you."

"Love you, too, Dad. Here's Devon."

"What's up, Dad?"

"Nothing, what's up with my main man?"

"Well, I just finished studying biology for my test on Tuesday. Now I'm getting my clothes ready for school tomorrow."

"Great, now that's the kind of stuff I like to hear, my son handling his business like a man. And I know you're going to pass that test because you have the Harris brain."

Devon laughed and said, "If Mom only heard you say that, she would flip."

"Well, it's not for her ears to hear, you get my drift?" Dee joined him in laughter.

"I gotcha, Dad, I love you. Hopefully we'll see you tomorrow."

"I love you, too. Best wishes on that test. I expect to hear you got an A. Please put your mother back on the phone."

Devon handed the phone to Myra, and she said hello. Dee then asked Myra to bring the Bible with her to the hospital tomorrow. She agreed, then put the phone on speaker so they could all pray together. As they grabbed hands, Myra told Dee they were ready.

Dee responded in a somber tone, asking Myra to begin the prayer. She motioned the kids to close their eyes, then bowed her head and closed her eyes.

"Lord, we come to you in total submission to your word, and we know that you have the power to do all things. We ask you, Lord, to be with Dee while he's in surgery; only you can give the strength and power to pull him through. And, Lord, we know that his life lies in your hands, so whether you take or spare his life, we ask that you keep us and guide us with your spirit; that we not lean on our own understanding, but on your word. It's through you that all things are possible. We believe and have faith that he will be okay tomorrow morning. We pray this prayer in Jesus' name. Amen."

And they all said "Amen."

"Well, you guys, get ready for bed now, except for Devon, of course," Myra ordered them.

"Oh, man, why does Devon get to stay up and we can't?" Trey whined.

"Look, I don't want to hear it, Trey," Dee interjected.

"Okay, Dad, good night," the three said simultaneously.

"Good night!" Dee replied.

"So, I'll see you tomorrow morning, baby. And get your rest. I love you, Dee," Myra sadly said.

"I love you, too, Mimi."

The Surgery

❧

"Today is the day ... Let me put Dee's Bible in my bag now, so I don't forget." Myra began the morning talking to herself. She walked into Devon's room calling his name to wake up. After a couple of nudges, Devon woke up, asking her what time it was. She told him it was five thirty, then gave him instruction to get Trey, Princess, and himself ready for school on time. She let him know she was leaving, then kissed him on the forehead. He mumbled okay and told her to tell their father they love him. She smiled, said okay, then left. When Myra got outside, she walked slowly to the car as though she was forgetting something.

She got in the car, started it, and put her head on the steering wheel. She began pleading to God for Dee to make it through the surgery. She thought to herself, "I can't believe this is happening today. I just hope everything turns out okay." Then she started the car and pulled out, knocking the trash cans as usual. While on the highway, drops of rain began to fall slowly on her windshield. A dark cloud formed in the sky, and a shower ensued. Myra quickly picked up the phone and called Cissy. Cissy picked up in a groggy and half-asleep voice, saying, "Myra, is everything okay?"

"Quick, what does rain mean on a day like today?"

"Huh, what are you talking, Myra?"

Myra's voice cracked, "You know, like they say when it rains on your wedding day, it's good luck, and sun on your funeral day is a sign you're going to heaven."

"Oh, girl, it doesn't mean anything, it's just rain," Cissy said with empathy, but fully awake all of a sudden.

"I don't know, Cissy. I woke up optimistic, and now I don't feel as confident."

"No, that's just the devil. Look, I'm going to get dressed now, and I'll meet you at the hospital."

"No, Cissy, the last thing you need to do is cancel on your clients. I'll be okay," Myra said, trying to sound hopeful.

Cissy wasn't convinced, so she replied, "But you're not okay now."

"Don't worry, Cissy. I'll call you after the surgery. Just pray for us."

"I always do, but you're sure you'll be okay, Myra?"

"Yes, Cissy. Like you said, it's the devil. I'll be okay. Thanks for the talk."

"Stay strong, Sis, I love you."

"Love you, too. Well, I'm already here, so I'll speak to you later."

"Okay, bye." Cissy hung up the phone, asking the Lord to be with her sister through the wait of the surgery.

Myra entered the hospital, went to the cafeteria to buy coffee, then proceeded to Dee's room. Before entering his room, she composed herself so she wouldn't seem dismal. She opened the door and, with the brightest smile she could put on, greeted Dee, "Good morning, baby. How you feeling?"

"Good morning, I'm a little nervous, but I'll be okay." Myra was satisfied to see she wasn't the only one with bad nerves, so she sighed and said, "I know ... me, too."

"Myra, if you don't mind, I'd like a few minutes alone before the surgery, so I can read my Bible."

Myra, relieved she didn't have to wait with Dee for the doctor, quickly said, "Okay, sure. I was planning on leaving in a few minutes anyway, so I could sign the rest of the papers for the surgery."

Before Myra walked out, Dee stopped her, saying, "Listen, Mimi, if I do pass, please let them use me to be a donor."

Myra held her head down to hide her tears and replied, "Well, as long as you agree to be buried, how can I say anything against it? I don't even want to have to make that decision."

Dee noticed her sad face, so he gently pushed her chin up and said, "Of course, I want to be buried. Where did you get the idea that I didn't?"

"Well, I still remember the conversation we had when we first got married. You said you'd want to be cremated if you died." Myra was crying at this point.

"Oh, please, Myra. I was young and ignorant when I said that. All I want is to be buried, with you next to me, when that time—God forbid—comes."

Myra kissed Dee on the lips, stopping him from talking, then said, "Well, enough of the death talk. Are you ready?"

"As ready as I'm going to be. Just promise me, Myra, whatever happens, you'll live life happy and strong, like I know you to be," Dee said, with tears rolling down his face.

With her voice cracking, Myra agreed, "I will, Dee, but only if you promise me you'll fight this with all the might God gave you."

Tears continued to roll down Dee's face as he looked at Myra's beautiful hazel eyes. He stroked her face and said, "I just want my family to be okay, please."

"We'll be fine, Dee. And stop talking like you're going to die."

Dee felt something, but he didn't know what it was. All he knew now was that he wanted Myra to promise him that she would do everything to make sure they're okay. Myra noticed his desperation for a response, so she said, "I promise you, Dee. Please, you're scaring me."

"Don't be scared," interrupted the doctor.

"Hey, Dr. D'Angelo, are you ready to work your magic fingers?" asked Dee, wiping the tears from his cheeks.

He gave a little chuckle, then said, "I sure am, but the question is, are you ready to be fully healed?"

"Oh, that would be music to my ears." Dee started to chuckle to himself.

"Okay, you have few minutes before we put you to sleep, so you can start saying your good-byes if you will. Mrs. Harris, the waiting room is fully stocked with coffee and muffins, so enjoy."

"Thank you."

Dee interrupted Myra, saying, "You know, I feel funny for some reason."

"What's up, baby? Are you feeling weak?"

Dee said with certainty, "No, actually I feel strong for some reason."

"That's a good thing," the doctor replied.

"Well, I guess I'll see you later, baby, I'm going to go sign those papers." Myra kissed Dee, then went to walk out.

"I'll see you later, Mimi. I love you."

"Love you, too, Dee."

Myra walked out, going straight to the nurses' station to sign the papers. When she was done, she went to the waiting room, grabbed a muffin, and sat down. At that moment, the door swung open, and another doctor entered.

"Mrs. Harris?"

"Yes," Myra said before looking up to see who was talking to her.

"I'm Dr. Thompson. I'll be assisting Dr. D'Angelo in the surgery. Once the surgery is done, I will come out to inform you of the status of the surgery."

Myra got up, shook his hand, but realized her hand was wet, so she apologized and thanked him. As he was shaking her hand, he noticed how nervous she was, so he said, "Mrs. Harris, trust me—your husband is in good hands."

"I know. I'm just a little nervous."

"Okay, well, I will be back in two hours; in the meantime, please enjoy the coffee and muffins, and if you like, you can put on the TV."

"Thank you, Dr. Thompson."

"You're very welcome."

Myra turned on the television, then shut it off again. She got up and started pacing the floor. She didn't know what to do with herself. She sat back down, leaned her head back on the wall, and closed her eyes. As she hummed Mary Mary's "Can't Give Up Now," she dozed off into a dream where she saw Dee standing across the room in a tuxedo. They stood, staring at each other, until Dee took the first step toward Myra and collapsed. Myra started screaming and running toward him, but the faster she ran, the further away he drifted. She finally reached him. She grabbed his head close and started crying, shouting. When she looked at his face to kiss him, she noticed blood coming out of one side of his mouth. She screamed out, "Dee, wake up. Wake up, Dee …" Just then a nurse came into the waiting room and gently nudged her while whispering her name. Startled by her presence, Myra looked around, confused. She realized her surroundings and replied, "Yes? What's the matter—is it my husband?"

"No, I just wanted to know if you're okay, Mrs. Harris. You seemed a little disturbed in your sleep, like you were having a bad dream."

"Oh, um, yes, I'm okay, thanks anyway."

"You're welcome. If there's anything you need, feel free to ask one of us at the nurses' station, okay?"

"Thank you." Myra smiled.

After waking, Myra realized she still had a few hours to wait before Dee made it through surgery, so she went outside to get some air. As Myra stood outside, she began to pray to herself, "Lord, only you can help me through this storm. I want to be able to make sound choices in light of everything that is occurring. I pray that my children receive your guidance in every way and that they look to you only for strength, power, and endurance. I pray for my husband through his surgery, that he comes through with a second chance at life. I truly believe, Lord, our work done your way will never ever lack your supply. And, Lord, I want to do it your way; please supply me with the knowledge and revelation to handle all, if any, issues that may arise as a result of the surgery. I am leaving it in your hands. I know that out of the heart, the mouth speaks, so I proclaim from my heart that you will provide for our family perseverance, resilience, and unity. This I pray in Jesus' name. Amen."

Myra then grabbed her phone to call Cissy, but saw a voice mail signal. As Myra checked her voice mail, she started thinking about Dee and the years they had shared with each other. She listened to a message left by Travis. Her first thought was, "Should I call him?" Then she thought if he was kind enough to see how she was doing, then she could definitely return the call. She hung up and called him. Waiting for Travis to answer, she got a funny feeling in her stomach.

"Hello," said a sleepy, yet sexy, deep voice.

Myra paused, and Travis said hello again, knowing it was Myra on the phone. "Myra, I know it's you," he said immediately after.

"Hey, Travis …"

"Are you okay?" Travis responded quickly, as if afraid to hear bad news.

"I'm okay, I just wanted to return your call," Myra replied hesitantly.

"I'm assuming they started the surgery already?"

"Yes, and so far it's been an hour. He has three or four more hours to go," Myra said anxiously.

"So you're at the hospital alone?" Travis asked, hoping Myra would say no. He hated the thought of her being by herself on this day.

Myra mumbled, "Uh-huh."

Travis asked Myra if she wanted company. Myra knew that's what she needed, but didn't want to impose. And in an unconvincing tone, Myra replied, "Oh, no, you have to go to work, I'm okay, Travis. I'm grown."

"I know you're grown, but you know grown folks need support, too. Plus, I'm my own boss; I don't have to go to work."

Travis was definitely not into being controlled by anyone or anything. And this was his way of making it known. Myra knew this about him.

In fact, that's what attracted her to him in high school. Myra pictured him in her mind and replied with a smile, "I know, but I think its better that I'm by myself. You know, it gives me time to think."

"Well, I think you should have company. I mean, if not me, at least your sister could have accompanied you today."

Sounding surer, Myra said, "Travis, I'm okay. I don't need a babysitter."

"No, but you need a friend."

Myra wanted to change the subject, so she asked him what was on his agenda for the day. Travis chuckled and said, "The usual undercover work, drug busts, and more."

At that moment, it became apparent how much Myra missed Dee. She missed him getting into his suit, kissing her on the forehead as he left for work at the crack of dawn. Myra paced back and forth, then said, "Hmmm, I can't wait to hear Dee tell me his plans for the day again."

"You will, Myra, just hang in there."

"Why now?" Myra asked in confusion.

In his level-headed attitude, Travis said, "Why not now? You ever asked yourself that question? Maybe this is an opportunity for you to find yourself and become independent."

"Please, Travis, I was going to do that anyway. It may have taken a long time for me to realize my passions again, but I'm aware of them now and it would be nice to live those dreams with Dee."

"That's the point. God does things on his time, not yours, Myra."

"Why do you always have an answer for everything?" Myra rolled her eyes.

"I don't. I just know that you're a woman of God, and it's time you act like one."

"Excuse me." Myra looked at the phone like it was Travis, as if to say "who do you think you're talking to?!"

Travis continued and said, "I'm being honest. You grew up with the word, yet you're acting as if you have no clue God has His own plan for your life."

Myra didn't appreciate Travis's bluntness, so she ranted, "You should talk, what about you? You grew up in the church, and now you don't even go."

"My issue is different, Myra. And although I departed from the church, I still believe in Him, just not the church."

"They're one and the same, Travis."

"I beg to differ. You don't need a church to have a relationship with Him."

Throwing in the towel, Myra said, "Okay, so we can agree to disagree."

"Isn't that always the case? Even when we dated, we didn't agree on things."

"True," Myra said with a chuckle.

"You see, I made you laugh."

"Yeah, you always knew how. Thank you, Travis."

"No problem, I just wish I could be there to lend a shoulder. What hospital is he having the surgery anyway?"

"He's in Johns Hopkins Medical, but you don't have to come, Travis. I feel better already. Anyway, I'm going back inside now. I'll call you back later with an update."

"Okay, just try to take it easy, Myra."

"I will, Travis, bye."

Myra stared in a daze for a minute, then went back inside. After getting off the phone, Travis felt uneasy with Myra being alone, but he got dressed for work anyway.

In the waiting room, Myra watched the news while reading the newspaper. After getting tired of hearing all the negativity in the news, Myra shut off the TV and decided to go to the cafeteria. She walked to the nurses' station to inform them of her whereabouts in case they needed her. As Myra entered the cafeteria, she noticed an elderly couple eating and talking. She stared at them and pictured herself and Dee doing the same thing in years to come. Myra smiled and walked over to the couple and explained how enthused and encouraged they made her feel. She went on to explain how good it was to see them smile together even in their golden years. It made her think there was still hope for her and Dee after all. The couple gave her some hopeful words and wished her the best. They spoke for a good half hour before Myra excused herself back to her table. As Myra walked away, the couple continued talking, laughing, and enjoying each other's company. Myra knew then that she and Dee shared a different chemistry, but it was never too late to have that kind of friendly marriage.

Just then, she glanced at the entrance of the cafeteria and saw Travis standing there, looking around for her. Shocked by his suit, Myra's face became flushed red, and her stomach began to flutter. She contemplated going up to him, but her legs felt too weak to move. Then he noticed her. Myra quickly pretended to read the newspaper as if she didn't see him. Clearing his throat, Travis looked down at her. Myra was so nervous, but agitated at the same time. She couldn't understand why she was acting like a teenager with a crush, when in her mind, it was the exact opposite.

Myra looked up to his clean-shaven, dimple-face smile and managed to utter, "What are you doing here, Travis? And all dressed up. I told you—you didn't have to come."

"I know, I wanted to come. How you holding up anyway?"

"I'm okay, just a little anxious, nervous, and everything else that goes along with having someone you love in surgery. So, what's with the 'Armani, *Men in Black*' suit?"

"I know it's not my typical jeans and T-shirt ensemble, but since I've been promoted, this is my uniform until there's some kind of bust. Then I can put on a dress."

They looked at each other and laughed. Travis pointed to her smile, leaned over, and whispered, "I always loved your smile. So, what are you having? Let me guess: coffee, light and sweet."

"Wow, you remembered, Travis." Myra was intrigued by his memory. The closeness also gave her a nudge in the rib.

Travis, though observant, wasn't trying to score points and said, "That's what you had the other night, remember?"

"Oh, right, at the diner."

"Are we having a senior moment?" Travis joked.

"Oh, you got jokes, Mr. Funny-man." Myra pushed his chest, feeling his very muscular pecks.

"Hey, at least I'm making you laugh."

"Yeah, you sure are."

At that moment, they paused and stared smiling at each other, as they walked onto the line to get coffee. Suddenly the cashier broke their gazes with an irritating, "Uh, hello, Do you want anything?"

Travis caught off guard, jumps to respond, "Uh, yes, one coffee, light and sweet. And a mint tea, and one teaspoon of brown sugar, thank you."

The cashier rolls her eyes and turns to get the order. Upon her return Travis smiles at her again and says, thank you in a soft tone, breaking the cashier's attitude and instead making her smile in return. This was his typical way of diffusing any tension or frustration.

After paying for both coffees, Myra and Travis found a table and started talking about everything from life to work, the old days, dating, and many other things. As time went on in the conversation, Myra wondered why she and Dee didn't have this kind of communication. Whether it was at home or when he was in the hospital, they spent their time talking about the kids, bills, what had to be done, and what wasn't being done. They barely made time for each other—unlike that elderly couple she saw earlier. Travis kept talking, but knew something was on Myra's mind. He asked her what was wrong, and she explained she wanted to have this kind of time with Dee when he came home. Travis told her exactly what she wanted to hear, to put a smile on her unsure face. But in his heart, he knew differently. Travis loved Myra unconditionally and only wanted to have happy thoughts at that moment.

Myra looked at him with tears in her eyes and thanked him for being such a great friend through all of it. She hoped they would continue their friendship, even after Dee's recovery. Travis reassured her he wasn't going anywhere and would always be there for her, no matter what. Suddenly Myra looked at the clock facing her and said, "Oh, my God, it's been two hours already. I need to get back."

"Okay so let's go," replied Travis.

They both stood up and walked toward the elevator to take it to the waiting room outside of the O.R. As they reached the floor, they heard a code being called over the loudspeakers. Then they saw the staff scurrying around to the O.R. in response to the code. Travis and Myra looked at each other nervously and proceeded to walk briskly to the nurses' desk.

Breathless, Myra asked, "Excuse me, nurse, is there something going wrong with my husband's surgery?"

"I'm sorry, I don't have that information yet, but if there is something going on, the doctor will inform me. I assure you, whatever it is, you'll be the first to know."

"Okay."

"When you do find out, can you please let us know?" interrupted Travis.

"Yes, I will let you know if there are any problems; meanwhile, have a seat and don't worry."

But as Travis and Myra started walking to the waiting room, they saw the doctor walking toward them. Myra turned her attention away, unable to bear seeing the doctor's sad disposition. She knew whatever news he was delivering, it clearly wasn't good news. She thought to herself, as long as Dee was still alive, they could overcome any complication.

"Mrs. Harris?"

"Yes," Myra replied, with a strange feeling in her gut.

"Um ..." the doctor hesitated.

"What!? Why are you hesitating?" Myra screamed out. She felt something was wrong, and by the look on Dr. D'Angelo's face, she knew ...

"I'm sorry, but ..."

Myra looked at the doctor with tears in her eyes. "No, no … whatever you're about to say, don't. You said he would be okay!" she shouted, as she leaned against the wall of the waiting room.

"I'm so sorry, but we lost him." The Doctor responded with the saddest expression.

"What do you mean, 'we lost him'? How could you? You said this would work!" Myra cried out to him. At that point, Myra felt so faint that her legs gave way. She began sliding down while putting her head in her face. The doctor stood in front of her asking if she was okay, but she didn't respond.

"Mrs. Harris … Mrs. Harris … can you hear me?" the doctor called out. Myra whimpers a response.

"The surgery was successful, but once we released the blood flow and began the suturing, he had a stroke and we were unable to revive h…

Suddenly Myra stood up, crying, "No, you're lying. My husband is still here. Where is he? I want to see him!"

Myra tried walking away, but her legs felt heavy. So there she stood begging the doctor to tell her where Dee was.

"Please, where is he? I just want to see him, please!"

The doctor knew it would impossible for her to see him at that moment. He then tries to express his sympathy, but to no avail. Myra told him in so many words that he had not one clue what she felt. Then asked him where Dee was again. Travis stood quietly in shock, having no clue what to do to help. He wanted to say something, but all of the old feelings of his father's death kept him from offering his sympathy. Myra grew impatient and demanding. When she notices her demands were not being met, she then turned to Travis pleading for his help. Travis baffled, saw his Mother's face as he looked at Myra. Screeching in pain, she held onto his shirt to get his attention. Travis snapped out of it and grabbed hold of her as she continued to weep. He gently rubs her head.

"Myra, listen to the doctor. Let him explain …"

"No, I can't wait here. I have to see Dee."

Myra grabbed the door. And after getting a nod from the doctor, Travis grabbed Myra.

"Travis, get off me." Myra pushed him away.

"Myra, I'll take you to see him after they move him ..."

"No, you don't understand, I have to see him. I have to talk to him. If he hears my voice, he'll wake up. Get off, Travis. *I said, get off!*"

Myra collapsed into his arms screaming and crying. Travis never saw Myra this upset, and it made him cry to see her in so much pain.

"It's okay. You'll see him, Myra," Travis said as he hugged her tight.

"*Oh, God!*" Myra belted out and continued to cry.

Dr. D'Angelo started to speak again, but Travis put his hand up, signaling for him to leave while he calmed her down. The doctor left.

"Come, Myra, have a seat."

"I can't do this, Travis, I can't ..."

"You don't have to do it alone."

"I want my husband."

"I know ..."

Just then Myra thought about Devon, Trey, and Princess, so she yelled out, "My kids, what am I going to tell the kids? They're expecting to see their father again. I can't tell them he died!"

"Maybe your sister can," Travis suggested.

"Oh, my God, Cissy, I have to call Cissy, where's my phone? *Where's my phone?*"

"You need to relax, Myra. You can call her in a few minutes. Let's go for a walk first."

Travis and Myra walked outside. After walking around the hospital grounds several times in a daze, Myra called Cissy while Travis called the office to cancel the rest of his meetings.

"Celestial Hair, Celeste speaking ... Hello."

In a cracking voice, Myra responded, "He-l-lo, Cis-sy."

"Myra, is that you, what's the matter?"

"He's gone ..."

"What! Girl, where are you? I knew I should've gone to the hospital with you."

"I'm at the hospital," Myra mumbled.

"I'll be right there ..."

"No! I ... I ... I need you to get the kids and bring them home, but ... but don't tell them anything ... I will tell them, okay?... Okay."

"Yeah, sure, whatever you need."

"Thank you, I ... I ... I'll be home in a little while, Cissy," Myra said.

Travis and Myra got off the phone at the same time. They looked at each other, but stood silent. There were no words to alleviate the pain Myra was feeling. All Travis knew was that he never saw Myra this upset, and it killed him to know there was nothing he could do to take away her hurt. He stretched out his arms, and Myra walked right into them. Myra held her head down as they walked back into the hospital. They got to the elevators, and Myra started walking away.

Travis grabbed her hand. She pulled away.

"I can't do this now."

"Myra, you have to," Travis ordered.

"No, I don't, I just want to go home."

"Listen, I know it's hard, Myra. I'm here with you."

Myra looked up, then back at Travis.

"Come on, you can do this, Myra."

"You don't understand ..."

"I do, Myra. My mother didn't get to do the same thing you're about to do right now, and she was sad for a long time; something about not seeing him for the last time shut her down completely. It was unhealthy for her, which made it bad for us, because we carried the brunt of her sorrow."

Myra thought about it for a few seconds and then mumbled, "Okay, I'll go, but stay close."

"I will," Travis assured Myra.

As they approached the nurses' station, Myra began to feel weak in the knees. She leaned on Travis to prevent falling. Travis let the nurse know that Myra just lost her husband.

The nurse looked at them cross-eyed and asked Travis who he was. Travis told the nurse he was Myra's brother. The nurse continued looking the same way and said, "She can see him, but you're not allowed to go with her into the room."

Travis then replied, "It is my understanding that any family members can see the body. And as long as I'm family, I will be going in the room with her, unless you would like me to call the administrators."

The nurse automatically changed her disposition and pointed them to the room. Myra was so out of it that she walked like a zombie down the hall. Travis went to open the door, but Myra pulled away.

"You can do this, Myra," Travis whispered.

Myra turned around and walked in the room. They walked over to the body. Myra put her hand on top of Dee's. She burst into tears, whispering, "I love you, baby." Then she lay her head on his chest as if she would hear his heartbeat. Myra then kissed his forehead. She began talking to Dee, "I know you tried, baby. But you have to wake up now. You hear me, baby? Wake up."

Travis put his hand on her shoulder, but Myra moved it away. Then Travis whispered, "He's not waking up, Myra."

"Yes, he is, Travis. He did the last time. I just have to keep talking to him." Myra wept profusely.

"Myra, he's not in a coma, he's dead."

Giving Travis a hard shove, Myra shouted, "*No, don't say that …* *Get out!*"

Travis just stared at Myra. Then he whispered her name, but Myra ignored him. As he continued to try to get Myra's attention, she kept talking to Dee. Suddenly out of nowhere, Myra screamed for Travis to get out, but Travis wouldn't move. Myra continued ranting, "*I said, get out!* He's going to wake up."

Finally Travis gave in and said, "Okay, Myra, I'll be waiting outside."

Travis walked out of the room and proceeded to the lobby to call Cissy at the shop from Myra's cell phone.

"Hello," Cissy answered on the first ring.

"Cissy, it's Travis, I'm here at the hospital with Myra, and she won't leave Dee's side."

"Are you serious? Wait a minute, how are you at the hospital?"

"Celeste, stop with the questions and get down here. Your sister needs you."

"I'm on my way, just stay with her until I get there, Travis."

"I am, just hurry up."

"Okay, bye."

"See ya."

Travis closed the phone, then headed back to the room. He waited for the elevator, but it took too long, so he took the stairs. When he got to the room, Myra was lying down beside Dee. The transporter in the room looked at Travis and said, "I've been trying to get her to leave, but she's determined to stay. Are you related?"

"Yes."

"Well, it's a good thing you came in when you did, because I was about to call security. I have to take the body for the autopsy."

"Thank you. Just give me a few minutes, please."

"You have five minutes. We do have to get the body to the morgue for an autopsy."

"You got it," Travis promised.

Travis walked over to Myra. He looked at her with tears in his eyes; just seeing her lying there reminded him of what his mother missed in not going to the hospital when his father died. Although he wished his mother had seen his father when he died, he believed his mom would have reacted the same way. Travis gave it another two minutes before he walked up to Myra, whispering, "Myra, we have to go now …"

Looking disoriented, Myra said, "Huh? Oh, no, I'm waiting for Dee to wake up. You can go, Travis."

Travis didn't know what to say other than that the transporters had to take Dee to check on him. But Myra wasn't having it and aggressively told Travis she didn't want anyone touching Dee. Then she pushed Travis away. Travis stepped back, watching Myra hold tight to Dee. He started pacing the floor, trying to figure out how he could get her to leave.

*   *   *   *   *

Cissy was doing eighty on the street to pick up the kids. She couldn't believe Dee was gone. All she could think about was Myra and the changes she must be going through. Cissy finally reached Trey and Princess's school. She was happy to see Devon followed her instruction to walk to their school, so she could get them home at the same time. The ride home was pretty quiet until Princess blurted out, "Hey, Aunt Cissy, why did you pick us up so early from school today? Is it because we're going to see Dad?"

"No, Princess, your mother asked me to pick you guys up."

"But I thought we were going to see Dad," interrupted Devon.

"I don't know, Devon. I'm just helping your mother, and right now she needs me at the hospital." As they approached the house, Devon noticed his aunt crying, but ignored it to avoid hearing any bad news. Although having her go to the hospital didn't necessarily show good news, he still had high hopes. For now, the kids took out their books to start on their homework.

"Here's twenty dollars, Devon; order some food if you get hungry." Then Cissy turned to the other two and told them to get started.

"Aunt Cissy?" Trey interrupted.

"Yes."

"Do you know if Dad's surgery went okay?"

"I'm not sure, Trey. Your mother knows more." Cissy hated lying to the kids, so she walked quickly toward the door to avoid being asked any more questions. Devon knew in his heart something was wrong, so he pushed the subject, "So you didn't speak to her at all about the surgery?"

"Devon, I don't know what you think you're doing, but now is not the time, okay?" Cissy gave him a hard stare.

Devon, not intimated by her looks, replied, "Yeah, right."

"Excuse me ..."

"Nothing, man, just go." Devon knew he was pushing her buttons, but didn't care at this point.

"Listen, Devon, I'm not your friend nor am I a man, so watch how you address me, okay?"

"Yes."

"Yes, who?" Cissy cut him off.

"Yes, Aunt Cissy," Devon replied as though he didn't want to be bothered.

Cissy ignored his attitude because of the unfortunate circumstances, but warned him that his mother had been through a lot for the day and that he shouldn't under any circumstances do anything to get on her nerves. Devon shook his head in agreement. However, Cissy knew it went in one ear and out the other. Cissy got in the car and sped off. She started feeling guilty for not being at the hospital. What bothered her even more was that Travis was there. That to her definitely didn't make any sense. However, that was a topic for another time. Cissy pulled up to the hospital garage, jumped out, and ran inside. When she got inside, she called Travis back to get the floor and room number. She took the stairs, ran to the room, and from the window observed Myra lying next to Dee. Cissy entered the room, and behind her entered the transporter with security.

Cissy gave them a crazy look and said, "Um, excuse me, why are you pushing up behind me like that? You don't know me. I don't play that."

"Ma'am, you need to step aside, so we can take the deceased," said one of the security officers.

"Listen, I just got here, let me talk to her and try to get her to leave."

The officers looked at each other, hesitating to give her a chance. And Cissy, being her sarcastic self, said, "I mean, it's not like he can go anywhere. The man's dead."

The security officer looked sternly at Cissy, then said abruptly, "You have two more minutes. The transporter has to get the body to the morgue for an autopsy."

Cissy didn't care how aggressive the officer was being; she replied, "To hell with the morgue, this is a woman who just lost her husband, and I'll be damned if you guys use force to get my sister out of here, so time me ..."

"Look, we're just following procedure, so please do not make it more difficult than it has to be," security pleaded.

Travis walked over to Cissy, pulled her away from the officers, and walked her over to Myra.

"Cissy, you're here to talk to Myra, not fight with the staff ..."

Cissy looked at Travis as if he was crazy for touching her and sarcastically responded, "Oh, really, Sherlock."

Travis nodded his head, convincing Cissy to do what she came to the hospital to do.

Cissy turned to Myra and whispered, "Myra?"

"Huh?... Hey, Cissy, what are you doing here? Where are the kids?"

"I came to check on you, sweetie," Cissy whispered.

"Cissy, I'm fine, I'm just waiting for Dee to wake up like before, remember?" Then she waved at Cissy to come closer and whispered, "The doctors think he's dead, but I know Dee is a fighter."

Cissy looked at Travis, then said, "I understand that, sweetie, but the only way we'll know for sure is if we allow the doctors to check him, okay?"

"They don't need to check because I know. I feel it in my heart."

When Cissy realized that wasn't going to work, she immediately mentioned the kids. If there was anything that would snap Myra out of this craziness, it was hearing about the kids. So she grabbed Myra's attention again, only this time she told Myra the kids were home waiting for her and what was she going to tell them when she went back home alone. She told Myra they had to go home. Myra grabbed Dee closer. The security officers stepped forward, but Travis signaled to them to wait. As they paused, Myra kissed Dee on the forehead, turned to Cissy, and said, "He's cold. He's cold."

She then got up from the bed and kissed Dee again on the cheek, while rubbing his head.

"Come on, Myra," Cissy said while putting her arms around her.

"Okay, but please be careful with him, please," Myra said to the transporter.

Travis interrupted and said, "I'll make sure they're careful, okay, Myra? Just go home, get some rest. I'll call to check on you later."

Myra put her hand on Travis's cheek and said, "Thank you for being such a great friend."

Travis took her hand, kissed it, and gave her a hug. Myra began bawling loud and hard. He rubbed her hair to comfort her.

"I can't believe he's gone. I can't …" Myra cried out.

Cissy began to rub Myra's back, then told her once again they had to go. Myra pulled away from Travis, looked at Cissy, and cried out, "Cissy, he's gone. I need him."

"I know, sweetie," replied Cissy, grabbing hold of her.

As soon as Myra got into Cissy's arms, Travis waved bye and signed that he'd call later.

Cissy nodded and continued to console Myra. The transporter began rolling the cart out, but Myra stopped him so she could take another look. She looked at Dee and said, "Cissy, he looks peaceful. He's not in pain anymore."

Cissy gently pulled Myra to leave. They both left, crying in each other's arms. As soon as they got into the car, Myra reclined her seat to relieve the pressure she was feeling in her head and back. Cissy handed Myra two aspirins and bottled water. Myra thanked her, then dozed off. On the drive home, Cissy started to get nervous about the kids' reactions when they find out their father had died. She couldn't fathom why things had turned out this way. In all the years they'd been married, she never once thought about one of them dying. And she knew Myra thought the same way. Cissy couldn't even imagine what Myra must be going through. She kept peeking over at Myra to check if she was okay. Meanwhile, Myra was deep in her sleep, dreaming of Dee. She had the same dream she had before, only they were at a white ball, looking at each other from across the room. And as she walked toward Dee, he moved further away. But this time, Dee didn't collapse. Instead, she couldn't reach him, and when she finally did, he wouldn't turn around.

A few minutes later, Myra jumped out of her sleep, looking around, confused about her bearings. Cissy looked, then asked Myra if she was okay. Myra shook her head yes, but internally felt alone and empty. The dream made it worse. As soon as Cissy was approaching the exit, she told Myra to gather herself up to greet the kids. Myra followed by putting her seat upright, then checking her face, eyes, and hair. She spent the rest of the drive looking out of her window, trying to compose herself. She thought of how to tell the kids, but came up empty. It was then she decided to totally to abandon the belief of God.

Release

M "ama!" Trey and Princess screamed out as they ran toward Myra.

"Hey, my babies ..."

Trey and Princess anxiously asked, "Mama, how's Daddy? When can we see him?"

"Okay, you guys, relax ..." Cissy tried to calm them down.

"No, it's okay, Cissy. They're just missing their father."

"Are you sure, Myra?"

"Yes, I got this ..."

Devon stepped back to take a good look at his mother's face and impulsively screamed out, "I knew it ... Why did you let him get that damn surgery anyway? I can't stand you ..."

Cissy immediately screamed back, "*Excuse me!* Your mother is not responsible for your father dying. Only God can give or take away life. Now you need to calm down before you get the other two upset."

"*He what!?!*" Devon looked in shock and grabbed his head. He walked over to the wall and punched it, making it crack. Devon thought his father had gone into another coma; he didn't think he had died. After Cissy realized the effects of her opening her mouth, she walked over to Devon and began to rub his back, but he shoved her hand off. Leaning on the wall, Devon started banging his head against it. Trey and Princess at this point were crying as Myra tried to comfort them. Cissy then put her arm around Devon. Only this time, he knocked her hand off, turned around, and yelled in her face, "*Man, to hell with God right now ... I want my father, you hear me?... I want my father ...*"

Devon fell to the floor, holding his head and crying. Cissy rushed over and wrapped her arms around him. Devon looked up into her eyes pleading, "*I want my Dad, Aunt Cissy ... I just want my Daddy, please ...*"

Cissy looked back with tears in her eyes and said, "I know. Devon, I know, baby ..."

"Baby, I'm sorry," Myra said while rubbing his head. But Devon pulled his head away, shouting, "*Don't touch me. This is because of you.*"

"Devon! Your mother has been through enough today ... Stop blaming her ..." Cissy said in sympathy.

"Man, this is bull."

"Uh-uh, don't you dare swear in front of us. I understand you're in pain, but you are not going to disrespect either of us, or I will knock your teeth out, boy," Cissy quickly interjected with a threatening look on her face.

"Man, I'm outta here ... I can't take this ..." Devon walked abruptly past both Cissy and Myra. Myra grabbed his hand, pleading for Devon not to go, but Devon pulled away as he told her, "Get off of me. I don't want to stay here and watch those fake tears come out of your eyes. You know you never cared if Dad lived or died."

"You know what?" Cissy interrupted with one hand on his shirt and the other hand in the air, in position to hit him. Myra turned to face Cissy, blocking her from landing a slap on Devon's face. She calmly convinced Cissy to let him go and that she couldn't handle his attitude right now. Cissy let him go and walked away. Myra pulled her hair back away from her wet and teary face. Then she looked at the mantle over the fireplace and saw the family picture from months ago; Myra collapsed to the floor and began to cry uncontrollably. Devon, not moved by his mother's emotions, then responded, "Yeah, you can't handle my attitude just like you couldn't handle Daddy's sickness either."

Myra continued to bawl as Devon walked out of the kitchen, then out of the house. Devon slammed the door shut, making everyone jump from the vibration. Trey walked up to Myra, asking, "Mommy, is it true? Daddy's really gone?"

Myra wiped her tears and nose and wept. "Yes, baby. I'm so sorry …"

Trey got down on the floor with Myra, looked her in the eyes, and said, "Mama, why are you sorry? God needed him … I don't blame you, Mama. God is in control of giving and taking away life, not you."

At that moment, it was unexplainable what Myra felt. All she knew was Trey had a special gift, a spirit she didn't want him to lose. So she gently grabbed his cheeks saying, "Promise me you will always keep that spirit."

"I promise, Mama," Trey replied as he started to cry.

Myra hugged him tight, then looked around the kitchen and noticed that Princess was not there. She didn't know what to think because Princess had never been the type to hide her feelings in any situation. Confused by her absence, Myra asked Cissy, "Where's Princess?" Cissy pointed upstairs, letting her know that Princess ran to her room after Devon slammed the door and walked out. Myra got up and headed to Princess's room. She hoped that Devon's behavior didn't make her too upset. His reaction was exactly what Myra knew would happen. She was hoping to not see it come to pass. She didn't want to deliver this kind of news to her children. As Myra headed toward the stairs, Cissy approached her and asked if she needed company. Myra kept walking and said, "No, I think I can handle this."

"All right, then, I'll make you some hot tea," responded Cissy.

Myra got upstairs and proceeded to knock on the door, saying, "Knock-knock."

"Mommy, I was just changing into the dress Daddy bought me before he went into the hospital … Are we leaving to go see him now?"

Myra plopped herself on the bed and said, "No, baby, I want to talk to you first."

Myra couldn't believe her ears. This was worse than she thought. *Princess is in denial of her father's death,* Myra thought to herself. Myra pulled Princess closer, putting her on the bed beside her. Princess then said, "Okay, Mommy, you have to hurry so we can go see Daddy."

"Well, that's what I wanted to talk to you about."

"What, Mommy?" Princess innocently replied.

"Daddy is not with us anymore. He died, but he's with God now, sweetie."

Princess put her head down and cried out, "Why did God have to take him away? I thought God wants his children to be happy. How can we be happy when he makes people die?"

"Well, I think God just didn't want Daddy to have any more pain. So instead of Daddy being here with us having pain, he took him to heaven where he wouldn't be in pain anymore. And now he's an angel."

"Yeah, but I thought the operation was supposed to do that," Princess angrily responded.

"Yes, Princess, but not all operations can help sick people," Myra replied, as she fought the urge to cry again.

"So why do the stupid operation anyway?" Princess started to take off her dress in anger.

"Well, Daddy wanted to try it to see if it would help him to live."

"I want my Daddy!" Princess yelled out as she ran into Myra's arms.

"I want Daddy, too, Princess." Myra couldn't hold the tears anymore, so she wept quietly.

With her mouth buried in Myra's side, Princess whispered, "Mommy?"

"Yes," Myra responded.

"Can I be alone right now?"

"Okay, but if you need me, I'll be downstairs."

Myra opened the door to walk out. In the hallway, anxiously waiting, was Cissy. She wanted to know how Princess was doing. Myra, looking a little relieved, said, "Princess is taking it pretty well. She was in denial at first, but now she just wants to be alone. I don't know, Cissy, I think she's going through mixed emotions right now. I think I'll just give her time to mourn on her own ..."

Cissy shook her head in agreement and handed Myra the tea. Myra thanked her as she walked downstairs to the kitchen. As Myra took a seat, she began to vent about not knowing where to begin. She posed the question to Cissy, but Cissy shrugged her shoulders, saying, "I don't know, but I know who would know."

"Who?" Myra asked.

"Mom!"

Myra told her she was right, but felt reluctant to call. She reminded Cissy they had not spoken in awhile and she felt funny calling her for help now. Cissy shook her head in disbelief, then grabbed the phone off the hook. Myra snatched the phone, telling Cissy she'd call later. Cissy didn't believe Myra, so she told her to call right now. Myra needed time to think of what to say to her mother, because she hated asking for her help. Especially since her mother put her through college and she had nothing to show for it. Every phone call to her mother ended with, "Since you're done having kids, why haven't you started your career yet?" Myra always left the conversation feeling as though she was disappointing her. Cissy knew this, but continued to badger her about calling. Myra finally came out and said, "Cissy, I need a day or two to think of how to ask her. It's not that simple."

Cissy hung up the phone and said, "Myra, it never is that simple with Mama, but it's Mama. And she'd do anything for her girls. You know that."

Myra leaned her head against her hand to think. And after a minute of pondering, she said, "You're right, I'll call her tomorrow. But for right now, can you do me a favor and try to get hold of Devon? I can't think of anything else until I know for sure he's safe."

"No problem, just give me all of his friends' and girlfriend's numbers. I know one thing, he better not snap at me, because I'm not you right now, I will smack him," Cissy replied, rolling her eyes in anger.

"Just don't be too hard on him, Cissy. He did just lose his father," Myra pleaded.

"Now I can't promise you that, it depends on his attitude. Where are the numbers anyway?"

"Over there in the nightstand; you can take them with you. I'm going to try to get some sleep." Myra stretched, then gave Cissy a hug good-bye.

"Okay, get some rest. And call Mama, Myra."

"I will, Cissy."

As soon as Cissy left, Myra went to her room to lie down. Trey and Princess came in a few minutes later to ask for a snack. After getting permission, they left to go to the kitchen. Then Myra got up to change into her silk pajamas and robe.

She plopped back down on the bed and looked around the room, stumbling across her wedding picture. She grabbed the frame and pressed it against her chest, crying. She thought, *This is so crazy. I married Dee in sickness and health, but I never thought those words would come to life.* Then she began talking to God: "Lord, where do I start now? I have no clue. Who would've thought the day I saw him awake again, it wasn't going to be forever. I should've known … Why, God, why bring him back to say good-bye? Humph, I still remember our wedding night: the mood was right, everything was in place, and best of all, there was nothing and no one to stop us from enjoying each other's company. Oh, God, why? I need to show my children that we can survive this. I know it won't be easy, but I just hope we can get past it. Show me how we get past it, please …"

Interrupting her thoughts, the phone rang. Myra leaned over, picked it up, and said, "Hello."

"Hey, baby …"

Myra looked up to the ceiling and whispered "thank you," then replied, "Mama, I'm forty years old …"

"And you're still my baby. You'll always be my baby. Don't you know that?"

"Humph, I see where I get it from. I say the same thing to your grandson …"

"Oh, how is Devon?"

"He's okay, I guess," Myra replied sadly, hoping her mother would ask what was wrong so she wouldn't have to come out and ask for anything.

"Baby, what's the matter? You don't sound too happy? Are the children okay? How's Dee?"

Closing her eyes to stop the tears, she whimpered, "He's gone, Mama …"

"What! When, baby?"

"He died this morning, Mama."

"And when were you going to call me, Myra? Or is the phone so heavy you can't pick it up to call?"

"Well, I didn't want to burden you with my problems, Mama. But Dee was getting worse and needed surgery right away. The doctors were able to do most of the work, and then …"

"Baby, I am coming out there first thing tomorrow morning. You can explain it to me then, because you sound too upset to talk right now."

"It's okay … I'm all right, Mama."

"No, you're not all right. Your husband just passed, and you have three kids to take care of all by yourself. Now I'm your mother, and I said I will be there tomorrow. In the meantime, get some rest and try not to get too worked up, baby."

"Mama, I don't know what I'm going to do. I don't even know where our insurance policies are or anything else for that matter …"

"Well, that's why I'm coming, baby. And where is your sister, isn't she there to help?"

"Mom, Cissy has been great, she was helping us with the kids every step of the way. I mean, no matter what I asked for, she came through …"

"Now that's what I like to hear, my girls looking out for each other. And where is Devon Jr.?"

"He left the house a couple of hours ago. He was in a rampage about his father's death being my fault …"

"Are you telling me that he blames you for Dee dying?"

"Yes, Mama."

Myra started to cry, but her mother told her to calm down, then asked if she knew where he was. Myra gathered her breath and said, "No, but Cissy went to look for him."

"And Cissy will find him. I just hope she doesn't jump on him."

"You know Cissy's crazy, Mama. I wouldn't put it past her. But in all honesty, Devon deserves every bit of craziness she gives him."

"Wow, he must be putting you through a lot."

"He hasn't been an angel for a while, and lately he thinks he's grown, acting like he can do whatever he wants …"

"Oh, really, so he's been asking for it, huh?"

"Don't get me wrong, he's not out all hours of the night, but he has an attitude that won't quit."

"He sounds like his father's child …"

"He sure is. I definitely never had an attitude like that when I was his age. But I must say, Dee came somewhat out of his attitude after the coma."

"Humph, I can't imagine that."

Myra heard the change of attitude in her mother's voice and said, "Oh, Mama, don't start …"

"I won't. Now get some rest, and I will see you in the morning. Bye, baby."

"Good night Mama."

Myra lay down on the bed, rubbing her hands on Dee's side of the bed. She started to feel a gut-wrenching pain in her stomach, instantly becoming paralyzed with sadness, not knowing what her future would hold. The thought of Dee's last request popped in her head. They hadn't solidified things. Myra already was feeling guilty about the attitude she gave Dee for even thinking of giving her such a challenging position at his law firm. What was she going to do was the question on her mind. However, the bigger question was, where did Devon go? She continued to lie down with her eyes closed, waiting to hear from Cissy.

*   *   *   *   *

In the meantime, Cissy was busy calling Devon's friends and driving around the neighborhood until she found out where he was. Cissy pulled up in front of a bar/pool hall, the place his girlfriend told her he goes whenever he's upset. Cissy got out of the car, slammed the door shut, and walked into the place. As she scanned the room, she noticed him in the back of the pool hall. At the same time, his best friend Kevin caught eyes with Cissy and alerted Devon. Devon looked toward the bar, then opened his eyes wide. As Cissy approached him, he continued to play as if her presence didn't scare him. At least, that was the impression he was trying to give. He called his next shot, then nonchalantly he greeted Cissy, "Aunt Cissy! What are you doing here?"

"No, the question is, what are you doing here, Devon?"

"I needed to get away, so I went to my boy's house, then we came here to chill."

"Oh, really?" Cissy realized he was trying to look cool, but she still grabbed him by the ear, wrenching it.

"Ouch, Aunt Cissy. It's not like I was drinking or something."

Cissy stepped up in his face, grinding her teeth, mumbling, "Boy, I don't care if you're sipping on a soda. You're only sixteen years old and have no business at a bar."

"It's a pool hall, not a bar, and besides, we're only playing pool and video games," Devon said with an attitude.

At this point, Cissy became overly filled with rage in her eyes and said, "Boy, did you hear me? I said you have no business in places like this unless you're twenty-one and a grown man. And since you're neither, you're leaving with me. Now you have a choice: you can walk out on your own, or I can walk you out."

Devon saw his aunt's fury, but still tried to test her, "Oh, really, how's that?"

"Oh, you think I'm playing? Okay," Cissy grabbed Devon's arms up behind his back, then pushed him into the wall. Devon's face hit the wall and his knees buckled, but he quickly jumped back up to save face. Suddenly he stuck out his chest and tried to walk briskly into Cissy's face; but out of nowhere, Cissy gave him a swift kick to the chest, knocking the wind out of him. Cissy then calmly walked over to Devon, grabbed his ear again, and tugged on it, making him stand up. Devon was in pain and scared at this point, so he pleaded for her to stop, but Cissy ignored his cry and said, "Well, it's either your ears or your balls, Devon. Which one do you prefer? Because I have no problem grabbing either. Now, let's go."

"Ouch! Okay, I'm walking. I'm walking. Aunt Cissy, please let me go, you're embarrassing me."

"Oh, like how you embarrassed your mother by lashing out at her, disrespecting her, then coming here like you're a grown man? Uh-huh, so I guess that makes us even. Now get in the car before I run you over with it."

Devon paused for a minute, giving Cissy a mean look. Cissy motioned to grab between his legs, so he jumped back quickly, saying, "All right, I am—I am …"

"And how often do you come here anyway?" Cissy asked.

"Just one time before this, Aunt Cissy …"

"Boy …" Cissy warned Devon to tell the truth.

After seeing the look on Cissy's face, Devon volunteered the truth and said, "Okay, okay, I've come here a few times. Aunt Cissy, how did you know I was here anyways?"

Cissy stared at him with a threatening look and said, "I have my resources. You just better make sure your behind doesn't come back until you're twenty-one. Now you wait here and call your mother. I'll be back."

"Where you goin', Aunt Cissy?"

"I'm going to have a word with the owner and get your 'boy' out of here too … I'm sure his parents are wondering where he is."

"No, Aunt Cissy, wait ..."

"What, Devon?"

"You can't go in there and grab up my boy like that, Aunt Cissy."

"Boy, don't tell me what I can and cannot do. I do what I damn well please."

"Please, Aunt Cissy, if you do that, it could ruin my rep in school."

"Oh, well, I tell you what, if he walks out quietly, your rep is good, but if he puts up a fight, then I can't promise you anything. What you need to do is call your mother like I said and let her know you're all right. Oh, and tell her that you're coming home with me tonight."

"But I have no clothes to change into for school tomorrow," Devon yelled out to Cissy, but she acted as if she didn't hear him. As she pulled open the door to the bar, she replied, "Well, I guess you should've thought about that before walking out on your mother. You see, you were better off having to deal with your mother, because she'll keep letting you slide until she gets tired, but with me—the only sliding you'll be doing is when I wipe the floor with you."

Devon put his head down in regret and said, "I'm sorry."

Cissy let go of the door, walked over to the car, and said, "I'm sure you're sorry—sorry you ever crossed me. Listen, Devon, I know you're upset about your father, but you're not the only one going through a loss. Trey and Princess loved your father, too. And your mother lost the love of her life, so instead of giving your mother grief, try helping her with both of your losses. Because, mark my words, 'The more misery you give your mother, the more misery I will give you.' And you know you don't want to deal with me. Am I making myself clear?"

"Yes," Devon responded in a low voice.

"Yes, who?" Cissy abruptly asked.

"Yes, Aunt Cissy."

*   *   *   *   *

At the house, Myra was dozing off. And as her eyes closed, the phone rang. She lay there wondering who was calling her from a private number. Finally she picked up on the third ring. In a sleepy tone, Myra said hello questioningly. It was Travis on the other end, checking to see if she was all right. Myra lifted herself from the bed, then changed her voice to sound more awake. Travis explained his concern for her. Myra stated she was fine now, but just missed Dee. Travis felt her pain, then explained she should pray, but Myra ignored him. She told him that praying was the farthest thing from her mind. Travis, in shock, said to Myra, "I know you're angry, but being angry at God is not the route you want to take."

Myra became furious and yelled, "God! Where was God when Dee was on the surgery table, Travis?"

Travis knew Myra was just angry, so he said, "God was there, Myra. And he'll always be there. Do you think maybe he just wanted to take Dee out of his misery?"

"Humph, that's exactly what I told my daughter. Then she gave me something to think about when she said, 'That was the point of the surgery, Mom.' So innocently, she only said what was truly in her heart."

"Myra, the only difference is she doesn't know God like you do. You clearly know God doesn't do anything for the sake of bringing his children pain. You want to know what helped my mother get through my father's death, Myra?"

"I give, what, Travis?"

"The Bible, Myra."

"Yeah, Travis, but your mother was a devout Christian."

"Yes, she was, but when my father died, my mother lost her way. I mean, even though she was a strong believer, her responsibility to take over fell to the wayside, until she consciously decided to read the Bible every day. She didn't believe in herself, and as a result, my sister and I had to take care of the finances and go to school—with no help from the church. I'm not complaining, but seeing my mother struggle with my father's death made me resent the church and everything having to do with belonging to the church. Imagine, here was the church my mother was married in, where I was baptized and saved, yet they couldn't bother to call or reach out to us."

"So, basically, you're carrying the same attitude I'm carrying toward God?" Myra asked.

"No, the difference is you're mad at God and I was mad at the church."

"Oh, wow, big difference. Like being mad at the temple of God is not the same as being mad at Him. Yeah, you keep telling yourself that, Travis."

Travis realized he was not going to get anywhere with Myra, so he explained that God wanted to see her over any hurdle or storm in her life. But midway through his explanation, another call came in, so Myra put him on hold to answer the call.

"Hello," Myra said with an alert voice.

"Hey, Mom, It's me, Devon. Aunt Cissy told me to call and let you know I'm okay. I'll be spending the night with her tonight."

"Devon, where are you?"

"I went out with Kilo, I mean, Kevin."

"All right, well, we'll talk about it tomorrow. I have to get to my other call."

"Who are you talking to, Mama?"

"A friend, Devon, I'll talk to you later."

"Bye, Mama."

"Bye."

Myra switched back to the other line, hesitating to continue the conversation with Travis. She knew the discussion was a little too tense for her at the moment, so she mumbled, "Hey, Travis."

"I'm still here," Travis replied.

"So, what were you saying?" Myra regretfully asked.

"Myra, I know you can do anything you put your mind to. And you can avoid having your children rush into survival mode at such a young age."

"Well, that will never happen. My kids could barely fend for themselves, let alone run the house. Plus your father died when you were in high school, Travis."

"True. Is your sister over there helping you?"

"No, she's with my oldest son."

"Well, you shouldn't be alone," Travis remarked.

"I'm not alone, I have the other two. And tomorrow morning, my mother will be here to help with the funeral arrangements."

"Oh, wow, how is your mother? I haven't seen her in a long time."

"She's great, looking good as usual."

"Great, I can't wait to see her," Travis anxiously said.

Myra took the phone away from her face to look at it. Then she got back on the phone and said, "And when were you planning on seeing her?"

"At the funeral, if I'm invited."

Myra sighed in relief because she wasn't sure what Travis meant by wanting to see her mom. Her first thought was that Travis had intentions of worming his way back in through her mother.

Once Myra realized Travis was talking about the funeral, she cut the conversation short by saying, "Thank you for the help in the hospital, and good night." Myra softly hung up the phone, lay back on the bed, and began staring at her wedding picture on the side dresser. She grabbed the picture and pressed it against her chest while breaking down into tears, screaming, "*Ohhhhhh God, why, why, why?... I don't want to be alone. I want my husband, and I want my life back. What am I supposed to do now? I have nothing without my husband. He was everything to me, and all I ever wanted was to ...*" Then at that moment, Myra heard a loud crash of glass hitting the floor. She quickly sat up and noticed the picture of Dee fell off the wall. He spoke with such certainty and command, telling her everything would be all right, being alone was temporary, and the only thing permanent in her life was He himself. He made it clear to her that her husband was not everything, but that *He—the Lord and savior—was everything* and that she had *nothing without Him … and not any man!* And to that, all she could do was cry; like a child being scolded by her father. As she cried, Princess entered the room asking, "Mom, are you okay? Please don't cry. I don't like to see you sad."

Myra gathered herself together and said, "I'm okay, Princess. I just miss your daddy. Go brush your teeth and get ready for bed."

"I did already. Can I sleep with you tonight, Mama?" Princess asked while jumping into Myra's bed, assuming she'd say yes. And like her assumption, Myra said yes, while moving over to give her some room. As Princess got under the sheets, Trey passed by. He paused, walked back, and asked to sleep with them.

Myra slightly smiled, then replied, "Sure, I can use all the company I can get right now."

Trey put his arm around his mother, asking, "Mama, were you crying?"

"Yes, Trey."

"Why? Everything's going to be okay … the Lord told me." Trey had often responded this way when Myra was upset, so she didn't give his comment a second thought when he said it this time.

She just continued to make room, while replying, "Oh, really, I bet He did. Now go to sleep you two, you need your rest. Good night."

The two kids said good night as they made themselves comfortable in the bed. Myra didn't get much sleep through the night. Every time she closed her eyes, she saw flashes of Dee. Some of them special days, like their first kiss, wedding day, and their first apartment. She would think about Dee's days in the hospital and the minutes before the surgery. Then suddenly Myra would jump up in shock because the dream was so surreal of him being alive. She spent half of the night staring at the ceiling, until finally she went to the living room and watched TV before falling asleep again. In the morning, she awoke to Cissy walking in with Devon by her side.

"Good morning, I brought your child home," Cissy said as she plopped down on the sofa.

"And?" responded Myra as if uninterested.

"And it's only temporary, I'm going to take him back to stay with me for a little bit."

Myra rushed to attention and replied, "I don't think so, Cissy."

"It's only until things are a little more settled, Myra. I mean, it makes no sense that you have to deal with Dee's death and at the same time Devon's 'I'm a man' attitude, when I can take him off your hands and you can get things together."

"Did Devon say he wanted to stay with you?" Myra asked as she turned her attention to Devon.

Relieved to hear his mother say no, he joined in, saying, "No, I didn't, Mama."

"Then what is this all about, Devon?" Myra continued to question Devon as if he put Cissy up to asking.

"I don't know; ask Auntie."

Once Myra saw that Devon had no part in this big idea for him to stay with Cissy, she turned to her and said, "Listen, Cissy, I know you are trying to help, but I think Devon needs to stay home with me."

Myra then walked away as Cissy tried to plead her case. In the kitchen, Myra grabbed a mug, poured herself and Cissy cups of coffee, and ignored her argument of Devon being better off with her. Cissy didn't know how else to grab Myra's attention, so she stepped in front of her, demanding her full attention as she explained, "Listen, Myra! I'm not trying to keep him. I just want you to have some peace of mind. I mean, the last thing you need is for Devon to decide to leave in the middle of the night, because he feels justified to use his father's death as an excuse to be mad."

Just then Myra heard from behind, "I think that's a good idea."

"MamaD!" shouted Trey and Princess.

"How are my little angels?"

"Fine," they answered simultaneously.

"Uh, Devon, are you waiting for a special invitation?" MamaD asked with a snide look on her face.

Devon kept his head down and said, "Sorry, hi, MamaD."

"Boy, pick your head up and greet me with your eyes."

Devon then stood up straight, looked his grandmother in the eyes, and said hello. Although he was happy to see her, there was sadness in his eyes.

"Hi, Mama," said Myra as she gave her mother a peck on her cheek.

"Hey, baby, how are you holding up?" MamaD held Myra's face to hers as she received her kiss.

"I feel better, but last night was hard. I kept dreaming of Dee all night."

"Mama, let me get those bags for you." Cissy grabbed her mother's bags.

"Oh, how is my little baby?" MamaD then remembered Cissy was in the room, too. Cissy rolled her eyes to the ceiling and said, "Mama, I'm not a little baby anymore."

MamaD knew that calling Cissy her baby was bothersome, but she didn't care. She continued with, "You know you will always be my little baby. By the way, did you ..."

"No, Mama, I haven't found a man yet," Cissy interjected quickly. Somehow she knew her mother was asking about her dating status. Every time her mother came, she had two major questions for her girls. To Myra, it was, "When are you going to open up your boutique?" And to Cissy, it was, "Did you find a man yet?" Cissy didn't think this time would be any different, so she rolled her eyes up with MamaD's back turned. She knew if her mother saw her crossing her eyes, that she would in a sense almost lose them, like the last time she was caught doing it. That was a day she would not forget; she remembered it like yesterday. She came home from college on one of her vacations, and MamaD asked her about school and began lecturing her on her study habits. All of a sudden, MamaD poked her in the eye and said, "You must want to lose your eyes, because the only thing they should be doing is blinking." And from that day until the present, Cissy made a conscious decision not to get caught rolling her eyes again. Interrupting Cissy's thoughts, MamaD replied, "Oh, so you're psychic now. I was just going to ask if you found another beautician to take the place of that crazy girl you had working at the shop. And besides, I lost hope on you finding a man. It's all in God's hands now."

Surprised by her mother's response, Cissy said with a smirk, "Yes, Mama, I did find a replacement. And you can start praising God now because I found a male friend, too."

"Oh, please, 'male friend' is just short for saying a 'booty call.'"

Everyone stopped and looked at MamaD as they yelled out her name.

"Mama! MamaD!" Myra, Cissy, and Devon screamed out at the same time.

"What? I know what you young people do these days; let's not fake the funk now."

"But you don't have to say it in front of the kids," responded Cissy.

"Why, they hear it every day. Am I right, Devon?"

Devon nodded his head yes in agreement with his grandma. MamaD continued to lecture Myra and Cissy, saying, "That's what's wrong with you new-age parents. You keep things like sex and every other thing that goes on in this world a hush, but at the same time, you don't keep them away from grown folk stuff on TV, radio, and everything else. You need to stop giving them mixed signals. And as far as Devon is concerned, he should stay with Cissy. I think it's a good idea, because you have a lot to take care of from now until the funeral."

Devon interrupted quickly to plead his case to his grandmother. "But, Grandma, if I stay home, I could watch Trey and Princess while you and Mama run around taking care of things."

"Boy, you need to stop. Since when do you want to help your mother?" interrupted Cissy.

Devon, looking upset by Cissy's interruption, said, "Aunt Cissy, are you serious? You forget I helped watch them when my father was in the hospital."

"No, but that was because you had to, not because you wanted to," Cissy came back with a smirk on her face.

"Well, I want to now," Devon answered while signaling Cissy behind MamaD's back to quit.

"Okay, so you can stay, but if you do one more thing to upset your mother, you will have to deal with me *and* Aunt Cissy this time. Do I make myself clear?" MamaD threatened.

Devon put a big smile on his face and promised to be on his best behavior. MamaD took his promise with a grain of salt. She knew Devon made the promise just so he could stay, but she had an even bigger surprise if he thought he couldn't keep his promise. The first job MamaD gave him was to take her bags upstairs so she could talk to Myra. Devon grabbed the bags, but before walking out asked if he can get his room door back. MamaD looks on in confusion, as Myra reponds, "Yes Devon, but don't let me have to take it down again." Devon shakes his head in agreement then carries the bags upstairs. Trey and Princess followed. Cissy saw Myra holding her head as she sat down, so she sat down beside her, rubbing her back to try to console her.

"Myra, are you okay?" Cissy asked.

Looking up, Myra said, "No. I'm … I mean, I don't want to start over. I want my husband back."

Myra looked at her mother with the look of "please make this all better, Mommy."

And MamaD comforted her by bringing Myra closer to her for a hug. Then she said, "I know, baby. It's hard at first, but one day eventually you'll be okay and see this all had to occur for the greater good. And you will move on ….."

Myra couldn't believe what her mother was saying, so she blurted out, "That's just it, I don't want that to happen. I don't want to be okay or move on. I mean, as sad as it sounds, Dee was my life."

"I understand that, baby, but he's gone and you still have life."

"No, Mama, you don't understand, he was my life." Myra shook her head in disbelief.

"No, Myra, he was a part of your life, just like the kids are a part of your life," MamaD corrected Myra.

"Mama, you don't understand. I don't know anything else but Dee and the kids."

"Humph, I see."

"What now, Mama?" Myra huffed, upset.

"Nothing, I just thought I taught you better," MamaD said in a disappointed tone.

"What do you mean by that?" Myra asked, aggravated.

"Well, I thought when you still have breath, you have a life, but apparently I'm mistaken."

"Please, Mama, not now." Myra was not up to the spiritual talk.

"So, let me get this straight, since my husband, your father, died, I should stop living life and become dead, too."

"Oh, come on, Mama, you know what I mean."

"No, Myra, I don't!"

Myra looked at her mother, shocked. It had been years since she heard her mother raise her voice sternly and aggressively. Myra covered her face with her hands as Cissy signaled their mother to take it easy on her. So Myra's mother took a seat on the other side of her, put her arm around her, and said, "Look, baby, in all of the years of raising you and your sister, I'd hope I taught you both what it is to be a Christian. Maybe I've failed or maybe you've forgotten, but in either case, I want you to hear this again. And this is something your grandmother said to me as a child when I didn't understand death or life. She said, 'Without fulfillment of the Lord, life or death will carry a meaning that can destroy your very existence.'"

"But, Mama, I feel like I don't exist now," Myra cried out.

"That's exactly my point, Myra. You need to reestablish your relationship with the Lord. If not, you will continue to feel incomplete and confused, like you do right now. Everybody has a life that consists of more than one person or thing, but God is the one that completes our lives; everything else falls to the wayside without him."

"Yes, Mama, but …" Myra mumbled as she held her head down.

MamaD then pushed Myra's chin up, so they could look eye to eye, because what she was about to say to Myra could only reach her heart by looking her in the eyes. MamaD wiped Myra's face and said, "No, Myra, there's no but, only free will. You can either choose to live or decide to die."

"Mama's right," Cissy interjected.

Myra wiped her face again, pulled her hair back, and said, "I understand what you're saying. It's just that …"

Myra paused to look at the family picture on the mantle above the fireplace. Cissy massaged her back and asked her, "It's just that what, Myra?"

In a daze, Myra whispered, "Huh?"

Myra looked at Cissy, confused, as if she had lost her train of thought. Cissy repeated herself, and then Myra remembered what she was about to say. She walked toward the picture, saying, "It's just that I … I miss my husband. I miss having him here. Him being in the hospital, I lost him for a time, but now I lost him forever."

"Oh, Myra, don't cry. We're here to help. And that's what we're going to do from this point on," Cissy told her.

"Am I right, Mama?… Mama?" Cissy gave her mother the eye.

"Yes, yes, of course, just as long as you understand I won't be a part of any pity party and will tell you when you've started one. Now I can't help you mourn or help you understand your loss without losing yourself in the process. God is the only one that can do that, but I can share what's helped me when your father died."

"Okay, so to start, Myra, you should get cleaned up. It will help you think clearly," said Cissy.

Myra got up from the couch and headed for her bathroom, when her mother asked her if she had called the funeral home. Myra shook her head no and said, "No, Mama, I wanted to wait until you got here."

"Okay, so I will make a list of all the things we need to get done while you're in the shower."

"Um, all right. Do you want some tea or coffee, Mama?" asked Myra.

"No, thank you, baby, go get yourself ready."

"Okay," Myra whispered.

As Myra walked off, Cissy and her mom sat back down to discuss how things were going while Dee was in the hospital. As they were talking, Devon walked in with his jacket on, heading for the door. MamaD got up from the couch and walked over to him, saying, "Uh, excuse me. Where are you going without asking permission?"

"MamaD, I was about to tell you I was going to my friend's house," Devon said in a pleading way.

"Oh, really, you couldn't possibly be about to tell me anything, because you're not old enough to tell me, you're still in the asking stage of your life. You got it?"

"Okay, Grandma, so can I go to my friend's house?"

"Well, then I'm confused, Devon, because having your jacket on and heading straight for the door means you already have permission. And since you're just thinking to ask now, then the answer is no!"

Cissy put her head down, chuckling because she was getting a flashback of how MamaD would get when Myra and she would think to overstep their bounds. It was all coming back to her. Devon, in a huff about MamaD's answer, blurted out, "What, why?"

MamaD took a step back to get a good look at him and said, "Because you should've asked first, boy. Next time you want to do anything, ask first. Besides, you know what they say when you assume."

Devon took a deep breath and ran upstairs to his room, wishing he could slam the door. Just then, Myra walked in the living room and asked what the two were laughing at.

Cissy responded, "Mama just shut Devon down about going to his friend's house."

Myra looked at her mother annoyed and said, "Mama, Devon is permitted to go out."

Paying no mind to Myra's aggravation, MamaD continued to laugh as she said, "Well, when he learns to ask first, then he can go."

"Mama, what are you talking about? He's seventeen years old. He's halfway out of the house."

"My point exactly, he's still under your roof. And until he is on his own, he must ask permission until he is out of the house."

"Oh, Mama, please ..."

Myra plopped down on the couch, aggravated at her mother's interference.

MamaD looked Myra up and down, then said, "You know, that's what's wrong with you parents today. You give these kids too much privileges without setting boundaries, then you wonder why the kids disrespect you."

"Mama, Devon has limits ..."

"Forget about limiting him, how about teaching him respect? How is he going to make it in the world if he doesn't acknowledge authority, Myra?" MamaD asked.

"Oh, he knows I'm in charge," Myra replied in assurance.

"Oh, and that's why he's been running amok, giving back talk, and acting like he's grown, huh?"

"Oh, so you feel like talking about me, Cissy?" Myra gave Cissy the evil eye.

"What! I didn't say anything," Cissy rushed to her own defense.

"So, what is she talking about, Cissy?"

"Uh, *she* is sitting right here, and you can ask me yourself, Ms. Myra Selena Lopes Harris."

Myra automatically changed her attitude because, like herself, when her mother used their full names, she meant business.

"Mama, I don't mean any disrespect. I just don't want you to concern yourself with the kids. They're a lot to handle."

"So, in other words, mind my business."

"No, Mama, I'm just saying ..."

Without giving Myra a chance to explain, MamaD started in and said, "Look, Myra, I raised your aunts, uncles, cousins, and you two. What makes you think I can't handle my grandchildren? Now as long as I'm here, they're going to learn to have respect, discipline, and obedience. Understand?"

"Yes, Mama," Myra replied while holding her head down.

"And I'm not saying you didn't teach them those things, but children will act like they have memory loss if you're not consistent with rules. And you are a great mother, Myra."

"Thank you, Mama."

They hugged each other, and Cissy looked on, feeling left out.

"Hey, I want some love, too," said Cissy.

They paused, looked at Cissy, then returned to their hugging. Cissy started to walk away when Myra said, "Hey—we're just playing, come get a hug."

All three hugged, then made their way to the kitchen. In the kitchen, they drank coffee as they discussed when and where to have the funeral. MamaD put Cissy on duty to call the funeral homes in the area. She asked Myra to either get one of Dee's best suits or buy a new one for the funeral. As Myra went to get the suit she had in mind, MamaD started calling the florist to order flowers for the wake and burial. Myra returned to the kitchen, with the Giorgio Armani black suit Dee wore to his "Honorable Black Men" awards ceremony. Her mother was still talking on the phone. Myra signaled to her mother to see if she liked it. And she responded with a smile on her face. Myra laid it across the couch and looked at his plaque on the mantle. She picked it up and began to read it. In walked MamaD, complimenting Myra on the suit. Myra smiled and continued to read the plaque. As MamaD put her hand on Myra's shoulder, Myra put her hand on top and began to sob. Reluctantly, MamaD asked, "Baby, when would you like to hold the wake and funeral?"

"I don't know. I guess I'll know for sure once Cissy gets back to us with some information on the funeral homes in the area."

"In the meantime, you can write the eulogy," said MamaD.

"Eulogy? I don't even know what to say, Mama," Myra responded with a helpless look on her face.

"Well, you could start with a short biography—what he meant to you, the family, and friends/coworkers. When you're done, I'll help with changes that have to be made. By the way, do you know where he kept the insurance papers, Myra?"

"Um, I'm not sure, but I can check his office."

"Baby, this is something you shouldn't be unsure about. They should be in a place where you can find them."

"I don't know, Mama. This is all too much for me! I have to go."

"Myra! Where are you going?

"I need a walk."

At that moment, Cissy walked in, wondering what happened in the short span of making phone calls. Just then, MamaD ordered Cissy to go with Myra on her walk, but Myra stopped short and refused the company. MamaD didn't like the idea of Myra being alone at this point. She was worried Myra wasn't in the right frame of mind, but there was nothing she could do about it. Myra made it clear that she was a grown woman who didn't need company for a walk.

"Devon!" MamaD yelled out.

"Coming, Grandma …" Devon was still angry. MamaD heard the difference in his tone, but couldn't care less.

"Devon, I want you to go to the supermarket and pick up a few things."

"Okay, but where's Mom?"

"Boy, am I sending your mama or am I sending you?"

"I just wanted to know where she went, Grandma."

"Well, she stepped out, so go do what I asked you to do before you stay in the house the whole week."

"Okay." At this point Devon was saying okay, but feeling like he wanted to say "shut up and just go back home." Cissy could see on Devon's face that he was very upset with MamaD's attitude, so she volunteered to go to the supermarket to prevent further tension. MamaD wasn't feeling Cissy's sudden volunteering act. Instead, she said, "I know, Cissy, but I want Devon to go. And, boy, why are you standing there? You need to get going. I would like to make dinner before the sun goes down and the moon rises."

"I'm out," Devon grunted to himself.

Devon walked away, thinking *Is she serious? It's ten o'clock in the morning. The sun doesn't go down 'til seven o'clock in the evening. Man, I know she's trippin'* …

"Mama, why did you send Devon to the supermarket instead of me?"

"I wanted to continue our talk about how things were around here," MamaD said sternly.

"The same as I said before, nothing different, Mama."

"So why does that boy act like he's man of the house?… And he has no respect."

"That's not true, Mama. He's just been going through a lot."

"Listen, he hasn't been going through any more than his mother, brother, or sister … That's not my point anyway."

Cissy was annoyed by her mother's criticizing, so she replied abruptly, "Well, what is your point, Mama?"

Mama D looked at Cissy as if she had lost her mind, then further explained, "My point is that I don't understand why he walks around here like he's king of this castle."

"Well, Mama, you know he's always been a little headstrong like his father, but his attitude started when Dee first went into the hospital," Cissy explained.

"Isn't that the truth? Dee always had a 'holier than thou' attitude, and so does Devon. I mean, don't get me wrong, Cissy. He was a good man and husband, but his attitude left much to be desired."

"I hear you, Mama."

*   *   *   *   *

Myra on her walk was wondering how she could make funeral arrangements when she and Dee never spoke about those kinds of plans.

She knew they both agreed to be buried, but that was all. And maybe that was all it should be. Just then, she came across a house she had admired for years. She closed her eyes, praying, "Lord, show me some direction, because I am lost and don't know what to do next. I love you, Lord, and as much as I hate to admit it, my mom is right—you are the center of our lives. Right now, what I need from you is a whole lot of strength and guidance through this ... Lord, I understand that life and death lie in your hands, so please help me to understand that you truly have a greater plan for me—just like my mother said ... I ask for these things in Jesus' name. Amen."

As soon as Myra finished the prayer, she opened her eyes and saw an eagle soar over the house she admired. Myra took a deep breath and whispered the verse Isaiah 40:31, which she was made to memorize and read, "But those who hope in the Lord will renew their strength. They will soar on wings like eagles."

She felt a surge come over and thought it was the Holy Spirit, until she realized her phone was vibrating. She answered in an aggravated tone, "Hello!"

"Hello, Myra, how are you doing?"

"Travis?" Myra asked because she couldn't hear anything but static. Yet somehow, she knew Travis's voice.

"Yes, I just wanted to check up on you and see if you needed anything."

"Thanks a lot, but what I need help with, you can't do anything about."

"Oh, yeah? Try me ..."

"Travis, I don't think you can help right now. If anything, you are making things more complicated."

"Oh, Mimi ..."

"What did you call me? Don't you ever call me that, Travis!"

"Myra, it's not like I didn't call you that in high school ..."

"I don't care, just never call me that again, you understand me?"

This time Travis became upset. He thought Myra had crossed the line of how she spoke back to him, so he assertively said, "Perhaps you think you're talking to your son, but in case you have forgotten, I am a man ..."

"And in case you have forgotten, I am not your woman anymore, bye."

Myra huffed to herself. She was infuriated at the fact that Travis would even think to call her the nickname Dee gave her for years. In the past, he always mocked Dee for coming up with it, because he believed his brain was not smart enough to come up with something better.

In reality, Travis was just jealous of Dee for being the man who turned Myra's eyes somewhere else other than himself.

The phone vibrated again, and she looked at the number this time before answering it. After seeing it was Travis, she didn't answer, but he continued to call until finally she picked up.

"Travis? What do you want? My mind is too preoccupied to entertain what you call a conversation."

"All I'm trying to do is help you by opening you up to talk; I know how hard this can be, Myra."

"Travis, how do you know hard it is? Did you lose your wife?"

"No, but did you forget my father died when we were in high school, and my mother practically went crazy?... Look, I'm not saying you're going crazy, but I remember the one thing that helped my mom was having a relationship with ..."

"I do not want to talk right now, Travis. Don't you understand that?"

"No, I don't, because you're shutting down, and you as a Christian know that's not right."

"Travis, you out of all people should be the last one to speak on Christianity. Stop being a hypocrite ..."

"Listen to me, Myra."

"No, you listen to me. I've heard enough about what your mother went through and what you and your sister went through. I get it, your mother found the Lord in the midst of her loss. But riddle me this, exactly when did her finding the Lord become your loss? You say I should read the Bible, stay in the faith, and reestablish my relationship with the Lord, but you who won't follow your own advice are not qualified to speak to me about any of this."

Travis quickly responded, "I receive that and will apply it at some point, but you must remember God never chooses those who are qualified but qualifies those He chooses. And I believe He chose me to speak to your heart and rebuke mine. So if you don't mind, please pray for me, and I'll pray for you, too. Bye."

Myra felt bad about acting so stubbornly with Travis. She also felt convicted about being childlike and immature in her walk. Travis made a point, and she received every bit of it. And although Travis strayed away from the word and the church, he still had spiritual wisdom and a relationship with God, but didn't realize it until now. Myra made sure to remember his last request and began praying for him right then and there.

*   *   *   *   *

At the house, MamaD was angry because Devon was taking so long to come back. Pacing the floor back and forth, looking out of the window every five minutes, and checking the clock for the time, she asked Cissy why he was taking so long. Cissy explained that this was a regular with Devon and that she shouldn't overconcern herself with his lateness. MamaD did a double take, then asked how Myra handled it. Cissy pointed out that she was the one that dealt with him because Myra had been so overwhelmed with Dee. She vouched for the fact that Myra became so enraged by Devon's overzealous behavior with his "becoming a Man", that she removed the door to his room along with all the other luxuries he had in it. Suddenly they hear keys unlocking the door.

"That must be 'Mr. Man' right now." MamaD remarked sarcastically

Sure enough Devon struts in slowly with the groceries. MamaD calmly walked over, then out of nowhere smacks him in the back of the head. Devon turned around quickly, noticing Cissy signaling him to stay quiet. Devon rolls his head back and forth in shock, trying to hold in his anger. MamaD started chastising him then pops him again. At that point, Devon lost his patience and snaps back, "Yo, what was that for?"

"When I ask you to do something for me, I do not expect you to lollygag."

"Lolly what?"

"Next time you come right back, you hear me boy."

"I did!" Devon balled up fists tight to refrain from losing it even more.

"Oh don't hand me that Devon. I know you were out there gallivanting the streets."

"Yo, for real… you buggin' grandma…"

Cissy then walked away. She did not want to witness the beat down Devon was about to receive. And soon as Cissy stepped into the living room, she surely heard a loud thump. MamaD had grabbed Devon by his jacket and with one swing shoved him against the wall in the kitchen. "Now you listen to me little boy. When you are speaking to any adult, leave the slang in the streets… Your mom sends you to school to learn English, not Ebonics. And the attitude, you check at the door because you are not a man, you are child. A man does what's asked of him, while a child does what they want to do. A man leads, while a child follows his friends. A man carries out his responsibilities, while a child avoids it all cost. And most importantly a man knows when to shut up, while a child rambles in ignorance, like you just did."

MamaD lets him go, the continued to lecture him.

"You need to learn – You can't be wrong and strong at the same time. You need to be humble when you fumble. Once you learn this, your mistakes won't become part of your character and repeat it self. You understand?"

"Okay, I'm sorry, MamaD." Devon held his head down in shame.

"Now I hope I made myself clear, because next time I might have to go old school and ask you to pull a switch. You hear me?"

"Yes MamaD …but what's a switch?"

"You'll see the next time you decide to do what you feel like doing," MamaD replied.

"Devon, go unpack your groceries," Cissy cut in.

"Are you serious? Why do I have to put them away? I already went to the store like MamaD asked."

MamaD then sat and listened to see how Cissy would respond to his deviance. Consequently, Cissy told Devon that if he didn't put the groceries away, he would definitely be going home with her; of course after he pulls a switch. She reminded him that he is to do what is asked of him. However Devon felt differently. He still didn't understand why he had to answer to all of the authority now being shoved in his face.

"You know what, Fine!" Devon then snatched the groceries off the table.

Cissy gave him the look as though she wanted to snatch him, but knew that putting her hands on him would only add fuel to the fire already blazing. So she chose to give him the benefit of a doubt. He did just lose his father. Plus she realized that hitting him was not having an affect on him anymore.

MamaD, on the other hand, didn't agree since hitting was the method she used on Myra and Cissy when they were younger. And it worked. In Cissy's mind, that was the difference between girls and boys. She tried to explain that boys at sum point would attempt to fight back. Yet, MamaD agreed to disagree. She believed that if a child was instilled with respect and good home training from the time they could speak, when they become young men/women they would already know to be quick listen and slow to speak: just as the bible teaches. At that point, Cissy couldn't argue with that. So she opted to discuss what Myra's mistake was with Devon. Just then Myra walked in the door. She looked at Cissy as if looks could kill. Of course, if that were the case, Cissy would be dead. Especially after talking like some sort of expert in raising kids. MamaD hurriedly interrupted so that an argument wouldn't erupt and explained she was the one putting her two cents in and not Cissy. And after saying her piece while she greeted Myra, it didn't stop Myra from cutting her eyes at Cissy and saying, "Thank you, Mama, for being here to help, but I think I know how to deal with my kids just fine, and Cissy, you need to stop sounding like you know so much about raising kids."

Cissy, on the other hand, wasn't fazed by Myra's attitude and retorted, "Well, I should, I practically helped raise yours."

"Girl, just because you spent a few months watching over your niece and nephews, it doesn't make you an expert on kids," Myra came back with, knowing it would strike a chord in Cissy since she didn't have any kids. And although it was a low blow, Cissy was still not moved and sarcastically said, "And just because you push them out does not make you 'mother of the year,' Myra." At this point, Cissy was in Myra's face, challenging her to a word for word. This was something they did from the time they were young, because they weren't allowed to fistfight ever. As it stood, Myra wasn't up for the challenge of words, or anything else for that matter.

Instead, she gave Cissy a once-over and walked away, saying, "Cissy! I am not up to your ignorance, so if you feel the need to be up in my face, then you need to leave."

"Fine! You don't have to tell me twice. I know when I'm not wanted." Cissy grabbed her purse and started to head for the door.

Just then, Myra figured she was up for the challenge and said, "I'm glad you could finally get that. I was wondering when you would realize I don't need you to raise my son."

It was clear Myra struck a big chord in Cissy's heart because she rushed in Myra's face as if she was ready to fight and said, "Your son, my nephew … it's all the same when it comes to blood. It's just sad when your stubborn behind can't see that!"

MamaD stepped in the middle of them to avoid it turning into a fight.

"Now wait a minute now … the last thing you two need to do right now is argue with each other, especially when it's about this manipulating, ungrateful son of yours, Myra … so both of you stop the attitude and make up."

"Mama, please, we are not little girls anymore. Ouch! Mama, you don't have to pinch me," Cissy replied while grabbing her easily bruised arm.

"Well, then, you know what to do, Cissy," MamaD said with an evil eye.

"I'm sorry, Myra. You are going through a hard enough time."

"I'm sorry, too, Cissy. I didn't mean to insult your non-having-children behind."

"Hey, I'm doing fine all by myself," Cissy said in response.

"You got that right. Anyways, what's for dinner, Mama?" Myra added.

MamaD loved to cook and feed people. And that would explain why she spent years catering events and running the family restaurant until the death of Myra and Cissy's father. As MamaD walked into the kitchen, she ran down the menu. "Well, we got barbecue chicken, macaroni and cheese, string beans, biscuits, and peach cobbler for dessert."

"Wow! Mama, you didn't have to go through all of that," Myra said as she walked up to MamaD to peck her on the cheek in appreciation for her help.

MamaD gently grabbed Myra's face to make eye contact as she said. "Well, I wanted to, and besides, when was the last time the kids had a home-cooked meal? Especially since Cissy was the one watching them while you were at the hospital."

Cissy folded her arms, pouting, then blurted out, "Hey, I resent that. I know how to cook. I just don't have the time."

MamaD looked at Cissy in an "oh, please" kind of way, then said, "You can resent it all you want, but we both know your primary dish comes in a microwavable box. Hence explaining the reason why you don't have a man."

"Mama!"

"What!… You know it's true, Cissy. If you put as much time into finding and taking care of a man as your shop, then maybe you would have a man longer than your microwave dinners cook."

That was a big exaggeration on MamaD's part, but it would have to be in order for it to take effect on Cissy.

"Devon, Trey, Princess, get down here for dinner," yelled Myra.

As the ladies prepared the dinner table in the dining room (the area they used only during the holidays), MamaD told Myra after dinner they'd write out the eulogy and program for the funeral. Myra hesitantly agreed as the kids came running down the stairs cheering.

"It sure smells good, MamaD," Trey said as he pulled out his seat and sat down.

"Thank you, Trey. But aren't you forgetting something?" MamaD replied as she looked sternly around the room.

Trey looked around the room, then jumped up from his seat to join hands with everybody to bless the food. He was used to praying before eating, but they typically sat down when they prayed. The only time they'd stand and pray was during Thanksgiving, Christmas, and Resurrection Sunday (known more as Easter). Just then Princess shouted out, "Grandma, are you going to move in with us?"

"No, Princess, why do you ask?"

"Because I miss you, Grandma, when you're not here, and you cook so good, it would be nice to eat like this every night."

"Well, baby, I won't be living with you, but I can definitely stay for a little while to help out your mother."

"Okay, but you should really think about moving in, Grandma."

"I'll think about it, Princess. Now let's pray. Devon, lead us in prayer."

Devon looked at her crazy, but dared not refuse, so he started, "As we bow our heads, God, bless this food we are about to eat for the nourishment of our bodies, for we know not everyone gets to have the same. And bless the hands that made it. In Jesus' name, we pray. Amen."

Everyone said Amen, then rushed to sit down and eat their food. Just then MamaD began to ask the kids about school. The boys simultaneously said school was fine as they explained who was on the basketball and football teams. Princess quickly intervened for attention and screamed out she was taking dance lessons. MamaD smiled at their enthusiasm to share the activities they participated in, but quickly diverted the conversation to wanting to hear about their grades. Trey interjected to brag about the straight A's he has been maintaining. Then Devon said in hesitation that he was doing okay, because he knew his average wasn't something to brag about to MamaD. MamaD was interested in hearing his overall average thus far, so she encouraged him to share. As Devon began to share that he had a B-turned-C average, Myra started in on why his grades had dropped. She rolled her eyes at him and said, "Yeah, because you make hanging out with your girlfriends and 'boys' more important than …"

"No, that's not true, Ma," Devon interrupted.

"So, what is it, Devon?" MamaD asked.

"I don't know. I don't want to talk about it."

"Well, it's on the table now, so you might as well share."

"Why, Grandma?"

"Because we're not raising you to be idle, but instead, productive."

"Um, Grandma, just so you know, I am productive. I'm captain of the football team, class vice president, and volunteering at the senior citizen home."

"Great, you have a full schedule, now how about maintaining your B average and work on an A average? After all, what you think about football is not all it's cracked up to be, especially if you, God forbid, get an injury and don't make it to the leagues," responded MamaD.

Devon was surprised and upset with MamaD's pessimism, so he mumbled, "Oh, really, whatever."

"Excuse me," Myra said, stopping Devon dead in his tracks before he continued to get fresh.

Devon put his head down, mumbling, "Nothing."

MamaD interrupted to explain to Devon that all they want is for him to become a productive man of God. And Myra added, "Like your father was."

Devon at this point couldn't take it anymore and said, "Mama, I keep telling you I am not like him and I'm not trying to be like him ..."

"Well, what's wrong with being like your father, Devon?" Myra asked.

"I'm not weak like he was," Devon screamed out.

Myra then became irate and shouted, "What! Who do you think you are to call your father weak?"

Devon balled up his fist, shouting at the top of his lungs, "*Mama, face it already. He couldn't fight for us ... he couldn't fight to stay here! Man, I'm outta here ...*"

"Devon, get back here," Myra shouted.

"No, Myra, let him go. He's mourning his father's loss, too," MamaD told Myra calmly.

Myra took a deep breath, releasing her frustration, and told Trey and Princess to get washed up for bed. As soon as they left the room, Myra looked at her mother and said, "Mama, how is it you want me to be stern with Devon, but yet tell me to let him get away with being rude?"

"Simple, it's all about listening and learning when to pick your battles with your kids, Myra. Devon wasn't trying to be rude; he's just mourning his dad. He feels Dee bailed out."

"Well, Mama, I don't know what else to do."

"Let it be for now ... Let him cool off and talk to him later. Devon has a soft heart, just like his grandfather. If anything, he's already sorry for what he said," MamaD said as she rubbed Myra's hand.

"I know he better be sorry," Myra added.

Cissy interrupted to let them know she'd put the kids to bed and then go home. And even though Myra thanked Cissy, she told her she didn't have to go home. Cissy told her she had to go home because a repairman was coming in the morning. Myra smirked and said, "So that's what you're calling it now."

"Oh, stop, Myra ... You know if I had a friend coming over, I'd say it."

"Would you really, in front of Mama?"

"Why not, she seems to know what a 'booty call' is."

"You know," Myra agreed.

Cissy looked at her mother smiling. MamaD, standing close to Cissy, nudged her with her elbow in response to the remark. Cissy then walked upstairs to help Trey and Princess get ready for bed. As she hit the top of the staircase, she saw Devon sitting at the foot of his bed with his head down, crying. She went to close the door for him to have privacy, but he mumbled, "Why?"

Cissy in shock stayed quiet and waited to see if he was talking to her. Devon repeated himself, but addressed her this time. Cissy, not knowing what to say, responded, "I don't know, no one knows why God decides to call someone home, but what I do know is that your father is still with you in spirit because he lives in your heart, baby."

Devon looked up at his aunt, and although he was seventeen, she saw the face of a six-year-old who had never heard of death. He tried to get up, but his legs were too weak to stand, so she kneeled in front of him.

As she grabbed his hands, she felt a teardrop fall. It had become clear to her that he was taking his father's death harder than everyone thought. She squeezed his hands tight and began praying over him. And at the end of the prayer, Devon looked in his aunt's eyes with appreciation and love. Cissy then got up and whispered, "I love you Devon, hang in there."

Devon responded, "I love you, too, Aunt Cissy."

In the hallway, Trey and Princess were heard bickering while having a tug-of-war.

"Give it back," Trey shouted while holding tight to the robe.

"No, I had it first!" Princess shouted back.

"I had it first, and you know it, Princess, it was in my bathroom."

"So, it's not yours anyway, Trey," Princess interrupted.

Suddenly a yell came from the foot of the stairs that put the fear of God into both of them.

"Hey, do not make me go up there, you two, because you won't like it," shouted MamaD.

"Mama, I got this," Cissy quickly interjected in a low tone.

"All right now, Trey, you take your father's robe, and Princess, here's your father's T-shirt with your picture on it. Good night, both of you."

Looking satisfied, they both answered, "Good night, Aunt Cissy, thank you."

Against All Odds

In Myra's head, she was going over what was done for the funeral. She couldn't believe it was already only two days away. She went down her list of things to do and realized she didn't complete the eulogy. Myra looked out of her window in despair. All she had written was the years Dee was born and died and who Dee left behind. She couldn't put into words all he had done, because aside from being successful at work, there was so much to share about who he was as father, husband, and Christian man. This was the hardest part of planning the funeral. She kept asking herself, "What do you write about a person you lose without making it a loss?" She didn't want her kids to perceive their father's death as just a loss, but also as a gift. The only problem was that she didn't believe his death was a gift any more than the kids would believe it.

Suddenly she remembered the old, but wise, adage, "Yesterday is the past, and today is a gift. That is why it's called 'The Present.'" All of a sudden, she became conscious of the apprehension she was radiating to her children about moving on with life. And if there was ever a better time to transform this experience, there was no time like the present to create a new beginning for her and the children.

Myra jumped out of bed in anticipation of what she needed to start. She grabbed the pen and pad from her nightstand, then made a list of everything she wanted to accomplish for the day. The first thing on her list was going to Dee's office to meet with his partner, then she would make all the necessary phone calls to his clients updating them on his passing, and finally, she wanted to write the eulogy and go to the funeral home. But first things first, she knew she had to beautify herself into a power suit for what she was about to do.

*   *   *   *   *

In the meantime, Cissy received a serious phone call at the salon from Devon's principal.

"Hello, Celestial Hair," Cissy answered.

"Hello, Mrs. Harris?" The principal asked in apprehension.

"No, this is her sister Celeste, how can I help you?"

"This is Principal Thomas at Eastside High, and I wanted to speak to Devon's mother or father about his attendance and behavior in school."

"Okay, so why are you calling my place of business?" Cissy snapped.

"Sorry, but we tried calling Mr. Harris on his phone and didn't get a response, and you are the only other person on our phone list."

"Well, you wouldn't get Mr. Harris on the phone since he passed away two days ago."

"Oh, my God, I'm sorry to hear that."

"You mean you weren't informed?" Cissy said more calmly, feeling for her attitude.

"No, I had no idea."

"I'm sorry, my sister and her kids have been going through a lot the last couple of days, so she probably forgot to call you."

"So that would explain Devon's behavior in school ..."

"What kind of behavior are you talking about?"

"He's been lashing out at the teachers, not participating with the workload in class, and today he threatened to punch his science teacher in the face."

Cissy pulled the phone away from her ear in disbelief, then returned, saying, "Oh, really, and when you say attendance, what are we talking—cutting classes or school?"

"It has been a little bit of both. He has fifty absences so far since the year started, and twenty-eight of them include cutting homeroom, which if homeroom is cut three times a week, it counts as one absence for the week."

"Are you kidding me?" Cissy couldn't believe what she was hearing.

"No, Ma'am, I'm not."

"Okay, the Ma'am has to stop. You can call me Ms. Cissy."

"Sorry, Ms. Cissy. Will you be speaking to Mrs. Harris today?"

"I most certainly will, Principal. I'm sorry, what did you say was your last name?"

"Principal Thomas, and from what I know, Mrs. Harris put your name down as a contact person when her husband was admitted into the hospital. I'm assuming you are the caregiver in her absence?"

"You assume correctly. As a matter of fact, I will be handling this myself. I ask that you continue to contact me until further notice if possible, Principal Thomas."

"Sure, no problem, and if you need any help, we do offer counseling to students who have lost any family member."

"Thank you for calling."

"No, thank you for showing an interest in your nephew … It's hard enough trying to get help from parents, but to see an aunt take part in the student's education deserves recognition, so I take my hat off to you … Enjoy the rest of your day."

"You do the same."

Cissy took a minute and looked at the clock as she hung up. She looked down at her appointment book and called one of the other beauticians to her booth to take care of her afternoon clients, since they only needed a wash and set. Cissy went back to doing her client's hair, looked at the clock, and assumed Myra and Mama were at the funeral home making the funeral arrangements.

*   *   *   *   *

Myra and MamaD were indeed at the funeral home, going over the final touches for the funeral. Myra was confused because she didn't know what kind of casket to chose.

"Mama, I don't know about the shades of wood," said Myra.

"Well, you can always go for the platinum casket," offered the funeral director.

Myra looked at the director as though he had two heads and said, "Um, excuse me, who is paying for all that? Unless you're paying for it, I'll go with the mahogany casket with white satin interior," Myra said in assurance.

"I thought that would make up your mind," he responded with a wink.

Myra smiled and grabbed her purse.

"Great, so we are all set," he said.

"Wait a minute, what about the suit?" MamaD interjected.

"What suit, Mama?"

"Do you plan on putting clothes on him, Myra?"

"Yeah, and he has his Armani suit in the closet. I showed it to you the other night, Mama."

"Don't you want to buy a new one, Myra?"

"Okay, Mama, how about I tell you the size and you go buy it? Right now, I have to go to the office ..."

"Heck no, it's not my husband."

"Okay, so what is wrong with him wearing one of his suits from the closet?"

"There's nothing wrong with it, I just don't know why you can't buy him a new suit."

"It's not a question of not being able to buy a new one, because money is not the issue. I don't see the point in buying a new suit for him to be buried in, and I don't have the time right now to take that into consideration. I have a lot of things to do."

"What things? You don't work, Myra."

"That's how much you know, Mama. I promised Dee before he passed that I would take over the firm until it meets the business quota in order to receive recognition in the Fortune 500. And after that, I would sell out."

"Now why would you take on such a thing, Myra?"

"Mama, I don't need this right now … I have to get to his office for a meeting."

"Baby, why are rushing into this? Your husband just died …"

"Mama, I have a lot to accomplish. The kids need to know that life doesn't end because of a death. Is that not what you have been lecturing me on from the time you came here? Plus, I know the office hasn't been running as smooth as when Dee was there."

"But doesn't Dee have a partner?"

"Yes, but Dee's last wish was his name being included when the law firm makes the Fortune 500. It is important for Devon to see his father accomplish his dream even though he is not alive. I mean, his firm would be the first in this state to achieve that."

Myra suddenly realized the power in those words. Here it was, she'd been fearful of starting over, but why? She had no clue. She just knew she was afraid. Just then Myra put her head down and cried over the lack of power, faith, and spirit she had been displaying. Here she was teaching her kids to have faith in God, but she wasn't doing the same. MamaD put her arms around her and said, "Oh, baby, don't cry … I just want you to be able to live out your passion, too, for once."

"Mama, I don't even think that's possible."

"Stop talking like that … You can do anything, Myra."

"How, Mama? When I have three kids?"

"Listen, I'm here, right?" MamaD said as she pulled up Myra's chin.

"But you will be leaving soon, Mama."

"And I could stay as long as it takes for you to accomplish your dreams, too, Myra."

"Mama, I can't ask you do that … Your home is in Charleston."

"Baby, my home is with my family; you guys are most important to me. I lived my life already; now it's time to live yours. So do me a favor and think about it, okay? And remember, 'For God did not give us the Spirit of fear, but a Spirit of power, love and sound mind' (2 Timothy 1:7)."

"I will, Mama. Oh, my God, what time is it?"

"Right now it's two, why?"

"Oh, no, I have to be at the office in half an hour." Myra wiped her face, checked it in her compact, then fixed her suit before leaving.

"Well, then, you better hurry up. Don't worry about me. I'll get your sister to pick me up."

"Are you sure, Mama?"

"Yes."

"Thanks for all your help, Mama."

"Anytime. Now go before you get there late. Bye."

"Bye, Mama."

Myra left, and MamaD went to eat at the shopping center. After eating, she took a walk around the shops to see if she'd see anything worth buying. All of a sudden, she saw a for-sale sign in one of the shops. She took down the number for Myra and proceeded to go inside, where she noticed seating and a fitting room area in the back. Mama thought to herself, "This would be perfect for Myra's boutique." She walked out of the store, called Cissy, and left a voice mail message to come pick her up in the shopping center.

*   *   *   *   *

Cissy was driving like a lunatic to get to Myra's house to check the mail before Devon got to it first. As she went into the mailbox, Devon came out of the house.

"Hey, Aunt Cissy, what are you doing here?"

"No, the question is, what are you doing here, Devon?"

"I'm always home by three, Aunt Cissy. Why you holdin' me suspect?"

"Maybe because you are, and since when are you home at three when you're typically at practice?"

"Well, today Coach gave us the afternoon off."

"Oh, really, so you guys are so good, he gave you the day off?"

"Oh, you didn't know … You better recognize, Auntie."

"Recognize what? You're a bold-faced liar. Your school called my shop today, Devon!"

Shrugging his shoulders, Devon said, "Yeah and …?"

"And the principal informed me that you have been absent from school and misbehaving in class."

"What!? Aunt Cissy, he's buggin'. No, I haven't. And what it sound like, me misbehaving, like I'm some five-year-old?"

"Well, apparently you are five, Devon, because you're going around talking back to teachers, threatening to hit them, and cutting homeroom."

"Man, he got it twisted."

Cissy popped him in the back of his head. Devon looked at her in rage, holding his fist, and said, "Look, I'm not Trey, all right? You can't be hitting me like I'm ten years old, for real."

"Excuse me, who do you think you're talking to, Devon?"

"Aunt Cissy, chill," Devon said, while holding her arms with his hands.

"No, you better chill, because you know I don't play, Devon."

"Yo! Seriously, you're buggin' …"

"Oh, I'm buggin', let's see how much I'm buggin' when I stomp the life out of you …"

"Yo, Aunt Cissy, seriously, if you touch me …"

"What?"

Cissy walked up directly into Devon's face, then walked out of the room and returned with a bat. She started swinging and hit his arm.

"Ow ...Aunt Cissy, Why you so violent, yo?" Devon jumped back, so Cissy couldn't pinch him.

"When you act like you have some respect, I'll stop being violent with you!"

"But I didn't disrespect you!" Devon pleaded with a smirk on his face.

Cissy didn't find anything funny, so she cracked her neck, jumped around practicing some blows with her fist. Devon suddenly wiped the grin off his face and looked at his Aunt like she was cuckoo crazy.

"Aunt Cissy, seriously, I am not about to fight you...."

Cissy just ignored him.

"And I'm not about to let you just hit me..."

"You could do what you want. I keep telling you, I fought bigger guys than you in the street. Fear is not one of my flaws."

"I'm sayin' what you want from me, Aunt Cissy?" Devon quickly replied.

"I don't want anything from you. Let's just fight the fair one, since you're such man!"

Devon shook his head in disbelief, ignoring the idea of putting his fists up to fight. He apologized for his disregard and asked her to put her hands down. Cissy looked him in the eyes and saw that he was being sincere, so she dropped her fists.

"Listen Devon, we're all on your side. You know that whatever you need anyone of us would give it to you, but when you don't do your part it makes it difficult for us to stand by you... "

Cissy grabbed his hand leading him to the couch.

"Look, I know it's hard right now to move on, but at least try, Devon. Do you think your father is happy where he is right now, watching you."

"I know, but you just don't understand what I'm going through..."

"You're right Devon, I don't know. But what I do know is acting as if you don't care anymore, won't help you get over the loss of your father. And neither will it make things better..."

"Easy for you to say – you don't have to figure out life on your own..."

Devon began crying as he rubbed his head with both hands. He lied back on the crouch and let out a raging scream.

"Why are you trying to figure out life on your own when you don't have to? You have your Mom, Grandma and me..."

Devon started rocking back and forth, banging his chest in anger as he began venting.

"It's not the same, okay? My dad was the one who's supposed to teach me how to be a strong man in this world. Did you know he planned a father/son trip this summer? Just me and him, man. No Trey, no Princess, not even Mom. You know. We were supposed to have that man-to-man talk, you know. And even though I didn't need it, I was lookin' forward to it, man. For real ... It's not like I didn't know, man. I knew when he was going for that surgery, it was going to be the end for real. I had a gut feeling ... Yo, this is crazy ..."

Devon tried everything possible to stop crying. He went from breathing heavy to pretending to laugh to pacing the floor. Finally he couldn't hold in his pain any more and started crying again as he balled up his fists and covered his face.

Cissy had never seen Devon like this. She started crying along with him because there was nothing she could do to take away his pain. In a whimper, she said, "Come here, baby."

Cissy tried to grab him, but he pulled his arm away and started shouting. *"Nooooooo! I hate this ... I hate him ... Why did he leave?... I don't want to be like this ... I don't want to be weak like him ... you hear me? I'm not weak like you ... so what! You left ... I don't care, okay, I don't give a shi—"*

"Now wait a minute! Devon, I know you're upset, but being angry at your father is not going to help ... You have to stop blaming him and make amends."

"Make amends? Are you serious? Yo, you are buggin' ... that's my word, yo."

"Then I guess I am 'buggin' as you put it, but in order to move on with your life, you have to first find forgiveness."

"Oh, really, and I'm sure you'll tell me how I'm supposed to do it. And what am I forgiving him for?"

"The same way you forgive a person who's alive—you realize he wasn't perfect and that he had no idea his sickness would take over his life and the surgery would lead to his death."

"I just can't, Aunt Cissy."

"Listen, you don't have to carry this alone, Devon. If you want me to pray with you on it, I can."

"No, it's okay, Aunt Cissy, I got this ... I'll do this on my own."

"Okay, Devon, I want you to ask the Lord to help you shape up in school, too. Your mother has a lot to deal with right now, and the last thing she should be concerned about is your not doing well in school. You know what I mean."

"True dat, true dat ... I hear you, Aunt Cissy."

"All right, so I'm going to get your grandma, Trey, and Princess. Could you do me a favor and order some food, because at this time I don't want your grandmother to get in and have to cook."

"All right ... No doubt, Aunt Cissy."

"And Devon?"

"Yes?"

"Please drop the slang by the time we get back."

"Okay, Aunt Cissy, see you later."

"I'll be back."

*   *   *   *   *

While Myra was in Dee's office, she decided to make some phone calls. One of the phone calls went to Travis. She wanted to let him know the information on the wake and funeral. While the phone was ringing, Myra went over some of the books and client folders belonging to Dee.

She couldn't believe that Dee's clients still had open or pending cases. And the books didn't match his caseload. It was almost as if his partner left Dee's clients out in the dark, but continued to charge them fees. Myra stood in shock, when all of a sudden Travis picked up.

"Hello."

"Hey, Travis, how are you doing?"

"I'm fine, how can I help you, Mrs. Harris?"

"Why are you being so formal, Travis? I'm not a client."

There were a few seconds of silence on the phone and no response from him, so she continued to speak nonchalantly.

"Anyways, I just wanted to let you know that Dee's wake is Thursday from six to nine and the burial will be Friday morning at ten o'clock."

"Okay, great, so I'll see you then. Thanks for letting me know."

"What, you're not speaking to me now?"

"Of course, I am. I just have company right now ... Can I call you tomorrow? Or did you need to speak to—"

Myra cut him off and said, "No, by all means continue entertaining your guest ... Bye."

"Good night."

Myra thought his behavior was strange but paid it no mind; especially since she had bigger fish to fry. She needed to make a list of what needed to be taken care of between today and tomorrow's meeting with Dee's partner, Charles. So she made her list, made her phone calls, and made a few memos for the rest of the staff. After finishing her tasks, she turned off the lights and left to go home.

Outside was so beautiful, she dropped the top on the car and unloosed her ponytail. She needed to feel the wind. Somehow it soothed her tension and stress. And although she was at the halfway mark in starting anew, she still didn't feel fully encouraged. She turned the dial on the radio, but couldn't find anything worth listening to. So she turned to the praise and worship station and heard Yolanda Adam's "Open Up My Heart." This was exactly the song she needed to hear. She took a detour home so she could hear the song in its entirety. As the song played, Myra went from feeling empowered to weak with emotion, then she felt faithful to unsure about her decisions. While listening to the words, it became apparent how much this song related to her life.

And as the song came to an end and Myra was pulling into the driveway, all of her fears, doubts, and pressure were released. In the driveway Myra sat for a few minutes taking in the beautiful air. She looked up at the sky, and it was full of stars. Ironically, as soon as she looked up, one of the stars happened to twinkle. At that moment, Myra thought, "God must be happy with me." Then she took the key out of the ignition and went in. Inside she found a note from the kids saying her plate of food was in the microwave and they missed her for dinner. Myra smiled to herself and took the plate, note, and bottled water to her room. There she found a card from Devon apologizing for his attitude lately and his promise he'd change it. Myra at this point didn't know what was going on, but whatever it was, she didn't want it to stop. She began to thank God for her day, her family, and the uncertain future. All of a sudden, it didn't matter anymore what happened because, like the song said, she was opening her heart to God and letting him take over her life. That alone was her peace and joy. She didn't need anything or anyone else. Just knowing the Lord had her back made Myra know how much power she contained within herself.

The next morning Myra woke to birds chirping, the sun shining, and the alarm clock blasting Mary Mary's "In the Morning." "Ironically fitting," Myra thought. She took off her eye mask and looked at her window, where she spotted a colorful hummingbird. She walked over to it and noticed it was making a home on her flower bed. Myra smiled, took a deep breath, and proceeded to get ready. After she was done, Myra greeted her mother in the kitchen.

"Good morning, Mama."

"Good morning, baby, what's on your agenda for today?"

"Today I'm going back to the office. I have a meeting with Dee's partner, then I'm coming back home to prepare some food for after the funeral on Friday," Myra said as she poured coffee into her thermal cup.

"Myra, why are you preparing food two days before the funeral?"

"Mama, I just don't want to wait until the last minute."

"Okay, but I have a number that I took down yesterday while I was at the shopping center. There's a space for sale, and the best part is it's already set up as a clothing store. When I went inside to speak to one of the workers, he told me the owner is retiring and is looking to sell to a buyer who will continue the same kind of business. So I think you should give the broker a call today. I mean, he's even willing to do a lease-to-buy agreement."

"Wow, Mama, you were able to get all of that info from just speaking to a worker? Thanks, I'll call them while I'm at the office."

"Okay, well, you have a nice day, baby."

"You too, Mama."

Myra then left for the office. On her way, she stopped and checked the mail. She saw a notice from the bank, some bills, and an envelope without a name or return address. Myra opened it up and saw a thank-you note attached to a check. It read, "Thanks for taking the time to represent me in my lawsuit. And although you took my discrimination case pro bono, I thought I'd send you something to spend on your beautiful wife and family as a token of my appreciation." It was signed Mrs. Louise Lucas.

The check was for three thousand dollars. Myra did a two-step all the way to the car. On the drive she thought of all the ways she could use the money. She could buy some materials for the store, or she could put it toward the copyright of the boutique's name, the tax ID, and the registration to the state. Myra was so ecstatic and anxious, she made a note to call the broker. Myra finally reached the parking lot of Dee's office and saw a car parked in Dee's spot. She parked next to it and went inside, wondering who the car belonged to.

Inside Myra ran into Dee's partner. She gave him a hug and said, "Hi, Charles."

"Myra, you look beautiful as always." Charles hugged her back, then held her hands out, admiring her suit. He always complimented her. He loved the way she carried herself, how she dressed, and how much she supported Dee in everything.

And although Charles admired Myra, he was just as happily married to his high school sweetheart, Marilyn. In talking to Dee, Charles always said Dee was blessed to have the whole package, but that he was truly blessed because he had a Proverbs 31 woman. That was their little joke, Myra gathered. But in actuality, she thought of it as friendly competition. Myra was beautiful, but Charles's wife was even more beautiful. Marilyn was a model in her early years and later turned professor, which are two different extremes in careers. Myra admired her, but resented the fact that she didn't follow her passion as Marilyn did. After twirling around and showing her suit off, Myra sat at the conference table and said, "Thank you, so get me up-to-date on our client accounts and what we have to look forward to for the next couple of months."

"Let me start by introducing you to a new partner, because he will be taking over all of the firm's clients and contracts."

"Oh, really, and when did this occur? Because the last time I checked, you and Dee were the only partners at this firm, Charles."

"Yes, but I guess Dee didn't tell you about our junior partner, Mark Thomas."

"Who is this, and why didn't Dee tell me this?"

"I don't know, but here he comes now … Mark, this is Mrs. Harris."

Mark looked straight into Myra's hazel eyes and said, "Wow, I saw you in Mr. Harris's picture, but it didn't do any justice to the beauty that stands before me. It is a pleasure to finally meet you. I'm sorry for your loss."

"Thank you, Mark. Isn't he the charmer?" Myra said while giving Charles the elbow.

"Oh, Mark, he just has a way with words," Charles added.

"Apparently. He talked you and my husband into making him a junior partner."

"As of today, he's senior partner. And I promise you, he is highly qualified for the position," Charles said as he signaled for Mark to take a seat.

Myra loved his charm, but she needed to know more about him, so she gave Charles the eye and said, "Oh, really? Well, I'm not convinced. What are his credentials, Charles?"

"He graduated at the top of his class, he's won over 90 percent of his cases in one of the largest law firms in Washington DC, and he is committed to the legacy of your husband and the law firm."

"Okay, pretty impressive, but is this commitment in writing, because it sounds like you had intentions of selling Dee out before knowing he was going to die, Charles."

Mark sat silently between the two, looking at each of them as they spoke. He made sure not to make eye contact, because that would only lead to him having to give his input.

"No, of course not, Myra. I just wanted to prepare for the worst case scenario. I mean, Dee was sick for a long time and in a coma for almost two months. And, yes, we do have a contract."

Not fully convinced, Myra gave Charles the corner of the eye look and said, "I tell you one thing, you better not think for one second you're going to take all of the credit in making the firm get into the Fortune 500. You would be sadly mistaken."

"Myra, you know I would never do that. As a matter of fact, you don't have to concern yourself with taking over where Mr. Harris left off because Mark is handling everything."

"How is that, is he Superman? Just yesterday I noticed a lot of Dee's cases open, pending, and left unresolved, Charles."

"Please. Myra, we're just trying to make it easier for you. And you were probably looking at an old database. Since Dee's last day here, we haven't gone in his office to update his computer. We didn't want to move his stuff until we knew for sure he wasn't …"

Myra was feeling relieved, yet overwhelmed at the same time. She didn't expect the changes, so she leaned forward, looking Charles in the eye, and said, "Forgive me if I don't sound grateful, but standing up for the best interests of my husband makes it easier for me, Charles."

"Myra, we both know you have no interest in this. Let's not pretend," responded Charles with a smile.

"You're right, Charles. I don't have any interest in law, but I'll tell you what I do have an interest in, and that's my husband's passion; and even though he is not here, I will make sure his dream comes to pass."

"Okay, suit yourself, but if you ever feel it's getting to be too much, feel free to let us know. We are here to help each other reach that goal," said Charles.

Myra started to get up, but paused, looked up, and said, "You know how you can help?"

Charles anxiously responded, "How?"

"Well, from now on, every decision that is made, communicate it to me, and can you please tell me where my husband's files are?"

"They're in Mark's office," Charles said in frustration.

"Do me a favor and have one of the assistants put them back in Mr. Harris's office, please."

"Look, Myra, since you have no intentions on going to law school or becoming a lawyer, those files can stay with Mark. And what is with referring to Dee as Mr. Harris all of a sudden? There's no need to be so formal; we're all family," Charles said, with a smile on his face to ease the tension.

"Oh, really? Well, as you may know, I do not have to be a lawyer to contact Mr. Harris's clients to update them on his passing and let them know they're not forgotten—which wasn't done yet. And Dee became Mr. Harris the minute you chose to make decisions without consulting with him and his family. Oh, and by the way, if you felt so much like family, why didn't you come to the hospital, Mr. Anderson?"

"Well, I spoke to Dee on the phone before the surgery, and he told me to just stay focused on the firm, Myra. He said he didn't need me to visit him, but wanted me to conduct business as usual. And speaking of making decisions, Dee and I decided long before his illness to take on a junior partner in situations like this where illness or death can happen," Charles recounted.

"Well, la-di-da, you deserve a special applause for all of your efforts and support. Let's bring out the champagne," Myra responded while clapping her hands.

"Myra, all of the sarcasm isn't necessary, but if it makes you feel better to get over the loss of Dee, make yourself happy," Charles interjected while picking up his files.

"I'm going to Mr. Harris's office. Please have his files returned, so I can go over them," Myra replied while looking candidly in Mark's eyes.

"Be my guest," responded Mark while holding up his hands out of her way.

As Myra walked off, Mark hesitantly added, "Mrs. Harris, if you need anything, please feel free to drop by my office, I will be—"

Myra quickly shut him down and said, "No, thank you, Mr. Thomas, all I need right now are the clients' contact information you're so graciously handling. Thank you."

"I assure you, Mrs. Harris, that all of Mr. Harris's clients are being taken care of. In fact—"

Myra cut him off again, saying, "Mr. Thomas, I am not interested in the way you're handling the clients. I would just like to know who they are and if you're winning their cases. Your credentials and boasting are of no interest to me. My only concern is your ability to gratify them so much so that they are satisfied and confident in your presenting their cases. Now if you will excuse me, I will be in Mr. Harris's office."

As soon as Myra got in Dee's office, she noticed her picture on his mantle. She took a seat on his soft mahogany leather sofa and stared at it. She could remember the day the picture was taken. They were on one of their annual wedding anniversary vacations without the kids, in Aruba. Myra thought to herself, "I could still fit into that two-piece, too."

"Knock-knock."

Myra looked to see who was entering the office. She realized it was Dee's assistant and quickly got up to greet her.

"Janice, how are you?"

"I should be asking you that, Mrs. Harris. Is there anything I could do to help you?"

Myra thought for a second, then she said to Janice, "Well, there is one thing you could do: tell me how Dee was on his last day here."

"Oh, Mrs. Harris ..." Janice responded, not knowing what to say.

"Please, call me Myra."

"Myra, he was just like he always was in the office, demanding but charming, and funny but intentional. Mr. Harris worked nonstop from phone calls to meetings, all while having a smile. It was always a pleasure to see him in action. He encouraged everybody to work at their best, and this day wasn't any different. Mr. Harris was his typical self."

"Was he?" Myra asked, but already knew Dee's way of being. She just needed to know if his day was normal or unusual. It made her happy to know that day was like every other day for him.

Janice wanted to share more, so she pointed to the leather sofa and said, "If I may, Mrs. Harris, uh, I mean Myra."

Myra smiled and invited Janice to join her on the couch.

"Your husband was great at being a lawyer, but he was even more of a pleasure as a boss. He knew how to make me feel useful and confident. And any chance Mr. Harris had, he would talk about you and the kids, whether it was with a client or just in a casual conversation. He definitely expressed love for his family."

"Well, he was always good at telling everyone else about how much he appreciates his family," Myra interjected.

"Isn't that always the case?" Janice said from experience herself.

Janice was a recent divorcee with one child. Her husband, from what Dee shared, was mentally abusive during the marriage, explaining the meek and shy traits of Janice's personality. And, of course, after their divorce, Janice's ex-husband somehow reformed himself and realized she was the best thing for him. And although Janice agreed, she couldn't rekindle anything with him because of the effect his behavior already had on their daughter. She did, however, continue to support their father/daughter relationship. Unbeknown to Janice, Myra applauded her decision—not because she didn't believe in second chances, but because Janice made a choice to show her daughter how a woman is truly to be treated. Now Janice was engaged to be married to a successful banker with just as sweet a personality as hers.

While other women might be intimated by having another woman in control of their husband's work life, Myra loved Janice and the role she played in Dee's life. She was the perfect assistant for Dee because he could be as demanding as he wanted without worrying about getting an attitude from her. And even though Janice seemed timid, she knew her job and did it very well without a complaint or a whine. Janice relieved a lot of stresses for Dee in that sense, and Myra appreciated it. Just then Myra leaned in to give Janice a well-deserved hug. Janice told Myra to hang in there and keep the faith. Myra thanked Janice by handing her a thank-you note and bonus check.

They stood up at the same time, and Myra walked Janice out of the office. Before Janice left, she turned around and thanked Myra for the note and check.

*   *   *   *   *

At the house, Devon was home alone as MamaD and Cissy took Trey and Princess to buy their clothes for the funeral. Devon was thrilled to have the house all to himself. This was the perfect opportunity for him to invite his girlfriend over. Devon called Shalise up with the "mac voice" as he called it and convinced her to skip school and come over. After several minutes of begging on Devon's part, Shalise finally gave in and told him she'd be right over. Devon hung up the phone excitedly and rushed into the shower. Now, even though he didn't know what time MamaD and Aunt Cissy were coming back from shopping, Devon knew it was always an all-day event. After his shower, Devon sprayed his Curve cologne on himself and around the room, then he gargled with mouthwash for two minutes to make sure his breath was fresh. He took a once-over look at his room to make sure everything was in its place, including the condoms, given out by his health teacher. A few minutes later, he heard the bell ring. Devon all of a sudden became nervous, but knew he had to repress it if he wanted to make a good impression on Shalise.

He opened the door, and there she was, smiling beautifully with innocence and sweetness. Devon looked her up and down before inviting her into the house. She had on a nice pair of hip-hugging skinny jeans, which accentuated all of her curves. Devon loved to see her in these jeans because it showed her thickness, but at the same time, her shapely tone. Shalise truly had the shape of a dancer, only she had a heavier top. Devon invited her into his room, where he had a sitting area in front of his TV. Shalise quickly sat down there and asked for something to drink. Devon went to get her some juice and Cheetos, her favorite. Shalise was impressed by the tidiness of his room. She always thought boys were sloppy, but Devon definitely broke the mold on that assumption. Devon plopped himself right next to her on the beanbag, making her slip off. She elbowed him in the gut, then laughed. Devon jumped on top of her after coming up for air and started tickling her. She screamed out, "Stop, Devon, stop."

"I'll stop when you give me a kiss," Devon whispered in her ear.

Shalise looked in his eyes and leaned up to give him a kiss, then said, "There, you happy now?"

"Very," Devon said as he stared at her for a few seconds.

Shalise asked him why he was staring, but he didn't respond. Finally he got up and pulled her to stand up with him. He gently grabbed the back of her neck and kissed her on both of her cheeks, forehead, then her lips. Shalise was weak at this point, so her knees buckled. Devon picked her up and brought her to his bed. After laying her down, Devon lifted up her shirt and pulled down her bra. He then got up to put on his CD of slow jams, then opened his drawer to get his condoms. He lay down beside her, and as he caressed her breasts, he asked if she was really ready.

Shalise looked at him and said in the sweetest tone, "I don't think I'll ever be ready, but if I had a choice on where, when, and who, it would be right here, right now, and with you, baby."

At that moment, Devon got chills and began having stronger feelings for her. It also made him feel guilty about putting her in the position to choose. Devon felt if there was ever a time to be a gentleman, this was the time, so he kissed her on the cheek, then said, "I don't think we should do this now. You're special to me, and if we're going to have a first, I don't want it to be rushed—and here, out of all places. You deserve better."

Shalise smiled and asked, "You're sure, Devon?"

"Girl, don't play with me; you look very tempting, but I'd rather wait."

Just then Myra got home and called out, "Hello, anybody home?"

But Devon didn't hear her.

Myra started looking around the house to see if anyone was home. As she approached the top of the stairs, she saw Devon's door closed, so she opened it. At that point, it was too late for Devon and Shalise to fix themselves up.

Myra, in shock, said, "What the hell, what is going on here?"

"Mama!" Devon blurted out as he jumped up and Shalise fastened her shirt.

"*Oh, no, you didn't just all-out disrespect my house. Boy, I can't believe you …*"

"I'm sorry. It's not what it …" Devon tried to explain himself.

Myra ignored him, looked at Shalise, and said, "Little girl, what are you doing in my son's room?"

"Mama, we were just hanging out and …" Devon intervened before Shalise could answer.

"It looks like there was more than that going on, with her shirt hanging off and her tatas hanging out … *Little girl, I'm going to ask you again, what are you doing in my son's room?*" Myra shouted in anger.

"Mama, this is my girlfriend and …" Devon pleaded.

But Myra wanted Shalise to answer, so she said, "I did not ask you, Devon. I asked her, and what is your name, anyway?"

"Shalise, Mrs. Harris," whispered Shalise.

"Sha what?" Myra sarcastically remarked.

"Shalise, and Devon asked me to come over."

"And you don't know better?… I mean, you must know that there should be an adult in any house you visit. Does your mother even know you have a boyfriend?" Myra asked.

"No. She doesn't know, but I didn't think I was going to stay long … and I know I'm not supposed to be here, Mrs. Harris."

"Please, all girls never think, until nine months later," Myra replied.

"Mama, please, stop being so dramatic. It's not that serious," Devon interrupted.

"Excuse me, I'll show you dramatic when I throw your butt out. You have no business inviting any girl into my house …" Myra gave Devon the up and down look.

"In my room! Are you serious?"

"In your room! Uh, do you pay rent or the mortgage, Devon? No, so until then, you stand corrected. This is a room you occupy in my house, which until now you used to sleep in."

"Oh, so now you're kicking me out?"

"Uh, did I stutter?"

"No, but can you at least let me explain, Ma?"

"Explain what, Devon? That you think you're grown and can do whatever you want to do?… Well, not in my house … Now take this girl home, and when you get back, you need to pack up some underwear and leave."

"How about I make it easier and just take my stuff now?"

"Oh, so you want to be a smart behind. How about you take the stuff your money bought." Myra knew that would get to Devon.

"What! Come on now, that's just one pair of jeans and a couple of T-shirts; I need more than that to go to school, Ma."

"Well, I guess you'll know better than to run your mouth in front of your girlfriend. And, by the way, Shalise, what is your mother's name and phone number?"

"My number?" Shalise asked innocently.

"Yes, you know, that thing my son called you on to come over ... I want to let her know what you were up to today."

"Mama, that's not even called for; we didn't do anything," Devon interjected.

"Boy, shut up before I smack you ... I say what is necessary, especially when you're in here playing house ... Now, what is your phone number and mother's name, Shalise?"

"It's (410) 555-2377, and her name is Henrietta Clarke."

"Good, I'm going to call her right now and let her know you're on your way, so Devon, do not make any stops, take her straight home."

"And where am I supposed to go?" Devon asked.

"I don't know, but you can't stay here," Myra replied as she grabbed the phone and called Shalise's mother.

"Hello."

"Hello, Mrs. Clarke?"

"Speaking, can I help you?"

"Yes, this is Myra Harris. I found your daughter Shalise here in my house, with my son Devon, about to do Lord knows what, but something they have no business doing and—"

"What!" Mrs. Clarke screamed out.

"Devon is going to bring her home now."

"No, do me a favor and keep her there, I will come and get her ... and if you don't mind, when I get there, I'd like to have a sit-down discussion with you and your son."

"No problem, but my son may not have a home by the time you get here."

"Hmph, I hear you." Mrs. Clarke replied.

"Yes, indeed ... I'm not turning a blind eye to this ... Listen, I'm not getting any younger, but I will be damned if I become a young grandmother."

"I know that's right," Mrs. Clarke agreed.

"Anyways, I'll see you when you get here, and we'll talk."

"Okay, bye, and thanks for calling, Mrs. Harris."

"Anytime, and you can call me Myra."

"Okay, bye, Myra."

Myra hung up the phone and told Shalise she spoke to her mom and she wanted to come get her herself.

Shalise plopped herself down on the couch, put her head in her hands, and mumbled, "Oh, my God, she's going to kill me."

"I doubt if she kills you," Myra replied.

"Mrs. Harris, you don't know my mom, she's kind of crazy."

"She didn't sound crazy on the phone … and as long as you don't get disrespectful, you should be okay … By the way, Devon, you need to start packing your things."

Then out of nowhere, MamaD appeared in the doorway and asked, "What's going on here?"

"Hi, Grandma, I'm moving out," Devon answered.

"Correction, I'm throwing him out. Hey, Mama, how did everything go with the shopping?"

"The shopping was fine, but what I want to know is what did Devon do now for you to throw him out?"

"Well, while I was out working and you were out shopping, Devon came up with the bright idea to invite his girlfriend over to feel on her tatas and play house."

"I keep telling her we weren't doing anything," Devon interjected.

"Excuse me, Devon, how can you possibly tell your mother anything other than sorry," MamaD responded.

"Grandma, I said sorry, but she won't let me talk or explain."

"And why should I let you talk if the discussions your father and I had with you didn't work? We told you when you are ready, let us know, so you would have protection," Myra interjected.

"First of all, I have protection; and second, leave my father out of it. I don't want to talk about him right now," Devon snapped.

"We are not talking about him, Devon, we are talking about you … Which, by the way, I'm through talking. Now get your things together."

"Where's he going? And why?" Cissy asked as she came in, catching everything late.

"Aunt Cissy, can I stay with you?"

"It depends. What did you do, and to whom did you do it, Devon?"

"Your nephew spent the afternoon playing house with his 'girlfriend,'" Myra commented.

"What! Boy, what were you thinking? Trey, Princess, go to your room."

Trey and Princess grabbed their bags and went upstairs.

"Aunt Cissy, we didn't do anything," Devon continued to explain himself.

"Please, if I hadn't come home early, you two would've been mixing sweat all up in and through my house ... *without any thought as to the consequences. Just get out of my face, Devon, before I hurt you.*"

Devon stepped away quickly, turned to Cissy, and pleaded, "Please, Aunt Cissy, I have nowhere else to go."

"Myra?" Cissy looked to Myra for approval.

Myra threw up her hands, then said, "Hey, that's your call, Sis ... I just don't need him here causing havoc when I'm trying to focus on the funeral and what my next move is."

MamaD, in disagreement, gave her input and said, "Now, what are we doing here, ladies? Myra, you cannot throw Devon out because he had a girl in his room."

"Who said? I pay the bills," Myra interrupted MamaD.

"No, correction, my father pays the bills—" Devon interjected, but before he could finish, Myra walked up to him and screamed at the top of her lungs in anger.

"*Let me explain something to you. All your father ever did was work blood, sweat, and tears so his family could have the best and be happy ... And you want to know how he was able to do that? Because I was here at home, working blood, sweat, and tears for you kids ... You would not be the best football player at your school if I didn't drive you to every single practice and training camp.*"

Devon wasn't touched by Myra's speech, so he cut her off and said, *"First of all, you did not make me the best football player. God did. And who cares what you or my father did? Does it matter now? He's dead! Don't you get it?"*

After screaming his head off, Devon grabbed his jacket and walked out. As he opened the door, Shalise's mother was about to knock. Instead, she walked in as she said hello to him. And although Mrs. Clarke had never met Devon before, somehow she knew it was him. Devon returned the greeting, but continued to leave. Myra called out for him to come back, but MamaD told her to let him go and cool off. Myra remarked that he forgot his bag, then walked away to the kitchen. MamaD invited Mrs. Clarke to sit in the living room and said, "Hi, I'm Devon's grandmother. You can call me MamaD. Can I get you anything, Mrs. Clarke?"

"No thanks, just my daughter if possible. Oh, and you can call me Rita."

"Oh, she just went to the bathroom, but she should've come out by now. I wonder what's taking her so long ... Shalise, your mom is here.... Shalise?"

Since there wasn't any response, MamaD turned the knob to open the door. And to her surprise, Shalise wasn't there.

"Oh, my God, where is she?" MamaD blurted out.

"What happened?" Mrs. Clarke asked.

"She climbed out of the window," Myra replied.

"No, she didn't," Cissy responded with uncertainty.

"Well, she's not in here, and the window is always closed," MamaD added.

"I am gonna kick her narrow behind," Mrs. Clarke said as she grabbed her cell phone to call Shalise.

"She must've climbed out when she heard Devon leave," MamaD assumed.

"I should've known it was going to come to this, from the last time they were caught," Mrs. Clarke let slip out.

"Excuse me. This happened before?" Myra asked.

"I'm sorry, but a couple of months ago, Devon brought my daughter home from a group outing; and when they reached my house, Shalise invited him in. I came home to find him running down the street after climbing out of her window."

"And why didn't you call me?" Myra asked in a concerned and aggressive way.

"At the time, I spoke to Shalise, and she told me Devon's father was very sick in the hospital and that it wouldn't happen again. Then she asked me to please not mention it … I'm sorry, I guess I should've said something," Mrs. Clarke replied.

"Wait, I just need to digest this … You mean to tell me you listened to a sixteen-year-old? Are you trying to have a grandchild?" Myra asked sarcastically.

"Hell to that, no," Mrs. Clarke replied.

"You must be, because it is beyond me why you didn't feel the need to have this discussion then. Whether or not my husband was in the hospital … These are sixteen-year-olds with raging hormones. Of course, she told you what you wanted to hear," Myra complained.

"I understand you're upset, but at the time, I didn't want to add to your burdens," Mrs. Clarke tried to explain.

"And keeping it from me, so that the two can get together again, made more sense? Is it me, or does that sound a bit ignorant?" Myra continued with her sarcasm.

"Call it what you want, but I did what was best for the situation … I apologize for not communicating, and I hope we can get past it," Mrs. Clarke replied patiently.

"Yeah, well, I don't see how we can discuss anything right now with both of them out there. And next time, can you please let me know if this happens?" Myra asked.

"Well, that's what we need to talk about. How are we going to convince them to make careful and responsible decisions?" Mrs. Clarke asked in confusion.

"Right now, I think they should take a break from seeing each other," Myra stated.

"I agree, but realistically, what are the chances that they will even follow our rules?" Mrs. Clarke asked.

"Well, I don't know about you, but my son knows better than to disobey me," Myra replied.

"Oh, really? So does he usually raise his voice and storm out of the house?" Mrs. Clarke asked, returning the sarcasm.

MamaD cut in to say, "Okay, now you two attacking each other is not going to solve anything, what you should do is work as a team and take a proactive approach toward guiding the kids into making the best decision."

"Mama, please, you know we would not be here if—"

"Be where, Myra? At least the young lady is not pregnant, and telling from Mrs. Clarke's disposition, she's not going to be ... You know a good parent when you see one, so stop behaving like you're the only one that can do right, because if I remember correctly, it takes two to tango, and *you* have not been able to control Devon for some time now," MamaD assertively stated.

"Yes, but—" Myra replied, but is interrupted by Devon and Shalise walking in.

Devon, holding his head down in shame, mumbled, "Hey, everybody."

"Where did you two go? Shalise, you know better than to leave. Now let's go." Mrs. Clarke grabbed her hand to leave.

"But, Ma ..." Shalise pleaded, but her mother stopped her by screaming, "*Now*, Shalise!"

Shalise walked quickly to the door, and Devon walked behind her to approach Mrs. Clarke.

Devon looked her in the eyes and said, "Mrs. Clarke, I apologize for talking Shalise into coming to my house today, and it will never happen again."

"Really, now why should I believe you, Devon?" Mrs. Clarke replied.

"Because we made the decision to wait and not rush into things …
I really care about Shalise, and I even love her. I don't want to pressure
her into anything she's not ready for. I mean it."

"I'm glad to hear that, Devon, but Shalise is still grounded and
won't be permitted to see you for a month, and more, unless her grades
show otherwise," Mrs. Clarke commanded as they walked out.

Then Devon shook his head in agreement, turned to Myra, and
said, "And, Mama, I'm sorry for disrespecting you … I know you
and Dad taught me better, but I've just been feeling lost lately, and I
thought—"

"Well, you thought wrong," Myra cut him off.

"Myra, let him finish," MamaD told Myra.

At this point, Devon didn't feel like he'd get anywhere with his
mother, so he waved his hand and said, "Forget it, let me just get my
things."

"Devon! Devon!" MamaD called out to him as she followed him
to the staircase.

"Grandma, it's okay. I'm just gonna stay at Aunt Cissy's house."

"No, Devon, your mother needs you here," MamaD said lovingly,
but Devon continued to go to his room.

"No, what I need is peace and cooperation. And right now, he's not
giving me any of them," Myra butted in to say, without a care in the
world for Devon's apology.

"Well, he was trying to make peace just now, but you shut him
down, Myra."

"Mama, I thought you agreed the next time he did something, he
would have to stay with Cissy."

"Yes, but this is not the time to do it—he just had a girl here
without your knowing. Now if that doesn't sound like him trying to get
attention after losing his father, then I don't know what it is."

"Okay, so now he gets to do whatever he wants and use his father's
death as a crutch; that doesn't make any sense, Mama."

"Myra, talk to him, he needs you right now," MamaD ordered Myra.

"Mama, I've done enough talking, I'm through." Myra threw up her hands.

Cissy saw the tension brewing between Myra and MamaD, so she intervened, saying, "Sis, I'll take him to my house for a few days until you cool off."

MamaD looked at Cissy angrily for opening her mouth and encouraging Myra's attitude.

Myra usually gave in to her mother's orders, but with Cissy by her side, she felt stronger, so she walked away, saying loudly, "Whatever, right now it doesn't matter where you take him, because I just want to be left alone."

Cissy turned around to get him, but he was already behind her and heard everything Myra just said.

Devon looked in anger at Myra and said, "So, you want to be left alone. Well, then I guess I'll leave you alone from now on. I'm outta here. I'll be waiting outside, Aunt Cissy."

"Devon, put your bags down, right now! This is ridiculous. You two stop with all of this anger," shouted MamaD.

"MamaD, I can't stay here. *You heard her. She'd rather be left alone than talk to me. I'm gonna give her what she wants and never come back!*"

Devon screamed so Myra could hear him in the kitchen. In the kitchen, Myra was in tears. She didn't know what to do with Devon, but she knew that talking to him was a waste of time, especially since she had already tried that without any success. At least she thought so. MamaD grabbed Devon's bag and said, "Yes, you can stay, Devon, so put your bags down and go in the kitchen. Talk to your mother. You only get one mother, and the Bible says you are to honor her."

"Mama, don't go against Myra's wishes," Cissy butted in again. She was trying to avoid Myra losing it on Devon in front of their mother.

MamaD walked Devon to the kitchen while saying, "Cissy, hush, I'm not going to have this animosity manifest itself during a time when the family needs each other the most. Now, Myra, you and your son need to have a sit –down because I said so, and if you have a problem with it, then I want to see you try and tell me ... Come on Cissy."

MamaD aggressively grabbed CIssy's arm as they walked out.

"I'm coming ... I'm coming, Mama" Cissy whined.

Myra wiped her tears then told Devon to have a seat. She looked up at him, grabbed both of his hands, and said, "Devon, when I got pregnant with you – your daddy and I could barely make ends meet, but it didn't matter because we had each other and that was enough. Then you were born and our whole world changed."

"Why?" Devon sat up erect and became really attentive. Before that moment he had never heard the history of his parents or his birth. Myra pulled her hair back away from her face to look Devon eye to eye as she continued to speak.

"Well, having each other just wasn't enough when we had you ... you became our whole world, the most important thing to us. Everything from that point on was about you, and still is. We just wanted to give you all of things we didn't have when we grew up..."

"And you did, Mama." After seeing the sadness in her eyes Devon felt the need to reassure her.

Myra smiles, "Devon, you are our firstborn, the perfect oldest of the family. We depend on you to set an example to your brother and sister. And when you do foolish things like you did today, you leave me no choice but to let you go and see for yourself how tough life can be on your own ..."

A tear rolls down Devon's cheek, "Mama I..."

Myra holds her finger up, signaling him to just listen. Devon shamefully put his head down, but continued to pay attention to what Myra had to say.

"Devon, you know for every decision you make there is a consequence, your father already explained that to you. So if you continue to do things without giving any thought to the consequence, you will set yourself up for the devil to create all kinds of chaos in your life. Furthermore, you should not put yourself in tempting positions that can lead to your disobedience to God. And having your girlfriend in the house, without an adult present was definitely not living obedient. Not to mention, babies come as a result. And If I hadn't come in when I did, you two would've been well on your way to making one.

"That's just it, Mama. When Shalise and I were about to do something, it didn't feel right. I felt like I was doing something wrong, like God was talking to me. The strange thing is it felt like Dad was there too."

"Well his spirit is in your heart if you take the time to reflect on who he was in your life." Myra gently rubbed Devon's head. And I could've taken advantage of the situation, but it just didn't feel right. I didn't think that was good enough. I want our first time to be special, not just a lay, you know what I'm sayin'?"

Myra couldn't believe Devon was being so open, which made her realize that MamaD was right. Devon needed someone to talk to, and she was glad MamaD made them talk.

Myra felt the urge to share her thoughts with Devon, so she said, "News flash Devon, that's what most girls think when they have their first boyfriend. Trust me, I know. I thought the same thing until I met your father. He showed me he liked me for more than just a good lay."

"Mama?" Devon looked at Myra like "do you really have to talk like that?" In his eyes, it was okay for him to talk like that, but it felt weird to hear his mother talk about getting laid.

Myra smiled, then said, "Well that's how you got here. What did you think, you were hatched?"

"No, but I don't want to equate you and getting laid in the same sentence," Devon said as he tried to hold in his laugh.

Myra paid no attention to his behavior and said, "Listen, just be careful out there with the girls. If they see you as ignorant, then they will do everything possible to keep you. Including having your baby."

"I know, Mama, Daddy already warned me. I'm sorry, Mama, for disrespecting and disappointing you again."

"Disrespecting me—you did, but I am not disappointed in you. In fact,

I am proud of you and the decision you made today ... Now go upstairs, put your things away, and get your suit ready for the wake tomorrow."

"Is everything okay in here?" MamaD asked from the doorway with hesitation.

"Yes, MamaD, it's safe to come in. And I'm staying," Devon said as he gave MamaD a big hug.

"Oh, thank God, because I don't like to see my family with tension, so promise me that you two will always find a way to work things out, please."

"We promise," Devon spoke for both Myra and himself.

"Well, I'm going home now. Good night. See you guys tomorrow." Cissy grabbed her bags to leave.

"Cissy, it's late; you should stay," Myra looked at her with a smirk.

"Myra, don't start, because I'm not staying here. I have a lot of files to update on the computer, and plus I open the shop tomorrow."

"Oh, well, in that case, do your thing, Sis. I'll see you tomorrow."

Cissy felt bad she had to leave, so she replied, "How about I stay over tomorrow, Myra?"

"That sounds good, Cissy. Be careful going home and call when you get in, okay? Good night."

"Good night ... Bye, Mama, Devon." Cissy pointed to her eyes, then pointed to him.

"Why you looking at me like that, Aunt Cissy?"

"Let's just say I got my eyes on you, Devon. I'm the eyes when your mom can't see."

"Aunt Cissy, I'm straight now."

"All right, now that's what I want to hear, peace, people." Cissy walked out.

"Man, Aunt Cissy is crazy, yo."

They all laughed as Devon left to go to his room. The evening was very peaceful in the Harris home. At dinnertime, everyone was in good spirits and enjoyed talking to each other without fighting. That night, MamaD suggested they pray together, then go to bed early.

The Wake

%a

T he next morning, Cissy went to the shop to open it up, and
who did she find in front but Lance, holding a bouquet of
flowers and card. Cissy shook her head in disbelief as she
approached him. She asked him what he was doing there, and he
replied, "Why didn't you tell me your brother-in-law passed?"

"I didn't see why that was any of your business," Cissy remarked.

"I have your favorite flowers," Lance replied, ignoring Cissy's
attitude.

"I see, but I'm not the one who lost a husband, Lance."

"These flowers are not for a loss, they're just-because flowers,
Cissy."

"Just because of what, Lance? Just because you made a mistake and
want a second chance?"

"Well, yes, but besides that, just because you're special. I want you in
my life again. I can't live without you being by my side. You know, when
someone dies, you're reminded of what's really important in your life. I
grew up with Dee. He was a great person with a great wife. They were
perfect for each other, just like us. And no one should live life alone—
which brings me to why I'm here. Cissy, I know I've made mistakes, but
I don't see why that should stop us from having a life together. I love you
with all of my heart, and without you it no longer works. I am nothing

without you. You are my better half, and God knows without you, I am not whole because he resides in your spirit. So I'm asking—would you make me the happiest man forever and marry me?"

Cissy put her head down in disbelief as she said to herself, "Please, God, speak to my heart. Is he serious about spending his life with me? I mean, I wouldn't mind marrying him, but not now."

Cissy was still in deep thought about their relationship when Lance tapped her and said, "So, what do you say, Cissy? Will you give me a second chance and be my wife?"

Cissy looked around, then found him on his knee looking up at her. And although God gave Cissy peace with the notion of marrying Lance, she felt it necessary to not make it easy for him. So she laughed while saying, "You got to be kidding me, Lance. You have a family."

"No, I have a son. I told you I don't want to be with his mother. I want you, Cissy, please."

Cissy stayed silent for five minutes, then said, "I don't know, Lance. I'm not ready for this. I'm not sure if I can handle sharing you for the rest of my life."

Then out of nowhere, a black Escalade drove by with some guys shouting, "Say yes to the brother."

Cissy laughed and asked, "So, is that your boys?"

And with a smirk on his face, Lance replied, "I have no idea where they came from."

"Yeah, I bet … Lance, I'm not ready for this right now."

"That's okay, I'm willing to wait. We deserve to take our time."

Cissy then said she'd think about it. Lance got up, put the ring away, and gave her a kiss. He told her he wouldn't give up, then gave a thumbs-down to his boys across the street. He got in the truck and shouted, "I'll call you later, baby."

Cissy shouted back, "Okay."

The whole day, Cissy was on cloud nine. And although Cissy was happy Lance proposed, she didn't get overexcited because Lance still had another life to think about. She didn't know if she was cut out for the baby-Mama drama, but she loved Lance and was willing to give it a try. She knew that, baby or not, they were a good fit, but this was something she had to pray on.

*   *   *   *   *

Later on that day, at the wake, Myra was getting the cards and programs organized when the wife of the funeral director walked up to her and said, "Hi, Myra, sorry for your loss."

"Thank you, Mrs. Adams."

"Myra, I just put the flowers where you wanted in the chapel. Do you need me to do anything else?"

"Just one more thing, can you keep Mrs. Bee away from me, because if she comes to me crying again, I just might lose it."

"Now is that any way to treat an old lady?" Myra heard from behind her.

"Excuse me, but I wasn't talking to … Travis, you came." Myra gave him a hug.

"Of course, I told you I would, Myra."

"I wasn't sure if after our disagreement that you would want to even be around me."

"You mean after your disagreement. You were the one really angry. I was okay."

Then Cissy walked in, smiling until she saw Myra hugging Travis. She then folded her arms while rolling her eyes and said, "What is he doing here?"

"Cissy, stop, we are grown-ups now. Please don't hold any grudges, because I'm definitely not," Myra pleaded.

"Whatever …" Cissy waved her hand.

"Hi, Cissy," Travis smirked.

"Hmm … It's Celeste to you, Travis."

"I'm sorry, my bad," Travis apologized.

"You sure are sorry …"

"Cissy, please!" Myra interjected with a threatening look as she signaled to Cissy "what's up?" Somehow Myra knew Cissy was anxious about something. Cissy then signaled back to Myra they'd talk later.

"Mama, the pastor is here."

"Oh, okay, Devon. Come here; I want you to meet someone."

Devon walked over in an aggressive, but friendly, manner. He was wondering who it was Myra wanted him to meet. Myra put her hand on Travis's back, then said, "This is Travis, an old friend of mine, Devon."

After hearing who Travis was, Devon became angry because in his mind he thought Travis was there to win his mother's heart, but he wasn't going to let it happen. He looked Travis dead in the eyes, then sarcastically said, "Good for him."

"Devon! Where are your manners?" Myra checked him.

"It's okay, Myra, he's just doing what boys do for their mothers. He's protecting you. I don't blame him," Travis explained to Myra.

"Well, I don't think so ... Apologize, Devon."

"What! No, I'm not ... I didn't do anything wrong."

"Myra, I said it was okay ... Devon, I know what you're going through. I lost my father too when I was your age ..."

Devon looked at Travis holding out his hand, then walked past it and said, "Yo, you don't know anything about me, man ... Come on, Mama, the service is going to start now."

Travis stepped in front of him. "You're right, I don't know you, but if you ever need to talk, I'm here, man," Travis said, while holding his hand out, again waiting for a handshake.

Devon looked at him up and down, then walked past Travis's hand and said. "No thanks, Dog, I'm awright ..."

"Devon, watch how you speak to him—he is an adult," Myra interjected.

"It's cool, Myra, that's how they speak nowadays. Devon, I got you ... Holla whenever you need to, all right?... And keep taking care of your mother."

"No doubt, that's my mom," Devon said as he mean mugged Travis.

"Go ahead in, Devon, I'll be right there," Myra pushed him forward.

"Mama?"

"Devon, I said I'll be right in. Now go to our seats and stop staring at Travis like that."

"Whatever! Just don't take too long, Mama."

"Excuse me, I'm the parent here. Now go …"

Myra then turned to Travis, apologizing for both Cissy's and Devon's attitudes. Travis stopped Myra from apologizing and told her he was the same way when his father died. Myra continued with another apology for her hostile attitude over the phone the other day.

Travis excused her again, saying she had a lot to deal with and he understood. Myra told Travis it was no excuse when all he was doing was being a friend, but she treated him like a bother.

Travis grabbed Myra's hand and said, "Okay, stop beating yourself up. I don't mind being a bother when it comes to you … just focus on you and your kids because they need you. And if you need any help, let me know."

"Well, I want to make it up to you; want to go with me for coffee after?"

"I'm sorry I can't. I have to meet my girlfriend at a business gathering," Travis replied with a sad face.

Myra pretended to shrug it off and said, "Oh, okay, well, I guess I'll see you later."

As Myra walked away, Travis grabbed her, saying, "But I don't mind going tomorrow after the funeral."

Myra looked at his hand holding her arm, and Travis quickly let go. Then Myra looked up and said, "No, that's okay, I just realized that this isn't going to work, anyway."

"What's not going to work, Myra?"

"Us hanging out, Travis … I'll see you later."

Myra walked away and went to her seat beside Cissy. Cissy moved over to make room for Myra, then leaned over and whispered, "So, Myra, what's up with Travis being here?"

"Cissy, he asked me to come. I guess he wanted to show his support. Anyways, the bigger question here is, what is up with you? Is there something you want to tell me?"

Cissy smiled, then whispered, "Well, when I showed up at the shop this morning, Lance was in the front waiting for me. He goes into this apologetic speech about not being able to live without me, then out of the blue he proposes to me. I told him I wasn't ready to share him and that the engagement would probably be long. He said he was willing to wait, and I said I'll think about it."

"Oh, my God, are you kidding me? Why didn't you call me? He's a great guy, Cissy. You can't let this one go," Myra said excitedly.

"There wasn't a reason to call you if I was going to talk to you now, Myra."

"You get proposed to, and there wasn't a reason to call, huh?"

"So how about you invited your ex-boyfriend to your husband's funeral and didn't mention anything to me. Give me a break, Myra."

Myra rolled her eyes jokingly, then said, "Oh, please, Cissy, that was so long ago. You need to give it a break. And do not bring Travis up again, especially in front of Devon."

"Why, Myra? It's not like you and Travis have a thing going on." Cissy shrugged her shoulders as if she disagreed.

"Because Devon was already in protective mode when I introduced him to Travis, and I don't want him to jump to any conclusions, you hear me, Cissy?"

"Mum's the word … Just one thing, Myra."

"What, Cissy?"

"Remember he broke your heart before."

"Are we in high school? I mean, you're getting ahead of yourself. I just lost my husband, no one is thinking of Travis that way."

"Please, Myra, everyone who knows your history knows you always had a soft spot for that man."

"The key word is 'had'; that is something I don't have now, Cissy."

"Okay, whatever you say, Myra."

"Anyways, let me go speak to the pastor, we'll talk later."

"You do that." Cissy gave Myra a suspicious look.

While Myra went to talk to the pastor, Cissy went to have a one-on-one with Travis. Cissy plopped herself beside him and whispered his name.

Travis looked at her and said, "Hey, Celeste, you came to keep me company?"

"No smart behind, I came to tell you to keep your distance from Myra."

"And you are telling me this because …?" Travis asked in a mocking way.

"Because you know you can reel her in and break her heart again."

"For your information, Celeste, I am a grown man who has a girlfriend and …"

"Yeah, like that would stop you from trying to make a play for my sister again, Travis."

"If I were you, Celeste, I would be more concerned about helping your sister get her identity back, because it's apparent that she lost it somewhere along the way in her marriage."

"Like I said, stay away." Cissy looked at Travis threateningly.

"Celeste, I am not a child nor your man, so please do not give me any orders. Good night."

Travis dismissed Cissy and returned to reading the program. Cissy got up and said, "I think you heard me."

Then she walked back to her seat as though she had told him, when in fact Travis basically put her in her place. Throughout the service, Myra was crying, with Devon holding onto her. The pastor's words were so eloquent that there wasn't any need for anyone to go up and speak. However, Devon went up to share his thoughts. Myra looked up in shock and with fear that he would say things out of anger.

Devon walked up to the pulpit and began with greeting and thanking everyone. He then cleared his throat, removed his shades, and looked around at everyone. His first word came out cracked so he excused himself, but someone attending shouted, "Its okay, baby, take your time."

Devon smiled and asked everybody in the room when was the last time they said "I love you" to their loved ones. Everyone in the room looked around but kept quiet. Devon shook his head in agreement, then said, "Just what I thought. Everyone here is guilty of not saying those three very easy, but never said, words. I myself am guilty of not saying them to the one person who made me who I am today, my father. Even though I saw him day to day, I didn't say often enough 'I love you, Daddy.'"

Devon put his hands over his eyes and began to cry, feeling guilty. Myra looked from her seat, but couldn't stay seated, so she walked up and stood with Devon as he spoke. Devon felt his mother's hand on his back, then he straightened up to finish.

"My father and I had a trip planned for the summer to go fishing. He was supposed to teach me about the 'birds and the bees' and 'girls' and life in general, but now it won't be happening. At first I didn't want to go, because I thought it would be corny to spend time with him, but as time went on, I was looking forward to it. I even went with him to buy the fishing gear. And even though we won't be going fishing, I still love you, Dad. And I just want everyone here to say it to the person seated on each side of you."

Everybody started saying it to each other as Myra and Devon did the same while walking down from the pulpit. Cissy said it to MamaD, then she turned to say it to the lady across the way, but she found Lance standing in the way. He bent down on one knee and said, "I love you, Cissy. Will you marry me?"

Cissy all of a sudden felt flushed. She looked back at her mother, who gave her a nod to say yes. Then Cissy looked at Myra and Devon, both of whom gave their blessing. Then Cissy looked at Lance and said, "I love you, too. And, yes, I will marry you."

Lance picked her up and swung her around while everyone applauded. He gave his boys at the back of the church a thumbs-up. And as everyone began settling down, the pastor closed the service.

Myra and MamaD were the first to congratulate them. Then Devon walked up to them and warned Lance to take care of his aunt. Lance gave him a pound and told him he did a great job during the service. Cissy agreed and said it was his speech that made her say yes to Lance. Lance then gave Devon another pound. As the family was mingling with the friends and visitors who came to the service, Travis walked up to Myra to let her know he was leaving. Myra gave him a hug and said, "Thanks for coming, Travis. And don't worry about coming to the funeral in the morning; it's going to be a brief service, and it's definitely not worth missing work."

"Myra, I know I don't have to come, but I want to. And since I have vacation time, I could use a little get away, anyways." Travis smiled as he held her hand.

"Well, excuse me, then I'll see you in the morning. Let's go, kids," Myra said as she grabbed her purse to leave.

"Mama, are we leaving all of the flowers here?"

"Yes, Devon, the funeral home will bring them to the plot tomorrow."

"All right … Um, Trey and Princess, get in the car. Mama's ready to leave," Devon directed them to the door.

Travis congratulated Cissy and Lance, then turned to Devon and said, "Devon, it was nice meeting you."

"No doubt, no doubt, Travis." Devon gave him a pound and continued to walk away.

"That was a beautiful service, Pastor Walker." Myra leaned in to give the pastor a hug.

"Thank you, Mrs. Harris. I assume I will be seeing you in church on Sundays again?" the pastor asked while giving her the eye.

Myra smiled, then replied, "I'm not sure about this Sunday, but most likely next week."

"Great, I'll be looking forward to seeing you, Mrs. Harris."

"Okay, and have a good night, Pastor."

"Good night, Mrs. Harris."

On the drive home, Devon and Myra talked while Trey and Princess fell asleep. Following them were Cissy, MamaD, and Lance. Lance's truck was in the shop, so he took Cissy up on her offer to drop him off. While driving home, Myra and Devon had conversations about everything under the moon. They even joked with each other about Cissy finally getting married. Devon came out and said, "If Daddy was here, he would crack every joke in the book on her for finally getting someone to marry her, you know."

"Yeah, he would definitely say something slick, like how much is she paying you?" Myra smiled, just remembering the words Cissy and Dee would exchange every time they saw each other.

In Cissy's car, MamaD was sound asleep while Lance and Cissy held hands. Cissy couldn't get over her engagement. At every light, she would let go of Lance and look at her ring. It was everything she wanted. She was just surprised Lance actually remembered. She had a two-carat pink diamond princess cut in a platinum setting with seven white diamonds circling it. At the last light before reaching Lance's house, he leaned over and kissed Cissy. And with one eye open, MamaD peeked and said, "You two are not married yet, so slow your roll."

Lance jumped, while Cissy didn't budge but replied, "Mama, weren't you sleeping? Why are you awake and in our business?"

"Excuse you. You are not too old to get smacked." MamaD flinched her hand, making Cissy jump.

Cissy then pulled into Lance's driveway and replied, "I guess you don't want me to get married, Mama—because you definitely almost got us killed."

"Child, please, you know if I wanted to hit you, that smack would've landed where it was supposed to," MamaD said calmly.

Lance said his good-byes, letting Cissy know he'd be at the funeral in the morning. He then turned to MamaD and thanked her for her support and blessings. MamaD gave Lance a hug, but warned him to do right by her baby girl.

*   *   *   *   *

At Myra's house, Devon was already in big brother gear. He carried both Trey and Princess up to their rooms, put on their pajamas, and put them in bed. When he came back down, he checked in on Myra, but she was already asleep. As he began to close her door, she mumbled she loved him. He smiled then replied, "I love you, too, Mama."

*   *   *   *   *

The next morning, it was sunny and hot. Myra woke up feeling energized but sad at the same time. As Myra had recently begun doing, she started with a morning prayer and dialogue with the Holy Spirit. To herself she mumbled, "Thank you, Lord, for waking me up and bringing me this far. This is it, the toughest part of our loss—the burial. We need you today. Please help all of us to get through this, Lord. I miss him, Lord, but I know he's with you and no longer in pain ..."

Interrupting her prayer, Myra heard Devon grunt loudly in his room, "Grrrrr! Damn it!"

Myra quickly jumped out of bed and ran upstairs to his bedroom to ask, "What happened, Devon?"

Feeling frustrated, Devon threw the tie to the side and screamed out, "I can't make this damn tie!"

Now usually Myra would not allow Devon to express himself in that tone, but she knew he was going through his own emotions toward the day they were about to face. Myra walked over to him, picked up the tie, and said calmly, "Here, let me help you. So, you're wearing your father's tie today, huh?"

With tears in his eyes, Devon innocently said, "Mama?"

"Devon?" Myra quickly responded.

"I don't know how I'm going to make it. Dad helped me with everything, my ties, he coached me with football. He never even got to meet my girlfriend. I really wanted him to meet her. And we didn't get to have that men's trip he ..."

"Okay, Devon, but he did get to teach you to drive and he did get to see you play ball with all of your heart, and most importantly, he did get to tell you how much he was proud of you and loves you ... He is in your heart, and he is a part of you. Lord knows you act and think just like him, so when you think of your father today, remember the good times you had with him. Now you could either choose to dwell on his death or you could take your experiences with him and pass them down to your brother. And count your blessings that you were able to have those experiences with your father; because ultimately Trey's not going to have any of those experiences."

Devon thought for a minute, then said, "That's true. Thanks, Mama."

Pretending to not know what Devon was thanking her for, Myra said, "Thanks for what?"

"For making me realize that I have been blessed with having Dad in the important times in my life so far. Oh, and for tying the tie."

"You're welcome, baby. Now let me go check on your brother."

"Mama, I'll do that—you just take care of yourself and Princess."

"Thank you, baby."

Myra then walked down the hall to Princess's room and began knocking on the door gently. As she opened the door, Myra said in a low tone, "Knock-knock ... good morning, Princess."

Princess replied, "Mama, you think Daddy will see me in my new dress?"

"Yes, baby, and he'll be so proud of his beautiful little girl."

"I miss him, Mama."

"I know. I miss him too, baby. But you know what I want you to do when you miss him?"

"What, Mama?"

"I want you to tell God what you want to say to your father, and he will pass the message on. Okay?"

"Okay, but what if he doesn't give him the message?"

Myra chuckled, then said, "He will, baby."

Princess, perturbed with Myra's answer, replied, "So why didn't God give him the message to come back home? I prayed and told God to send Dad back home, but when I woke up, he wasn't here."

Myra had to think fast, because she wasn't expecting Princess to come back with that reply, so she said, "Well, that's because Daddy already went to live with God, and he has to stay and help him."

Princess was a typical six-year-old who couldn't let only one question be answered but had to dig deeper to satisfy her mind and thoughts, so she interrupted Myra saying, "But, Mama, I thought you said God is all powerful and can do all things. Why does he need Daddy's help?"

Myra then plopped down on Princess's bed, put her on her lap, and said, "Yes, Princess, he can do all things, but God has so many people to help and is so busy helping everybody in the world that he needs angels to help get all of his work done—just like how Grandma came to help me or how Aunt Cissy helps me."

"And just like how my teacher has someone to help her in class?"

"Exactly, God has the same kind of help."

"So he chose Daddy out of all people—Daddy couldn't even help you around the house."

Myra started laughing while tickling Princess, then said, "You're too funny, you little monster ... Now get your brothers and go downstairs and eat breakfast while I get ready. I smell MamaD's pancakes already."

As Princess walked away, Myra tapped her on the bottom, as she said, "Okay, Mama."

Myra then went to her bathroom and saw Trey sitting on the floor with Dee's robe on. She walked over and squatted down, then asked, "What's up, little man?"

"Nothing. Devon helped me get dressed, but can I wear Daddy's robe? I just want to have something of his with me today."

"Well, I don't think the robe is going to fit, but I have the perfect thing for you to wear of Daddy's."

"What?"

Myra got up, went into her adjoining room, and grabbed Dee's necklace with his picture locket of the family. She returned to the bathroom and told him to stand up so she could put it on. Trey smiled and said, "Mama, I didn't know Daddy had a necklace."

As Myra struggled to lock it, she replied, "That's because Daddy never wore it. Even though I would buy him jewelry, he didn't like wearing it."

"Except for his wedding ring, Mama," Trey interrupted Myra to say.

"Yes, except for his wedding ring. Now, how's that? Do you feel better now?"

"Thank you, Mama, you're the best."

"Okay, now how about you go eat breakfast, before it gets too late."

"Okay, see ya." Trey ran out of the room and headed for the kitchen.

Myra turned around, locked the door, and started the shower. As Myra headed for the bathroom door, her cell phone rang. She looked at the number and saw that it was Travis. After contemplating for a minute whether to answer it or not, she said, "Hello."

"Good morning, Myra. How are you doing?"

"Hey, Travis, I'm actually okay. What's up?"

"I'm sorry, but I'm not going to be able to make today. Something—"

"Listen, don't worry about it, I told you you don't have to come to the funeral," Myra said softly but in an agitated tone.

Travis could hear her aggravation over the phone, so he said, "I just have a case that has to be closed by today, so—"

"Listen, Travis, you don't have to explain anything. Just go and do what you have to do," Myra interrupted.

Travis then said, "Are you sure you'll be okay?"

And out of nowhere, Devon called out, "Mama, hurry up; we have to go before we're late!"

Myra signaled Devon that she was coming, then said, "Listen, Travis, I have to go. I'll speak to you later."

"Okay, so I'll call you later, Myra."

"Okay, bye, Travis." Myra hung up before listening for a response from Travis. And although Travis knew Myra had to go, he was hoping to speak a little longer. Myra, on the other hand, didn't care to speak to Travis at that moment. Her mind was on the day ahead, and she didn't see the point in harping on whether anyone could make it or not, especially Travis.

*   *   *   *   *

As Myra drove off, she did the traditional knocking down of the garbage cans, which put a smile on everybody's face. Princess even giggled a little bit. Myra smirked and said softly, "I know your father is probably laughing his head off right now." The kids agreed and for the remainder of the ride, they took turns remembering funny moments they had shared with their father.

As they approached the church, everyone was looking at them as if they were crazy. They never saw a family act happy and peaceful on such a sad day. Even MamaD had to ask if everything was okay. Myra laughed some more before explaining that the kids and herself were just talking about Dee and the good times. MamaD smiled, then told Myra she was proud of the strength she was showing. Myra smiled back, then said, "Thanks, Mama, but I can't take credit for something that comes directly from God. He is my source and my strength so far." MamaD gave her a hug, then said, "Thank you, Lord, for speaking to my daughter's heart."

They proceeded into the room so the service could start. Myra walked up to the casket first. As she looked at Dee, she mumbled, "He's so handsome and peaceful. I'm going to miss you, baby. I love you."

Just then the pastor walked up and whispered to Myra he was ready to begin. Myra leaned into the casket and kissed Dee's forehead, then stood up only to have her knees buckle.

Devon quickly got up to help keep her from falling, then he walked her to sit down. As they sat down beside each other, Devon put his arm

around her as Myra laid her head on his shoulder. The pastor walked to
the pulpit at the center of the stage and began his sermon with asking
the congregation to stand and recite with him the "Lord's Prayer." Myra
couldn't stand up so she stayed sitting down. Devon, of course, had to
stay seated because Myra was leaning on him. Cissy sat on the opposite
side of Myra, holding her hand. MamaD, Trey, and Princess stood up,
but without wanting to. They looked around as everyone in the room
simultaneously began softly with,

> Our Father, who art in heaven, Hallowed be thy name.
> Thy Kingdom come, Thy Will be done
> On earth as it is in Heaven.
> Give us this day, our daily bread
> And forgive us our trespasses
> As we forgive those who trespass against us.
> And lead us not into temptation
> But deliver us from Evil,
> For thine is the Kingdom, the Power, and the Glory
> Forever and Ever. Amen.

When they were done, the pastor asked everyone to take a seat as
he began his sermon,

"We are here to celebrate a man's going home to be with the Lord.
Although it would be easy to mourn his death instead, it is not God's
plan that we should be sad at this time, but be happy and rejoice in the
life that he lived.

"Devon Livonius Harris Sr. lived life as a man of integrity and
discipline. It showed in most areas of his life, with his family, his work,
and most importantly, his faith. And though he may have not been the
healthiest always, he strived for it always. I've known Devon since he
was a teenager, and he was always in some kind of sport or activity or
just stayed exercising. But like so many of us, we reach a certain age and
time in our lives where our health is no longer a priority. This is not what

God wants for us—he blessed us with a temple, and in keeping this temple, we must learn to love, care, and maintain it. Folks, I'm saying if we can maintain, love, and care for all the material things in our lives, then we can easily take a lesson from Mr. Harris's death and appreciate the body and life God has blessed us with. God doesn't want you to remember his times of sickness, but remember his times of health; don't remember his mistakes, but remember his accomplishments; and most of all, don't remember him in death, but remember him in life.

"God be with you, Mrs. Harris, Devon Jr., Treyvon, Princess, and his extended family and friends—remember the Lord is with you always. And now I ask Sister Jenkins to sing his favorite song 'His Eyes are on the Sparrow' for the last viewing and greeting to his wife and family."

As everyone began to walk up to the casket, Myra buried her face into Devon's shoulder. Devon, not knowing what to do, started to caress Myra's hair and rub her arm. Cissy, on the other hand, stood up to greet the friends and family who came to show their support. As more and more people went up, Myra became more upset. Finally MamaD came over and, with Devon's help, talked Myra into accepting everyone's condolences. Devon convinced his mother that he would be beside her. Then Myra lifted her head, wiped her tears, and gave Devon a peck on his cheek.

Myra stood up and told Cissy to have a seat. With tears in her eyes, Cissy asked Myra if she was sure. Myra shook her head yes. Cissy hugged her and took a seat between Trey and Princess. Princess quickly jumped on Cissy's lap, hiding her face. Myra sat back down, grabbed Devon's hand, and smiled as the rest of the family and friends came up to view the body and express their sympathy.

After the last viewing was done, the pastor closed out the service with instructions to everyone on where the burial would be. On the way to the cemetery, Myra, Cissy, MamaD, and the kids rode in the limo, as everyone else followed in their cars. It was a quiet but peaceful ride. Myra attempted to think of how she'd face that moment, but couldn't bring herself to think about it. Devon, on the other hand, fell asleep, along with Trey and Princess.

Time After Time

〽️

Back at the house after a peaceful, but emotional, burial, Myra jumped right into preparing the food for the expected guests. Cissy and MamaD looked at each other, then signaled Devon to get Myra out of the kitchen. Standing behind Myra, Devon put his hand up, signaling his noninvolvement in doing what they wanted. Finally, after a brief pause, Cissy told Myra to go sit down and greet her guests. Myra refused until MamaD stepped in and convinced her that her place was out there talking to her guests. MamaD, in so many words, let her know that it would help her grieve. Myra didn't agree, but went along with her mother's request. Myra then took off her apron and stepped out of the kitchen. As soon as she reaches the living room, one of her girlfriends walked in and began giving the apologetic sympathy speech.

"Myra, I'm sorry for your loss; that was a beautiful service; if you need anything, please don't hesitate to call," her girlfriend said while rubbing her back.

"Thank you, Wanda, but your just coming today helps me. Thanks for showing your support," Myra replied after moving over so Wanda couldn't rub her back.

Just then another longtime friend walked up, saying, "Myra, I'm leaving now. Call me if you need anything, okay, girl?"

"I will, and thank you for coming, Juanita, bye."

After saying bye, MamaD walked up from behind to ask Myra something. Hesitating to open her mouth, MamaD softly said, "Myra?"

"What!" Myra shouted in annoyance.

MamaD jumped back to avoid making Myra more upset, then she mumbled, "I'm sorry, I didn't mean to bother you."

Myra realized she had just snapped at MamaD and quickly fixed it by saying, "No, I'm sorry, Mama, it's just that everybody is feeding me pity, and I—"

"Myra, it will be over soon," MamaD interrupted.

"Well, I can't take it anymore; I have to get out of here." Myra began walking toward her room.

MamaD followed her and said, "Well, where are you going, Myra?"

Myra paced the floor as she replied, "I don't know, Mama. I just need some time to myself, to think, reflect … I want to be happy again, but right now, I don't think I'll ever be happy."

MamaD stopped Myra from pacing and said, "So, why don't you go to the cabin this weekend? I'll stay with the kids for you."

"Thank you, Mama, but there's so much to do around here. I can't ask you to do that," Myra replied with tears in her eyes.

"I know you can't ask, Myra. That's why I'm offering. Listen, Myra, Lord knows I know what you're going through. I've been there. And I wish someone was there to send me away by myself. So accept my offer and go to the cabin. The kids will be fine here."

MamaD leaned in to hug Myra.

As they hugged, Myra asked, "You're sure, Mama?"

"Girl, I said go. Now if you ask one more time, I'll change my mind …" MamaD pulled away, looking Myra in the eyes.

And with tears in her eyes, Myra replied, "Thanks, Mama, I appreciate it … I'll just pack some things, then I'll go out there and help you and Cissy."

"It's okay, Myra. I'll tell the guests you're getting some rest and send them off. Lord knows, half of them only came to eat anyway," MamaD smiled, making Myra chuckle. Myra knew her mama was just being honest as she always was, so she didn't bother to reply.

After packing some clothes and napping for an hour, Myra picked up the phone, but hung it up again. She was contemplating whether she should invite Travis to go to the cabin with her. Being in limbo, Myra finally conjured up the courage to call him.

"Hello, Home Designs, how can I help you?"

Cracking her raspy voice, Myra nervously replied, "Hello, can I speak to Mr. Dewitt?"

"I'm sorry, he's not here right now. Can I take a message?"

"No, but isn't this his cell phone number?" Myra looked at the phone confused.

"Yes, but the phone lines in the office are down, so he left his cell phone for business use."

"Oh, okay, thank you, bye."

Myra started to hang up, then suddenly heard the receptionist yell, "Oh, wait a minute, Miss, he just walked in."

"Hello," Travis said in a rush.

Myra was so nervous she just came out and asked, "Travis, are you busy this weekend?"

"Myra? I don't have anything important to do. Why? Do you need me for something?"

"Um, you know what? It's nothing, forget it, Travis."

"Myra, I know you called me for a reason, so tell me, what did you want?"

"I was just going to my cabin for the weekend, and I was wondering if you were able to come with me, but you know what, it's not a good idea. So forget it."

"Wow, that sounds great, but why don't you think it's a good idea?... I wouldn't try anything if that's what you're insinuating. I do have a girlfriend, Myra. You can rest assured, I don't need to add any more drama to my life."

"I'm sorry. I didn't mean to imply anything. I just think our friendship should stay in its place."

"Now, Myra, you know better than to think this trip would be any more than just a friendly retreat. I got you, girl. Now, you want to meet me in the office in an hour? Here's the address."

Myra grabbed a pen and wrote down the address. They said their good-byes, and Myra continued to gather a few more things. As she brought her overnight bag to the living room, the kids rushed to her side, asking where she was going. Myra answered them, and immediately Trey and Princess asked to go with her. MamaD stopped them. Myra plopped down on the couch and explained to the kids she just needed a couple of days to rest and plan her next move to make them a happy family again. Even though they weren't satisfied with Myra's explanation, they gave her a hug and kiss good-bye. Devon, however, understood very well, so he gave Myra a peck on the cheek and told her to get a lot of rest. Myra gave everyone a hug one last time, including Cissy. Only Cissy looked at Myra suspiciously. Myra rolled her eyes at Cissy, then said she'd call her from the car. MamaD intervened and told Myra to make sure she stop to get gas, not talk on her phone while driving, and get her rest. Myra shook her head in agreement, then headed for the door.

As Myra got in the car, she played her Yolanda Adams CD, which almost always prepared her mentally, physically, and spiritually. She put Travis's address in the GPS and pulled out of the driveway. This was the first time she pulled out without touching the trash cans. And although she didn't notice, the kids did as they watched from the window.

The office was calculated at twenty minutes away, but somehow Myra made it there in ten minutes. As Myra pulled into the parking lot, Travis was standing outside with a small tote.

While opening the trunk, Myra asked him if that was all he was taking. Travis joked that only women overpack. Myra elbowed him, then they hugged and got in the car. Travis got in the passenger side with a pen and pad to make a list of what Myra wanted to figure out on this trip.

Travis first asked Myra to stop at a coffee shop so he could get some coffee, snacks, and the newspaper. Myra, of course, obliged, but warned him to not be a bossy passenger because she has low tolerance for being told what to do while driving. He smiled and told her he'd behave.

On the drive, Travis first took a nap. Then he read the newspaper. When he thought Myra was becoming restless, he offered to drive, but she refused. Instead, she preferred he would just talk to her. Appropriately timed, Travis pulled out the pen and pad again and began probing Myra about what she wanted to get out of this trip. Myra looked at him crazy, but she knew that was the kind of man he was. Everything pertaining to goals had to be structured. And although he wasn't as anal as Dee, Travis was just as organized, structured, and disciplined. Myra appreciated having people like them in her life, so she told Travis the first thing she wanted was some sleep. Travis agreed and wrote it down. Then he asked Myra about her plans to open the boutique.

Myra cut him off, saying, "Travis, you know I have to work out the details of Dee's law firm first."

"I know that, but I suggest you get your plans for the boutique on paper while you're figuring things out." Travis turned to a clean page.

"I appreciate your suggestion, but that's not how I do things, Travis. I have to accomplish one thing at a time."

"And who told you this? You're a woman—"

"What is that supposed to mean?"

"Women can do more than one thing at a time, so how is it you can't?"

"Travis, doing domestic chores and running errands are a no-brainer. But making business plans or negotiating business deals definitely takes a clear mind and undivided attention."

"Yes, but writing the plans down on paper are a no-brainer, too, especially since I have the experience."

"I get your point, Travis. So put down that I have to call Dee's partner for a meeting. Then you could put down some terms of conditions for me."

"Now that's what I'm talking about. Myra is back! I love it when a woman takes charge."

"Travis, you're retarded."

"Hey, whatever, as long as you are doing you, I don't care what you call me."

"Thanks for coming, I needed this push."

"No, I should be thanking you, Myra, for allowing me to be a part of this transition in your life. I love doing anything that has to do with the improvement of life."

And for the duration of the ride until they reached the cabin, they planned, talked, laughed, and cried. As they entered the cabin, the first thing Travis noticed was the 11 x 14 portrait of the family. He complimented it, then plopped down on the sofa, suggesting that was where he was sleeping, but Myra told him he could sleep in Devon's room upstairs. He smiled, then asked her what was for dinner.

Myra returned the smile and told him to order some food as she dropped the town restaurant menus in his lap.

The weekend was full of plenty of talking and planning, but at one point, Myra did break down at the thought of Dee not being alive to share in accomplishing her dream. She didn't see her life this way. And even though Travis was being a great support, it wasn't the same. On their last day, Travis made breakfast. then went for a jog. Upon his return, Myra was clearing the table. Travis began doing the same and, not paying attention, bumped into her, knocking the glass out of her hand. She bent down to pick up the pieces, but slightly cut herself. He ran to get a wet napkin and applied it to the cut. They looked at each other for a moment, then softly kissed.

*   *   *   *   *

"Knock-knock, I'm home … Hey, Mama," Myra announced as she crept in slowly.

"I hope you had fun, because I'm going home tomorrow," MamaD said, upset.

"What! Why, Mama?" Myra rushed behind her mother into her bedroom where she was packing her clothes.

"Myra, you told me you needed some time to think and reflect, not have a secret rendezvous with some old boyfriend." Mama looked at Myra in disapproval and in disappointment.

Confused by her mother's upset, Myra said, "What are you talking about? What makes you think I am having a secret anything, Mama?"

"Why else would you go with that man Travis?"

Immediately Myra thought to herself, "I can't believe Cissy told Mama. I'm going to have her head when I see her." Myra then took a deep breath and said, "Listen, Mama, I didn't go to the cabin to do anything other than what I said I would do. Believe me, there's nothing going on between Travis and me."

"So tell me, why is it, do you think you need a man to relax and so-call 'reflect'?"

"Mama, you remember Travis, he's been my friend for years. And he's the only one who could objectively give me his opinion and advice without being biased."

"Really, Myra, because the Travis I remember was the one that broke your heart; he was a player with a playboy attitude."

"Mama, that's in the past, he's a grown man, who's a father and a chief detective … He was also there to give me support and advice on what I was going to do with my life besides taking care of the kids and Dee's law firm."

"Well, I can't fault him for that, but you know, I do not like being lied to."

"I'm sorry, Mama, but I didn't exactly lie. I just didn't mention Travis was accompanying me."

"You just failed to mention your friend going, which is a secret that leads to a lie, Myra!"

"Hey, what friend?"

"Devon, how long have you been standing there?" Myra asked, looking as if she was a deer caught in headlights.

"I've been standing here long enough to know you went away with some friend that Grandma doesn't approve of ... So, who's your friend?"

"First of all, I don't have to answer to you, Devon."

"What! Daddy wasn't even buried a week yet, and you already hanging with some idiot."

"Devon, calm down! I'm not dating anyone. It was just Travis."

"What! You gotta be kidding me, Mama ... Anyone can see that dude is just playin' you."

"Devon, I am a grown woman, so stop it—and Mama, nothing happened, okay?"

"Well, it doesn't matter because I still have to go back." MamaD continued packing.

"Please, Mama, you can't go now ... I have a lot of stuff I want to do before you go. And you're the only one that can keep the kids in line while I get everything done. I need you now more than ever, Mama. Please stay." Myra put on a pleading face while laying her head on her mother's shoulder.

"Myra, I don't know ... I'll think about it."

"All right, peoples, I'm out, I'll be back later," Devon interjected.

"And where are you going? Just because your mother came back does not mean you can do whatever you want."

"MamaD, I haven't been out all weekend."

"So that means you pick up and go when you want without asking?" MamaD replied with a hard stare.

"Grandma, can I go to the mall?"

"No."

"Mama!" Devon blurted out to Myra, begging her to do something.

Myra intervened unconvincingly, saying, "Mama, let him go."

"Myra, hush. I said no, and it's no. And the next time you ask your mother to butt in, I will make sure you won't see the mall ever again. You hear me?"

"Okay, she's not having it right now," Myra mumbled as she walked away, throwing her hands up.

Devon tried to plead his case again. "Grandma, can I go to the mall, please? I don't have any work to do for school, my chores are done, and I washed up Trey and Princess."

After a brief pause, MamaD finally replied, saying, "Yes, but be home by six."

"What, MamaD! That's only two hours away," Devon complained.

"Well, then, I guess you really don't want to go," MamaD replied nonchalantly, but sternly.

"Oh, forget this … I'll be in my room." Devon walked away, angry.

MamaD didn't pay Devon any attention. Instead she continued to pack and talk to Myra. Myra started talking about the trip and what it did for her. She showed MamaD her to-do list and business plan. MamaD smiled with delight. Myra joined her, along with a hug. Just then the phone rang.

"Hello!" Devon answered abruptly.

"Good afternoon, can I speak to Myra?"

"Who this?" Devon asked with an attitude.

Before Travis could answer, Myra walked into the living room angrily, and with aggression snatched the phone, saying, "Devon, give me the phone."

Devon looked at Myra as if he had just been betrayed, then walked away replying, "Whatever, man, I'm out."

Myra looked back at him threateningly, then got on the phone, saying hello softly to Travis.

"Myra, I just called to see if you got in okay and to tell you I enjoyed myself at your cabin this weekend."

"Thank you, Travis. I enjoyed myself as well—although I did come home to some drama."

"What happened?"

"My sister told my mom we were together at the cabin, and she was highly upset when I walked in."

"Wow, your sister still has a big mouth."

"You know! Wait until I get her on the phone."

"Why was your mom upset?"

"She thinks I lied by telling her I needed to get away and not mentioning you coming with me, not to mention she thinks we're dating now."

"What! Are you kidding me?" Travis said as he laughed at the thought of even remotely dating. Myra joined him in a hearty laugh, then went on to ask him where he was. After saying he was home, he implied that Myra wanted to see him again. And before he could say another word, Myra calmly shot him down. She hung up the phone, then grabbed her jacket. Before walking out, Myra looked in the mirror on the wall behind the opened door.

Suddenly MamaD walked up to Myra and looked at her suspiciously. MamaD cleared her throat, making Myra jump.

As soon as Myra realized it was her mother, she went back to applying her lip gloss and said, "Mama, I'll be back."

"Where are you going now, Myra?"

"I'm going to Cissy's shop … I need my hair done for the board meeting tomorrow at the firm."

"All right, see you later. And be careful."

"Okay, Mama, bye." Myra quickly pecked her mother on the cheek, then walked out.

*   *   *   *   *

At the salon, the music was turned up loud, especially when Cissy was in a good mood. Simply being was cause for her happiness these days. However, Cissy's happiness would be cut short by Myra's attitude as soon as she walked in.

"Excuse me, Miss Cissy …"

"Myra, you're back; how was it?" Cissy replied in shock.

Rolling her eyes and talking with her hands, Myra said, "Don't you, 'how was it' me. How could you tell Mama I went with Travis?"

"Myra, you did that one to yourself."

"How do you figure?" Myra replied as she put her hands on her hips.

"Mama was trying to call you all weekend to see how your weekend was going. And to let you know Princess was sick. But when you didn't answer your phone, she questioned me. And you know, once Mama starts asking questions …"

After hearing Princess was sick, Myra immediately forgot about being upset with Cissy and cut her off to say, "Princess was sick! Why didn't she tell me this?"

"She had a short stomach virus, but I think she was missing you more than anything else. And why tell you when all it would do is make you want to come back home—especially when you needed the getaway?"

"Okay, so why did you have to tell Mama who I was with?"

"Myra, you know Mama, she kept picking, probing, and prying—and when that wasn't working, she gave me the look."

"Oh, my God, are you kidding me?"

"I kid you not. I felt like I was in high school all over again … If anyone should be upset, it's me."

"*You*! Why should you be upset?"

"Yes, because you put me in an awkward position. You could've at least picked up the phone and told me what to say. I mean, what were you doing that you couldn't pick up the phone?"

"Don't even try it, Cissy, nothing happened."

"Are you sure, because it definitely didn't look that way."

"Nothing happened, okay, Cissy?" Myra rolled her eyes.

"All right, but if I find out in nine months that something happened, you know I won't be happy."

"Trust me, if something happened, you'd be the first to know. Besides, no more babies are coming out of me."

After one look at each other, they laughed, then Cissy asked Myra what she wanted done to her hair. Myra told her what she wanted, and Cissy pointed her to the back. In the meantime, Myra's phone was ringing, and Cissy called her attention to it. Myra paused after noticing it was Travis. This was the last person she wanted to speak to in front of Cissy. Myra walked away quickly so Cissy wouldn't hear the conversation. Before sitting to get her hair washed, Myra answered in a low tone, "Hello."

"Myra, what are you doing tonight?" Travis rushed in to say.

Myra didn't know what to think, so she aggressively replied, "I'm not doing anything, why?"

"I have a friend who wants to meet you to—"

Upset at his response, Myra said, "Travis, I am not ready to date."

"No, Myra, this is about business. This guy has a lot of connections with fashion moguls. He happens to be in town for one day and free for the evening. And he's willing to meet with you and give the ins and outs about the industry."

"Are you serious? Oh, my God, I can't believe this. Okay, so what time?" Myra said in excitement.

"How's nine o'clock?"

"That's great. I should be done with my hair before then."

Myra went on to say her good-byes, but before she could, Travis cut her off and said, "Oh, and Myra, if there would be anyone I would set you up with, it would be me."

"Travis, you need to stop before you lose your girlfriend."

"Well, I don't mind, if you don't."

"Anyway, I'll see you later, Travis."

"Bye," Travis said hesitantly.

As soon as Myra put her phone down, Cissy said anxiously, "Who was that?"

Myra knew Cissy would make a big deal out of the phone call, so she casually said, "Oh, it was just Travis. He wants me to meet his friend, who has connections with a lot of fashion moguls, so I can open my boutique."

"Oh, really? Wow, well, that's one point for Travis."

"You need to stop talking mess and hurry up. The meeting is at nine, Cissy."

"All right, all right, but you know something, after all these years, Travis is still good-looking."

"Yes, girl, but he has a girlfriend, and I'm not ready to date."

"And I wasn't talking about you, anyway," Cissy said with a serious look on her face.

Myra jumped back in disbelief and said, "No, you didn't, Cissy."

"Relax, I was just joking, but you should've seen the look on your face." Cissy continued to laugh at Myra.

Myra, on the other hand, wasn't amused at all and replied, "Girl, please, what look?"

"Uh-huh, you know how you looked at me," Cissy teased with a nudge.

Myra cut her off and said, "Anyways, are you finished?"

"I'm putting the conditioner on now, as we speak … So, what are you planning to do, Myra?" Cissy asked inquisitively.

"Well, I'm planning to open my boutique for couture clothing; and through that, I will start drawing my own designs, make them, and sell them in the boutique."

"Now that's what I'm talking about …" Cissy gave Myra a high five.

Myra continued to give Cissy the info about Travis's friend who happened to know all the ins and outs of the fashion industry and who's who. Excited about Myra's plans, Cissy cut Myra off to ask her what she planned to do with the law firm. Myra went into detail about the meeting she intended to have with Dee's partners the next morning to sell out Dee's portion of the firm. Cissy went from excited to shock that Myra would think to sell—especially when she struggled over Dee's proposition for her to take over the firm. She went on to thank Travis for his meddling, which Myra called encouragement. Cissy expressed her happiness for Myra, and then asked what had changed to make her have this new go-getter attitude.

Myra smiled for a minute, "Well I received an eye opener this weekend from Travis. It was a blessing.

"Oh really, what's that?" Cissy asked in a serious, yet suspicious tone, as she walked Myra to her chair

Myra ignored her reaction and said, "All of these years, I've been putting my energy into everyone and everything else, instead of myself and what I want to do. And what did that do for me? …Nothing."

"True, but Myra, this is nothing new. You already knew that. I want to know what changed."

"Well it really came to me a few weeks ago, before one of the hospital visits with Dee; that I met with Travis and he reminded me – who I use to be."

"Wait a minute, you mean to tell me you've been talking to Travis longer than you told me?"

Myra rolled her eyes and ordered Cissy to stay on course. Myra proceeded to talk, explaining how Travis took her by the hand, figuratively speaking, and wrote step by step what her plans should be over the next few months to a year. Myra then shared they're accidental moment, but clarified no feeling from her erupted. Cissy, of course didn't believe her. However that wasn't something she was about to share with her. Instead she changed the conversation and started speaking about the biggest mistake women make when they get enraptured in a man. Myra, at first thought Cissy was implying that – that was what she was doing with Travis. Nevertheless, Cissy had to clarify her opinion, "What I'm saying Myra, is as soon as a woman gets married or even a committed relationship, she forgets who she is and her desires, and focuses on just being Mrs. So-and-So, 'Miss Wifey', or worse a 'Baby Mama' (without a life). It's redundant and ridiculous."

Myra looked at Cissy with the corner of eyes, "I'm sorry Cissy, but that's not completely true."

"Oh yes it is. I don't know too many women who are in committed relationships and doing their own thing without feeling at some point guilty of not paying more attention to their children or better yet their husband or man.

"Well, then, I guess you know all the women in the world," Myra said sarcastically.

"No, I don't, but name one woman you know that does it all or did it all without losing herself, Myra."

"Well, Mama's one and Aunt Lori."

"That's true, but if you know this, what happened to you?"

"Love. And that's what I'm about to do from this day forward—love myself."

"I hear that, Sis. Anyway, you're finished. And let me know how it goes with Travis."

"All right, I'll talk to you later … Thanks, Cissy."

As Myra entered her car, she pulled down her visor to freshen up her makeup and frizz up her hair. When she was done, she blew herself a kiss, then closed the visor and pulled off. Myra knew where to meet Travis, but had no idea if it was close or far. She put on the radio and heard "Heavenly Father" by Alicia Myers. Suddenly she began singing with the song:

I want to thank you, heavenly Father,
For shining your light on me.
You sent me someone who really loves me and not just my body.
I know it couldn't happen without you, oooh, without you …

As the song continued, she reminisced about high school, being in her senior year, and meeting Dee for the first time. She had a major crush on him, but, of course, never bothered to show it. Instead, she played it off as if she didn't like him, but somehow he knew she felt otherwise by the way she'd smile at him. This song was just as much her favorite today as it was then.

Ten minutes later, she pulled up to the restaurant, where there was valet parking. The parking lot was filled with high-class cars and limousines. At this point, Myra was impressed. Although she knew where she was meeting Travis, she had never been there. Myra was intrigued by the ambience and elegance of the décor. Myra walked into the entrance, and the hostess told her where to go.

As Myra looked around, she tried to find Travis. In her mind she thought he couldn't be too hard to find, being that he had a yellow/tan skin tone. Travis was average height, but built to perfection. He was muscular without bulk. He had deep dimples with average size luscious lips. And his eyes were hazel, like Myra's. She used to picture having children just like the two of them, only it made her laugh at the thought of them not having any color. Myra continued to look for Travis, and suddenly from afar, she saw a man waving his hand trying to get her attention. As she walked closer, she heard Travis calling, "Myra! Over here."

When Myra noticed him, she grabbed both of his hands and said, "Hi, Travis."

Travis, at this point flabbergasted by her beauty, said, "Wow, you look amazing."

"Thank you. So, where's your friend?" Myra asked as she kissed Travis on both sides of his cheeks.

Travis pulled out her chair, then said, "He's on his way, but what do you want to drink?"

"I'll just have some sparkling water," Myra told the waitress. As the waitress walked away, Travis tried to make conversation, saying, "So, tomorrow is the big day, huh?"

Myra looked around the restaurant, taking in the tranquil feel it had. From the turquoise dim lights, to the plush velour lounge chairs on one side of the room, down to the leather and smooth suede chairs at the carefully designed tables. After taking it all in, Myra took a deep breath and said, "Yes, I am planning on meeting with Dee's partners, and hopefully get them to buy out Dee's portion of the firm."

"You don't sound too confident, or should I say excited," Travis responded while winking at the waitress behind Myra.

"Wow, Travis, you couldn't be more obvious." Myra rolled her eyes.

"What are you talking about?" Travis gave the "dumb look."

"Oh, please, Travis. You're sitting right in my face, flirting with the waitress, winking your eyes. Give me a break."

"I'm not flirting, I was just letting her know that we needed her service."

"Yeah, right, sure. Anyways, I just feel like I'm not keeping my word to Dee." Myra changd the subject to avoid having an unnecessary argument.

"You're not keeping your word, but you are looking out for his best interests. He wanted you to wait it out with the firm until next year, so he could get recognized in the Fortune 500. At least you're doing that much—and quite frankly, that is enough. You have to live your life now."

"Hey, Trav." Suddenly they were interrupted by Travis's friend.

"Mike, my man … what's good my brother from another Mother? I'd like you to meet Myra, the friend I was telling you about."

Mike took a step back, holding his heart, then said, "Wow, she's beautiful, nothing like you described her."

"Excuse me," Myra said with an attitude.

"I'm just joking," Mike quickly replied.

"Don't mind him, he's a joker. You'll get used to it, Myra," Travis interrupted.

"So, you want to open your own boutique. What's your target market, and what level of fashion do you want to supply?" Mike got down to business, quickly putting the jokes aside.

Myra didn't know completely everything, but she didn't make it obvious. Instead, she stepped up her game and said, "Well, my target market would be women twenty-five years and older, any size or shape, and I want to see high-end fashion, you know, couture."

"I see, so you like high-quality clothes?" Mike asked.

"Yes, I've always liked quality clothes."

"Well, you definitely have the face and body for it," Mike commented.

"What does that have to do with anything?" Myra responded as if she had just been insulted. She didn't see what one had to do with the other.

Mike looked at Myra in shock at her blunt attitude. Being careful with words, he said, "Relax, I'm just saying the world of fashion is flaky toward women who don't have the look. And you have to come correct to even be recognized."

Myra leaned over with a look very serious and said, "Okay, but I'm not trying to be a model, so my look has nothing to do with opening a boutique or designing clothes. I've seen plenty of designers who do not have the look, but their eye for fashion is fierce. And another thing, I'm not getting into fashion because of how I look, I'm doing it because I like to look good and make other women look good, regardless of beauty."

"I see you mean serious business. And it's obvious you know fashion, telling by the way you're dressed." Mike changed his chauvinistic tone and addressed Myra accordingly, but at this point she has lost her tolerance and moved forward with her assertive attitude.

Myra then sat back and said, "Okay, so who do you know?"

"Anyone and everyone, I'm in fashion marketing."

"So you basically advertise for the popular clothing lines?"

"Yes, but I'm tired of it now. Right now, I'm looking to slow down and work on the inside of fashion." Mike winked at Myra, insinuating they should work together.

Myra, however, played as if she had no idea what he was talking about and said, "So, you were hoping you could work for me?"

Laughing at Myra's sarcasm, Mike suggested sweetly that he would like to work with her. Myra thought he meant as business partners, but he proposed that he market her boutique to the most famous couture designers, in turn receiving 20 percent of what she made in sales. Myra paused for a minute, then told him she had to think about it. Mike expressed his hurry to start this new venture and tried to convince Myra that her boutique could become an international franchise. Myra doubtingly asked if he really thought so. Travis cut in to explain that Mike was very energetic and a go-getter.

Myra told Mike to let her know what he could bring to the table, and in the meantime, she'd put her proposal together and do some research. She arranged that they would meet again in a week, giving them both time to have the information they needed to move forward. Mike handed Myra his card, and in exchange Myra called his phone so he could lock in her number. Mike then pulled away from the table to say his good-byes.

Myra shook his hand to seal the deal, saying, "It was nice to meet you, Mike—or is it Michael?"

"It's Michael, but you can call me Mike. And the pleasure was all mine. Have a good night."

"You do the same, Mike. And, Travis, I'll be speaking to you later."

Before Myra could leave, Travis held onto her in a hug and said, "Why are you leaving? Let's hang out for a little bit."

"Travis, you know I have an important meeting in the morning."

"Myra, please, just ten minutes."

"Just ten minutes, Travis. A girl needs her beauty sleep."

"Oh, stop! You know you're already beautiful, Myra."

"I know, but you can never get too much sleep at my age; so anyway, what's on your mind?"

"Nothing much, I just enjoy talking to you."

"Travis, that's what you have your girlfriend Jasmine for."

"I enjoy talking to her also, but we have a history, not to mention a chemistry that I don't think either one of us can deny," Travis said with a smirk on his face.

Myra chuckled to herself, then said teasingly, "History, we do have—chemistry, I don't think so, Travis."

"So you're not attracted to me?" Travis asked in disbelief.

"Travis, my attraction to you left in high school when you played me for that …"

"Don't say it, because I didn't play you—you told me not to call you anymore."

"Only after I caught you flirting. And with that being said, you definitely found someone else to call, permanently." Myra rolled her eyes at him.

"You can't still be angry at that, Myra. I was just a teenager, then. I'm a man now, and I don't think or act the same way."

"Travis, it's too little too late."

"Is it? Because I see something in your eyes."

"Yeah, sleep. Give me a break, Travis. You're not even my type."

"Oh, really, and what is that type, Myra? I have a job, I don't live with my mama, I can give you anything you want, and I know everything about you."

"A-ma-zing, you're right up there with God, only he's constant, and you're … Well, let's just say the only constant in your life is your ability to breathe, and even that can go at anytime. Travis, my husband just died. I'm definitely not thinking about dating right now. And if I was, it wouldn't be with you."

"Okay, well, I'm insulted. Why do you say that?"

"What about your spirituality, Travis?"

"Here we go." Travis shook his head in disagreement.

"Here we go is right. You know that's important to me, Travis." Myra rolled her eyes again.

"I believe in God, Myra."

Myra knew that was true, but she also knew he had a different lifestyle. She tried to think of a nice way to explain herself, but couldn't find the words, so she blurted out, "But I have a different walk from you."

"Oh, so, because I don't go to church, I'm a sinner, Myra?" Travis snapped.

Myra looked at him in shock, then snapped back, "No, because you don't live righteously makes you a sinner, Travis."

"Myra, don't judge me," argued Travis.

"I stand in judgment of no one. I just lost my husband, who was also my best friend, lover, and most importantly, my brother in Christ. So when I'm ready to share my love with a man again, he will have to be all of that and more to me."

Travis abruptly cut her off and said, "And that makes him better than me?"

Refusing to be nice as she continued to explain her feelings, Myra said, "No, that makes him the person who set the bar for anyone else who comes into my life. Listen, I enjoy your company, but a man of faith is important to me in a relationship, so can we just stay friends?"

"We can be friends; I mean, I do have a girlfriend," Travis responded, trying to play it off but Myra could see the disappointment in his eyes.

Myra tried to put a positive spin on the discussion by replying, "Well, at least you have somebody. You're doing better than me right now."

"You'll meet somebody, when you're ready." Travis stood up to excuse Myra from the table.

"I'll call you tomorrow after the meeting. Bye, Travis."

"Yeah, good night, get home safe."

*   *   *   *   *

The next morning, Myra drove her convertible to the meeting at the firm, her hair blowing in the wind while she listened to her gospel mix CD. As she pulled into her parking spot, she noticed the newly blocked parking space made for Mark Thompson. Myra looked in the mirror visor to fix her hair and makeup. Walking toward the building, she had the attention of the construction workers across the street and the security guard in the firm's entrance. She was wearing her Manolos stiletto heels with her black pin-striped skirt suit and a royal blue silk camisole. The skirt was just above her knees, but at her height, all they could see were her legs. Myra knew they were staring, so she walked with careful precision and confidence. She was never much of a shaker, being that her hips and behind always had their own language and didn't need the extra push. Plus, her mom always said, "Girl, when you're blessed with a body like ours, the only time you need to shake is when you dance. Otherwise, keep your moves to yourself." And Myra always did just that—only this time she was strutting herself, but in a ladylike manner. Today she carried a confidence that went beyond her looks. Today was about time. It was her time to have power, her time to have love, and her time to conquer fear, remove it, then make time for herself along with her passion for fashion.

As Myra walked into the office, Charles greeted her with "Good morning." Myra returned the same, along with asking him if everyone was in attendance. Charles hesitated to let her know that one of the key partners was not there yet, but continued to explain his absence, "Almost, Mrs. Harris. We're just waiting for Mark; he had an early deposition for one of our clients, but his secretary is here and she can take notes."

Annoyed, Myra sarcastically replied, "Great, so I called this meeting because I wanted to propose a buyout. As I told you in another meeting we had, at first I wanted to be involved with the firm for Dee's sake, and because I gave him my word I would stay until next year in his name, so that he is a part of the Fortune 500 goal. But as I see it today, I don't feel that is necessary, especially since this is his firm and he has already put his time in."

"I agree, Myra, but how much do you want?"

Without blinking her eyes, Myra said, "I want his half of what was already made and his name to continue to be part of the firm for our children's sake. In his name, I want 20 percent of the profit to go into a college fund for each of my kids, which I have already established."

Charles took a look around the room, then said, "That sounds doable. Let me get the paperwork together, and let's say by Friday morning, it will be ready for signing."

"Great, I'm glad we agree, Mr. Anderson. And by the way, I will be bringing my lawyer in with me on Friday; it's nothing personal, I just want to be sure everything I want is in writing."

"No problem, Myra. I wouldn't expect otherwise."

"Oh and Mr. Anderson, I want you to also include Mr. Harris in the article when you get printed in the Fortune 500 magazine."

"Myra, I wouldn't have it any other way."

"I want to thank you, Mr. Miles, for being so cooperative and considerate."

"Please use my first name, Myra. Dee was not only a business partner and a friend, but he was my family. And I consider you and the kids my family, too."

"Well, on Sunday, we're having the usual after-church dinner at my house, and you are more than welcome to come with Marilyn and the kids."

"It would be our pleasure, Myra."

"Okay, well, I'll see you guys then."

"Sure. Oh, what time?"

"We'll be eating at the usual time, five o'clock."

"Great, then we'll see you at five."

"Okay. Bye, Mr. Charles."

They pecked each other on the cheek and hugged, then Myra left. As Myra walked out of the room, the staff stared at her—which was nothing new being that she was the wife of the head partner at the firm. The staring never bothered Myra, and she wasn't about to let it bother her now—especially since she was elated with the idea of making her dream possible.

When Myra got into her car, she put her head down to pray, saying, "Thank you, Jesus. I have prayed on this, and you have delivered, as always. Lord, I have to say, I didn't think I could do this, but you showed me otherwise, and I finally see where you're leading me. I know now you have something greater out there for me. Thank you, thank you, thank you." At that moment on the CD, Myra heard one of her favorite songs come on. She thought, "Ooh, this is my song, it came at the perfect time. I've got to turn this up."

Great is your mercy towards me
Your loving kindness towards me
Great is your mercy towards me, day after day....

Myra continued to listen to the song on her short drive home. As she approached the red light, she had a flashback of her conversation with Dee on their honeymoon about their plans for the future. After his injury, all Dee would talk about was becoming a lawyer and one day having his own law firm. And Myra was all for it, but at the same time, she had her own agenda. She wanted to open her own boutique, and at some point sell her designs in it. However, having children took priority, and her plans had to be put on the back burner. At this point, Myra thought to herself, if only Dee were here to see me now. He would probably be proud, but aloof at the same time. Dee was okay with Myra's dreams—he just felt his career was more stable and less time-consuming. As if running a law firm is any more stable or less time consuming. All she knew was Dee couldn't be more wrong, but there wasn't ever a right time to bring it up for discussion—except for his hospital stay, and even then, he made a stink about it. But this was Myra's time, and nothing and no one was going to discourage her from accomplishing her dreams—not even Dee. Just then a tear rolled down her cheek as the cars behind honked their horns because the light had changed. Myra then drove off, crying at the thought of missing Dee and not being able to share this moment with him.

After crying for two minutes straight, Myra pulled into her driveway, wiping the tears from her face. She wanted to show MamaD it was time for a celebration. Myra pulled herself together, then walked into the door, shouting, "Mama! Mama!"

MamaD came walking out of the kitchen, saying, "Yes, Myra, why are you shouting my name? The kids are studying."

Ignoring her mother's snappy attitude, Myra replied, "I did it, Mama!"

"You did what, Myra?" Mama responded with a smile on her face. She always loved to hear when Myra or Cissy achieved anything, and this day wasn't any different.

"I found my way ... I went to that board meeting and asked for half of the profit of the business in a buyout. Dee's name will stay with the firm, so the kids will receive 20 percent of the profit, which will go toward their college fund every year until they're ready for college. And his partner is going to make Dee part of the article in the Fortune 500 magazine. They're going to talk about Dee's part in the development of the firm—just like Dee dreamed about."

"Oh, Myra, I knew you could do it—you just had to find your way through the Lord." MamaD hugged Myra tight to show how proud she was of her.

Then Myra pulled away to say to her mother's eyes, "And the Lord helped me there ... Words can't express what I'm feeling right now. Thank you so much, Mama, for staying to help me with the kids."

"Oh, please, child, it was nothing. You're my daughter. I just want you to be happy. Now, let me guess, you're feeling independent, free, and possibly excited about life."

"Yes, yes, yes ... Mama, go get dressed because we have to go to dinner and celebrate," Myra said in a rush.

"But I already cooked, Myra. You know I don't like to see food go to waste."

"Okay, well, how about on Friday after the meeting when we make it all official?"

MamaD smiled as she placed her hand on Myra's cheek and replied, "That sounds good."

After sharing a brief smile, Myra then giggled and said, "Well, I'm going to the shop to get Cissy, so we can celebrate tonight, because I feel too good to stay home tonight."

"Um, Myra, your sister went on a date."

"What! She didn't tell me about any date ... Man, I can't believe this." Myra heard the phone ring, but ignored it because of her disappointment in having nobody to celebrate with.

"Mama, the telephone, it's for you!" Trey shouted from the family room.

"Thanks, Trey!" Myra picked up the phone in the kitchen, then said hello.

"Hello, so how did it go?" Travis asked in a low but deep tone.

"Wow, I can't believe you cared enough to call."

"Why not? Believe it or not, I am interested in you finding happiness, even if it's not with me, Myra."

"It went great, Travis," Myra responded as if she had just lost her best friend.

"You don't sound like it went great."

"No, it's not that—I came home all excited and ready to celebrate, but nobody's available to celebrate with."

"So I guess I'm nobody, huh?"

"Travis, I don't feel right asking you to hang out with me when you have a girlfriend."

"Listen, if I don't mind, why should you? Meet me at the Blue Lounge in an hour."

"Are you sure?"

"If I wasn't sure, I wouldn't tell you to meet me, Myra. And besides, I'm not married, I just have a girlfriend."

Myra took a deep breath, then replied, "Okay, so that makes a big difference, Travis?"

"Look, do you want to celebrate or not?" Travis asked in an annoyed tone.

"I'll meet you in an hour. Bye." Myra hung up the phone, then saw Devon standing behind her in the reflection from the glass cabinet.

"Who's that, your 'friend' again?" Devon made sure to put a sarcastic quote around "friend" as he asked Myra the question.

"Yes, Devon."

"Damn, Ma, Daddy hasn't been buried for two weeks, and already you're seeing someone!"

"First of all, watch your mouth; and second of all, I am not seeing anyone. He just wants me to get a chance to celebrate."

"No, he's just pretending to be your friend, so he can hit that ..."

"Boy, hush, I don't usually go out and have fun, so why do you have to rain on my parade?"

"Whatever! I'm going to bed." Devon walked out of the kitchen abruptly, leaving his wind to blow the papers off the refrigerator.

"Mama, I'll be back," Myra said, ignoring Devon's attitude.

"Okay, baby, have fun."

"I will."

Just as Myra left, Devon appeared in the kitchen again and said, "Grandma, do you know she's going out with that man again?"

"Devon, stop being in your mother's business," MamaD replied.

"Her business is my business!"

MamaD rolled her eyes, then said, "Excuse me, who are you shouting at? Devon, you are her son, not her father."

"Yeah, well, I'm the man of the house now, so …"

"First of all, Devon, you're not the man of anything. You will be a man when you stop whining and let your mother live her life, instead of creating a problem where there is none. Do you want to see your mother by herself for the rest of her life?" MamaD replied.

"No, but why does she have to start dating so soon?"

"What makes you think she's dating him, Devon?"

"It's the way she sounds when they're talking on the phone, like if she's talking to my dad and …"

"Okay, stop right there. No one can come close to what your dad was to her … and what's wrong with her being happy again?"

"Nothing, forget it, you don't understand." Devon held his head down in annoyance.

"Devon, just be happy for your mother, like she is for you."

"Okay, Grandma, good night."

"Good night, baby."

*   *   *   *   *

Myra drove to the Blue Lounge at full speed. She mulled over what to say when she saw Travis again, knowing their last conversation wasn't pleasant. She wasn't sure how his attitude would be after letting him know in so many words he wasn't her type. As she pulled into the valet parking, the attendant paid her a compliment and winked his eye. Myra thought, *Please, don't even look my way. I have enough going on in my life,* but smiled politely, hoping someone would drive up behind her. That way, there wouldn't be an unnecessary cat-and-mouse conversation. At that moment, he asked her for her number. Before she could turn him down, another car pulled in, saving her wasted time. She told him she was running late, then walked away quickly. As she walked into the lounge, she called Travis on her cell to locate him.

"Travis?"

"Myra, I'm walking toward you. I have my hand up."

"Okay, I see you now." Myra closed her phone.

"You look nice."

"Thank you, you don't look too shabby yourself." Myra giggled at her corny, but sarcastic, joke.

Smiling himself, Travis pointed them in the direction of their table in the back. Myra commented on how nice the tables were set up as she mentioned she has never been in the back. Travis saw this as the perfect opportunity to mockingly say, "You mean to tell me, Dee never brought you here?"

"Please, we barely had time for family day, much less each other," Myra replied.

"Now why is it your husband couldn't find the time for you? I mean, you are beautiful, intelligent, classy, and so much more. I mean, I could never understand why men court the woman before marriage, but after, they stop spending time with her, then they expect the spark to still be there."

"Don't get it twisted, Travis, we had plenty of spark, just no time to ignite it," Myra snidely remarked.

"Exactly my point. Marriage or kids shouldn't stop the fun between couples."

"Is that why your marriage didn't last, Travis?" Myra continued with her attitude.

"No, Myra, but if you must know, she cheated," Travis replied with a slight attitude.

Myra was taken aback by this new revelation, so she said, "Oh, I'm sorry to hear that."

"Hey, no need to apologize. I'm happy now, but if you saw me about a year ago, then I would say you should feel sorry. It was a blessing to my life."

"How did you get over it?"

"I didn't, that's why we're divorced … I tried to stay, but every time I touched her, I didn't see her the same way—I just saw her differently."

"Wow …" Myra took a deep breath.

"But on a happier note, we're good friends, and even better coparents. And now I believe congratulations are in order for you." Travis grabbed his glass of wine.

"A toast to my future," Myra said in an excited tone.

Travis cut her off quickly to say, "Better yet, to our future."

"What, stop playing, Travis." Myra looks at him confused, but hoping he wouldn't try to make an advance toward her. She liked Travis, but wasn't about to start anything with a person not spiritually grounded.

Looking into Myra's eyes, Travis continued, "Who's playing? Myra, you are so beautiful and …"

"Wait a minute, stop, Travis! I told you …"

"Myra, let me speak. Since our breakup in high school, I always had you in my heart. And no matter how many times I tried to move forward with other people, I compare them to you. In the end, I wind up wishing I never lost you in the first place."

"Funny, my sister seems to think the same thing about me when it comes to you, but I don't think so." Myra spoke without confidence.

Seeing Myra's unsure belief in what she was saying, Travis got close and leaned in close to her face, saying, "Oh, you don't think so, why?"

There was a short pause as Myra took a deep breath again, then moved back in her seat and changed the subject. "Anyways, about today,

I put my offer on the table, and the partner agreed. We sign the papers on Friday morning."

"Why are you avoiding the question, Myra?"

"I'm not avoiding anything—I just think this is a discussion for a different time."

"All right, so let me hear the details." Travis gave in so he could hear the details of the meeting.

"Okay, so I'll be getting half of the profit thus far. Dee's name stays as part of the firm, and from that the kids will get 20 percent every year from the total profit. That, in turn, I'll put into their college fund. And to top it all off, Dee will be included in the Fortune 500 article, which was his dream."

At this point, Travis was sitting right next to Myra. He heard all she had to say, but still made a sensual innuendo remark that had nothing to do with the subject at hand.

He started to lean in closer, but Myra didn't move. He realized she had stayed put and went for her lips.

"Travis, *stop!*" Myra leaned back with hesitation. She loved feeling his breath on her neck and the touch of his hand around her shoulder, but Lord knows, she wasn't ready to explore kissing another man just yet. And although she was attracted to him, too, all she could think about was Dee.

"Myra, it's true; I'm so attracted to you right now. Humph, you smell good." Travis sensed her feelings of wanting more, so he gave her a peck on the cheek.

Myra found herself getting aroused, so she grabbed her purse, then said, "Okay, I have to go."

"Myra, wait." Travis grabbed her hand.

"I can't do this, Travis … I'm not ready for this."

"But—"

"I have to go, good night." Myra pulled her hand away.

"Let me at least walk you out," Travis pleaded.

"No, it's okay, I'll be okay, Travis." Myra walked away in tears.

"Okay, but call me when you get in," Travis said loudly, trying to speak over the music.

Myra got outside, and as she waited for the car, the attendant who hit on her earlier tried again to get her number. This time she didn't hold her tongue. She told him in so many words to get lost, but, of course, without being nasty. The attendant walked away, and her car pulled up. Myra got in and skidded off. She entered the highway at top speed, hoping to get home quickly so she could wallow in her tears. She just wished she had her husband back at this point. Myra couldn't see how she would find anyone like Dee. Travis was a good person, but he didn't possess what she needed in a man. She thought, if only he was a Christian, but there was no point. He was who he was, and transformation was the furthest thing from his mind. Myra pulled in, turned off the car, and walked quietly into the kitchen from the garage.

"You're back early," MamaD mumbled from the couch in the living room. Myra looked through the opening and said, "Mama, I need to talk to you."

"What's the matter, baby?"

"Is it possible for me to find love again? I mean, Dee just died, and I'm having a hard time trying to think about starting anything with another man—even though I'm attracted."

"Anything's possible, but are you sure it's love?"

"Mama, I get butterflies when I see him; and if he calls, I don't want to hang up with him. I'm not sure what it is I'm feeling. I mean, I think I'm in love with him."

"Honey, if you love the man, then go for it, but take your time. There's no rush. You have your whole life ahead of you."

"But my husband just died, how would that look?" Myra couldn't grasp what MamaD was saying.

"Who cares? It's not like you're getting married. You're just dating. And besides, who died, you or Dee?"

"But, Mama, he's not a man of Christ."

"Well, now, that's a personal preference, and an important one in this family. If you truly love him and you show him your walk, then maybe he just might come around. But I thought Travis was a Christian."

"Who said it was Travis, Mama?"

"Child, please, a mother knows, especially when you're swooning around the house when he calls. And let's not forget about your getaway weekend."

"I don't know, Mama. How can I accept a man who does not accept the Lord?"

"Myra, you are making too much of this. You're just dating the man, you're not starting a relationship with him. It sounds like you should be discussing this with him."

Just then the phone rang, and MamaD picked it up.

"Speaking of the devil … Hello?"

"Good night, Mrs. Lopes, how are you doing?"

"I'm okay, Travis, thanks for asking."

"Did Myra get in yet?" Travis asked anxiously.

"Yes, she's right here." MamaD handed Myra the phone.

"Hello."

"Hey, are you okay?"

"Yes, I'm okay. I'm in the house, right?" Myra didn't know what else to do but to be abrupt in her response.

"No, I mean are you okay, you know, with what happened earlier tonight?"

"I don't know, Travis. I don't know what to think or feel right now."

"Myra, I can't stop thinking about you … From the day I saw you again, you've been on my mind."

"It's been the same for me, but we're not compatible, Travis."

"Who says? I say we try. You never know, Myra."

"Travis, I don't want just a love, a friendship, and an attraction … I want a spiritual connection with you."

"Myra, I told you before, I don't have to go to church to be considered a man of God."

"No, but you have to walk the walk. You still drink, go to clubs, and not to be in your business, I know you're not celibate."

"First things first. I do not drink to get drunk, I just have wine on occasion. And I only go to high-class lounges, not a club. And although I may not be celibate, I am monogamous."

Proving her point of how opposite their spiritual beliefs were, Myra cut him off to say, "You see, how can I get involved with a man who's of the world?"

"Myra, let's be honest, you weren't exactly a virgin when we were dating."

"Excuse me! That was before I got saved, and anyway, we're not talking about me right now." Myra looked at the phone as if Travis could see her mean mugging.

"I disagree. I think we are talking about you. As a matter of fact, you are avoiding my question to date and take it one step at a time."

"Travis, you have a girlfriend." Myra threw it out there as if that would help her case.

"Yes, but I would give that all up for you."

Shocked, Myra changed the conversation. "Travis, are you going to Michelle's barbeque?"

"Yes, are you?"

Relieved he didn't push the subject, Myra said more happily, "I'm not sure … I want to, but it depends if my mother will watch the kids."

"You know she will … Why don't we go together?"

Myra rolled her eyes up, thinking *he just doesn't give up, does he?* She looked at the phone, then said, "Travis, you have a girlfriend."

"So? I don't have to go with her."

"I don't know, I'll think about it, Travis. I'll call you after the meeting tomorrow."

"All right. Have a good night and sweet dreams."

"Good night, Travis." Myra smiled at his last comment.

$$* \quad * \quad * \quad * \quad *$$

"Good morning," Cissy said loudly as she entered the kitchen.

"Good morning, Cissy."

"So, today is the day?" Cissy nudged Myra, then smiled.

"It is D-day," Myra smiled back.

"Have you thought about what you're going to do?" Cissy looked at Myra with a smirk on her face.

"I told you about my plans for the firm," Myra said as she continued to make breakfast. Then she looked back at Cissy, saw her smirk, and said, "Oh, you're talking about Travis. I guess Mama told you, huh?"

"Of course, she told me. What did you think I was talking about?"

"My meeting."

"Oh, please, girl, I want to know if you're giving Travis another try. You already know what to do about your plans."

"Well, I haven't decided yet what I'm going to do about Travis, but I know I want to take it slow ... you know, as friends."

"Good for you."

"Hey, what are you two talking about?" Devon walked straight to Myra to give her a kiss, then kissed Cissy.

"Devon, have a seat, I want to talk to you."

"Oh, boy ... what now, Mama?" Devon let out a sigh.

"Boy, hush ... You remember Travis?"

"Yes."

"I'm thinking of dating him." Myra stood by waiting to see Devon's reaction.

Devon looked down and said nothing for a few seconds. Then out of nowhere, he got up from the table and ranted, "Oh, hell, no ... you see, Auntie, I knew it."

"Did you just curse?" Cissy paid no attention to his point but gave him a warning look.

"I'm sorry; I can't believe this!" Devon paced the floor in anger.

"Boy, what are you talking about?" Myra said to Devon.

"You are actually falling into this man's trap." Devon threw back his head and covered it with his hands.

"Devon, there's no trap," Myra said abruptly.

"Oh, really? So, what did he tell you—you're beautiful, and he thinks you two can be more than friends, and let me guess, he can't stop thinking of you."

"Okay, first of all, your Mama is no fool," Cissy interjected.

"You could've fooled me," Devon retorted.

"Excuse me," MamaD stared straight at Devon.

Devon failed to see her demeanor as intimidating, so he replied, "Not now, Grandma."

MamaD moved toward him to set him straight, but Myra stepped in to say, "Listen to me, Travis and I have a history you don't know about."

"So you cheated on Dad?" Devon looked at Myra in shock.

"No, boy! He was my boyfriend before I started dating your father." Myra shook her head in disbelief.

"So? That doesn't mean anything, Mama."

"No, it doesn't mean anything, but I am interested in seeing where our friendship could go … and I like him."

"No, you don't, you're just lonely," Devon mumbled.

"Yes, I am lonely, but I like him, too, Devon." Myra saw how calm Devon got, so she walked over to him, putting her arm around him.

Then Devon moved away from her and continued his upset. "Whatever! You were just waiting for Daddy to die, so you can move on."

Myra stood in shock. She never thought Devon would say such a thing. And she didn't like it. So Myra walked over in his face and screamed, "How dare you!" Then she calmed herself down and continued to plead her case. "Don't you know that no one can take your father's place? He was the love of my life."

"Really, because you have a funny way of showing it … How can you even think about another man so soon?"

"Okay, listen to me, Devon, he makes me happy, happier than I've ever been in a long time, he supports me, and he is the only other man besides your father who I loved."

"Oh, so now you love him? Wow!"

"Devon, please, I'm not saying become his best friend, but at least be happy for me."

"Mama, I love you, but if you think I'll be all hunky-dory about this, then you got it twisted."

"Okay, as long as you don't disrespect him."

"As long as you don't bring him here, there won't be any reason to disrespect him."

"Devon, please."

"I'm out …" Devon walked out of the kitchen to go back to his room.

"I don't know what I'm going to do with that boy …" Myra put her head down in disappointment.

"Sis, let him be—he'll come around," Cissy said unconvincingly.

"Yeah, it's not like he has no choice." MamaD tried to comfort Myra.

Myra hugged her mother, then said, "I'll see you later, Mama."

"Have a good day, baby."

"Bye, Cissy," Myra nudged her lovingly.

"Let me know what happens!" Cissy blurted out as Myra continued to walk out.

"Okay," Myra shouted back.

* * * * *

At the firm, Myra walked to the head of the conference table, where Charles, Mark, and both their secretaries were waiting. First, Myra said her good mornings, then she introduced her lawyer, Mr. Doyle, to everyone in the room. A second later, Janice walked in, and Myra asked her to get coffee for both her and Mr. Doyle. Upon Janice returning, the meeting commenced. But before they started, Myra requested that they say a prayer. The partners agreed, so they gathered hands and Myra led them in a short, but powerful, prayer. As they all said Amen, Charles passed the agreement of buyout to Mr. Doyle for him to read over. Mr. Doyle began to read the agreement. And as he read it, he asked Myra if she had any last-minute requests. Myra explained her full satisfaction, then thanked the partners for their generosity and compassion. As Mr. Doyle finished, he asked Charles and Mark if they were fully satisfied with the terms of the agreement before they all signed. Both of them give him a thumbs-up, then Myra signed her name. The partners then signed their names. Upon completion of the meeting, everyone shook hands, then stood up to talk about more interesting topics, like politics, finance, and of course, sports.

Myra couldn't help but feel bummed out about Dee missing out on masculine-type discussions. Naturally he would have a lot to say. When Charles realized the expression on Myra's face, he walked over, then comforted her by reminding her about dinner after church on Sunday. Myra then smiled.

On the drive home, Myra called Travis to tell him she sealed the deal. The phone was ringing over and over with no answer. Finally, after the fifth ring, Travis picked up, coughing and sneezing as though he was dying.

"Hello, Travis?" Myra asked in confusion because he didn't sound like himself.

"Yeah."

"Ooh, you sound awful."

"Yeah, I have the flu, but how did it go today?"

"It went excellent, but why don't you get your rest, and I'll call you later," Myra suggested.

"Are you kidding? I've been waiting for your phone call all day, so tell me how does it feel to be an entrepreneur?"

"I'm not an entrepreneur yet, but it feels great to be independent."

"Well, I say from the moment you made the decision to do a buyout and start your own business, you became an entrepreneur."

"Okay, so I'll come over and tell you face-to-face about today. And I'll even bring you a bowl of soup."

"No, Myra, the last thing you need is to get my germs," Travis quickly cut her off.

"Man, please. I've been around all kinds of germs from my kids, so getting any germs are slim—especially when I already had my flu shot."

"But you need to get your research together to meet Mike on Monday."

"Why do I get the feeling you're pushing me off?" Myra asked aggressively.

"Myra, I'm not pushing you off. I just want you to get your work done."

"And I will, after I visit you."

"But you don't need to visit me now. You can tell me over the phone."

"Travis, if your girlfriend is there, just say so."

"Myra, if she was, I would, but you fail to realize that I don't need to be taken care of … I am a grown man who can take care of himself."

Not intrigued by Travis's admirable man speech, Myra got upset and said, "Yeah, right … Do me a favor, Travis. When you're finished playing games, call me."

Travis knew Myra's next move, so he blurted out, "Myra, don't hang up. Myra!" but it was too late. She had already ended the call.

Myra took the long route driving home so she could think about her next move. She knew she had to call Mike, the guy Travis connected her with. As far as the business plan, she was proud to say she finished most of it, except for the budget plan. That was something Travis was going to help her with, but now she felt compelled to do it on her own. Myra began mulling over what numbers were needed for the business plan. She knew she had to consider the cost of clothing racks, hangers, and mirrors, but the construction of the boutique was another bridge to cross. Myra had no clue where to begin to map out the look of the store. Although she hoped the broker for the store her mother saw would come through, she didn't get word yet. And this would be the icing on the cake—buying a place that was already constructed as a clothing store.

Just then her cell phone rang, and it was the broker to make an appointment to meet with her. Myra set a date and time, then hung up, screaming from excitement. She couldn't believe the owner was also interested in meeting her. Most times the sellers meet the buyers at the closing of the deals. But she could tell this was no ordinary person, but instead, extraordinary. This could only be God-sent. No one else could make all these plans go through all at the right time.

As Myra drove up the driveway, she called Mike. And when she got no answer, she left a voice mail message. "Hello, Mike, this is Myra. When you get this message, give me a call. I would like to meet you tomorrow at three. I'm thinking of a different location, maybe at the seaport. Let me know what works for you. Speak to you later, bye." Myra ended the call, turned off the car, and went inside the house. Upon entering, she caught Trey in the kitchen getting cookies. Looking like a deer caught in a car's headlights, Trey looked at Myra and said with his mouth full of cookies, "Hey, Ma, how was your meeting?"

Myra pretended to act as if she didn't notice and replied calmly, "Very good, Trey ... Did you finish your homework?"

Feeling relieved he didn't get in trouble, Trey turned his back to chew the cookies fast, so she wouldn't see them. Then he answered her question, "Yes, I finished my homework, but I still have a project to finish."

"Okay, so should you be sneaking cookies or getting the project done, Trey?" Myra squinted her eyes giving him the "you know better" look.

Trey smiled, then apologized for not asking and sneaking the cookies. Myra accepted his apology, but reminded him to not wait until the last minute to finish his schoolwork. She went on to tell him the same thing MamaD would tell her when she was in school, "If you snooze, you will lose, so do your part to get a fresh start. God helps those who help themselves first." Myra then leaned down and kissed him on the forehead. Trey ran off, chanting it over and over until he reached his room and closed the door.

"Hey, Sis, how was the meeting?" Cissy asked as she entered the kitchen.

"It was great," Myra replied in short, with a slight frown on her face. Suddenly the conversation with Travis entered her mind. And she just wanted to end their friendship so that she wouldn't get hurt again.

"So if it was great, why do you sound aggravated?"

"Nothing," Myra pretended to cheer up while pouring herself a glass of water.

"Myra, I know you—what's wrong?"

"I said nothing, Cissy." Myra walked away and headed for her bedroom.

Princess walked out at the same time and said, "Mama?"

"Yes, Princess."

"Can you help me get my pajamas on?"

"Sure." Myra was glad Princess threw off the badgering being done by Cissy.

"Uh, Princess."

"Yes, Auntie?"

"I need you to ask Grandma if she can help you, so I can talk to your mom, okay?"

"Okay, Auntie."

Myra couldn't believe Cissy sent Princess away just to find out what was wrong with her.

"Now, again, why are you looking so pissed?"

"I said nothing. Just leave it alone, Cissy."

"*No,* I'm not going to leave it alone … You are obviously upset about something, what is it?"

"Okay, fine, since you keep badgering me. I just fooled myself into thinking I could be more than friends with Travis, and I can't."

"Isn't it too soon to be considering a relationship? I thought you were just going to date and take it slow."

"Hmm, you think?"

"Come on, Sis, you know how Travis is." Cissy gave Myra the eye.

"You see, that's the thing. I looked at Travis and saw him differently. For the first time, he was being authentic and not just giving me lines, but genuinely expressing his feelings for me, but—"

"But then reality hit, and you realized he's the same Travis from high school."

"No. He's not the same, he's a better person. I'm the one that hasn't changed. I've always been the nurturer, wanting to take care of everybody and not myself. Here it is, I have everything working out for myself, and instead of staying focused on my passion, I'm thinking about winning his heart, with no regard for mine."

"Okay…?" Cissy didn't know where Myra was going with all of this, so she said nothing else and listened.

"Like when I spoke to Travis earlier, I offered to go over to bring him soup because he has the flu, but he said everything and anything to keep me from doing just that. I was going to tell him how the meeting went today while I fed him his soup. You know, to be there for him like he was for me, and he told me no."

"Okay, so was his woman over there?"

"That was my first reaction. He tried to say he can take care of himself—in so many words, then he says he knows how I am. He knew I had intentions on going over to take care of him."

"Okay, you lost me, what's the problem?"

"He's not like Dee … He doesn't need me waiting on him hand and foot—he's capable of taking care of himself. And he made that very clear on the phone."

"Shoot! That's a good thing, Myra … You want to start your own life, right? You don't need to turn into Mrs. Suzy Homemaker again."

"Right, but that's not all," Myra agreed with a smile.

"What now?"

"I realize that not only I haven't changed, but when I lost Dee, I didn't know what a real relationship was until Travis. With Travis, it's just not him taking from me, but him giving to me. And we're not talking material stuff either."

"Well, that's a good thing."

"I never experienced that with Dee. Don't get me wrong, he was a good provider, but that was all he was … Dee gave me what I needed and not what I wanted. And what I wanted was based on conditions. I can start my business after he completes what he's doing. I can have the money to start my business if I stay and work for his law firm for two years. I can spend time with him after he's done with his loads of cases. You know what I mean, Cissy—you've witnessed it."

"Wow, I see what you're saying."

"When I lie down at night, I think about Dee, but my heart is with Travis … All I do is cry, I get no sleep, and when I get sleep, I dream of Dee. Everything is always about Dee … I don't know how I can move on if I can't get Dee out of my system."

"Why are you in a rush to get him out of your system? I mean, I understand you want to move on, but why so fast?"

"Cissy! How am I ever going to get ahead in anything I want to do if I can't get past Dee's death?"

"It's only been two weeks, give it some time."

"I want to, but at the same time, I want to start over, I want to start my business, I want to be happy, I want to live again, damn it, I want to have sex …"

"Myra!"

"Please don't act surprised, Cissy. I haven't done anything in awhile, and I wish Dee was still here … I want Dee, I want to feel his hand going through my hair, caressing my skin and holding me tight." Myra started to cry.

"Come here, girl … It's going to get better. Tomorrow we'll go to the barbeque and have a good time, and I'll stay over tonight to keep you company."

"I don't think I'm going, Cissy," Myra mumbled. She knew Cissy wasn't going to accept her answer.

"Why?"

"First off, Travis is going to be there."

"And?" Cissy retorted with an attitude.

"And I don't want to see him … I just had a disagreement with him. I just don't want to see him right now."

"Listen, Sis, it's not like you're his girlfriend—he probably paid you no mind anyways … Come on, you need a day off to relax and hang out. Besides, we haven't hung out with our girls in a long time." Cissy gave Myra a gentle push, with a smirk on her face. She knew this always made Myra do what she wanted.

"Fine! I'll go, but I don't want to stay a long time."

"We won't. I'll see you in the morning."

"Where are you going?"

"I have a date with Lance."

"Hmm, that's the second one this month … We are serious, huh?" Myra said that to say Cissy had a habit of finding fault with her relationships. This was her way of protecting her heart.

"Oh, yeah, we're planning the wedding!" she replied as she walked out.

"Have a good time."

"Oh, trust me, I will." Cissy gave Myra the "I'm gonna get me some" look, then walked out.

Myra laughed and mumbled, "That girl is nasty." She changed into a nightgown, then put the TV on and lay down. A few minutes later, she dozed off. Then out of the blue, the phone rang. Myra jumped up out of her sleep, looked at the caller ID, then lay back down. It was Travis, but she wasn't in the mood to discuss anything with him. All she wanted to do was sleep, then work on her budget plan for the store. After the fourth ring, the answering machine picked up. Travis was first asking Myra to pick up as though he knew she was home. Then he went into a long, but unnecessary, speech about why he didn't want her to come over; which she had already heard when they were on the phone. He spoke so long that the machine cut him off. And she just chuckled her way back to sleep.

As Myra dozed off, she began dreaming of Dee. In the dream, Dee smiled and held his hand out to Myra. He told her that he missed her, then kissed her on the forehead. Myra dropped a tear. He gave her a hug and said he had to go, but that he didn't want her to be sad because he felt better. And all he wanted was for her to stick to her plans and continue being the great mother she was. Dee let her go and started to back away. And Myra cried out for him to stay. He told her she'd be fine and to make sure she finds love again. Myra woke up holding his pillow.

*   *   *   *   *

The next day at the barbeque, Myra wore her aqua-blue halter-top dress with her hair up in a ponytail and a swooped bang, and her snake-print Manolo sandals, which had a touch of aqua blue and earth-toned rhinestones. Cissy, on the other hand, had on her dark blue skinny jeans and sleeveless Bohemian top. It matched perfectly with her bronze-color skin. She also had on a pair of leopard-print Manolo sandals.

As they both entered the backyard, the men stopped and stared. This was the usual case with them. It was something about their presence that came across as charismatic and bold at the same time. This was also something they picked up from MamaD and her sisters. They always told them, "People treat you the way you carry yourself. So if you act like a lady, then that's how they will treat you. However if you act another way – then you better believe that's the kind of treatment you will receive."

Myra and Cissy found their way to Michelle's kitchen to say their hellos. Of course she was busy still preparing the food. As soon as they walk in, Michelle rinses off her hands and runs toward Myra.

"Hey Diva!" She hugs Myra tight. They stay that way for about two minutes as Myra starts to cry in her arms. She didn't realize how emotional it would be to see Michelle after Dee's passing, even though she was the one responsible for getting them together.

Myra and Michelle met in the tenth grade. They were in practically all the same classes. Although Dee was in the eleventh grade, he had a certain interest in the girls of a lower grade. They later concluded that it served Dee's ego better to be with someone younger. Michelle however, was a challenge to any boy at the time, whether young or old. It was one of those strange outcomes that don't normally happen. After dating briefly, Myra realized Dee wasn't her type. So Michelle thought Dee would be a perfect match for Myra, especially since she was the more passive/assertive type. And twenty years married definitely proved it was a perfect match. Whereas Michelle was an "independent/strong minded" young lady, who couldn't be bothered with the superficial involvement of a football player like Dee. Dee was all talk about his plans and himself. And Myra was the perfect listener.

As Myra and Michelle let go of each other, they share a smile. Then Michelle turned to Cissy, "So Cissy, I heard congratulations are in order."

Cissy holds out her hand to show off her ring.

"Oh my God! Somebody get my shades to block the rock that's blinding me."

"Chelle, you are so crazy!'

"Girl, you know you and Paul are the only two that still call me that?"

Paul was her husband, who was also part of the high school click. The ladies hug, then Michelle hands them each a glass of wine to toast to Cissy's engagement. After the toast, Michelle goes right into announcing Travis possibly stopping by. Cissy shrugs her shoulder and walks away. Myra doesn't show any emotion. But somehow Michelle could read into it.

"I hope you don't mind. But my mother would have my head if she found he's in town and I didn't invite him."

Myra and Cissy looked at each other and giggled. Michelle looked back, confused. The look alone let them know to explain what was so funny, so Myra stopped chuckling and said, "Girl please... you know its inevitable for me not to see him."

"Yeah, and what are you not telling me." Michelle flung the kitchen towel to her butt.

"There's nothing to tell … Anyway, we'll talk later, because he's walking this way right now."

"Hey, ladies, looking beautiful as always. Uh, Myra, can I talk to you for a minute?"

"Travis, this is not the time or the place," Cissy stepped in between to say.

"Cissy, I know you're concerned for your sister, but I would like to hear that from Myra."

By seeing Cissy's reaction to him, Michelle then folded her arms and mean mugged him, too.

"It's okay, ladies," Myra said.

"All right, don't say I didn't warn you," Cissy mumbled as Myra grabbed his hand and walked him outside. As he was walking behind her, he looked at her silhouette and smiled at the gorgeous view.

Before she left, Myra pushed Cissy and mumbled, "Be quiet, Cissy."

"What is that all about, Cissy?" Michelle asked curiously.

"I'll tell you later. Now, where's the real drinks?" Michelle pointed her to the refrigerator.

Meanwhile, Myra and Travis started walking down the hill in Michelle's backyard. She had about two acres of land behind her seven-room, three-bathroom mansion. Oh, yeah, her husband owned a landscaping company his father left him. As soon as they reached the gazebo, Myra sat down on the wooden bench and said, "Okay, Travis, let's not have a big discussion about what happened on the phone. What do you want to talk about?"

"Trust me, I wasn't, but it's interesting to me that you would even think that you getting upset on the phone would be of some great concern to me."

"Excuse me …"

"Listen, I'm not into playing games. I left that in high school, but it only behooves you to know that when I left my mother's house, I left being taken care of by any women. Now I thank you for having concern for me while I was sick, but I am not in the business of having women take care of me, I can do that on my own."

Myra started clapping her hands and said sarcastically, "Well, bravo, but I'm not in the business of being impressed by your self-sufficient yet insensitive ways … I thought I could come over and see how you were doing, but you were too busy being on your own, you didn't consider it as a friend helping a friend."

"Listen, I get that you were being a friend, but you just finished taking care of one man, you don't need to jump into taking care of another."

"Hold it right there. Taking care of my husband was a responsibility that I wanted to do; you are just a friend, who by all means I am not obligated or required to take care of. I was just being thoughtful. And, you know what, the thrill is gone."

"Oh, so, it's like that now? I didn't accept your help, and now you don't want to be friends anymore."

"Yes, it is, Travis. Because I realize now that I was fooling myself into believing you and I could eventually take our relationship to another level. But you're too stubborn to see who I am and allow me to be—"

Travis noticed his girlfriend walk in, so he cut Myra off, saying, "Well, then, I guess I'll be seeing you."

Myra was shocked by his response, but downplayed it and agreed, "I guess so."

"Listen, I'll call you tomorrow, Myra, my girlfriend is here."

Travis started to walk away when Myra said, "Yeah, uh, don't do me any favors, Travis."

Travis didn't bother to look at her, but replied, "Have a good time."

"Whatever! Your girlfriend is waiting."

Travis walked off, and Myra sat back down. She started to cry, but stopped herself. She felt there wasn't any point in crying when she knew all along it wouldn't work between them. For the rest of the night, Myra worked the room as Travis sat back watching. Myra made sure to flirt as much as possible and dance in front of him. Although she said she wasn't interested in Travis, her behavior said otherwise. Travis continued to look, but then became upset at one point when he saw the guy she was dancing with keep trying to pull her closer. Myra, of course, wasn't going for it and pushed the guy away a few times. Finally Travis got so fed up, he pushed the guy into the barstools on the deck. The man threw his hands up as Myra stepped in between to stop Travis from doing anything else. He looked down at Myra, swiped her hands away from him, and walked out without saying a word. Myra stood there feeling like she had lost another person she cared for.

*   *   *   *   *

The next day, Myra worked on her business plan some more. And Cissy helped her until Lance called her to come over. Myra made no big fuss, but knew she would now start worrying about Travis and how he was feeling or thinking of her. As Cissy walked out, MamaD walked in, catching Myra in a daze, looking worried. So she put her hand on her shoulder and said, "Baby, if you're going to worry, no sense in praying, and if you're going to pray, no sense in worrying."

Myra looked up at her, smiled, and said, "I know, Mama."

Then the doorbell rang. Myra got up from the dining room table, walked to the door, and yelled, "Who is it?"

"Travis!"

Myra thought, *Oh, my God, what is he doing here?*

MamaD signaled to Myra she'd be in the yard with Trey and Princess, then told her to open the door.

"Travis, what are you doing here?" Myra looked him up and down, thinking, *Oh, my God! He looks so fine.* He was wearing a navy blue velour sweat suit with a white wife-beater T-shirt underneath. And his chest looked very much buffed.

"Hey, Myra, I was thinking about you all day. I tried doing a lot of things to get you off my mind, including jogging, but here I am."

Myra was happy to see him, but gave him the cold shoulder. "Oh, really, how convenient, since you didn't think about me yesterday at the barbeque."

"Are you serious? I can't believe you're acting so upset when you told me we wouldn't work. But let's not get into all that." Travis grabbed her hand.

"Travis, I don't have time for this right now, what do you want?" Myra pulled her hand back.

"I want to know why you're so angry."

"Okay, now, either you're just playing ignorant, or you truly don't have a clue how to deal with women."

"No, I don't have a clue on how to deal with you."

Myra looked at him, saying to herself, "I can't believe he just said that." Then she folded her arms and began telling him about himself. "First you call it putting me in place with your self-sufficient bullcrap. Then you act like you care about me and who I am. You can't even accept my natural way of being a nurturer. And to top it all off, you invite your girlfriend to a barbecue you just asked me to attend with you. And now you come here acting like something is wrong with me. How dare you!"

"So I guess you're upset." Travis put on his baby smile. Myra rolled her eyes. Then he said, "You mean to tell me if Dee had walked into the barbeque, you would've stayed talking to me and not acknowledged him?"

"No, I would not continue to talk to you, but then again, I wouldn't invite him to an event after asking you to accompany me. But what I am saying, it's you we're talking about. I should've not expected you to do anything differently."

"See, that's the thing, why are you setting any expectations at all?… It seems to me if you want to have happiness, then you would create it apart from what you expect from anyone or anything in life."

"So, you're the authority on happiness now?" Myra rolled her eyes at him.

"Look, I'm not an authority on anything, I just know that the person I choose to be with has to love herself enough to not set any limitations, concerns, or expectations … I mean, isn't that what the word teaches you?"

"Oh, don't even try to go to church on me now. After you just finished telling me the church is of no interest to you."

"I was talking about the Bible, but since you insist on saying I'm not saved, sanctified, and holy, was it not you who told me church can be anywhere?"

"Oh, so you have all the answers today," Myra replied with an attitude.

"No, I just know what I want, who I want, and I'm not afraid to say it's you." Travis bent down to make eye contact as she held her head down.

Myra looked at him, giggled, and said, "Travis, if you wanted me, you would meet me halfway."

"Halfway, where, Myra?" Travis threw his hands up, looking around in a joking manner.

Myra got upset again, then said, "Look, forget it, I'm not ready for a relationship with anyone."

"Even me."

"Especially you," Myra replied as she looked at the ground.

"Look in my eyes and say it."

"Travis, leave me alone."

"No, I want you to look at me and say it." He gently pulled her chin up.

"Travis, stop!" Myra moved his hand and looked back down.

"Look in my eyes. I mean, if you truly want me to leave you alone, then saying it to my face should be a snap." He leaned down again to see her eyes.

Myra covered her face as she said, "I don't want … I don't want … look, this is stupid."

"Hmmm, hmmm, that's what I thought." Travis started giggling while putting his arms around her. Myra stood there for a minute, enjoying his embrace. But as soon as she felt herself enjoying it too much and he had dodged the topic at hand about his spirituality, she pushed him off and said, "Okay, you have to leave."

"Why you keep pushing me away? What are you scared of?"

"I'm not scared of anything—I just know this is not going to work."

"Myra, you don't mean that."

"Yes, I do, now go please before my kids come back in." Myra stepped back into the doorway and waited for him to leave.

But instead, Travis stood there replying, "Myra, please—"

Cutting him off, Myra replied, "Travis, it will never work, now go."

"Why, because I know you too well?"

"No, because I don't ..." Myra paused, looking to see if the kids were coming in.

"You don't what, Myra?"

"I don't know how to be in a relationship with a man like—"

Travis cut her off. "Myra, you were married for twenty years."

"Yeah, but it was different. We had a spiritual connection."

Travis nodded his head in disappointment and said, "So, we can take it slow ..."

"No, I'm not ready ... please, just leave it alone and go." Myra grabbed the door.

Travis looked at Myra with tears in his eyes and said, "Okay."

Noticing his eyes whelping with tears, Myra said, "I'm sorry, Travis."

"Call me if you need anything."

"Yes, okay, bye."

"Can I get a hug?"

"One," Myra held up one finger.

As he hugged her, he whispered in her ear, "Myra, I could hold you all night."

"Okay, Travis, let go ... Let go, Travis." Myra pried his arms from around her.

"Whatever you do, I wish you the best." He gently rubbed her cheek.

Feeling uncomfortable with his touch, Myra looked back again as she said, "Thank you, you too, Travis."

"Bye, Myra."

"Bye."

Myra hurried and closed the door, then walked quickly to her bedroom. She shut the door and held her mouth as she wept. She was crying because she couldn't have a relationship with her first love again. Myra slid down to the floor and stayed crying until it was time to go to bed. She never knew this would have such a big effect on her, but it did. And even though the kids hadn't gotten to know him, they were getting used to hearing his name. Devon didn't want her with anyone, no matter what. Of course, he wasn't over losing his father. Myra always loved Travis. He wasn't superficial; although he thought Myra was very beautiful, he saw more to her. When she was around him, she talked for hours about everything and anything, especially about herself. Ever since high school, he would listen to her talk for hours without mentioning a thing about himself. They spoke at length then as well as now. The only problem they had was the perfect denominator, their spiritual connection. Being raised a Christian, there was no doubt in her mind that if Travis couldn't share in the same foundation, they wouldn't last.

Finding Love Again

༄

One Year Later

"Okay, Mike, so what's the plan for tomorrow?" Myra asked her marketer while sitting in the boutique.

"Well, Mr. Venucci is coming in to show off his designs at two. Then Ms. Santiago from Venezuela and designer of Tan Bella is coming to show her fall line of fit jeans at three."

"Okay, great. Well, let me start clearing some racks, and you can call the boutique in Paris and tell Mr. Frantz we need an inventory printout by tomorrow morning."

"I sure will. Wow, I knew we would do great together. I mean, look at you, making *Allure* one of the most popular couture boutiques here and abroad."

"Oh, please, I couldn't have done it if God didn't bless you into my life. Oh, and Mike, I need a ..." Myra turned back but stopped short as she saw him standing there, looking strikingly handsome.

"Excuse me, can you tell me where I can find a sexy dress for my future bride?" came a voice from the front of the store.

Just then Mike came from the back and said, "Myra, what did you say you nee—" He stopped dead in his tracks and looked in shock at Myra and Montel on his knee.

"Montel, what are you doing?" Myra whispered.

"Myra, this past year has been incredible. You walked into my life and changed my heart; you brought me happiness again. And so I'm asking that we continue to be happy, together. Myra, will you continue to make me the happiest man in this world and marry me?"

Myra put her hand over her mouth as she looked at the two-carat princess cut diamond ring with three one-carat white diamond stones on each side. A tear fell from Myra's eyes as she said, "Montel, I don't know what to say."

"Say yes, girl," Mike nudged her.

"Yes," Myra said.

"Yes?" Montel asked, unsure if she was answering him or repeating Mike.

"Yes, Montel, I'll marry you."

"Yes! She said yes … Okay, okay … oh, my God, I can't believe you said yes … so I guess we should tell the kids together." Montel grabbed Myra and lifted her up off the floor.

"Uh, how about you leave that to me?"

"Okay, let's have a celebratory dinner tonight."

"Okay, how's seven?"

"Okay, seven, seven it is … I'll see you later … Oh, and Myra, I love you."

"I love you, too, baby."

"Wow, you're getting married, girl," one of the employees said.

"I know … I have to call my mother and sister."

Myra picked up the phone and called Cissy first.

"Hello, Celestial Hair."

"Cissy?"

"Myra?"

"Yes, you are never going to believe this."

"What?"

"I'm getting married."

"What?" Cissy heard her, but couldn't believe what she was hearing.

"I'm getting married."

"I heard you ... I just can't believe you're doing this."

"Doing what, Cissy?"

"Why are you getting married so soon?"

"Celeste, I have been with Montel a whole year, and I love him."

"Yes, but you said it yourself you're not in love with him."

"Yes, I did, but I realize I'm happy with him, and that's what's important."

"Is it? When you were with Dee, was it just happiness that kept you two together?"

"No, but I will never have a love like Dee again, and I'm not willing to hold my breath on it, either ... Now, can you be happy for me?"

"Don't get me wrong, I'm happy for you. I just want you to be sure."

"Well, I'm sure."

"Have you told Mom yet?"

"No, I'm going to call her now. And by the way, we are celebrating tonight."

"Okay, what time?"

"We're meeting at the Blue Lounge at seven."

"Okay, so I'll see you then."

"Okay, bye."

Myra ended the call, then quickly called her mother.

"Mama." Myra was so happy she picked up.

"Hey, Myra, how you doing, baby?"

"Great, Mama, Guess what?"

"What, sweetheart?"

"Mama, I want you to guess."

"Myra, I can't remember what I was supposed to do two minutes ago, and you want me to play guessing games now. Please, tell me your surprise, girl."

"I'm getting married."

"Oh, really? Well, are you ready for that?"

"Why is everyone asking me that?"

"Well, I'm not everyone, I am your mother, and I'm more concerned about your true happiness than some run-by-night wedding. Don't you remember, I asked you the same thing when Dee proposed to you?"

"Yes, Mama, but I'm very happy."

"Okay, but how do you define happy, Myra?"

"Mama, there's nothing to define. I'm just happy."

"Baby, I just want you to continue to make wise choices, rather than settle for a lifelong decision that could end up regret."

"I will, Mama, I will. Anyways, we're celebrating tonight at the Blue Lounge, at seven. Can you come?"

Slurring her words in an unenthusiastic way, MamaD replied, "I'll be there, with bells on."

"Thanks, Mama."

"See you later."

"See you." Myra hung up the phone.

*   *   *   *   *

A couple of hours later, Myra arrived at the house, anxiously waiting for the kids to get home. She quickly put her preseasoned chicken in the oven, started steaming the vegetables, then jumped into the shower. The time was passing fast, so she made sure to get in and out. Once she was done, she put on her Baby Phat jeans and a T-shirt. After she was dressed and applied her makeup, Myra started playing with her hair. She had run out of ideas for her hair. Her hair was long, and she grew tired of wearing it down, in Shirley Temples, and in a bun. It had been the same way for too long, and it was time for a change. There was no time like the present.

Montel was not as quite as distinguished as Travis, but he loved the Lord. He was average height, with a cute smile and a lot to offer. He owned a real estate company in Washington DC, which was thirty minutes away. His children were older, so he had no baby Mama to really answer to. And best of all, he had some nice qualities, although he could be somewhat overbearing with his need to take care of her. If he wasn't reminding her of what was or wasn't healthy to eat, then he was always giving unwanted advice on anything from the kids to her business and any situation that would come up. In some ways, he reminded her of Dee. Only Dee was more self-consumed. Montel would give her and the kids anything they asked for all of the time.

Myra looked at the clock on her nightstand after realizing the kids should've been home already. She entered the living room and paced the floor. One would think she was wondering about them, but in actuality, she was trying to figure out how she was going to break the news of the engagement. She went over a speech several times, but nothing would prepare her for when the kids finally arrived home.

"Mama, we're home," Devon mumbled in a low tone, thinking Myra would be upset about their being late.

Nervously, Myra smiled and said, "Hey, you guys, how was your day?" Myra greeted them with a hug.

Devon was worried until he saw his mother's behavior. He knew something was up, so he plopped down on the couch and said, "What's up?" with a serious look on his face.

"Well ..." Myra started fiddling with her fingers. "Okay, first, I want to know, do you guys like Montel?"

Trey and Princess looked at each other, then they looked at Myra, simultaneously saying, "Yes."

Devon didn't say anything, but rolled his eyes up and blurted out, "Oh, boy, where are you going with this? Because I hope you're not planning to move him in here."

Myra became frustrated with his attitude, then realized he was just being overprotective. "Now, Devon, why you have to be the one to go there?"

"'Cause, man, I mean I don't have a problem with him, but our house is full enough," Devon hissed and looked down, shaking his head in disappointment, as though he already knew her next response.

"That's not what I wanted to talk to you about anyway. Besides, Devon, our house has the same amount of people, with the exception of your father."

"Exactly, and it should stay that way."

Myra realized in that moment Devon had gone from overprotective to just plain territorial. In one year.

Devon huffed angrily then said, "Anyway, Mama, what do you want to talk about?"

Myra hesitated, then she slowly said, "Well, Montel asked me to marry him, and I—"

Before Myra could finish, Devon shouted, "Oh, come on!"

"Devon, shut up, let Mom speak," Trey screamed out in Myra's defense.

"I said yes."

Devon jumped up, swinging his hands, blaring, "I knew it … I knew it … You know what? I'm leaving anyway, so it doesn't matter."

Myra turned her attention to him. "Devon, that's not the point, I want you guys to be okay with it." After she didn't see Devon giving in, she turned back to Trey and asked him what he thought.

"I don't know, Mama, I guess that's good."

Myra looked up and mumbled, "Princess?"

"I like him, but do you have to marry him?"

"All right, what's up, you guys? Why are you guys acting as if you don't like Montel?"

"I like him, but I'm just not ready for him to be my father right now," Trey said quietly so as not to anger Myra.

"Oh, Trey, he could never be your father. And no one can ever be your father, Princess."

"But what will we call him?" Princess asked with an innocent look on her face.

Devon hissed again and said, "You call him Mr. Montel! What else? That's his name."

"Devon, please, you're making this impossible. You'll never be happy to find me with anyone, so just stop." Myra sternly stared at Devon.

"No, I'm not happy to see you with Montel!"

"Why?" Myra pleaded with Devon.

"The man tries too hard; no man is that nice unless they're up to something."

"Well, he's not, Devon."

"So you know everything now?"

"No one can really know everything, Devon. But I know he cares about you guys a lot. And you know what I think? You guys need a day together to hang out alone, just the guys."

"Mama, I've been around him enough."

"But you don't know everything about him."

"Exactly my point, Mama. You've been dating him almost one year, and all I know about him is that he loves the church, looking good, and just happens to like everything we like. Give me a break. Sorry, but I'm not interested."

Myra knew she couldn't convince him, so she changed the subject and said, "Yeah, well, we're celebrating tonight, so—"

"So that means nothing to me," Devon cut her off. He was angry at the fact that even though she was asking their opinion of him, she had already made her decision. Trey felt otherwise, but had only one concern.

"Mama, I want you to be happy, but I don't want to move."

"Who says you have to move, Trey?" Myra gently rubbed his face.

"Montel lives too far away, and I like my school here." Trey looked up at Myra with tears in his eyes. As a tear rolled down his face, Myra wiped it, then said, "Trey, we're not moving."

"So he's moving in with us?" Princess quickly asked.

"Of course, I would never bring you guys out of your element, so get that out of your head."

"So what are we going to do with Daddy's stuff?" Princess then asked in wonder.

"What stuff, Princess?"

"His clothes. His office has all of his things in it. Where are we going to put it?"

"It's just office things; we can move them to the basement."

"No, you can't!" Devon jumped right into the conversation.

"Okay, Devon, don't yell. The stuff can stay there; I need a home office anyway."

"Mama, don't get married … I'm happy with everything like this," Princess said in a low tone.

Myra looked at her with a smile and said, "You know what? How about we talk about this another time? I'm going to Aunt Cissy's shop. And Grandma is on her way to stay with you guys."

"Bye, Mama!" Trey and Princess shouted.

"Bye, you guys, Devon, please give them dinner." Myra grabbed her bag and walked to the garage.

"Okay, Mama."

*   *   *   *   *

At the shop, Cissy was finishing her client's hair when Myra walked up and said, depressed, "Hey, Celeste, give me a wash, set, and cut, please."

Cissy looked at her weird. She knew something was wrong, so she said, "Well, you don't sound like a person getting married."

"Well, I don't know how that can ever be possible when the kids aren't exactly excited about it." Myra let her hair down out of a ponytail.

"Oh, Sis, I'm sorry. What, Devon has an attitude?"

"Humph, not just him, all three of them are not happy about the news."

"Oh, Myra, don't worry about it, they'll come around. They just need more time to adjust to the idea."

"I guess."

"What do you mean, you guess? Are you sure you want to marry Montel?"

"Yes, I mean no. I mean I don't know. I'm not comfortable with the idea of marriage if my kids aren't."

"That's understandable, but why are you making the kids the reason why you're doubting marriage?"

"Because whatever decision I make for myself, Cissy, will affect them. And I'm not about to destroy everything I put into the kids for the past year, just for the sake of having a husband in my life."

"I hear that, but at the same time, you can't make that the only reason why you're not comfortable with getting married. If you really love someone, you make adjustments, especially when it comes to choosing a man to be in your life."

"I don't know. There was something not quite right when I asked them how they felt. Not even Trey was happy, and you know he goes with the flow with everything."

"Myra, they have been around Montel for a whole year. He's a Christian brother with a great heart, and he cares for the kids a lot."

"Yes, but why are they so uncomfortable if he's so great?"

"The bigger question is, why are you so uncomfortable?"

"What do you mean? I'm fine."

"Myra, when you love someone, it's a sure thing. No one or nothing can make you think twice. Not even the kids. Now, how short do you want your hair, girl?"

Myra looked in the mirror, then said, "I don't know; give me a bob." Cissy gave her a crazy look, but grabbed the scissors anyway.

"That's another thing. Since I've been in close relationship with the Lord, I haven't received confirmation yet to get married. I don't know. All I can do is pray."

Cissy agreed, then showed Myra her new hairdo. Myra smiled from ear to ear. She fiddled with her bangs a minute, then gave Cissy a tight hug. After they hugged, they said their good-byes until they would meet later on at the Blue Lounge.

Cissy closed the shop and rushed home to get ready. Outside of her apartment, there was a bouquet of flowers with a card, which read,

"Roses are red, violets are blue. I can't wait until you become Mrs. Redding, too. XOXO, Love, Lance." Cissy smiled.

*   *   *   *   *

"Mama, I'm home, and I hope you're read—Mama! Why aren't you dressed?"

"Because I'm not going."

This was the last thing Myra needed. She was already second-guessing herself. And now MamaD wasn't going to go.

"Why?" Myra followed her to the kitchen.

"I'm not up to it, baby, but I'll stay with the kids."

"Are you sick, Mama?"

"No, I would just like to stay home. You know I don't like all of that loud music. But I'll make a nice dinner on Sunday, and we can celebrate then."

Myra wasn't exactly happy that her mother wasn't going, but at least she offered to cook for Montel on Sunday. "Okay … Um, I'm going to get ready."

"Well, you better hurry up, because it's six o'clock now. And, Myra,…"

"Yes, Mama?"

"Your hair looks nice."

"Thanks, Mama. And, Mama, please say a prayer for me."

"Baby, I always pray for you."

"I know, but I'm back-and-forth with the idea of getting married."

"Well, first of all, it's only an idea if you were just talking about it, but you're not. You're engaged. And secondly, when you are in love, there is no back-and-forth. Did you feel this way with Dee?"

"Honestly, at first I did, but then I realized he truly loved and cared for me. I wanted to marry him, but of course, I didn't have to worry about involving the kids. It was just about us."

"Sweetie, I know you want to make sure the kids are part of your decisions, but don't fool yourself into thinking that your decisions are contingent upon the kids. It's what God shows you and tells you. It's what's in your heart. 'Uncertainty only leads to unhappiness,' so go to the Lord and ask for his guidance in your decision and let that be your answer, instead of struggling with it by yourself; and remember, 'out of the heart, the mouth speaks,' so those feelings you're talking about come from your heart. Listen to them."

"Thank you, Mama." They gave each other a hug and kiss.

"Now go and have a good time, baby."

"Okay, Mama."

Myra went to her room to change. She put on her form-fitting red dress and her favorite red sling-backs.

*　　*　　*　　*　　*

At the Blue Lounge, Cissy sat patiently waiting for the happy couple to show. She was also wondering why Lance pulled out at the last minute. It was kind of unusual, but she didn't have the gut feeling of him doing something wrong. He was a contractor, so his jobs could go on to well into the night. As soon as the waiter came and asked for her drink of choice, she saw Montel.

After telling the waiter to bring her an apple martini, she shouted, "Hey, Montel, over here."

Montel walked over, saying, "Celeste, you look good."

Cissy laughed, replying, "I know. Where's Myra?"

"You mean she didn't get here yet?"

"No, but that's okay because I have to talk to you." Cissy smiled to ease his discomfort.

"What do you need, Cissy?"

"Why do you always assume people need anything from you? I don't need a thing from you, but to know exactly what are your intentions with my sister. Because she's come too far for her to not be happy." Cissy sipped on her martini, giving him a minute to respond.

"But she's happy with me."

Cissy leaned forward, saying, "The question is, 'Are you happy with her or with the thought of being with her?'"

"They're one and the same, Cissy. What are you getting at?"

"I'm not getting at anything. I just want to know what are your intentions."

"Well, my intentions are that your sister be taken care of with every fiber of my being. And that being said, your sister just walked in." Montel smiled as she walked up, so she wouldn't think they were having a heated discussion.

"Just make sure you do what you say," Cissy managed to squeeze in before Myra reached them.

"Hey, guys," Myra kissed Montel on the cheek.

"Myra, you look beautiful as always. Baby, you cut your hair. It looks good, but I thought you liked your long hair."

Myra noticed his fake smile, but refused to make a big deal in front of Cissy. So she gave him another kiss, this time on the lips, then said, "Thank you, baby, and you look sharp yourself. Hey, Sis, I hope you're ready to celebrate. Where's Lance?"

"Oh, he had to work late, but I'm definitely ready to party." Myra checked her forehead because typically Cissy would be upset and frowning. But this time, Cissy didn't seem bothered.

"What do you want to drink, sweetie?" Montel asked Myra.

"A glass of white zinfandel would be fine."

"Wow, don't you think that's a bit much?"

"You asked me what I wanted to drink, Montel."

Cissy looked like "Oh no he didn't", as if Montel was out of line to question what Myra was drinking, then took another sip of her martini.

"Yes, but if you're driving, Myra, having wine is not a good choice."

"Montel, I hardly think one glass of wine is going to inhibit my capacity to drive."

"Okay." Montel started to head for the bar.

"Oh, can you get an order of buffalo wings, also?"

"It's after seven o'clock, Myra."

"And?" Myra looked him up and down.

"And eating after certain hours leads to unwanted fat."

"Excuse me, but I'm not concerned for my weight," Myra replied in frustration.

"Montel, are you serious?" Cissy interjected.

"Celeste, I got this," Myra cut her off.

"Let's not make it a big deal. I will get the buffalo wings, I just …" The two looked at him with their arms crossed. Montel threw up his hands and said, "Never mind."

"What was that all about?" Cissy asked Myra after he'd left.

"I don't know, Cissy, but I was not about to have him dictate what I eat, especially when I know when I'm hungry."

"And you look good, too," Cissy added.

"Good? I look great," Myra showcased herself with her hands.

They started giggling, then Cissy mumbled, "Okay, here he comes." They sat up straight and pretended they were talking about the shop.

"Okay, here's your wine, and the wings are on their way."

"Thank you, sweetie."

"My pleasure. I want to make a toast to my future bride. Myra, you mean everything to me, and I'm happy you picked me to be your husband. I'm anxious to take care of you and start our lives together."

"With the kids," Cissy cut in to say.

"Yes, Celeste, with the kids. To our future," Montel held up his glass of apple cider.

"To the future," Myra said with a smile.

Suddenly the DJ sent out a surprise shout to Myra from Montel, then played Jagged Edge's "Let's Get Married"—the remix version with Run-DMC's background music. They danced to that song and well into the late night.

*   *   *   *   *

The next day, at Montel's house, Myra woke up to Montel lying by her, staring. She opened her eyes as he whispered, "Good morning, beautiful."

"Good morning, handsome." Myra smiled.

"You had a good time last night, huh?"

"Yes, didn't you?"

Montel smirked, "In a way."

"Why you say that?"

"Well, I don't want you to take this offensively, but when I was telling you to hold off on the wine, I was just uncomfortable with you drinking. As a Christian …"

"Montel, there's a difference between drinking to be drunk and having one drink. I had one small glass of wine last night." Myra rolled her eyes.

"I have to say I'm still not comfortable with it. But anyway, about the appetizer thing, it was for your own good. Health is important to me."

"Look, I appreciate your concern, but the last time I checked, I was told I was a healthy woman. And that's coming from a doctor, thank you."

"I just want you to stay that way."

Myra couldn't believe what she was hearing. "So, in other words, you don't want me to get fat."

"Well, it sounds bad when you say it like that. Baby, I just don't want you to gain unnecessary weight."

"Well, I never have in the past, and I won't now. So please, don't bring it up again." Myra got up and went to the bathroom.

"I'm sorry." Montel sat up, wondering what to say next. "So, when do you want to get married?"

Myra rolled her eyes up. The last thing she wanted to talk about was wedding plans when she was still upset. "I don't know, I was thinking in the fall."

"Why not at the end of this summer?" Montel responded.

"Because that's not enough time, Montel, to prepare and make arrangements."

"Oh, so you want a big wedding?"

Myra came out of the bathroom fully dressed and said, "Oh, please, I had that already. But I don't want a run-by-night wedding, either."

"But you could get help from your mom and sister with the planning."

"I'll think about it, Montel. But for now, I love the idea of having it in the fall." Myra started to gather her things when she saw Montel sitting on the edge of the bed staring at her. Myra stopped what she was doing and mumbled, "What?"

"When are you going to start packing?"

"Packing for what?"

"I figured since we're getting married, you and the kids would move in with me."

"Well, you figured wrong, honey. I can't move out. My kids are comfortable there, and changing their living and school environment will obviously take them out of their comfort."

"Are you concerned for their comfort or yours?" Montel looked straight in her eyes, hoping she wouldn't take it the wrong way.

But just as he thought, Myra rolled her head and eyes, saying, "Excuse me?"

"In other words, I'm just wondering if maybe you're still hung up on Dee's death."

"No, I'm not. For your information, everything that's important to me is by my house—the business, my family, and my kids' school. Are you forgetting that I begged my mother to move closer to me, and my sister and I are getting closer and closer every day? And now you think I'm going to move a half hour or more away? You have to be kidding me."

"So, are you expecting me to pick up and leave what I have?"

"No. I learned a long time ago from a friend to not expect anything from anyone, but I know one thing: I have a family to think about. And if getting married is going to interfere with that, then I don't think we should do it." Myra took off her engagement ring and held it out for Montel to take it.

Montel gently put her hands down and said, "Oh, come on, Myra, it's just a minor thing. We can work out the details later."

"No, Montel, this is a big detail. A detail I'm not willing to budge on." Myra put the ring on the dresser. But Montel managed to drop it into her purse without her knowing.

"Okay, so why don't we talk about it this Sunday, after church?"

"Montel, that's only a day away. Whether it's today, tomorrow, or the next day, it's all the same. We have a decision to make." Montel put his head down, shaking it as if he was confused. Myra looked at his reaction and said, "You know what? I don't think this is going to work."

"Myra, just give it some thought before you start ending things between us. Can you at least think about it? I love you, baby."

"Do you love me? Because if you do, then you wouldn't ask me to only think about you and what you want. You would try to not just make me happy, but at least consider my kids. Did you even think about them? Or did you think at all?"

"Myra, it's not like that. I just want to make you happy."

"But I'm not happy right now, Montel. As a matter of fact, I was happier when we were just dating."

"I'm sorry to hear that." Montel looked at the time and realized he was going to be late meeting one of his clients. "Well, I have to meet a client, so can we continue talk about this after church on Sunday?" Montel picked up her chin, giving her a sensuous kiss.

"Fine. Just know that if we can't agree on any major decisions, my answer will remain the same."

"Okay, so which service are you going to?"

"The usual time."

Montel knew that meant nine o'clock. "I'll see you later."

"Okay." They walked out together.

"Okay, bye." Montel opened Myra's car door for her. "Myra?"

"Yes?"

"I really do love you. And I can't see my life without you."

"I know. So we'll meet in the lobby after the service."

"Yes, of course."

Myra started the car, and before she pulled out, she looked at him and said, "Have a nice day."

"You, too."

Montel walked away as Myra pulled off. She spent her drive wondering what she was going to do.

*   *   *   *   *

Cissy, on the other hand, couldn't be better. Although she was still a little confused about Lance not making it the night before, she didn't dwell on it too much. Cissy was getting dressed for their picnic when the phone rang; it was Lance on the other end. Cissy got excited until she heard him explain that he had to change their time to meet. All of a sudden, she was upset. She started telling him off, then she hung up the phone. Cissy wasn't an emotional person, so she normally wouldn't waste her time crying, but this was an exception. This was the first time she put her heart on the line. In the past, Cissy would always find a way to end relationships; but after the death of her sister's husband, she realized life was too short. She didn't want to spend the rest of her life trying to find Mr. Perfect. Especially when there wasn't such a thing. In her eyes, there was a Mr. Redding, and he was perfect for her. Cissy wiped her tears, grabbed her keys, and stormed out of the door.

She had no idea what she was about to say or do, but she knew she was going straight to Lance's office to see if his story checked out. God help him if he had lied. According to him, he had to meet with a business associate. And that was exactly what he had better be doing. He had already messed up once. And now he had a six-month-old son as a result. On the way there, Cissy fumed at the thought of him lying to her after how far they had come. Cissy finally reached his office on a construction site. She walked in abruptly and came in contact with his secretary. The secretary was nice and friendly, although she seemed to be a little nervous.

That was when Lance walked in with his supposed business associate, who happened to look more like a date. "Celeste! What are you doing here?"

"I just came to confirm my suspicions. I guess I'll be leaving now." Cissy turned to the lady who had walked in with Lance and said, "Whatever he says, don't believe him. It's all bull----!" Then she takes off her engagement ring and shoved it in Lance's chest. Lance grabbed it with one hand and grabbed Cissy's arm with the other. Cissy looked down at his hand as if he was crazy. Then he quickly lets her arm go and asked her to let him explain. She walked out the door, and he followed her.

"Cissy, wait! She's an architect! I needed her for a special job."

"Yeah, I bet it was a special job. Is that what you're calling it now?"

Lance finally caught up to her. Out of breath, he mustered up, "I promise you, Cissy. It was a business meeting."

"Oh, really? And do all of your associates dress with low-cut blouses and miniskirts? Do they all look like streetwalkers, Lance?"

"Cissy, please, calm down and let me explain. Better yet, get in the car."

"What! I'm not getting in your car. You must think I'm really stupid!"

"Please, Cissy."

Cissy looked into his eyes. Her mama always told her if she wanted to know if a person was telling the truth, "Look into their eyes." She got in his car.

Hesitant, she looked at him from the corners of her eyes, "This better be good, Lance."

Lance smiled and closed her door. He got in and pulled off. Cissy commented, "You're very blessed that I love you so much."

Lance smiled in agreement. However, Cissy wasn't smiling at all. Ten minutes into the drive, Cissy asked Lance where he was taking her. He replied, "You'll see."

"Look, Lance, I'm not up for the games."

"Cissy, relax, I'm not playing any games. My playing days are over."

"Yeah, but you're still sneaking around. How am I supposed to trust you if every second you're canceling our dates and having meetings with ladies who are half-dressed?"

"I think you're exaggerating just a bit."

"Don't tell me what I'm doing! Did I ask you?"

"I know, baby, I'm sorry."

"Yeah, you're sorry all right … You know, I've the mind to just—"

Cissy stopped short, looking at the view. It was the same view she had described to Lance months back. Two minutes later, they pulled up to a beautiful lot of land. Cissy looked around, confused, and asked, "Where are we?"

Lance turned off the car, walked over to her side, and said, "Close your eyes."

Cissy gave him the eye as if to say "What are you up to?"

"Come on, close them, Cissy."

Lance then covered her eyes and walked her a few feet over to a lot with a wood base, foundation, and two stories. As they got in front of it, Lance removed his hands and watched Cissy's reaction. She looked in shock; her mouth dropped open, and she was speechless. She looked at Lance, and without making her ask, he answered with a yes. She jumped onto him in excitement, and he swung her around. They kissed, then ran onto the foundation. He walked her through the house his company was building for them. Cissy was on cloud nine. She felt so touched that he would do such a thing. Then Lance went to his car and got the picnic basket. After laying down the blanket in what was going to be the living room, he got on his knee, looked up at Cissy, and said, "I wasn't prepared to show you the home today, but you opened the floor,

Nanette Ramsay

and now I see this is the perfect opportunity to tell you what's in my heart. I've loved you for a long time, but never knew how much until the day you left me. Now you know, I'm not a man of many words, but you bring out the best in me. When I don't know, you do; when I can't, you can; and when I give up, you push. And that is why I'm asking you again, Celeste Marie Lopes, to be the better half of me for as long as you'll have me … Will you marry me?"

Celeste thought for a second, making Lance more nervous, then belted out, "*Yes, yes, I'll marry you!*"

Lance then hugged her tight, lifting her a few inches from the ground. They then sat, fed each other, talked, and laughed at her reaction to his putting off their picnic. Cissy was sorry she had called their architect a streetwalker. But Lance reassured her he would apologize on her behalf. However, Cissy wouldn't think of having him do her dirty work. She was all "woman." And if she was wrong, she would clean it up herself. Lance loved that about her. He appreciated her independence, strong will, and honesty. She was everything he needed in his life.

* * * * *

"Good morning, I'm home."

"Mama!"

"Hey, Trey, Princess. Where's Devon?"

"Oh, he's still sleeping," Princess blurted out.

"What! At this hour, I'm surprised your grandma didn't wake him up yet." Myra looked at the clock on the microwave.

"Well, that's because he came in late last night from one of those stupid dances, remember?" Trey explained.

"Oh, my God, I forgot." Just then MamaD walked into the kitchen. "Thank you, Mama, for watching the kids."

"No problem. Just don't go waking that boy up yet."

"I have to. I want to know how it went," said Myra as she headed for Devon's room.

"Knock-knock ... Devon."

"Um, hey, Ma."

"Hey, baby, how was the dance? I'm sorry I forgot." Myra sat down at the edge of his bed.

"That's okay. It was great. I had a lot of fun." Devon sat up, rubbing his eyes.

"Did you take pictures?"

"I took a lot of pictures, especially of Shalise."

"I see you two are still going strong. I'm happy to hear that."

"Yeah, she's mad peaceful and caring. I really like her. I think I even love her."

"Wow, so have you shared that with her yet?"

"Oh, I'm sure I will. I don't know when, but I will."

"Well, what are you doing today?" Myra was hoping he was free to spend some time with her.

"Nothing so far. Grandma makes my plans when she's here."

"Well, not today. You and I are having a mother/son day. So get up, get ready,"

"What about Montel? Don't you guys have to make wedding plans?" Devon was making a face, mocking Myra.

Myra changed her mood and mumbled, "I don't know about that."

Devon wasn't fully supportive of the engagement, but he didn't like seeing his mother depressed, either. "Mama, I'm sorry if I made you feel bad about getting married. I definitely wasn't trying to break you guys up or nothing like that. And whoever you choose to marry, I'll be happy; as long as he makes you happy."

"Oh, baby, you didn't make me feel bad. I just realized it's not going to work out with Montel."

"Why?"

"We share mutual feelings for each other, but with different life plans. Plans I'm not willing to accept right now. And unless we come to a compromise, I'd rather not get married."

Devon, a little relieved, tried to make Myra feel better, saying, "Not for nothing. I don't think he's the one for you, Mama."

"Devon, you don't think anyone is for me except your father," Myra nudged him.

"That's not true. I'm not caught up in my father like that, Mama. Remember, I'm seventeen now. I don't expect you to be by yourself for the rest of your life."

Myra looked at him in amazement. Then she moved closer to him and whispered, "Funny you should say that. Someone once told me 'you should never have any expectations, limitations, or worry.'"

"Who told you that, Dad?"

"No, Travis."

"Wow, that was good lookin' out."

"Okay, so get ready, because it's a beautiful day and I don't want to waste it."

"Okay. And by the way, Mama, I didn't have a problem with Travis; it was just too soon."

"Oh, really?" Myra shook her head in disbelief.

"Really, he was nice and something about him seemed real, not fake. He didn't seem like he was trying to change or appease you."

"Hm, appease, huh? What a big word."

"Oh, stop, Ma, you know I'm smart. I can speak intelligently when I want to."

"You sure are, and I'm proud of you." Myra gave him a hug.

"Mama, what ever happened to Travis?"

"I don't know, but I'm sure he's happy wherever he is. Anyway, that's history."

"You should call him up."

"Oh, please, I'm not even thinking about him. Besides, I have to resolve some issues with Montel."

"Any issue you're having with Montel, you wouldn't have with Travis."

"How do you know that?"

"I don't know, but you seemed a lot happier when Travis was around. Believe it or not, I pay attention."

"I see that. Well, that's a lost cause now, so I'm not even going there. Anyways, get dressed, Devon." Myra got up and headed out.

"Okay, I'll meet you downstairs."

Myra walked downstairs, where she heard Cissy and Lance sharing their news on the house Lance was having built for her. Myra got excited for Cissy. She gave her a big hug, then turned to Lance and said, "Good job."

He blushed and said, "Anything for my baby."

Devon then walked in, giving kisses to the ladies and a pound to Lance. MamaD asked where they were off to, and Myra said, "We're going out to eat, then maybe do a little shopping."

Devon got excited, saying, "Oh word ..."

"Relax, we're not talking shopping spree," Myra shut him down.

They walked out and Myra handed Devon the keys for him to drive. Devon smiled at Myra. She rarely let him drive, but she knew he would be leaving for college soon and wanted him to have more experience behind the wheel. As Devon drove off, Myra started talking about college and how he should carry himself. She let him know that under no circumstances was he to have unprotected sex. And even if a girl said she was on the "pill," that he needed to protect himself anyway. Devon took everything his mother said in and reassured her that having kids was not something he was planning anytime soon. They spent the rest of their drive talking about Shalise, her plans for college, and how much he was going to miss her if they didn't go to the same school.

Their day together was beautifully spent. They didn't have one disagreement except for the clothes Devon chose to buy. Myra admired Devon's individuality because he had his own sense of style. But he only carried an eye for the most expensive items. She didn't mind; how could she when her passion for style was just as luxurious? She also didn't mind that he paid for half of it. Devon was good in that sense. He didn't and never had looked for any handouts. Myra could truly say that this was something he picked up from his father. Devon would use any and all money he received from birthday gifts, allowance, and work. Myra loved his sense of worth and value.

*   *   *   *   *

The next morning, Myra rushed around in a huff because the kids weren't getting ready as they were supposed to.

"Devon, hurry up, or we'll be late for church," Myra yelled from the bottom of the stairs. As she walked back into the kitchen, she mumbled, "That boy gets on my nerves sometimes."

MamaD laughed and commented, "Myra, you know he's just like his father. He has to look his best."

"Yeah, well, if he doesn't get down here in the next minute, I'm leaving!" Myra yelled out so Devon could hear her.

Then out of nowhere, Devon slid into the kitchen, tipping his hat, then dusting his shoulder and popping his collar. After his supposed "Big Pimpin'" rendition as Myra called it, Devon smiled and said, "Big D is here, and you can definitely look but can't touch, 'cause you might get burned. Holla!"

"Ugh, what's that smell?" Trey blurted out, making Devon angry.

"Shut up, Trey!" Devon jumped at Trey with his fist up.

"No, you shut up," Trey said as he ran to Myra's side.

Myra looked at both of them and said, "Both of you, shut it up! Today is Sunday. Let's make it a peaceful one for once. And, Devon, you put on way too much cologne."

"I did? Then let me go change my shirt." Devon started to walk back upstairs, but Myra yelled out, "Uh-uh, boy, it's too late for that. We have to go."

"But, Mama, I'll be quick. I'll meet you in the car," Devon put on a baby face.

Myra rolled her eyes up and replied, "Okay, one minute. Let's go, you two."

Myra started the car, then put it in drive. Just as she was about to pull off, Devon pulled open the back door and jumped in. Myra huffed loudly in aggravation, but Devon paid her no mind.

Their church was only ten minutes away. But because it was one of those mega churches, seats were taken quickly. Myra liked seating in the front, so she would wake an hour and a half earlier than necessary just to sit and wait for the service to start. Today, on the other hand, she'd be lucky if she even got a seat at all.

Upon entering the church, Myra received a text from Cissy that she was sitting in the second row in the center section and had saved some seats for her, the kids, and MamaD. Myra was so relieved, she calmed herself down and anticipated meeting Montel. She scanned the room for him, but didn't see him. At the same time, she noticed Devon looking around, too, so she leaned toward him and asked, "Devon, who are you looking for?"

"Shalise is meeting me here."

"Oh, so that's why you had on so much cologne," Myra commented.

"Uh-huh, and spent all morning getting ready," MamaD added.

Devon smirked at their comments and replied, "No, I always do that."

"Yeah, you just took longer today," Myra responded, teasing him.

"Oh, there she is … Shalise!" Shalise turned around, then smiled when she saw him in his suit. She quickly walked over, "Hey, Devon. Hi, Mrs. Harris." She gave both of them a hug.

"Hello, Shalise. It's nice to see you again and in church. Shalise, this is my mom. You can call her MamaD. The last time you saw her, it wasn't under normal circumstances. And I didn't get to introduce you to her."

"Okay. It's nice to meet you, MamaD." Shalise held her hand out to shake hands.

MamaD looked at her crazy and said, "Child, give me a hug, I don't shake hands."

"Okay, let's go to our seats." Myra continued to look around for Montel.

"Now who are you looking for Myra?" MamaD asked.

"Montel. He said he was coming today, but that's okay. He did say he would meet in the lobby after church. I just thought I might see him coming in."

Suddenly inside, Myra heard the service about to start.

"Praise the Lord," the choir director shouted.

"Praise the Lord," the congregation responded softly.

"I said, praise the Lord. Get on your feet and start praising the Lord! He woke us up this morning. He planted our feet on the ground so we could walk this morning. He opened our mouths to speak this morning, and he opened our eyes to see this morning. You don't hear me. I said *he opened our eyes to see this morning* ... Can I get Amen?"

"Amen!" the congregation shouted out. The choir director loved encouraging shoutin'. It was almost as if that was the only way the congregation could prove their love for the Lord.

"Hallelujah!" the choir director shouted out. Then the choir went into singing "Blessed."

Blessed, blessed, blessed, blessed.
We're blessed in the city. We're blessed in the field.
We're blessed when we come and when we go.
We cast down every stronghold, sickness and poverty will cease
For the Devil is defeated, we are blessed!

Myra was clapping along while praying at the same time. In the midst of praise and worship, she thought it best to speak to the Lord now, so she could get a word in season. "Lord, I ask you to guide me in making the right choice. Lord, you know what's in my heart; and because you give us the desires of our heart, I hand my choice to you. I have faith that you will continue to bless my path. And because you have been the only constant in my life, I will only accept what is right in your eyes. Even if it hurts. For I know, Lord, that with all pain, there is also joy. Thank you always in Jesus' name. Amen."

Myra opened her eyes, enjoying the rest of the song. She felt powerful and free again. It was like a big weight was lifted off her shoulders. As she looked at the couples near her, she noticed how genuinely happy they appeared to be. And she knew that was what she wanted for once. Not this picture-perfect romance, which only looked good. But something beyond what it looked like. To have a love that showed the truth, with all its shortcomings. Myra could honestly say this wasn't even something she had shared with Dee. Although they had shared a "happiness," it was all in the looking good, and not the truth.

The service began with the pastor praying with the congregation. Then he went into his teaching.

"Yes, Lord, turn to your neighbor and say, 'It feels good to be blessed, and it's good to know you're blessed.'" The congregation greeted each other, then the pastor continued to speak.

"Because we are blessed to see another day, we're blessed to see each other again. We didn't take our last breath yet. *We are here, and we are blessed!* And speaking of blessings, we are going to start the service with testimony from our congregation. And who can better tell you about blessing than your own sisters/brothers of Christ? Well, while the first person coming up hasn't been here in a long time, he has found his way back. Congregation, you know the saying, 'You raise up a child in the word, and he shall never part.' He is a true example of that. His parents were a part of the church for years before their passing."

Myra wondered who this could be. She looked around but didn't see anyone waiting to speak. Finally she stopped looking and started to read the order of the service program.

"And he's back now to share his testimony of rebirth through Christ Jesus. Welcome Mr. Travis Dewitt, everybody."

Myra heard the pastor, but couldn't believe it. She thought to herself, "Did he just say Travis? Oh, my God, my heart is beating so fast. What is he doing here?" Myra took a peek, then looked back down, saying to herself, "I can't believe that is actually him on the stage."

All of a sudden, Devon whispered to Myra, "Mama, that's Travis."

"I know," she whispered back.

"Yo, we were just talking about him yesterday."

Myra replied, "I know." Then she told him to stop talking so she could listen. Myra was so confused but happy at the same time. She was confused about Travis being in church but was happy to see him in attendance. As she waited to hear him speak, Cissy leaned over and said, "Is Montel here, too?"

"I don't know, but it doesn't matter. I don't have any business with Travis. Now shush, so I can hear his testimony."

"How is everyone this morning?" Travis started out saying.

Myra smiled proudly and thought, "I'm impressed."

The congregation, including Myra, responded, "Blessed and highly favored."

Travis looked around at the well-dressed congregation and joked, "You definitely look blessed." Everyone laughed, then he continued to speak. "I've been away from the church about nineteen years now. I like to share this because it shows how long I was separated from the church and still I return, unbroken and unashamed. I was raised in a word as a PK, also known as a 'Preacher's Kid,' but soon after my father's death, I began to slowly depart from the church. And although I remained knowledgeable of the word, it meant nothing without the relationship with him. Out of college, I met and married who I thought was my soul mate, when really she was my means to finding a soul mate. After two years of marriage and one child, I came to find out I was not my wife's only one. In fact, there was a question of paternity. And, men, you know that is the biggest blow to us as men. But I moved on, and my daughter, who is now seventeen, is on her way to college. I'm Proud to say she has recently been born again with me."

"Amen!" the congregation cheered.

"Thank you, family. You see, for the past seventeen years, I believed that the only good God saw in me was through my father, and after he died I immediately thought God couldn't possibly care about me. Because if he did, why would he take my father? Why would he make it so I had to take care of my family when I was still in high school? Although I didn't know it then, I realize now it was all God. I mean I can't believe He loved me so much that I am alive and here today in church. He brought me so far.

You see, congregation, the devil is a liar! Because there was a time when I changed women like I changed my underwear. I wasn't living consistent with the word; my flesh felt good, but my spirit was uneasy and lost. I felt like the children of Israel, when God was giving those commands and ways to live righteous, but they ran away covering their ears because if they knew the word, they would be held accountable in God's eyes. I kept trying to cover my ears. My mother would speak in my ear, and I would cover them to avoid the guilt. Then a year ago, my sister in Christ and soul mate spoke some words in my ear, and I covered them again to avoid the guilt again. Finally, the Lord said, 'wake up!' He said, 'I've been speaking to you, and you've been ignoring me. Now, wake up! I sent you your soul mate, and you let her go.' In my mind, I was thinking, 'But, Lord, I didn't deserve her.' Again, the devil is a liar. And you know what the Lord said to me?"

The congregation shook their heads no, all at the same time. Travis laughed to himself as he continued to speak.

"The Lord said 'If you didn't deserve her, why do you think you saw her again after twenty years?'

And so I thought, 'You have a point there'."

The congregation laughed while clapping.

"And here I am in church telling you that even though I struggled to take care of my mother and sister, I still made it through the military to then become an officer in blue and now chief detective. And I did all this while raising my daughter. Thank you, Jesus."

The congregation shouted in agreement, "Amen. Hallelujah!"

"You see, that's how I know God was always there. He never left my side. And even though I lost my father on earth, my Father in heaven never forgot about me."

Everyone clapped loudly. Travis looked around at the congregation. Myra, at this point, wondered what or who he was looking for. A couple of seconds later, Travis cleared his throat, paused, then continued, "Family, I came up here to share my testimony, but I also want to share my soul mate. I don't see her right now. I've been looking, but the light is so bright. Anyway, I know she's here because she is the only woman, along with my mother, whose love of the Lord made me realize the love I was missing. I want to show you, family, who she is. So, Myra, please stand up wherever you are, so I can see you."

Everyone shuffled around looking for the blessed woman who was asked to stand for this hunk of a man. Myra pretended to be looking for something in her purse as she said to herself, "Did he just say my name? No, he didn't say my name."

Devon shook Myra abruptly, whispering, "Mama, he's talking about you ... Get up!"

"Baby, he's calling your name," MamaD added.

Myra smiled in her heart as a tear rolled down her cheek. She looked at Devon. He nodded, giving her the go-ahead. Then she looked at MamaD and Cissy. They smiled and signaled her to stand up. Myra took a deep breath and stood up, saying, "Here I am, Travis."

Everyone in the congregation looked on as Myra walked out to the center aisle of the church. Nervously walking up, Myra thought to herself, "Thank God, I was only in the second row." Travis met her halfway down the steps of the stage with his hand stretched out to her. Myra smiled at him, but didn't give him her hand yet. Travis tilted his head, looked into her eyes, and without saying a word, convinced her to join him. So Myra put her hand into his, and Travis pulled her into a tight hug. The congregation began to clap and cheer for them as they continued to hug.

"Family, I'd like you to meet my friend, my soul mate, and my sister in Christ, Myra Lopes. Living righteous was always an ultimatum but never a choice until I came in contact with this beautiful woman right here."

The congregation clapped their hands as a few members shouted an Amen in agreement.

"She let me know she wasn't having the foolishness. And she let me know in so many words that she wasn't in any way Burger King and allow me to (as they say) 'have it your way'."

Everyone laughed as they clapped some more. Travis then turned to Myra and said, "Myra, I love you! I'm in love with you and always have been since high school. I just thought we could have a relationship without the spiritual foundation. But I've come to realize that you deserve more than some run-by-night relationship. And I'm glad you didn't settle for less, because I wouldn't be here to say I want to spend the rest of my life with you with God as our pilot."

Travis got down on one knee as Myra gasped for air and put her hand over her mouth in shock. "Ms. Myra Lopes, will you make me the most blessed man in the world and marry me?"

Myra started crying. She looked out at the kids, when out of nowhere, a voice spoke out, "Excuse me!" It was Montel, walking down the center aisle toward Myra and Travis. Myra jumped back and shook her head, hoping he wouldn't make a spectacle of himself. But with his ego bruised, Montel had to state his claim. "My brother, this is my fiancée."

Travis cut him off to say, "I'm sorry, but I don't see a ring on her finger."

"Oh, well, then you must not know," Montel spoke aggressively as he took a step closer.

Cutting him off again, Travis took a step forward and assertively said, "My brother, all I know is you have no ownership here. Myra can choose where her heart lies. And it's clear that if it was with you, she wouldn't be standing next to me."

Montel was now furious and embarrassed, so he began breathing heavy, then blurted, "Travis is your name, right? Aren't you the same one who, if I stand corrected, broke her heart not once, but twice?

There's no way she would choose you over me. I'm not the one who will break her heart again." Montel licked his lips as if he had won. Then he gave Myra a look as though she would be making the wrong move by accepting Travis's proposal.

Myra stepped back a little, and Travis turned to her, saying, "Yes, I did break her heart, but I didn't break her spirit."

Montel tried to exploit him some and said, "That's the difference between you and me. I never did anything to hurt her."

Travis continued to look in Myra's eyes. And without looking at Montel, he said, "No, the difference between you and me is time. And, brother, you have bad timing. This is our moment."

Montel realized his ploy wasn't working, so he resorted to using his long standing with the church and addressed the pastor. He put his hand over his heart, as if to say he was genuine as he said, "Pastor, I apologize for having this discussion in the sermon. I realize this isn't the time or the place to talk about—"

Travis cut him off, still focusing on Myra. "I disagree. We're talking about love. And I couldn't think of a more perfect place to discuss love than the house of the Lord. And, right now, I love you, Myra. I know I may not be the man of your dreams. And I can't give you the world, but I know you are my world. My life is good, but you make my life worth living. And I can tell you now, I can't see my eyes open up tomorrow if you are not there to spend the rest of your life with me. So, Myra, will you grace me with your presence every day for the rest of your life and be my wife?"

Montel spoke up, "You can't be serious. Myra, are you really going to fall for this Travis character? I'm the one for you. I don't have to succumb to any lines or false pretenses. You know I make no mistake in what I choose in my life, and I chose you. I'm here and will always be here. So, tell me, are you going to chance having a life with him and his games, or a life with me? Because I'm telling you, you won't find any man who loves you as much as I do. Myra, look at me."

Myra looked at Montel, and with tears in her eyes, she whimpered,

"I'm sorry, Montel, I know you will find the perfect woman for you, but it's not me, because I just found the man who loves me more."

"So, is that a yes?" Travis smiled at Myra.

"Yes, yes, Travis, I will marry you!" Myra gave him a kiss, then Travis put a ring on her finger—the same ring she was looking at in the magazine she kept at her cabin. Travis noticed on their trip that she had the page marked. And being the well-trained man he was brought up to become, he made sure to get it for this moment. After putting on her ring, Travis shouted over the congregation's cheer, "Pastor, did you hear that? She said yes."

The pastor stepped to the microphone and said, "I heard her. Congratulations. Well, that's all for today. And thank you for your testimony and message of love. We all know now that following your heart is following the Lord. Remember, he will always make a way when you think there is no way. Make it a blessed week, and congratulations, Travis and Myra. You are truly blessed."

The congregation began to disperse as Montel walked away in anger. In the crowd, Myra whispered in Travis's ear, then she went to find Montel. She looked around for a minute, then finally saw him in the back. She pushed through the crowd, walking in his direction. She tapped him on the shoulder and said, "Montel, I know it's hard to hear right now, but I do love you. Our life wasn't going in the same direction, though. It was too much work to figure things out. And love shouldn't have to work so hard to stay together. I know love doesn't come that easy, but I know it comes unconditional—and to be fair, there were conditions when it came to us."

"How could you say that?" Montel replied, his eyes welling with tears.

"Montel, you love the way I look. You love that I make you look good. And you love the fact that people see us as the perfect Christian couple."

"Myra, that's what any man wants."

"No, that's what you want. And with conditions, we were bound to break up or end up resenting each other. I love our friendship too much to give it up, so please accept my offer as your friend for life and know that if you ever need to talk, you can call me." Myra held out her arms.

Montel embraced her, then said, "You make sure to make yourself happy first no matter what the circumstances, and if he hurts you, call me."

"Okay, thank you."

Just then Travis walked up from behind and greeted Montel. With his hand out for a shake, he said, "My brother, I'm sorry."

Montel kept his hand down, looking Travis up and down. Then he abrasively said, "Oh, don't be sorry, because you have the responsibility of protecting her with everything you have. If you don't, then you'll be sorry."

"Is that a threat?" Travis looked at him sternly.

Montel changed his disposition and said, "Just think of it as a warning."

Travis smirked, knowing where Montel stood, and replied, "Trust and know that she'll be well taken care of. But it definitely makes me happy to know you care enough to be bothered."

"Yeah, right. Anyways, Myra, take care of yourself." Montel then walks away as he shook his head in disbelief.

Devon quickly walked up, "Hey, Travis."

"What's up, Devon?"

"Yo, I'm sorry I treated you ill the last time."

"Listen, what you call ill, I call anger. And then it was all about you angry at losing your father. I understood that then, and I understand that now."

"You awight," Devon shook his hand.

"Excuse me, Devon," Myra corrected him.

"I mean, you cool with me, dog."

Travis smiled at him, then said, "No, it's not dog. If you're going to call me anything, call me brother, homie, maybe even sir. But a dog is just what it is—a dog."

"Yo, my father used to say the same thing."

"Welcome to the family, Travis," MamaD interjected as she hugged Travis.

"Thank you, Mrs. Lopes."

MamaD pulled back, looked at Travis, then replied, "Just take care of my daughter, and you'll be all right with me."

"Oh, believe me, I will. The Lord led me here, and this is where I am staying."

Myra then walked up, introducing Trey and Princess. And even though Travis had already met them, it wasn't under the best circumstances. Trey shook Travis's hand while Princess blurted out, "Do you like Da Bratz?"

Travis looked at Myra for help. And after she left him hanging, Travis picked up Princess and replied with uncertainty, "Yeah, they're my favorite, Princess."

Princess turned to Myra, saying, "Mama, he's good to go." Myra laughed and gently squeezed her cheek.

Just then Cissy walked over with Lance and introduced him to Travis. Then she walked up to Travis and said, "You finally won her over. Not too bad, future brother-in-law." Travis flashed his cute smile, but Cissy didn't return the smile and said, "Don't try to win me with that smile—that only works on Myra. You hurt my sister, and I will hurt you."

Smiling, Travis replied, "Believe me, unless I have a death wish, your sister is going to be fine." Then he looked at Myra and said, "I can't believe you come with a warning label."

"Honey, with greatness comes great responsibility," Myra responded with a smile as she showcased herself.

"Amen to that," replied MamaD as they all joined in in laughter and love.

*   *   *   *   *

Myra made herself believe she was complete with Dee, but her reality check revealed her only sustenance in life was the spirit of Love. Death played a significant role into her getting this true revelation. Though Travis was also an intricate part in Myra finding herself again, she didn't have the same dependency on him as she had on Dee. This new Love she found was different. It was nothing short of amazing, yet something unimaginable, but so fulfilling and real at the same.

And though there was always something missing in the life of Myra, Dee, Travis, and Cissy, their roots of an early spiritual foundation helped them find what they yearned for. In her marriage to Dee, Myra became what was expected, but not who she was, unfortunately revealing itself to her when she thought all was lost. In spite of the fact that often times Myra questioned her life, she drew strength in hoping her family will always be complete.

Life is interesting in how men do such a great job in protecting and providing for the family, and fail to capture the voice of reason and 'Love'. It is also interesting how women like Myra view submission to her husband the same as living life through her husband or putting dreams on hold. Misfortune only lead her to a wholeness she found in Travis.

Being rough around the edges didn't leave much to be desired, but Travis brought Myra to a place of motivation. History was their key element. However, the lack of a Spiritual connection was their breakdown. That missing link was all things but a deal-breaker; hence creating space for Love to take place in Travis's life again.

To Cissy, love came to everyone else but her. Until the day it came right up to her and broke her heart. It was the day she realized sometimes Love has to hurt, especially in matters of the heart. The break-down allowed the spirit of forgiveness to reassemble the broken pieces of her life and filled her up with a Love she never experienced before. And although her heart is filled with love again, it was always with her. Only this time her commitment to Love not only comes from her heart, but within her Spirit.

Myra once questioned whether or not love does exist after death. Although she didn't realize it during the pursuit of finding herself, the fulfillment Myra sought had been there all along. And while her journey was very challenging, she realized 'Love was always there, and in all things …but not always considered. Today she holds this scripture to be true and dear:

"God is Love, and whoever lives in love – lives in God, and God in Him." 1st John 4:16

God Bless

Breinigsville, PA USA
27 October 2010
248138BV00001B/2/P